BLOOD SECRET

ALSO BY JAYE FORD

Beyond Fear

Scared Yet?

Published in Australia and New Zealand

(Coming soon worldwide)

Already Dead

Darkest Place

For news on the international release of these Jaye Ford titles, sign up for her newsletter on her website at www.jayefordauthor.com

BLOOD SECRET

JAYE FORD

isbn 978-0-6487532-5-4 (paperback)

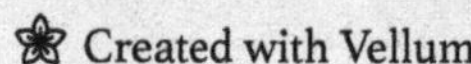

To Mark and Claire

PART 1

GONE

1

Max turned at the lake's edge and took his eyes off the road to absorb the one hundred and eighty degrees of stunning, hot pink sunset in front of him. He'd watched the sun rise and fall over this stretch of water his whole life and it could still knock the breath out of him. Tonight, a gentle breeze skipped across the water's surface, shattering the reflected image of perfection into a million pieces. If he was a philosophical man, he might come up with some crap about his life and the gust of wind he knew was heading his way, but he wasn't so he didn't try, just held onto the magic a moment longer.

The small roundabout up ahead was just a kink in the quiet lakeside road and Max was going straight through but he worked back a gear anyway, in no hurry to start the rest of the evening. He was in the bend, almost at the adjoining street, when the car approaching on the left jerked forwards suddenly, launching itself into the intersection, it's silver chassis suddenly large and solid and right in front of Max's grille.

He slammed the brake. Rennie gasped. In unison, they were launched into their seatbelts and thrown back into the upholstery. As the compact four-wheel drive coasted past Max's much larger work ute, a pale-haired kid eyeballed them through the driver's window. No fear in his face, no apology.

Max thought briefly of the wreckage his bull bar might have caused and made the words large on his lips. 'Good driving, mate.' He flattened his palm on the horn to reinforce the message but the car continued without pause, the driver lifting a fist to the window and flipping his middle finger.

Max shook his head, shoved the stick back into gear. 'You okay?'

Rennie still had a hand pressed to her chest. 'Yeah, I'm fine. What a jerk.'

'Doesn't look old enough to have a licence for more than five seconds.' Max checked the rear-view mirror as he continued through the roundabout, saw the four-by-four had started another loop around it. Beginner's version of a donut. Idiot.

'Your reflexes were all over it, though,' Rennie grinned.

'You like my reflexes?'

'One of your best features.' She glanced around the car. 'We forgot the wine.'

It wasn't the only dumb thing he'd done tonight. 'We can pick up a bottle on the way.'

She nodded, watched him a second. 'About before . . .'

She didn't mean the kid in the roundabout. 'Don't worry about it.'

'It's just . . . I didn't think . . .' She stopped, restarted. 'Are you all right?'

Not close to all right. 'Yeah, babe. Just been a long week.'

'Anything you want to talk about?'

He was sick of thinking about it. 'No. Let's just go say happy birthday to Trish,' he said. 'Have a few drinks and chill out for a while. Okay?' He made it sound like 'Okay with you?' but meant, 'Let's leave it at that, okay?'

She didn't push it. It didn't mean the subject was closed. He followed the road that wound along the water's edge, a black path tracking the ins and outs of the rocky foreshore. Beside him, Rennie scooped her hair into a twist at the back of her head.

'Leave it out,' he said. 'It looks good.'

'Are you kidding? I didn't have time to dry it properly. It's a mess.'

No different from usual, as far as he could tell. Not exactly blonde, not exactly brown, it tried hard to be neat but never quite made it. 'I like it.'

'Good reflexes, no taste.'

'What the . . .?' The roundabout was three or four bends behind them. Max figured the kid had had a little fun burning rubber around the traffic island then kept going in the direction he'd been heading. 'The car from the roundabout, it's behind us.'

Rennie turned in her seat to see for herself but he stopped her with a hand on her arm. 'Why? What's he doing?'

'Sitting on our tail.'

'What, he followed us?'

'Looks that way.'

Rennie ducked her head to the passenger side mirror. 'I can't see him. How close is he?'

'Close enough for a nosebleed if I hit my brakes.'

The kid wasn't just a smart-arse now. He was dangerous, his right-hand tyres drifting into the oncoming lane on the narrow, winding road. Max's fingers tightened around the wheel, anger firmed his jaw. He didn't have the patience to deal with this tonight. He checked the mirror above the dash again. The four-wheel drive was so close he couldn't see it's headlights. There were two silhouetted figures inside: the driver hunched forwards, one hand punching sign language insults through the dark; the other a small head outlined against the front passenger seat. Max wanted to pull over and give the kid a mouthful.

'He's a jerk, Max. Just head to the car park like it's no big deal. Like you don't even know he's there.'

She was right. Only an idiot tailgated a dual cabin ute around bends doing sixty k at dusk and there was no point explaining it to the guy who was stupid enough to do it.

Despite his urge to pull ahead of the kid, Max kept an eye on the jostling and baiting, his foot light on the pedal as he drove the long way round to the strip of shops at ten clicks under the limit - just to make the point - turned left and headed past the cafe. The party was already underway in there, people standing about, balloons clinging to the ceiling, a pile of gifts on a table in the window. No paying guests tonight. And no parking left out front. He turned between the news agency and the bottle shop, then again into the parking strip behind.

'Is he still there?' Rennie asked.

'Yep.' All the way into the car park.

Max pulled into the first available space, half a dozen from the top of the row. The kid kept going, speeding up as he headed down the lane, screeching as he slowed for the corner. Turning off the ignition, Max watched until the car paused at the exit at the far end. 'Well, folks, that's the entertainment over. Come on.'

But the four-wheel drive was still sitting there with its rear lights glowing as Max hit the auto lock. He stood shoulder to shoulder with Rennie for a moment, staring down the length of the car park at the vehicle.

'What do you think he's doing?' she asked.

'Probably using his GPS to locate his brain. Forget him. Let's go say happy birthday.'

He took Rennie's arm and she nudged him with her shoulder. She wasn't big on public displays of affection, preferring to stride rather than nuzzle in close, but he knew what a nudge meant. They were okay. At least for now.

Almost at the top end of the row, Max heard a noise, checked over his shoulder and felt his hackles rise. The kid was coming back and he wasn't looking for parking, that was for damn sure. He was hustling up the next lane, pointing a finger at them in some kind of aggressive incitement.

Max's hand tightened on Rennie's arm. 'Let's wait here a second.'

Pebbles scattered as the kid's car took the corner at the top of the row, more skittered about as it ground to a halt, blocking the end of their parking lane. Max took half a step in front of Rennie.

'Max.' She said it like a warning.

'We'll just see what he wants.'

As the window came down and Max waited for the driver to make the opening gambit, he took a closer look at who he was dealing with. The kid would need ID to prove he was eighteen. Clean shaven, nice shirt, teeth straight enough to have cost some parent a bomb. And the car was a long way from a hoon vehicle - a toy four-by-four that had probably never felt the dirt of off-road.

The boy kept his hands on the steering wheel as he lifted his chin and spoke with schoolyard belligerence. 'What did you say to me?'

Max hadn't said anything yet, unless he meant back at the roundabout. 'I said, Good driving, mate.'

The yell was sudden and stunning in its vehemence. *'You're the shit driver! You could've hit me. Don't you know the fucking rules?'*

Max hesitated. A lesser reaction and he might have met aggro with a little of his own but this was way over the top. He kept his voice at conversation volume. 'Yeah, I know the rules. You're meant to give way to your right. Are you even old enough to have your licence?' He cocked his head at Rennie and started walking.

That was when Max saw the girl in the passenger seat. Sixteen, maybe. Sweet kid, if you could tell that at a glance - pretty dress, nice hair, a little make-up, like she'd gone to some effort, like maybe she'd kissed her mum and dad goodbye on her way out. Max met her eyes for half a second. She dropped her gaze. Didn't look like she was having a great time.

As he and Rennie drew level with the kid's front fender, there was a rev of the engine. Not a quick *hrrumm* as it slid into gear but an extended growl from a foot working the accelerator. The driver didn't say a word, the car didn't move, but Max's skin tingled at the intended threat. Without a hitch in her stride, Rennie slid the strap of her shoulder bag to her hand and bunched it in her fist.

The car rolled slowly forwards, keeping pace with them as they walked, the fender at their sides, the cab behind them. It stopped with its bumper almost touching the rear panel of the last parked car in the row, blocking their way out.

Oh, man, the kid was pissing Max off now. He backtracked to the driver's window, stayed out of arm's reach. 'What is your *problem*?'

'I was on the roundabout first,' he said. 'The rules say the first one on the roundabout gets right of way.'

Did he think it was a race? 'I don't know where you learned to drive but you should be asking for your money back.'

The kid's chin came up. He tried for a sneer but his face wasn't mean enough to pull it off. 'Don't you believe me? You calling me a liar?'

Max wanted to laugh. Who picked a fight over road rules? Who picked a fight with that corny line? But wariness stopped him. There was a tonne of metal under the kid; he'd already used it to try to run them off the road and he'd brought a cannon to a yelling match.

Max glared at him for a second, trying to let the face of experience warn him to drop it. Rennie's hand curled around his forearm.

'Come on,' she murmured.

He resisted, not wanting to turn his back, not wanting to fold for a *boy*. But she pulled at his arm and he caught the uneasy look in her eyes. Walk away, Max. You're the grown-up. Not so grown up he didn't want the last word, though. 'No, mate,' he finally answered. 'You're a real stand-up guy. Have a good night now.' He glanced at the girl as he stepped back from the window. Her face was averted, her neck flushed with embarrassment.

'*I will,*' the kid barked like a tough guy who'd won the scrap. He made a big deal of shoving the stick into first and over-revving as he pulled away. He yelled his final gesture out the window as he headed into the narrow road that led to the street. 'Rich fucks!'

If it hadn't been for that, they might have crossed the lane to the bottle shop a little shaken up, wondering what the hell had just happened. But his parting words topped off the absurdity of the moment. Max raised his eyebrows at Rennie.

She raised hers back at him. 'He thinks we're rich.'

'Probably should've checked our bank statements before he fired that one at us.'

They were both laughing as they stepped into the roadway, out loud, letting go of the edginess. Max channelled De Niro in *Raging Bull*: '*You calling me a liar*?' He didn't hear the tyre spin until it was a squeal. Until the four-wheel drive's brake lights glowed red through a cloud of smoking rubber as it reversed fast down the narrow road at them.

2

Max hauled Rennie the rest of the way to the kerb with him as the car screeched to a stop beside them.

They were on the passenger side of the vehicle now, the young girl staring straight ahead, eyes on the windscreen as the window rolled down. The boy shouted past her. 'Are you laughing at *me?*'

'You need to calm down, mate. You're driving a lethal weapon, not a bloody toy.'

'Don't fucking tell me what to do. You're the bad fucking driver. You're a fucking arsehole.'

And the kid was a coward, Max thought. Yelling abuse across a girl's lap, hiding behind a steering wheel. He was debating the merits of walking around and dealing with him face to face, man to kid, when Rennie raised her voice.

'Okay, you've made your point. You can go now.' She sounded calm, conciliating but her bag was at her side like she was ready to swing it and her runner's legs looked set for flight.

The boy ignored her and poked a stiff finger at Max. 'I know what you drive.'

Max's shoulders tightened. 'What's that supposed to mean?'

'Figure it out, cocksucker.'

'Is that a threat?'

'Yeah, it's a fucking threat.' The kid kept one hand on the steering wheel as he stabbed a finger at him across his flinching passenger.

Max clenched and unclenched his hands. Rennie bent towards the passenger window and spoke loud enough to make her own point. 'You all right?' she asked the girl.

The girl didn't look at her.

'Don't stay in there if you don't feel safe.'

'Hey!' the boy barked at Rennie.

'Hey!' Rennie shouted back. 'You're not the only person in the car.'

'What the fuck has it got to do with you?'

The insult was aimed at Rennie and, for a red-hot second, all Max wanted to do was take aim at the kid's belligerent chin. But she was right; he wasn't the only person involved here. Any pushing and shoving and Rennie and the girl would be caught in the middle. Max clamped his teeth together, made his voice slow and patronising. 'Insulting a woman from the safety of your car, you're a real hero.' He flicked a hand at him like he wasn't worth the effort, stepped between Rennie and the vehicle and took her arm. 'Come on, babe.'

The kid yelled some more as they headed towards the bottle shop, threatening to find them, muffled taunts coming from behind the windscreen. Then the evening fell suddenly quiet. Just their footsteps on the concrete path, darkness almost complete, the four-wheel drive idling behind them. Not moving. Not leaving.

'You okay?' Max asked Rennie.

'What the hell is he doing?'

'Trying to be an arsehole would be my guess.'

'He's making a good job of it.'

The bottle shop was set back from the roadway, two parking spaces out front and a delivery driveway that led to huge glass doors. As they turned towards it, the engine at their backs revved quietly. Max listened for the sound of it moving off, heard only the pop of gravel under its tyres as it rolled slowly forwards. Inside the shop, a queue of customers waited under bright fluorescent lighting, blind to the night outside. The four-wheel drive slid into view - not heading for the street but steering left, its headlights flaring in the glass as it crept towards them like a large, menacing animal.

Max lifted a hand to Rennie's back, pressed her ahead of him, watching in the window as the grille squared on both of them, the bumper inching towards their calves. Then the heat of the engine was on his thighs and something tense and agitated hardened inside him. He slid his hand around Rennie's waist and drew her to the side wall with him. The car didn't come any closer. Just idled in the driveway, blinding them in its headlights. No yelling, no revving. No need. The threat was clear.

Christ, would the kid run them down? Outside a bottle shop? He'd done nothing rational so far, no reason to think logic was part of the decision-making now.

Max glanced at Rennie. Her body was rigid, braced, as though sudden movement might scare the revving beast into action. Then he saw her face. In the five years he'd known her, she'd only hinted at the ugly fragments of her past. He'd never asked more than she wanted to tell, just understood she was trying to put it behind her. Now he wondered if it was the kid or the memories that had rooted her to the spot. Either way, he wanted to do something to erase the fear in her eyes. It shouldn't be there, not while he was with her.

'Keep walking, Renee,' he told her quietly.

As she turned away, he started towards the driver's side, adrenaline flooding his muscles. It was a long time since he'd thrown a punch. But that's what the driver was after so he was going to call him on it, see if the kid had the guts to throw the first one. He was young and fit looking and Max was patched together, but he had age and bulk and experience. An arm appeared out of the driver's window, flipping the bird over and over. There was yelling, too. Max couldn't hear the words but it didn't matter. He had the gist of it.

It was Rennie's voice that pulled him up. She was standing in front of the windows, squinting in the glare, mobile phone in her hand.

'I'm calling the cops. I've got your number plate.' She called out the letters and numbers like she was reading a vision test to a live audience. Not unnerved anymore. Cool, determined, in control. She didn't wait for a response, just hustled to the shop, threw open a door, waved her arms around and shouted, 'That kid out there, he's threatening us with his car.'

Heads turned, the guy behind the counter looked at her then out into the driveway.

It was too much for the coward behind the wheel. He gave a final, pissed-off rev of his engine and reversed out, a little squelch of rubber as he headed for the street. Max stood in the lane and watched him all the way, proud of Rennie, a bit ashamed he'd reached for the clenched fist option.

She was checking the racks of red wine by the time he found her. No one had made a dash for the driveway. No heroes in here, either.

'You okay?' he asked her.

She dodged the arm he tried to put around her, kept her eyes on the wine. 'What do you want to drink?'

'What? I don't know. Rennie?'

She ignored him.

'Renee?'

She swung around. 'What, Max? What the hell were you doing out there?'

'You're mad at me?'

'Yeah.' She squeezed her eyes shut for a moment. 'No.'

'Nothing happened, Rennie. He's gone.' He put a hand on her arm, high up near the shoulder and felt a faint tremble inside her. 'We're buying wine. We're going to a party.'

'Shit.'

He wasn't sure if it was directed at him or the kid or something else. 'Okay?' he said, meaning both 'You're okay' and 'Let's forget about it, okay?'

She crossed her arms, took a breath, turned back to the rack. 'Red or white?'

. . .

THE CROWD in Skiffs had generated enough heat to remind Rennie how late they were. Pav would be desperate.

'Rennie! Max!' If Trish noticed, she didn't care. Her arms were wide, a flute of champagne in one hand, no apron, no work-issue black, no busy face. Good for her.

'Happy birthday!' Rennie waited until she was wrapped up in Trish's arms. 'Sorry we're late.'

'No time sheets tonight, sweetie. And Eliza's here, already working off her birthday present.' When Trish and Pav had been going over the guest list, worried about the cost and trying to rationalise that they didn't need so many people to celebrate her fiftieth, the staff had announced their joint gift. They were donating a few hours each to help in the kitchen and front of house so all that Trish and Pav had to cover was the food. Trish had shed a few tears. She'd probably shed a few more by the end of the night, Rennie guessed. But for the moment, she stretched her neck up to receive a kiss on the cheek from Max, then raised suggestive eyebrows at them both. 'I hope it was something fun that held you up.'

Rennie exchanged a brief, deadpan glance with Max. It started out that way a couple of hours ago. 'Not exactly.'

'A kid just tried to run us down in the car park,' Max said.

'Oh my God. Are you okay?'

'Just shaken up,' Rennie told her, answering the question in Max's eyes at the same time. She figured that was how she'd looked.

'Well, come and get a drink and forget about it. You're having a good time tonight. On me.'

Trish was already having a good time, apparently. She took Rennie's hand, did a little sashay as she swung under it then led her towards the counter, where several bottles of bubbly were sitting in ice buckets. 'Help yourselves, lovelies.'

'Lovelies?' Rennie chuckled.

'You won't live that one down in the morning,' Max said.

'It's my party and I'll *lovely* if I want to,' Trish sang, waltzing off to someone new.

As Max poured, Rennie scanned the crowd. Lots of familiar faces. Customers, friends. Trish and Pav didn't differentiate much.

Max held a flute out to her. 'Here, have a drink.' He said it like it'd have to do until he could find her a sedative.

'I'm fine,' she snapped. He thought the kid in the 4x4 had scared her. She had been scared but not for the reason he thought. In that moment in the driveway, with the car idling at their calves, the ghost of her past had walked right through her. Five seconds of heart-pounding dread and urgent, fast-tracked decision-making - then it was over and she was telling herself it wasn't time and this was Haven Bay and when had she got so slow? And now, fifteen minutes later, the trail of anger and recrimination that had followed was still working its way through her system. It was everything and nothing to do with Max but she was mad and he was treating her like she might faint.

She took the champagne from him, sipping as though she needed nothing more than a taste, and looked for Pav's head - big and bald on top of pick handle shoulders. He was always easy to find but he wasn't out there and she felt a twinge of guilt. 'I'm going to help Pav in the kitchen.'

'I'm going to check the car,' Max said.

'What?' Rennie grabbed his elbow as he turned to go. 'Don't be ridiculous. That kid's probably still out there.'

'Yeah and he might do a job on the car. You heard what he said.'

'You've got insurance. Better the car than you.'

'Bloody smart-arse kid. He deserves . . .'

'Don't be an idiot, Max.' It was intended for Max's ears only but at the other end of the counter, Trish glanced over with a grin. It fell when she caught sight of Rennie's face.

For a moment, Max did nothing but look affronted. 'What, Rennie? Is it what just happened or what happened before?'

The 'before' had made her wonder if he'd been a participant in any previous conversation or whether he'd spent five years just nodding and pretending to agree and thinking about soccer or work or . . . who the hell knew? 'I thought you didn't want to talk about it.'

'So it's *before*?'

She shook her head in frustration. 'I've got to go.'

'Come on, Rennie, give me a break here.'

'*Now* you want to talk about it? In the middle of Trish's party? When I'm meant to be helping Pav.'

'No. You're right. Let's not talk about it. Let's just file it with all the other stuff you haven't told me.'

She pulled in a breath as though she'd been winded. 'Where did *that* come from?'

'Nowhere. Forget it. Forget the lot. Go help Pav.' He took a champagne bottle from its ice bucket and walked into the crowd.

3

'Rennie, Rennie. My best girl!' Pav called across the kitchen from the workbench. Not sounding too desperate.

The small space smelled of fresh coriander and mint and the heady aroma of garlic in the marinated beef skewers cooking on the grill.

'I'm not your *girl.*' Rennie waved at Toby, the seventeen-year-old dishwasher and dogsbody, and stood at the workbench opposite Pav, a half-filled platter of rice paper rolls between them. 'I'm your manager, chief waitress, stand-by barista and free party staff. Anything ready to go out?'

'Two minutes. Hey, you're shaking. Have some bread.' Both of his hands were busy arranging the platter so he used his head to point at the baskets of Turkish bread behind her.

'I'm not hungry; it's adrenaline. A kid tailgated us to the car park and tried to run us down with a four-wheel drive.'

'Then drink, drink.' He touched the tip of his tongs to the base of her champagne flute, pushed it towards her mouth, making throaty sounds that could have been 'up, up' or something else entirely in Polish. Or maybe some other language he'd picked up between

Warsaw and Haven Bay. She gulped, felt the alcohol hit its mark and was disappointed she needed it more than she'd expected.

'So road rage comes to sleepy Haven Bay, huh?' Pav said.

'Who would've thought?'

'I was in a road rage thing once. Some guy pulled a knife on me.'

'No shit. A knife?' Toby called from the sink.

Nausea did a quick roll in Rennie's stomach. She'd wondered why the kid had stayed in the car. Wondered if the taunting was to get one of them close enough to use a weapon. Christ, and Max had been walking right up to him. She shook it off. This was Haven Bay. 'Let me guess. Berlin.'

'No, Kings Cross, Sydney. This guy got worked up about a parking spot, started yelling at me and whipped out the knife.'

'What kind of knife?' Toby asked.

'Some little pocket blade.' Pav picked up a long, wide chopping blade from the workbench and grinned. 'Nothing like a real tool.'

'What did you do?' Toby asked.

'I showed him where the fillet knife got me.' He turned his left palm face-up. He was wearing gloves but Rennie knew the old, jagged scar that ran from the inside of his thumb to the veins on his wrist like a lifeline - a warning for kitchen hands working with slippery dead animals.

'Told him I was ex-KGB, trained in hand-to-hand combat, and I could crush his face before he could get close enough to cut me.'

'Good one,' Toby laughed.

Rennie's grin was half amusement, half disbelief. 'Seriously?'

He shrugged. 'He was a moron. Wanted to know if I'd met Gorbachev. I let him shout me drinks while I bullshitted all about it. Here, this one's ready.' He slid the platter towards her, the rice paper rolls teamed with bite-sized Thai fish cakes. 'A favourite dish at the Kremlin, you know.'

She took the platter, not sure how much Pav was bullshitting tonight. He definitely wasn't ex-KGB but he wasn't a monk, either. He'd left home at fifteen, had lived all over the world, worked in all sorts of kitchens and other places he didn't talk about. If half of what he said was true, she empathised with why he'd stayed here. Nothing ever happened in Haven Bay. It was the safest place on earth. One of the reasons she was still here.

Rennie grabbed a pile of napkins on the way out and swapped small talk for finger food as she made a circuit around the cafe. Customers introduced their partners, a few people laughed that they hadn't recognised her without her usual black, some joked that they'd like a flat white and a skim cap.

Naomi waved her over to one of the tables that hadn't been stacked in the courtyard out the back. She took a couple of seconds to get to her feet and Rennie shifted the platter to one hip so she could hug her without squashing the pregnant belly.

'I swear you're bigger than you were two days ago,' Rennie said.

'And I swear this baby is ready to come out.' Naomi laughed.

'You look gorgeous tonight,' Rennie said. Even eight and a half months gone, a little puffy around the face and not sleeping enough, she looked gorgeous. And it wasn't the silky dark hair and perfect skin. It was an inner thing with Naomi, something lovely on the inside that made her shine on the outside, perhaps brighter by the fact she didn't know it. 'That colour really suits you.'

'Aw, thanks. Can you please come and live in my bathroom and keep saying stuff like that until I've shrunk back to normal size?' She picked up a satay stick in each hand. 'It could take a while.'

'Sure, no problem, but James might have an issue with it.' She stood on tiptoe and did a quick once around the room, not seeing the taller, bigger version of Max. 'Where is he?'

She pulled a face. 'Working. He probably wouldn't notice if you were living in the bathroom. He's been putting in really long hours. I've hardly seen him. Is Max the same?'

Max and James were cousins, and James and Naomi were married, which Naomi claimed made her and Rennie family. De facto cousins-in-law or something. It was a stretch and Rennie had no desire to be part of another family but it was nice that someone like Naomi wanted to include her. Max and James were also business partners. They owned a franchised branch of MineLease, an equipment hire company that provided massive machines to the coal mines around the Hunter Valley.

'He was holed up in the study after dinner all week,' Rennie said. She didn't add he was preoccupied and a tad tetchy. More than a tad.

'Only this week? Well, at least he comes home. James's been working late for a month or more. Says he can't get anything done with me around so he stays at the office.'

'Maybe he's trying to clear his diary before the baby comes.'

'Maybe. Are they working on the same project?'

Rennie shrugged. 'I don't know. I haven't asked. I've been painting a lot.' Max was already in bed when she'd come in from the studio every night this week.

'Oh, I meant to say,' Naomi turned and swept her arms wide like an orchestra conductor, 'I *love* it. Not as much as I love the mural you did for the nursery but it's fabulous.'

Rennie eyed the huge canvas on the wall. She'd given it to Trish yesterday - her actual birthday. She and Pav must have hung it for the party. That in itself felt like a gift, when it was meant to be the other way around. 'Thank you.'

'Are you happy with it?'

As far as Rennie could see, there wasn't anything to be unhappy about. She wouldn't be painting if it wasn't for Trish and Pav, and spending the time and sweat on a piece for either of them always felt like gratitude. 'It's not me that counts. But it's hanging on their wall so it must've got a thumbs up.'

'More than that. Trish was showing it to everyone who walked through the door when I got here.' Naomi pulled a face, pushed a fist into the small of her back. 'I need to sit down for a bit. Come back and say hi sometime.'

Rennie finished her circuit and went back to the kitchen. A couple of the other waitresses had turned up and she sent them out with platters, ordered Pav to go and mingle with his wife then pulled on an apron. She wasn't a chef but she could handle a cafe kitchen. Pav had done most of the work; she just had to keep the food moving on the grill, through the oven and in and out of the fridges.

It wasn't all work, though. She made occasional forays into the party, collecting empties and scraps as she caught up with guests. When the speeches were made, she toasted Trish with a tall, fast glass of champagne and relaxed a little more. Max was over by the gift table, surrounded by other guests. She had no idea where the red wine was that they'd bought, just hoped he was using it to soften up his sharp edges. Whatever was up with him, she seemed to be making it worse.

It was after eleven when Trish declared, 'Enough!' and marched Rennie out of the kitchen. She sat her down in a circle of late-stayers and thrust more bubbly at her.

Well, if she insisted. Rennie slid down on her chair until she was almost horizontal, crossed her legs at the ankles and looked around at the remains of the evening. Naomi was beside her, looking exhausted and rubbing circles on the mound of her belly. Eliza had stayed and was sipping champagne and grinning at Trish, who was still talking up a storm. She'd have a killer headache in the morning. There was another small group on the other side of the room, women with their heels off, picking at the last of the dessert trays. Actually, there were only women inside - and from the baritone laughter coming from the footpath beyond the doors, Rennie guessed the remaining men had set up camp outside. Typical.

She tipped her head back to look through the door into the street. All she could see was Pav propped against a two-hour parking sign and chuckling at something out of view. She imagined Max doing the same further down the footpath, surrounded by whoever else was out there - there had to be at least eight of them if their partners inside were going home with them. Rennie was tempted to shift her chair to watch him. She figured he would have had a few drinks, forgotten their earlier thing and settled into his usual chilled-out Maxness. The easiness that drew people to him. That had drawn her and made her stay longer than she'd planned.

Pav wandered in a while later, collecting glasses on his way, raising his eyebrows when he saw her. 'I thought you'd gone.'

'Not when there's bubbly to be finished.' She held up her half-full glass.

'How are you getting home?'

She rolled her eyes. 'Has Max had too much to drink?' He was meant to be driving tonight. It didn't matter - they could walk. Give them a chance to make up before they did it properly at home.

'No idea. Where is he?' Pav asked.

'I thought he was outside with you.'

'No.'

Rennie looked out the door, as though Pav had it wrong. Terry Bickson, one of the regular breakfast customers, had taken his place against the two-hour sign. Rennie hauled herself out of the chair, walked the few steps to the entry and stuck her head out. There were six of them gathered around the signpost, two leaning on a car, the rest standing with legs splayed and arms crossed like they were playing Simon says. James was among them; it was the first time she'd seen him all night. Max wasn't there.

She leaned out a bit further and looked both ways along the street. The path that ran in front of the shops towards the lake was empty. In the other direction, two male bodies were sitting on the kerb at the corner. Both were too wide to be Max.

A little bewildered, she scanned the cafe, thinking maybe he'd pulled up a chair and dozed off while he was waiting for her but he wasn't inside, either.

'When did you see him last?' Rennie asked Pav at the coffee counter.

He stopped stacking the ice buckets and thought for a second. 'A while ago.'

'How long is a while?'

'An hour. Maybe two.'

That long? When had she last seen him?

During the speeches. She'd raised a hand to get his attention across the room but Trish had delivered her birthday goodwill from in front of Rennie's painting and he hadn't seen her.

Back at the circle of late-stayers, Rennie interrupted Trish. 'Has anyone seen Max?' All she got was head-shaking and a yawn from Naomi. Okay, well, he was probably off having an alcohol-fuelled deep and meaningful with someone. Wouldn't be the first time. Outside, she edged a shoulder between Terry and Gordon Frey, asked if they'd seen him. Angus McDonald, leaning on the car, hitched a thumb towards the lane.

'He said he was going to check his car.'

Uneasiness took a few quick steps up her spine. 'When?'

'Dunno. 'Bout an hour ago.'

She glanced down the street towards the two bodies squatted on the kerb, thought of the knife in Pav's road rage story and heard the kid's voice in her head: *Yeah, it's a fucking threat.*

4

The bottle shop was closed and it was darker in the lane than when they'd arrived. The pub on the other side of the car park was open but there was no activity along its well-lit back wall, just the muted thump of music from inside. The only clear sound was the clump and scuff of four pairs of feet as Rennie led the way to the car.

James was the one to suggest the posse. Terry had fronted up with an enthusiastic 'Yo', although Rennie wasn't sure alcohol and age shouldn't have ruled him out. She'd called Pav from the doorway. He was big and loud and he could apparently bullshit his way out of a knife attack.

She slowed at the first full view of the car park. Glow from the pub and the road and two dim street lamps created a frame of light around its darkened centre. There were only a few cars left: a dark sedan halfway down the first row, Max's bulky, white dual cab with the company logo on its side and a sprinkling of other vehicles. No small, silver four-wheel drive.

It didn't mean it hadn't come back.

Pav and James outpaced her to the ute, splitting up when they reached it, walking down either side to the front bumper. As they exchanged glances at the other end, Rennie felt apprehension sharpen inside her.

'Anything?' she called.

'No.' James turned away, peering at the darkness, hands on his hips.

Pav walked along the other side of the car, checking the chassis, stopping at the back passenger door. 'There's a dent here.'

'That was already there,' Rennie told him. It was driven around mine sites and MineLease's machinery plant; dents happened.

'We should do a walk around the car park,' James said. 'I'll take the pub side.'

Pav headed towards the exit end and Terry ambled unsteadily beside Rennie as she checked the boundary at the rear of the shops, looking over the fence into each courtyard. Five minutes later, they were back at Max's car.

'It's too dark to see into the courtyards behind the shops,' Rennie reported.

'What would he be doing back there?' James asked.

She folded her arms across the uneasiness in her chest. 'He might not have planned it.'

'Nah. It'd take more than a young bloke and a girl to dump him over a fence,' Terry slurred.

His idea of teenage girls was obviously outdated. It was the boy she was worried about, though. 'He might have come back with mates.'

Pav looked about a bit more. 'Maybe. Maybe he went back to the cafe. Did you check the toilets or out the back?' No, she'd just jumped to the worst conclusion. Old habits die hard.

He wasn't in the single bathroom at the cafe, or out back with the bins and the stacked tables, or in any of the doorways on either side of the road, or the public toilets at the end of the street. Terry went back to Skiffs, too tired and drunk to maintain interest, but Pav and James continued with her to the park. When the light from the shops had faded behind them, they stood together in darkness, searching the black, bony shapes of trees and playground equipment silhouetted by the sparkle of lights from the other side of the lake.

'*Max!*' Rennie called, half expecting to see a figure separate itself from the shadows: Max oblivious to the fuss he'd caused.

Pav cupped hands to his mouth and made more noise. '*Max!*' The sound seemed to hover above the water before dying. James took a few steps in the other direction and shouted. No answer, no movement.

As Rennie started towards the shore, Pav said, 'He wouldn't come out here.'

She hesitated, unsure. Max would never wander about in the dark, not on his own, not after what he'd been through. 'That kid was out of control, though. He might've . . . I don't know, if he got him down by the water's edge ... If he ... I think we should . . .'

'Okay, let's look.' James caught her elbow as she stumbled on something in the dark. He had none of Max's charm, could be aloof and a tad dour but he was tall and broad and she was grateful he was out here with her.

Reflected light from across the bay gave the shoreline some clarity and she called Max's name in both directions. All she saw was water lapping gently on the pebbles, its staccato slaps the only sound in the still night.

'He's not here,' Pav said finally.

She pushed a hand through her hair, clenched her teeth on the fear wedged in her throat, not sure if it was another old habit or intuition.

'We can look some more if you want but we won't see much,' James said.

They could drive a couple of cars to the road barriers and turn the lights to high beam, she thought, but the park was only one pocket of the reserve that wound for kilometres along the lake's edge. 'No. I guess not. Let's go back to Skiffs.'

There were just a handful of guests left by the time they returned and Trish had wrangled them into shuffling the tables and chairs back into place for the morning. 'He could've gone home,' she suggested when Rennie gave her a rundown of the search.

'His car's still out there.'

'He might've walked so you could get home.'

'He wouldn't have left without telling me.'

'Have you checked your phone? Maybe he tried to call.' She headed for the kitchen with Trish on her heels, hoping she was right and wondering why he'd phone when she'd been right there in the cafe. Was he still ticked off? Enough that he couldn't talk to her? Max didn't get that ticked off.

She picked through the contents of her bag, reminding herself she hadn't needed it in a pocket when everyone she knew had been at the party. Thinking about the way home on foot in the dark. And the kid in the car who'd threatened to find him.

There was one new text message. From Max.

Luv u b

Rennie read it twice, her forehead tightening in a frown.

'Anything?' Trish asked.

She held it up to show her.

'What's the "b" for?'

'I don't know. Maybe he didn't finish it.' Maybe he was texting when the kid interrupted him. 'He sent it at nine fifty-seven. That's nearly three hours ago.' She hit speed dial.

Trish edged closer. 'Who are you calling?'

'Max.' She hung up. 'It went straight to message bank. I'll try the house.' She smiled thinly at Trish as she listened to it ring. Pav came into the kitchen, stood at the workbench and watched.

'Max, it's me,' Rennie told the answering machine. 'Are you there? Pick up.' She glanced at Trish, then Pav, and shook her head. 'If you get this, call me.' She put the phone down, ran a hand through her hair and closed her eyes. This was Haven Bay, safest place in the world. 'I'm calling the cops.'

• • •

'IT WAS a silver five-door four-wheel drive, a late model Subaru,' Rennie told the police officer. She was still in the kitchen, pacing between the workbench and the cooktops, talking into her mobile. Edgy. Pav moved quietly about, stacking the fridges with leftovers, wiping surfaces. Listening probably. She didn't mind.

Rennie repeated the registration number she'd called out in the driveway of the bottle shop.

'Did you see the driver?' The cop was male, sounded young and the road rage story had piqued his interest. She gave him a description of the angry kid and his passenger - hair, clothes, eye colour, his watch, her jewellery. The stuff she noticed.

'That's a pretty detailed description. Have you seen them before?' he asked.

'No. I just pay attention.'

'Did Mr Tully know either of them?'

'No.'

'Is there any reason Mr Tully might decide to leave the party without telling anyone?'

'No.'

'Could he have had a fight with someone?'

They'd snapped at each other. It wasn't that kind of fight. 'No.'

'Has he had work problems?'

She remembered the conversation with Naomi, the long hours he'd been working. 'Not that I know of.'

'Does he have any medical issues?'

'No.'

'Is there a chance he might want to harm himself?'

Not since she'd known him. 'No.'

'Okay. I'll put his details in the computer. If you haven't heard from him by tomorrow, you'll need to come into the station and make a statement. And bring a recent photo.'

Rennie rung off. 'I'm going to look for him.'

'He could be anywhere.' James was in the doorway.

'I know. But I can't just go home, not without looking. I'll drive back along the lake. Maybe he tried to walk. Maybe the kid found him. I don't know, maybe he just fell over in the dark.' She tossed her phone in her handbag and dug out the car keys.

'Should you be driving?' Pav hauled his apron over his head. 'How much have you had to drink?'

'Not that much and I feel stone-cold sober.'

'Well, I'm over the limit, for sure, but I'll come with you,' Pav said.

'I'll take Hilltop Road and meet you at your place.' James saw the question on both their faces. 'I'm fine. I've only had a couple beers.'

'What about Naomi?' Rennie asked.

'She's gone already. Eliza took her and Trish home.'

She felt a sudden rush of gratitude. They're friends, Rennie. It was another reason she'd stayed. 'Okay, let's go.'

She drove slowly, retracing Max's route. The water was a black satin sheet that stretched all the way to the opposite bank. At the shoreline below the road, she couldn't tell where the rocks ended and the lake began. On the right, the rough edge of bitumen met lawns that sloped upwards to unlit houses. The only illumination came from a bright moon, well-spaced street lamps and Rennie's high beam.

Pausing at the mouth of the roundabout, she noticed the fresh skid marks circling the island. 'This is where it started,' she told Pav.

She took her time cresting the hill and heading down the other side before turning into their street, where Max's grandmother's old timber house came into view, the light on the porch glowing softly on the new charcoal-grey paint job. Relief was her first thought, then she couldn't remember if they'd flicked it on before they left.

James's car was identical to Max's and already in the driveway when she pulled into the carport. He was talking as he opened her door. 'No sign of him on the way over. I took a bit of a look around the back while I was waiting but it's pretty black out there.'

Getting out, she eyed the house - the porch light was the only one she could see.

'Maybe he went to bed,' Pav said.

That's what Rennie wanted. To go inside and find a Max-sized lump in the bed, put a hand to his forehead and feel him burning up.

Sick. Sick enough to phone a cab or get a lift with another guest, too overwhelmed to find her or leave a message. Sick enough to deserve forgiveness for scaring her.

She unlocked the front door, found the light switch and in the moment before the darkness vanished, she saw a body soaked in blood. Then it was gone, replaced by the incandescence flooding the corridor and cool, still silence.

She didn't call out in case he was in pain. In case there was someone waiting for her, too. It was Haven Bay but some things never left you.

Pav and James walked around her, their height and bulk reassuring. Lights came on, the bathroom exhaust fan started up and went off again, the back door rolled open. Rennie moved quietly down the hall to their half-closed bedroom door and edged a shoulder inside. Pale squares of light spilled through the window across a rumpled doona and cast-aside clothes. Her paint-crusted overalls and a bra, his T-shirt and shorts - the remains of their impromptu passion before the party. No Max on the bed or on the floor or squeezed into the wardrobe.

'There's no sign of him out the back,' James said when she met him and Pav in the living room.

'Or anywhere inside,' Pav said.

'It doesn't look like anything's been touched in the bedroom,' Rennie told them.

She glanced beyond the glass at the back of the house. The floodlights were on now, illuminating the deck and the yard and the converted garage. 'I should check the studio.'

'It's just your painting gear out there, isn't it?' James asked as he and Pav followed her out.

'Max keeps stuff in there, too. And we had a . . . tiff. Maybe . . .'

'He put himself in the doghouse,' James finished.

'Yeah, maybe.'

He hadn't done it before. Max believed in never letting the sun go down on an argument, even if the sun had to go down and come back up before it was settled. It wasn't a concept Rennie's family would understand but his parents lived by it and they were still going strong. With a failed marriage behind him, Max liked to take advice from the experts.

The pungent smell of paint wafted into the night as she pushed open the door. The single room had been her home for a year until Max convinced her to move in with him. Her old bed was still there, canvases leaned against the walls, paint tins and other detritus stacked in the corners. The centre was clear except for the easel and her current work. No Max.

'Did you look for a note?' she asked Pav when they were back in the living room.

'I couldn't see one.'

'Okay.' She nodded. 'Right. Thanks. *Shit.*' She squeezed her eyes shut for a second. It's not what you're thinking, Rennie. 'Okay. We wait then.'

Pav and James exchanged a glance and she realised what they'd thought. The 'we' was something else from her past, back when it was just her and her sister making urgent decisions. 'No, sorry, I don't mean you guys need to wait here. You should go home.'

'I don't mind staying,' Pav said.

'Me either,' James added.

Pav had opened Skiffs at six am and worked through to the party and James had been doing overtime at the office on a Saturday. 'Thanks but you both look wrecked.' Worried, too. Pav's hands were clamped to his hips and James's eyes were everywhere, as though he expected to find Max tucked into a corner. 'I'll ring you when he turns up.' She walked to the front entry as she spoke. 'After I've hit him over the head.'

'Then you can hold the phone to his ear while I tell him he's a bastard for making us send out a search party in the middle of the night,' James said as he stepped past her.

Pav gave her a quick, firm hug. 'I'll clock him when he comes into the cafe tomorrow.'

Rennie smiled a little, trying to believe it. When they'd gone, she dialled Max's mobile for the fifth time, listened to the first words of his recorded voice and hung up, worried about filling his message bank with pleas to call when she might need to leave more important information.

Like what, Rennie? This was Max, not her sister. Back then, she'd have been telling Joanne where to meet her. Right now, there was nothing more important to say than, 'Let me know where you are.'

She kept the phone in her hand as she surveyed the room. Max had inherited the rundown, shotgun-style cottage not long before Rennie met him - one of Haven Bay's original miners' residences sitting on a small rise that sloped gently down to the lake. Max had lived in the studio flat off and on for years. When Rennie moved in there, he'd been renovating the house, staying up nights and knocking out walls, converting the pokey old rooms on this side of the hallway into an all-in-one living room/kitchen that now looked onto both the street, at the front, and the water, at the back.

Maybe he had left a note. Somewhere obvious only to Max. She checked the pages stuck to the fridge with magnets, the junk basket under the telephone. Maybe he was distracted or in a hurry. She shook the local phone directory, checked the bookshelves, the coffee table, the buffet and hutch, the magazine rack. Or he could have been sick, a little confused, stumbling drunk. She opened the fridge, the freezer, looked in the pantry, cupboards, drawers, the oven, the TV cabinet. Then she stood at the panels of glass at the back of the room and watched the dark yard. Frustrated, worried, cross. Where the fuck are you, Max?

Okay, think. If he came home, he might have gone to the study. She crossed the hallway and swung the door open on the small third bedroom that he'd filled with desk space and shelving. There were definitely signs of a struggle in there but it always looked like that. Organised chaos, he called it. Talk about living in denial.

There were plenty of notes. Post-Its stuck to the edges of the shelves above the desk, lined up like little coloured flags. She ran her eyes briefly over them - dates and phone numbers and cryptic messages. Nothing starting with, 'Hey Rennie, I'm going . . .'

She couldn't think why he'd go to the second bedroom but looked anyway. It was the same as it'd been for two weeks - double bed, curtains open, wardrobe closed. In the bathroom next to it, Max's towel and a pair of board shorts were in the tub, his electric razor still plugged into the socket. Standard Max mess.

She kept going to their bedroom and threw open the doors to his side of the wardrobe. Bits of clothes were snagged in the drawers, tops stuffed into the shelves, wire hangers weighed down by jeans and shoes tossed in on top of each other. The shelf above the drawers was cluttered with . . . stuff: handkerchiefs, stray socks, pens, a tube of suncream, a leather belt. She picked up a bunch of papers and flipped through bills and receipts, a trivia night scoresheet, a program from a funeral. An old, bowl-shaped ashtray was full of small bits and pieces he must have emptied from his pockets. No notes for her. No clues to where he was.

She shut the doors and looked around the room, hearing her sister's voice in her head: *Safest to assume the worst first.*

Rennie had bagged all that up and shoved it in the back corner of her psyche five years ago but it was so ingrained that she didn't know how to do it any other way. Tonight, she'd assumed the worst and acted on it. Not like they used to but she'd called the cops, searched the road and the house and now she was here, eyeing off the clothes on the floor, remembering Max's hands as he'd peeled hers off, his mouth on her skin, his breath on her face and the irritated words that'd followed.

And another 'worst' crossed her mind.

5

She pulled up the text from Max again.

Luv u b

Back at the cafe, she'd thought 'b' might be for 'babe' or 'by the way', as in *Luv u babe* or *Luv u btw.* He'd sent both of those before. Maybe *Luv u back in a minute.* He never included punctuation - easier to write, harder to read. Now she wondered if it was something else.

Luv you but...

But what? Love you but I need some air. Time to think. I can't stand it any longer. Can't stand *you* any longer. Oh fuck, had he left her?

She picked the clothes up, laid them on the bed, sat down beside them and heard her sister's voice again. *We don't get to have what other people have and you're a goddamn fool if you think you can.*

The phone split the silence like a shriek. Rennie launched herself off the bed and grabbed the handset from the bedside table. '*Max*?'

A beat of silence. 'Can you put Dad on?'

'Hayden?'

'How many kids has he got?'

Rennie clenched her teeth. Hayden's attitude was like a

programmed message scrolling across his forehead in neon lights: *My Parents Suck, Their Partners Are Dog Turds on My Shoe.* Tonight, it was the last thing she wanted to hear down the phone. 'Max isn't here.'

'He's not answering his mobile.'

'No.' She knew nothing about bringing up children or how to handle fourteen-year-old boys but she figured telling him his father was missing would do more damage than good. Besides, he might not be missing. He might be back any second. 'Can I give him a message?'

'Tell him to pick me up at the train station in fifteen minutes.'

She glanced at the alarm clock. 'You're on a train?' It was nine minutes past three in the morning.

'Well, duh.'

She ignored the sarcasm and thought about the text. *Luv u b . . . uzzing off to pick up Hayden.* Maybe the train was late, or Hayden missed an earlier one, and Max had been waiting at the station all this time with a dead phone battery. 'Did Max know you were coming?'

Hayden's answer was laced with defensive hostility. 'Dad said he'd come and get me anytime. So tell him to come get me, okay? I'll be there in fifteen.'

The phone went dead and Rennie tossed it on the bed. She wanted to wait here, stay by the landline, let Max in when he got here and make sure he was okay. Apologise, if that's what it took. Why tonight, Hayden? She scribbled a note for Max - *Picking up Hayden from the station. Be back soon. Don't go. Please* - grabbed her handbag and left the lights burning for him as she walked out.

Hayden was sitting on steps under a streetlight when she pulled into the car park. He sauntered over like he had half an hour to fill before he needed to get there, chucked a backpack in the boot and opened the front passenger door.

'Oh, it's you. Where's Dad?'

Hi Renee, thanks for coming out in the middle of the night. 'He's not home tonight. Are you okay?'

'Yeah.' He answered as though she'd asked if he was human, clipped his belt in and turned his face away, staring out the window as she drove into the street. He smelt of cigarette smoke and sweat and greasy takeaway food. There were traces of Max in there: the chocolate- brown eyes, the soft, wavy hair, the full lips. She wanted to like him, for Max's sake.

Whatever made Hayden jump on a train in the middle of the night, it was clear he didn't want to talk to her about it. It was probably just as well. If it was another argument with his mother, Rennie didn't want to get involved, and anything she had to say wouldn't be what he wanted to hear. Max told her to remember what it was like to be Hayden's age. He used phrases like 'teenage angst' and 'spiralling hormones' and 'pushing the boundaries'. They weren't the things she remembered from her youth and Hayden had parents who loved him and two homes that were safe. She would have sold her soul for half of that at his age.

She tried to sound casual. 'When was the last time you spoke to Max?'

'I speak to him all the time, all right?'

She must be categorised as step-parent-on-his-back tonight. He'd never pulled his head out of his hormones long enough to notice she wasn't interested in being any kind of parent. 'Did you speak to him before you caught the train?'

'No.'

'Anytime today?'

'No.'

'So coming up was a spur of the moment thing?'

'Yeah.'

'And your mother didn't mind?' There'd been heated words before over when and for how long he came and whether Max would be at the station when the train got in.

He shrugged.

'She knows you're here, right?'

'No, all right.'

Shit. He'd run away to Max. And Max wasn't here.

It was almost four a-m when they got home. The doors were locked, the lights still on, no messages on the phone and the note on the counter hadn't moved. The alcohol from the party had morphed into a headache and Rennie's eyes felt like they'd been dipped in salt. Hayden dumped his backpack on the floor in the living room, his body on the sofa and flicked on the telly.

Rennie raised her voice over the bass beat coming out of the speakers. 'Turn it off and call your mother.'

'I'll text her.'

She took the handset off the wall, turned the TV off and held the phone out to him. 'Call.'

'It's the middle of the night.'

'Exactly.'

He swore under his breath. 'You going to stand there and listen?'

'Yes.' She could do the one-word answers, too.

'Don't you trust me?'

'No.'

He slumped on the cushions like it was a protest and dialled, not bothering this time to keep the cuss under his breath. She heard the drone of a single ring, then Leanne's voice. *'Hayden?'*

Rennie recognised the high-pitched urgency in the word and it made her want to tell Hayden to make it quick, that Max might be trying to call. But the kid thought his father was out for the night and his mother deserved a few minutes of reassurance. Rennie stayed long enough to make sure Hayden passed on the right information then left them to it.

She kept her mobile in her hand as she wandered through the house, checking the rooms again and the notes on the fridge, trying the locks on the back door and peering restlessly into the night.

Then not so restlessly.

She moved closer to the glass, focused deep into the yard where the outer edge of the floodlighting touched the hedge at the fence line. Something had moved out there. She flipped the latch, rolled back the door, stood in the opening and listened. The sky was a black, starless dome, the air felt warm and cool at the same time. She could smell the sweet tang of jasmine and the earthy pong of blood and bone. She heard a faint, dull thump. Like a bump on a timber paling.

Taking a couple of cautious steps onto the deck, she stood for a long, silent moment, not sure what she'd heard or where it had come from. The mobile trilled in her hand and she jumped like it had fired an electrical current.

A message from James: *He's not at the office. Heard anything?*

It was a little comforting to know someone else was as worried as she was. She tapped quickly: *Not back. No messages. Thanks 4 looking. Hayden here. Haven't told him. Talk later.*

She killed the screen and walked to the end of the deck, sensing the darkness being held at bay by the floodlights as she listened again. Her skin bristled as another unwanted memory scuttled through her, reminding her that dark was good and bad.

'Max?' She called it softly, inquiringly, nowhere near a shout but in the dead quiet of the early morning it sounded like she'd spoken into a megaphone. No answer. No noise at all. 'Max?' She said it louder, a little sharper. Heard nothing but her heart pounding.

The reserve was on the other side of the fence, a continuation of the park beside the shops. The walking and cycling track that ran through it was also a shortcut from the main street for residents along this side of the bay. Maybe he'd taken it, done an ankle and spent hours limping home. Rennie jumped soundlessly off the end of the deck into the centre of the glow from the floodlights. Maybe now that he was almost home, he couldn't get any further. As she crossed the lawn towards the gate, the illumination on the grass at her feet grew dimmer and her steps hesitant.

Something made her stop. She couldn't have named it but it froze her mid-pace, a couple of metres from the fence, the nerve endings on her scalp standing to attention. She listened, waited. No sound, no breeze, just an uneasy, apprehensiveness creeping into her bloodstream.

'Max?' she breathed.

A whisper of sound reached her from over the fence and she was moving before her brain had time to decipher it - fast, bent, diving for the hedge. She hit the ground on her hip, rolled to a crouch, ready to run. Wanting to. Telling herself to wait. *Wait,* for God's sake. It might be Max. She slid her eyes along the garden and the fence, sweat prickling in her hair, panic grappling for a hold. If it was Max, he wasn't on this side. She lifted her eyes, finding the top of the palings in the darkness. Her pulse pounded in her ears, in her throat. Shit, *shit.* Get a torch, Rennie. And something to swing.

She ran for the lights of the house, feeling the fear shrink behind her with the darkness, shaking the remains off it like soot as she passed through the door. She fumbled through the drawer in the buffet and hutch, found the torch. Her hands were trembling. Come *on,* pull it together.

The thump of a drumbeat starting up made her spin around. Hayden was off the phone, sprawled on the sofa, feet on the coffee table.

'Turn it off,' she called quietly.

He angled the remote and eased the volume down.

'Turn it off, Hayden.' It came out as a growl.

He turned his head, looked ready to complain then changed his mind. The sound died with the picture and the silence of the night rushed back in through the glass. Rennie glanced briefly at the darkened yard, crossed the room to the kitchen and pulled a long, straight-bladed carving knife from the block on the counter.

'What're you doing?' Hayden followed her to the door, more cynical than curious.

'Stay here.' She expected to hear his footsteps behind her as she crossed the deck, figured it was disinterest not obedience when they didn't.

Hesitation said fear, she told herself, and held the knife in her right hand, torch in her left and walked with purpose. Long, determined strides, shoulders squared, chin up, all front and no substance.

She stopped where she'd crouched two minutes earlier, made her voice firm, not even close to a whisper. 'Max? Are you there?' No reply. Just a shoosh in the canopy of the gums along the path as a breeze lifted. She tightened her jaw, stepped up to the gate, pulled it wide and stood in the gap, torch raised, the handle of the knife solid in her palm. Nothing in front. Or to the left. She moved the beam through a semicircle to the right and her breath caught. At the edge of the light, past their fence, near the neighbour's gate, was a still, dark mound.

Oh fuck. A body.

No. Wait.

Keeping her back to the palings, she edged towards it, slowly now, wanting to know, not wanting to see. If it was Max, he wasn't moving. The breeze lifted again and something dark flapped at one corner of the mound. A coat tail? Max hadn't worn a coat. A shirt? He'd worn pale blue. Four steps away, she knew it was a tarp, could see a bright metal eyelet and hear the crunch of heavy plastic - and her skin turned cold. Was he wrapped in it? No. Oh Christ, no. She wanted to run, to turn around, get the hell away and not look back. *Don't, Rennie. It's not that.* She held her ground, gripped the knife tighter and, straightening her torch arm to stop it trembling, she edged closer.

It was the wrong shape for a person. Too square, too . . . even. Then she was standing above it, looking down at grass clippings spilling from under black plastic. She stretched out a toe and gave it a push - soft, unformed, disjointed and nothing like a body. Bloody hell. She was relieved and worried and shaken up and annoyed. This was Haven Bay. There weren't bodies and she didn't need to be walking around with a knife. Max was okay. He'd be back. There was an explanation. She just didn't know what it was yet.

She turned to go and recognised the caution that held her to the spot. It came from the other version of herself, the one that wasn't called Renee. That was suspicious and guarded and alert - and other things she didn't like to think about. It was warning her not to get careless. And here, in the dark, with a knife in her hand, Rennie paid attention.

She worked the torch beam around her and stayed close to the fence as she made her way back to the gate. She pulled it hard behind her, jogged back across the lawn, eyeing Hayden as he watched her through the glass.

'What were you doing?' he asked as she came in, making it sound like she must be nuts.

'Checking the gate. You should go to bed.'

He followed her to the kitchen. 'Why'd you take the knife?'

'I thought I heard something. Your bed's ready. Find a towel for yourself in the hall cupboard.'

He didn't. He stood at the end of the counter, watching as she ran the tap to rinse her perspiration off the knife.

'What were you gonna do with that?'

She dried it with a towel, keeping her hands busy to hide the shakes.

'Were you gonna kill a cricket or something?'

She slid it back into the block.

'Were you down there casting a spell? Ooh, abracadabra.'

She lifted her eyes at the sound of his nasty laugh. He was a moody, pissed-off, self-absorbed teenager. He played his parents and said hurtful things. He thought he was tough, probably figured jumping a train in the middle of the night was cool. She was tempted to tell him the truth - that his father was missing, that there were times in life when a bloody big knife in your hand was exactly what you wanted. But he was just a soft, needy kid. He'd caught a train because he wanted his dad. She didn't want to strip that from him. What she wanted was Hayden gone so she could focus on finding Max.

'Is your mother coming to get you?' It wasn't Max's access weekend and Leanne made a point of sticking to their arrangement.

'Nah. She says there's no time before the flight so I have to stay here now.'

'What flight?'

'To Cairns.'

'You're meant to be going to Cairns?'

'Yeah.' His smile was laced with victory. 'I told her she couldn't make me go. We went to the same resort last year and it was crap.'

Rennie's jaw tightened. The soft, needy kid had put his mother through hell because he didn't like the *resort*.

Shit, Max. Where are you?

6

Rennie slept for a couple of hours, if you could call closing your eyes and stuttering in and out of awareness actually sleeping. Her ears were trained on every sound, her body was conscious of the empty space in the bed and her mind rolled and pitched with fear and worry. And with memories that had found their way out, that didn't belong here, that couldn't hurt Max but could still scare the crap out of her.

The last time she woke, the porch light was glowing through the window in the pre-dawn darkness and she thought Max had come home, slipped under the sheet and the life she'd always believed could exist had returned. She'd felt his warmth at her back, an arm draped over her hip. He'd stretched a little and groaned sleepily with the start of the slow, wrenching process he went through to drag himself from sleep every morning. Four and a half years of watching it and it still made her smile.

Rennie had spent too long in a different kind of life for her waking moments to be anything other than instant attention. Max, on the other hand, started with eyelid fluttering and throat clearing. It was followed with various combinations of dazed sitting, head scratching and face rubbing. She'd learned not to bother trying to get any sense out of him until he'd fought his way out of the fog. She usually left him to it, pulling on running gear while he was still squinting at the daylight, glad for him that his nightmares were confined to the darkness and not for the world around him.

This morning, though, she'd only dreamed his presence. He hadn't tiptoed in and fallen into the clutches of slumber without waking her. He wasn't there and she had no idea where he was or where to look.

She watched the sun come up standing at the bay window in the living room, holding a mug of peppermint tea between her palms and thinking how Max called it her cat piss juice. But it was the kid in the four-wheel drive that she kept seeing in her mind, yelling abuse at them through the window, his face distorted with hyped-up rage, and the sensation it left her with was tense and agitated - and familiar.

Rennie had lived with the hollow ache of dread in her gut all her life. She recognised it like other people knew hunger and tiredness. She was three years old when her mother fled with Rennie and her older sister, escaping their father's escalating paranoia and violence. It was meant to save them but it started an obsession that would imprison them all for life.

As a kid, Rennie used to dream through the eyes of another girl, someone with a different set of emotions and responses, who would see bright colours - lime greens and hot pinks and sky blues - instead of the muted, dark shades of fear. Awake, she used to tell herself she would have been that girl if fate hadn't dragged her into another life.

For the past eleven years, Rennie and Joanne had been free of their father's pursuit but the dread remained, at least it did for Rennie. It was the soundtrack to her life, the volume rising and falling according to her circumstances. For the last five here in Haven Bay, it'd been mostly a whisper, sometimes almost too quiet to hear.

This morning, it made her want to run. Not away, not like last night. She wanted the adrenaline-depleting comfort of a fast, exhausting pace. Sweating off the edginess had always made her feel less vulnerable and more capable. She still did it every day, along the lake mostly and mostly because she loved it. She tried not to think about the other reasons.

She forced them out of her mind now.

The sun had burned off the soft light of dawn and she went outside, glimpsing only briefly at the calm expanse of water beyond the fence before crossing the lawn again. The cloud cover that'd hidden the stars last night was gone and there was the promise of heat in the early morning glare.

The garden along the rear fence was in full colour now, not the shadowy shapes of last night. A glossy-leafed, waist-high hedge was the backdrop to purple-covered lavender, a gardenia with its first creamy buds, grasses with feather-duster heads and other plants Rennie didn't know the names of. Max was the gardener. She just pulled and dug where she was told, hosed and pointed proudly like she had something to do with it when the vegetables came in. Yesterday afternoon, Max had turned the soil around the whole garden, going at it as if it was a workout instead of leisure, adding compost from their bins and whatever was in the big bags he'd hauled home from the nursery. He once tried to explain the science behind it all and she'd feigned interest for about half a minute. This morning, she was grateful for his enthusiasm, that the soil was plumped up and spongy and footprints would be easy to find.

She walked the length of the bed, finding only indentations where she'd crouched and listened. She unlatched the gate and stepped out. A magpie squawked as it flapped from the canopy of gums at the edge of the lake. A high breeze made the leaves sing as though there was a choir hiding in the branches whispering 'shhh'. Left and right, there was only the long strip of grass and the bike track, a straight line of fences bordering one side, the eucalypts and water along the other. The mound of grass clippings that had freaked her out last night didn't look anything like a body in the daylight. Perhaps it hadn't last night.

She walked to the lake's edge, casting her eyes around the boats floating by their moorings, stepping onto wet pebbles at the shoreline to get a better view in both directions. The humps of upturned dinghies were the only interruption to the gentle curve of the bay.

It was when she was trotting back to the gate that she saw why the tarp covering the grass clippings was still flapping in the breeze. House bricks held down three of its corners. A fourth was lying about a metre from the tarp. She glanced at her fence then back at the brick. Its trajectory was moving away from their yard. She remembered the noise she'd heard from the back door and how she'd stopped in her tracks halfway across the yard. Had someone gone through the gate then bolted as she approached? Had they stayed close to the fence line and knocked the brick off its corner as they ran?

The brick could have been like that for days, she told herself. Could have been dislodged by the kids that rode up and down the path on their bikes. She walked to the house trying to ignore the pressing, uneasy thought of someone in the shadows, watching as she'd crept about with a torch and knife, as she'd called for Max and freaked out.

Inside, Rennie dug out the old dog-eared address book that Max kept in the drawer under the phone. He hadn't used it in years, at least not for phone numbers, just digging it out occasionally to jog his memory for a name or a family or an old address, turning the yellowed pages as though it was a priceless relic, claiming the history of his life was between its A-Z tabs. His nostalgia had always bewildered Rennie but this morning, as she flipped to the P's, she was glad of his sentimentality.

His old sailing buddy Pete answered at a shout. 'Yo, Max. Spoke to him. All sorted, mate. Thanks.'

She'd expected to wake him. 'Pete, it's Renee.'

'Oh hey, how you doing?'

'I've been better.' She explained about the party and the search afterwards. 'Have you heard from him?'

Pete's voice dropped a few decibels with concern. 'No, not this morning. The last I spoke to him was Friday arvo. He found a guy who could crew for me today.'

It was Sunday, racing day at the yacht club. Max and Pete had sailed on the lake together since they were kids. They'd started in two-man sabots - and still had the trophies - then tried anything they could crew on until Pete eventually put the money together for his own racing yacht. Max had been his tactician for years - they had trophies for that, too - but for as long as Rennie had known him, Max had never crewed for Pete. The hip that had been crushed in a mine cave-in six and a half years ago didn't cope with crawling around a boat and he tried to keep weekends free for Hayden. Instead, he'd become the go-to guy for crew. Max could find a spare sailor during a national championship if Pete needed one.

'Will you let me know if you hear from him?' Rennie asked.

'I can do better than that. I'll do a ring-around and ask if anyone else's had a phone call.'

'Thanks, Pete. Can you tell people not to ring unless they've heard something? I don't want to tie up the phone.' She gave him her mobile number then phoned the commodore of the Haven Bay Sailing Club, the president of the soccer club, the captain of the team Max coached, apologising for calling so early and getting a 'No, haven't heard' from all of them. Then she tried his office manager, Amanda, who had already heard from James, and two friends from his days down the mines. Between them all, there were calls being made all around the lake.

She put the address book in her handbag with her mobile and wrote two notes: one for Hayden telling him she'd be back later and to make his own breakfast; the other for Max - *I'm worried. Call me. Please.* She put his in an envelope with his name on the front and sealed it in case Hayden was tempted to help himself. Taking a photo from the buffet and hutch, she pulled the picture from the frame and slid it into her purse.

At the second bedroom, she stuck her head in, turning her nose up at the smell. Hayden had only been in there a few hours and it already stank of smelly shoes and BO. He was on top of the covers in boxers and a T-shirt, looking like he'd been knocked unconscious falling from the ceiling - flat on his back, arms spread, legs jumbled, mouth gaping.

He'd told her, like she was stupid, that he didn't have to go to school on Monday - he was at a *private* school, they broke up *three weeks* before Christmas. In the restless early hours of the morning, she'd considered driving him all the way to the airport to meet his mother. Rennie didn't want him here while Max was missing. Yeah, okay, Max might be back any second; he might breeze through the door and say, 'Hey, babe.' And if he did, she didn't want Hayden in earshot while Max explained why he'd stayed out all night, didn't want Hayden's adolescent sneer in her face if it got messy between them. And if Max didn't, if he stayed missing or if he was . . . found, she didn't want Hayden around while she tried to deal with it.

And Hayden wouldn't need her brand of coping if things turned bad. She didn't know about kids. She'd never had any of her own and didn't intend to. Her DNA was flawed; every member of her family had been screwed up and scarred by it and she had no intention of passing that on to a child. Besides, the life she'd had and the things she'd done hadn't given her the skills for bringing up a normal human being.

Her old hatchback was in the garage but the memory of the kid and his four-wheel drive made her take Max's big work car instead, making a detour before heading to the police station in Toronto and going back along the road they'd taken to the party. It wasn't the quickest route to the cafe and she remembered her impatience as Max had headed that way last night. But she'd seen his wistful gaze at the sunset, guessed the lure of it had been too much once he'd glimpsed it from the top of the hill.

Now she took the bends slowly, alternating her gaze between the rocks on the edge of the lake and the lawns that sloped up to the houses, not really sure what she was looking for. Footsteps, skid marks, clothing, a wallet.

She continued to the main road, turned and drove to the strip of shops where Skiffs was nestled between a bakery and a gift shop, and which was all but deserted this early on a Sunday morning. At the T-junction where the street met the lake again, where Pav and James had crossed with her to search the park, she went right and kept going for Garrigurrang Point.

The point was at the tip of a long, narrow finger of land that stretched out into Lake Macquarie forming the safe cove of Haven Bay on the northern side and the more exposed Winsweep Bay on the south. The road followed the water's edge, forming a loop around the base of the hill that split the peninsula into its two sides.

The neighbourhood was not yet roused for the day: garage doors were closed, blinds drawn and there was only a single walker with a dog. She rounded the tip of the finger, slowing to cast an eye over the picnic ground.

One car was parked at the end near the small jetty, presumably belonging to the man and child standing on the dock with fishing rods. She continued back along the south side, passing the main road again, this time heading out of town towards the highway and the police.

Haven Bay wasn't big enough to warrant a cop of its own. It was one of a string of small communities on the western side of Lake Macquarie and despite being on the shores of the largest saltwater lake in Australia, perfect for sailing and fishing and surrounded by large chunks of national park, tourists tended to drive right past, on their way to the vineyards in the Hunter Valley or the spectacular beaches of Newcastle and further up the coast. It was too close to Sydney and too far off the freeway for most people to bother with the detour, which was just fine with the locals. More than fine for Rennie. As far as she was concerned, the name said it all.

Twenty minutes later, she was outside the police station, parked at the kerb and uneasy about being there. She had plenty of memories involving cops; most of them included sirens and flashing lights and the urge to run and hide. She got out of the car, reminding herself not all the memories were bad. Some of the cops she knew had helped - and that was what she needed now.

She spoke with the officer at the front desk, a young woman, not the guy from last night. It didn't matter; the details were on the computer. Rennie handed over the photo - Max at her birthday dinner last year. He'd put on a barbecue, Pav brought seafood marinated in coriander and chilli and Trish came loaded with new and outrageously expensive paints and brushes that Rennie gushed over. Naomi and James were there, too, Naomi excited they were finally trying for a baby, James as unreadable about it as he was on everything. The picture was taken on the deck, Max working the barbecue, smiling, happy, being Max.

The officer pulled out a missing persons form and found a pen. 'You're the person who made the phone call last night?'

'Yes.'

She read from the screen. 'Your name is Renee Carter?'

Rennie hesitated. 'Yes.'

'What's your relationship to Mr Tully?'

'I'm his partner.'

'Business or de facto?'

Neither explained what they were. She would never marry and she wouldn't stay forever but they were . . . together, entwined, connected. She felt more for Max than she'd thought capable of feeling for anyone. 'De facto.'

The officer asked her to go through the details again, taking them down by hand - when she'd last seen Max, where they'd been, who they were with, what he'd been wearing, where she'd looked, the text message. And the incident with the kid in the four-wheel drive. Rennie had no problem repeating the licence plate number. It wasn't the kind of detail she forgot. Then she signed a statement and it was official: Max was missing.

7

'Does Mr Tully have any favourite places, somewhere he might go?' the officer asked.

Rennie checked her watch, impatient with the cop's unhurried questions and slow, neat handwriting. It was after eight; Max had been gone nearly twelve hours and urgency felt like a nervous tic in her gut. But she had enough experience of police procedure to know they followed the steps whether she was shouting or not. She took a breath, tried to think where Max might go.

He was a social guy. There weren't many people in Haven Bay he didn't know and he liked to have a drink with his mates, with James. But he didn't stay out and forget the time, or flop on someone's lounge if it was late, or sleep in the car if he'd had too much alcohol to drive. He called or texted if he was late and he always came home. 'His office, maybe. But his cousin checked and he wasn't there. I've called friends, too. No one's seen or heard from him.'

'Anywhere he likes to go on his own?'

He loved the lake. They'd watched sunsets and sunrises and storms making their way across. But he didn't go there on his own. Quiet and alone wasn't his thing - being trapped in a collapsed mine put an end to that.

'Maybe the reserve at Garrigurrang Point. We take fish and chips out there sometimes.' In summer they ate on the jetty, in winter they stayed in the car keeping out of the wind. Except there was nowhere in Haven Bay to buy fish and chips after ten o'clock.

The officer wrote it down. 'Anywhere out of town? Family or friends he might visit.'

His parents retired to their old holiday spot in Yamba on the Far North Coast and his sister lived in Perth. Not exactly places he could drop into. He had a couple of school friends in Sydney he caught up with every now and then but she didn't think he'd go on the spur of the moment. 'No.'

'Is he taking medication that might make him confused?'

'No.'

'Has he been unwell recently?'

'No.'

'Is there any reason he might want to go somewhere for a while?'

'No.'

'Has he had been involved in any conflicts?'

'Only the one with the kid in the four-wheel drive.'

'Okay.' The officer put her pen down and gathered the papers she'd been writing on. 'Thank you for your assistance. I'll update the computer with your information and we'll continue with our inquiries.'

Was that it? 'Have you checked the licence plate number I gave you?'

'We'll be following it up.'

'What about hospitals?' Last night she'd imagined him lying hurt somewhere but maybe there was more to it. 'It's possible he was injured and someone found him and took him to get medical help.'

'Our inquiries will include calling the local hospitals.'

'That kid threatened him. If he assaulted him, he could've stolen his wallet. He could be unconscious or confused in a hospital without ID.'

The officer didn't nod, didn't take a second to think about it, didn't acknowledge her theory in any way. 'It's worth keeping in mind, Ms

Carter, that people are reported missing every day and most of them are located quickly and without our help. As I said, we'll be following up on the information you've provided and we'd appreciate it if you let us know if you hear from Mr Tully or find out where he is.'

It was said firmly, although not unkindly, and the message came through loud and clear. Road rage kid or not, the cops weren't rushing to put a search party together. People went missing all the time, no reason to panic yet.

Easier said than done, Rennie thought as she headed to the car. The cops didn't know Max like she did.

She'd told him only fragments of her ugly story - few people knew all the details. The fact he hadn't pressed way back when they met was one of the things that had made her stick around to see what was behind his silly grin. It turned out he was a better man than she'd thought possible. Almost too good to believe so soon after she'd finished the court-ordered counselling.

But he had his own ugly story and he understood what it was like to be left alone, he knew about starting over and that trust was a hard-earned commodity.

Rennie drove back to Haven Bay, heading for Skiffs instead of home. If Max rang, he'd try her mobile first - and she couldn't face pacing the house, waiting for the cops to pull a finger out and dealing with Hayden when he woke up hungry and cranky.

She planned to call the hospitals herself but first she wanted to take another look around the car park in the daylight, see if she could find some hint to what had happened there last night... if anything *had* happened. She could also drink about a litre of Pav's double-shot cappuccino. He'd be at the cafe by now, despite the party and the late night. Trish might even make an appearance - and company from either of them wouldn't go amiss.

It was past nine o'clock when she turned into the main street. It was a warm, sunny Sunday morning, a little confused about whether it was late spring or early summer, not yet pumping out the Christmas heat, and there were more than a few Haven Bay residents now out enjoying it. There weren't enough shops or locals to generate a crowd but those that were there had their weekend faces on. Several adults chatted on the footpath, some little kids in sports uniforms were running about, there was a queue in front of the bakery and whatever club or school was taking their turn at the cake stall was doing an okay trade.

Rennie parked behind the strip and went back to where Max had left the car last night. Keeping her eyes to the tarred surface, she walked all the way around the blue sedan that was in the spot now, looking for scuff marks, stains, broken glass - anything. She got on her hands and knees, checked under the chassis, then beneath the cars on either side and in front.

'Lost something, luv?'

An old guy in equally old shorts and T-shirt was standing above her, waiting to open up the blue sedan.

She stood, brushed her hands on her jeans. 'Yes, but it's not here.'

When he'd reversed out, she squatted over a dark circle in the centre of the space, rubbed a finger over it, held it to her nose. Oil.

Her phone pinged with an incoming message. She grabbed it from her back pocket and shaded the screen with her hand.

Max home yet? It was James.

She wasn't sure she'd ever had a text from him before last night. He and Max were close but her friendship was with Naomi. It wasn't that she didn't like James, more that they'd never really taken to each other. She was wary and needed a good reason to make a friend; he had a face that was hard to read, was stand-offish, unresponsive and smart in a way that made her conscious of her own interrupted education. She'd wondered more than once what kept him and Naomi together. Naomi was effervescent and sensitive, while he was sensible and even. Maybe they balanced each other out.

And he was obviously concerned about Max. *No. I listed him as missing person wth police an hour ago.*

On my way to check the plant. Will keep in touch.

MineLease housed and serviced its mine machinery at a plant outside Toronto, closer to its clients. Maybe the security alarms went off last night and Max had gone out there. Maybe that's what he was telling her in the text last night. *Luv u b back soon.* But if that's where he went, where was he now?

Let me know either way, she texted back.

She started a wider search of the car park, working her way down one side of the parking lane and up the other, then retraced the path she'd taken with Terry in the dark along the back of the shops, looking over the fences into the courtyards behind. There were chocolate wrappers, empty chip packets and drink bottles. A five-dollar note, a dog collar, three pens and a small screwdriver. Nothing that told her anything about Max. What had she expected? Clues to a scavenger hunt? She ran a hand through her hair as she eyed off the far lane. It was probably pointless to look over there, just as pointless as the rest of the search. But she couldn't *not* check it.

She walked along the rear of the cars that faced the pub, turned at the top and headed down the row pointing into the middle. Potholes, shiny pieces of glass, a soft toy dinosaur that looked like the victim of a hit-and-run. Halfway down, overlapping the white line between two parking spaces, was a mark that drew her attention.

It wasn't an oil stain. It was an uneven, ragged-edged splat of dark liquid. About the size of a large hand with half-a-dozen smaller satellite drops like a spill from a cup. Except the substance that had congealed in the gravel wasn't milky or coffee-like. It was . . . rust coloured. She knelt, held a finger over it then pulled it back as realisation pitched in her gut.

Blood.

8

Rennie shot to her feet, eyes flicking around the car park, instinctively alert. She glanced down the laneway beside the hotel, automatically registering it as the best escape route: out to the street and across the road to the path she'd run hundreds of times. She turned back to the blood, searched the tarmac and under the car next to it. There was no more, just the one large splat and the tight gathering of drips.

It wasn't a nose bleed; there was too much of it for that. She remembered the blood from wounds she'd inflicted, spilling as a hand slipped from a gaping wound, dripping from red fingers. No, there wasn't enough here for a gunshot wound. Not nearly enough. It had to be from an injury, though. The position suggested a fight beside a parked car or in the roadway. A slash from a knife maybe, or a gushing head wound. She lifted her gaze to where they'd parked last night. Two rows over, six spaces further up the line. Would Max walk over here to have it out with the kid in the four-wheel drive?

Did it matter? The fact was, Max was missing and there was blood in the last place he was known to have been. She pulled out her phone and dialled the police again.

Half an hour later, Rennie was still waiting for the cops to arrive -

annoyed it was taking so long, wondering if Hayden would ignore the phone if he was in bed, worried that Max might try to call while she was using the mobile. Unsettled, too, knowing the discovery of blood at another time, in any other place, and she wouldn't have waited. Would already be on the expressway driving fast.

She'd reversed Max's car into a parking spot opposite the blood so she could keep an eye on it, making sure no one ran over it before the police got there. She used the time to google hospitals on her phone, finding pen and paper in the glove box to write down contact numbers and names of people she spoke to. There were three public ones in the region - Belmont, on the other side of the lake; Wyong, to the south; and John Hunter in Newcastle. The closest was a thirty-minute drive, even late at night. She called them all and was put on hold for minutes at a time while she waited to speak to someone in Emergency. As she sat, staring at the stain in the roadway, questions ran through her mind. Why was there only a single patch of it? Had it been staunched quickly? Had someone grabbed a towel from the back of a car or ripped off a shirt and wadded it on the wound? Maybe the bleeder got in a car and bled some more on the upholstery. Or maybe they'd been bundled in, unwillingly, forcefully.

None of the hospitals had treated or admitted a Max Tully and there were no confused patients without ID.

She tried a private hospital and a clinic. Then Cessnock and Maitland hospitals - both were an hour away at least and an unlikely choice if you were in Haven Bay and needed medical attention in a hurry, but she figured they were worth a try, to cross them off the list if nothing else.

When a man climbed into a sedan in the car space beside the blood, Rennie tapped on his window and asked him to steer clear of the stain on his way out. Five minutes later, as a woman prepared to drive into the spot, Rennie stood in front of her BMW and waved her arms about before asking her to find another place to park.

Both times, she got straight back in her car, not wanting to linger in the open. It was something she'd never felt the need for in Haven Bay but tension had settled deep in her spine and, like a child with a security blanket, her brain looked for the comfort of old habits. Maybe the caution wasn't out of place today. The kid from the four-wheel drive was a loose cannon. He knew what she looked like and he might have another car or friends with vehicles she wasn't watching for.

When the phone buzzed, she'd been dialling a number from Max's book. Trish's photo on the screen made her close her eyes briefly, disappointed it wasn't Max but grateful to hear from her. 'Trish. Hi.'

'Hey, hon.' Her voice was groggy and a little husky, like she'd been woken out of a deep sleep and forced to speak. 'How you doing this morning?'

Rennie remembered the champagne-induced state Trish had been in at the end of the night, imagined her still in bed, dry-mouthed, bleary-eyed, hair and mascara a scary duo, and decided not to rush straight into it. 'I've been better.'

Trish cleared her throat. 'Ditto. Did Max turn up?'

'No. I made an official missing persons report with the police about an hour ago.'

'Oh, hon, that's not good. Where are you now?'

Rennie glanced at the blood across the laneway. 'In the car park behind Skiffs.'

'Are you arriving or leaving?'

'Neither. I'm waiting for the cops. I found blood.'

There was silence for a moment then confusion in her voice. 'Blood? What do you mean blood? A lot of blood? Where?'

'A patch of it on the pub side of the car park.'

There were stuttering noises on the other end of the phone, as though Trish was sorting through a response that made sense. 'I'll come down.'

She sounded like she might struggle walking to the bathroom to look for painkillers. 'No, it's okay. You should stay home and nurse your hangover.'

'What, and not share the wonder of the mountainous bags under my eyes this morning? No, I'm coming down. And I'm bringing coffee.'

God, coffee. The next thing she needed after Max - finding him, holding him, beating him around the head - was strong, hot coffee. 'Thank you.'

She hung up, held tight to the phone and wondered what she'd do without Trish and Pav. Wondered where she'd be now if they'd closed half an hour earlier the day she arrived in Haven Bay.

Rennie and her sister, Jo, had left Victoria the morning after Rennie's court-ordered counselling finished, both of them restless and ready to move on after the forced year-long stay. They drove straight up the coast, stopped for a late lunch south of Sydney, pushed on north for another hour, then decided to call it quits for the day. The sign to Haven Bay was the first they saw with symbols for food and a caravan park. Jo was driving when they hit the small, tidy main street. She did a single, despondent lap and said, 'One pub, one cafe, we ain't going to be here long.'

But the caravan park was on the water's edge and the lake that afternoon was breathtakingly lovely - sailing boats skipping past, wisps of cloud, soaring gulls and a breeze that filled Rennie's lungs with what felt like the first fresh air she'd breathed in ... a lifetime. Maybe it was the counselling, maybe it was the sense of freedom or maybe it was the one personal goal the psychologist made her write down before she finished that final session - *sketch a place through all its seasons.* Whatever it was, after years of moving and running, Rennie had a sudden, urgent, burning longing to be still.

They needed food and a stiff drink first, though. While Jo took the car to see what else the bay had to offer, Rennie walked the main street. Trish's short-cropped, flame-red hair was hard to miss as she hauled tables from the footpath. Rennie followed her in, saw at first glance it was more than a pie, chips and milkshake joint. She hadn't discussed it with Jo but their standard operating procedure had always been if someone landed a job, they gave it a minimum two weeks.

Trish slapped her hands on the counter and doubled over

laughing when Rennie asked if they needed staff. 'Kitchen hand, waitress, barista?' she'd tried.

Still laughing, Trish turned her head to the kitchen and called, 'Hey, Pav!'

'What?' he'd bellowed from inside.

'Come see what just walked in.'

'Trish, come *on*. I haven't got time for this.' He came to the door anyway, stood with his hands on his hips, more hot and bothered than angry by the look of him.

Rennie had no desire to get caught in the crossfire of someone else's argument but Trish shot her a glance, including her in a smug look of triumph and Rennie decided to give it a second to see where it went.

It turned out Pav had just chucked a tantrum, stomping about only moments before, ranting about having no staff, the impossibility of finding staff, the glut of lying, stupid, money-pinching staff he was sick of firing and who were all too lazy to drive out to Haven Bay for work. Ra, ra, ra. He'd apparently shaken a fist at the ceiling, demanding the god of cafe owners to take pity on him and send someone with experience and maturity who could cook and make coffee and wait tables or any of the above. Then Rennie walked in and gave Trish her potted work history: fifteen years of cafe work and she'd have a go at anything they threw at her. Ten minutes later, she'd whipped up a cappuccino, passed Pav's barista test and he was showing her the kitchen while Trish rang a friend to organise a better cabin at the caravan park.

Two weeks later, when Jo was bitching about the lack of shifts at the pub and wanting to move on, Pav and Trish asked Rennie if she wanted to earn some extra cash helping them paint the inside of the cafe. That exercise had set her on a path she'd never seen coming. Of creativity and belonging like she'd never known or expected. Things she'd ached for but had never been within reach. Things her sister thought were a load of fairytale bullshit that would only hurt her.

Joanne was a hard case. The day she turned eighteen, she'd inherited custody of fifteen-year-old Rennie. She'd had no life, only a screwed-up family, bad memories and the burden of responsibility. Rennie figured that gave her every reason to have no faith in the concept of something better. But they'd once spent four months in a normal home with a mother and father and three laughing, joking, sports-mad kids and Rennie knew it existed. As she told the psychologist, though, she just didn't think that kind of life was in her reality. She didn't resent it; it was just the way it was, like every other ugly detail of her life.

Dr Foy tried to tell her she had as much right to a home as anybody else, that she deserved to love someone who would love her back without wanting to hurt her, that she didn't have to live in the shadow of her father's violence forever. It sounded nice and Rennie had agreed - she just didn't believe it.

Then she met Max. Gentle, patient, willing to accept whatever she was able to give. He hadn't asked why, was just happy to help her find a new way to live. He encouraged her to get lost in her painting, made her laugh as though she'd never done it before, like the girl in her dreams. And taught her about love.

She should have left. Jo told her; Rennie had told herself. But she didn't, and most days she convinced herself not to think about it. Her father was sentenced to fifteen years. She and Jo wasted six of them being wild and reckless and free of him until it ended in violence of Rennie's making - and three days a week on Dr Foy's couch. Then she'd landed here and spent five years learning to live like everyone else, knowing it wouldn't last forever. At best, she had four to go before she had to shut it all down and run again.

Now though, as she kept watch on the splat of blood and waited for the cops, she saw how her sister could be right. That the fairytale could hurt her as much as her parents had. To have it, to hold it, breathe and exist for it - then have it ripped away.

9

Rennie was shielding her eyes from the late morning glare, watching two uniformed cops string crime scene tape around the blood, when Trish found her. She had a large takeaway coffee in each hand, passed one over then used the free hand to give Rennie's shoulder a gentle rub.

'How you doing, hon?'

Rennie didn't know how to answer that so she gave her an update instead. 'They're sending out a detective and a crime scene officer.'

Trish pulled in a breath.

'Apparently, it could take a few hours for them to get here.'

'A few *hours*?'

She wanted to throw her hands up and shout, *Yeah, hours. Goddamn hours, can you believe that?* 'Uh-huh.'

Trish switched from shoulder-rubbing to a quick squeeze of the arm. 'Is this what you found?' She stepped to the now completed enclosure of police tape.

'Yep.' Rennie gulped at the coffee, feeling its heat make its way to her stomach and the caffeine hit the tension in her shoulders.

'What do they think?'

Rennie glanced at the two officers who were back at the patrol car talking by the open driver's door. 'They agree it looks like blood and that in light of the missing persons report, they need to take samples.'

'So they think it's got something to do with Max?'

She shrugged, frustrated, irritated. 'Not necessarily. They take the samples in case it's required later as evidence. In case it turns out Max didn't pop off somewhere in the middle of the night by choice but is actually lying bleeding somewhere while they're standing around talking.' She turned her back on them, drank more coffee.

Trish moved to her side. 'Hey, you don't know what's happened. It might not be his blood. I heard there was a fight at the pub last night after we closed up. Someone else might have been bleeding out here.'

Rennie nodded. 'Yeah, you're right, you're right. He might not be hurt but it still doesn't explain where he is. It just feels like a bloody waste of time standing around in the car park when I could be ... I don't know, *not* answering the same questions from every cop I speak to. I keep telling them he doesn't go off in a huff and he wouldn't leave without telling me. Max wouldn't do that. What the hell else do they need to know before they do something more than *this*?' She pointed at the crime scene tape with her coffee cup and glanced at Trish for corroboration. Trish's eyes didn't meet hers straightaway. They flicked to the blood, the patrol car moving slowly away, the single police officer left behind before settling on Rennie again. There was sympathy in her expression but that wasn't all. She seemed hesitant and Rennie remembered Trish and Max went way back.

When Skiffs opened ten years ago, Max was the first person in Haven Bay to get past Trish and Pav's newcomer status. In what Trish described as their concerted effort to become valued members of the community, she and Pav befriended the other shop owners, insisted on local tradesmen for the renovation of their old cottage and sponsored a couple of sports teams. Which was how Max found them. He was a stalwart of the sailing club, veteran of the soccer club and lover of a hearty laugh, the last of which made the three of them instant friends.

Rennie reminded herself she didn't own the licence for worrying about Max. 'Sorry. You must be upset, too.' Trish opened her mouth to speak, closed it again. Maybe there was more to it. 'What?'

'Excuse me.' It was the cop and he was speaking to a woman beside the people mover that was now trapped behind the crime scene tape. 'Is that your vehicle?'

'Yes.' She had a shopping bag in one hand and car keys in the other.

'I have to ask you to leave it there. This area is part of a crime scene.'

She was one of the tennis mums who came in for a coffee once a week in their short skirts and runners. Right now, Rennie couldn't think of her name. 'How long will it take?' the woman asked.

'It'll be a few hours,' the officer told her.

'I've got to pick up my kids in twenty minutes.'

'I'm sorry but you won't be able to move your vehicle until we're finished here.' He walked towards her, pulling a notebook from his shirt pocket. 'And I'll have to get some personal details from you.'

She frowned. 'What for?'

'Hey, Maureen,' Trish said, edging around the tape. Maureen glanced over as if she hadn't looked past the cop and the tape before now. 'Can you believe this? My car . . .'

'Max Tully's gone missing,' Trish interrupted. 'And that blood might have something to do with it.'

'It's blood?' Her eyebrows shot up as her gaze found Rennie. 'I heard Andrew saying something about it in the newsagency. I thought I must have heard wrong. Max taught my kids to sail. What happened?'

Haven Bay was like that. Everyone was connected. That meant Rennie, too. She didn't want to go through the details again but Maureen deserved some information in return for her impounded car. 'Trish had her fiftieth birthday party at the cafe last night. He went out to the car and . . .' *disappeared into thin air* '. . . no one's seen him since.'

Maureen's eyes flicked back to the blood and the cop. 'Well, don't worry about the car. It can stay there as long as you need. I'll get Mum to come down.'

Rennie finished off her coffee, eavesdropping as Maureen told the cop the stain was there when she'd parked two hours ago. When she'd left, the officer had stood to one side of the people mover and folded his arms.

'What happens now?' Rennie asked him.

'I'll stay at the crime scene until the forensics are done.'

'What's the other officer doing?'

'The patrol car is needed for general duties.'

'So . . . what? You just wait here?'

'That's right.'

'You don't go and, I don't know, *investigate*?' She heard the sarcasm in her voice and saw the cop square his shoulders.

'A detective will be here shortly. He'll want to speak to you but you don't have to wait here. I have your details. Just make sure you keep your phone on so he can contact you.'

'My partner is missing. I'm not going to turn my phone off.'

'Rennie,' Trish said quietly, 'why don't we go sit in the cafe for a while?'

She didn't want to *sit*. The sitting and the waiting and the standing around were making her uneasy and irritated. She clenched her teeth, closed her eyes, heard her sister's voice in her head. *We don't wait. Get your backpack. We're leaving.*

Trish slipped a hand around her forearm. 'Have you had anything to eat today?'

Rennie pushed the memory down and shook her head. 'No.'

'Then come on. You need to eat.'

Is that what other people did when they couldn't make sense of what was going on? Comfort themselves with food instead of hard-and-fast rules and backpacks and distance?

Trish didn't give her a lot of choice, steering her in the direction of Skiffs, looking back at the cop as she did so. 'Can I get you a coffee, officer? I own the cafe in the main street.'

'Oh, yeah?'

'A cappuccino?'

'Two sugars.' He dug around in a trouser pocket.

'It's fine, my shout for guarding the . . . well, you know. I'll send someone out with it.'

Rennie sat on the edge of a chair at Trish's desk. It was really just a small table like all the others but tucked into a corner by the counter where she could plug her laptop in.

'Wait there while I organise some food.' She pointed at Rennie as if she were a beagle that might bound off if left unattended.

'I'm waiting.' Rennie rubbed her hands over her face and through her hair, then folded her arms tightly. Most of the tables were full, pretty standard for a Sunday with the mix of late breakfasts and early lunches at this time of the day. Life as usual. Except for Max.

Trish's computer bag was beside the desk, her laptop not yet unpacked. Some of the ordering and accounts for the cafe were done here but most days Trish sat and did what she'd been doing for thirty years - writing. She was a journalist by trade, had used it to work her way around the world. As Trish described it, not a war zone junkie or a save-the-planet type but scraping together a living writing inspiring, entertaining fluff. Mainly travel, some fashion, food and film, and the odd personality piece - if she bumped into someone high profile she could talk into an interview and photos. All in good fun, she said. No tell-alls, an occasional junket to a luxury resort and plenty of hospitality work to help pay the travel expenses.

She met Pav in Serbia when it was still a part of Yugoslavia. He'd been working in a dodgy, backstreet restaurant and had to leave in a hurry so they did it together. Rennie never heard the why, just that they travelled for ten years, Pav talking his way into kitchens while Trish wrote articles about street markets and fashion houses, alpine dinners, jungle treks and the glorious places she found off the beaten track. They came back to Sydney to nurse Trish's dying mum and when she'd finally, painfully, passed away, Trish brought Pav out to Haven Bay to show him the old holiday house before it was sold. And they never left.

Now she wrote magazine articles and a popular blog, ran a travel website and organised the occasional tour, all from Skiffs. Someone else who'd given away one life for another in Haven Bay.

'Pav's making your favourite,' Trish said as she slipped into the chair opposite.

'Thanks.' French toast, she thought, and another memory surfaced - the first time she'd eaten it, the morning after a bloody and terrifying night when Sergeant Evan Delaney had taken Rennie and her sister home for some of his wife's cooking. It ended up being the start of the four-month stay during which she'd scoffed down Claire's French toast with lashings of maple syrup every Sunday morning. Pav's version was a little fancier with spiced fruit compote and Greek yogurt on the side but it was still comfort food. And it reminded Rennie she needed some help.

'Hayden turned up last night,' she told Trish. 'Rang from the train *at three am* wanting Max to pick him up at the station.'

Trish's eyes widened in surprise. She'd known Hayden since before he started school, before Max's ex-wife Leanne took him to Sydney to live. 'Did Max know he was coming?'

Rennie shook her head and told her about the 'Oh, it's you' greeting, the conversation with Leanne and missing the plane to Cairns. 'I thought. . . *hoped* Max would turn up this morning and Hayden wouldn't have to know anything about it. And I wouldn't have to try to sit him down and talk to him.'

'Where is he now?'

'I left him asleep in bed. Which is the next issue. I think I should hang around for this detective but I want to ring the house to see if Max has called and I don't know what to tell Hayden. He's a kid, he shouldn't be told over the phone that his dad is missing and I'm not sure I'm the right person to deliver the message.'

Trish cocked her head. She loved Hayden and she knew Rennie struggled with him. She also understood what Rennie meant about not being the right person. She hadn't tagged her Don't-Fuck-Me-About Rennie for nothing. 'What about Naomi and James? Maybe they could be there when he's told.'

Aunty Naomi and Uncle James were distant-enough relatives and too great a source of good times and nice gifts to warrant Hayden's sneer-and-grunt treatment. 'Good idea. What about calling the house? Any suggestions how to handle that?'

'Could Naomi phone and ask for Max? See if Hayden's spoken to him?'

'Yeah, that could work. I'll call her.'

Trish reached for the cordless phone behind the counter. 'Here, use this so you don't tie up your mobile.'

Rennie stood as she dialled, unable to sit still any longer, edging around customers to the street entrance and peering out as she spoke to Naomi. She'd heard from James and sounded anxious and apologetic that she didn't have better news. There was no sign of Max at the plant so James had gone back to MineLease and found nothing changed from last night.

As Naomi talked, Rennie watched a kid coast past on a skateboard. He crossed the road, hit the kerb on the lake side, found air and landed shoulder first on the grass. Yesterday, she might have grinned. Today, she just scanned past him to the figures in the park, looking for Max-like bodies among the walkers and joggers and bike riders.

She told Naomi about Hayden, asked if she could ring the house without spilling the beans and come around later to help break the news.

A family group had gathered in the park. It looked like children, parents and grandparents. Food was being laid out on a picnic table, kids were crawling and running and falling over. A couple of men checked out the communal barbecue, another man had a camera out taking snaps of the lake, the park, the kids. Then turned around and aimed the lens at the street.

Rennie eased away from the door, watching him from inside the cafe: older, thin, a brimmed hat covering his face. Tourists weren't unheard of in Haven Bay, she reminded herself, and the main street hadn't changed much in a hundred years. Plenty of reason to take photos, even the locals did it. But today, with her past on rewind, it made her uncomfortable.

'Rennie?' Naomi asked on the other end of the phone.

'Hmm?'

'I said, when do you want to tell Hayden?'

Never. She knew what it was like to be a kid and get bad news and she didn't want to be the messenger. But pretty soon Hayden would want to know where his father was. 'Give me an hour.'

Trish was at the table when she hung up. As she sat, Eliza appeared with the French toast. 'It's horrible why he's here and everything,' she said, depositing the plates. 'But I just took the coffee out to the car park and how hot is that cop?'

It was a tad tactless, but Rennie smiled. Eliza was twenty, at uni part-time, four days a week at Skiffs, and when she'd started there in her last year of school, she'd been self-conscious and, as far was Rennie was concerned, too sweet for her own good. Rennie had made it her mission to toughen her up. Taught her how to handle the customers, to fend off the leery ones and stand up to the complainers - and how to cuss in the kitchen and rib Pav without mercy.

The cop comment made Rennie proud. 'I wasn't really paying attention. Did you stop for a chat?'

A soft pink crept across her cheeks. 'Just for a second.'

'Good for you.'

She grinned proudly. Trish dismissed her with a shunt of her head, looked back at Rennie, her face suddenly solemn. Rennie's stomach tightened. 'What?'

'This situation with Max, it might not be what you think.'

What Rennie thought was that something like this belonged in her other life. 'I don't know what to think.'

Trish reached across the table and took Rennie's hand. 'He's done this before.'

10

Something shifted inside Rennie. She pulled her fingers from Trish's grasp. '*What* has he done before?'

'Disappeared.'

Rennie didn't want to believe her, wanted to tell Trish she had it wrong, that Max had never done anything like that, that he *wouldn't.* But Trish had no reason to lie. Still, there was an accusation in her voice when she spoke. 'When?'

'Look, I didn't want to say anything in front of the cop . . .'

'When?'

'When he and Leanne were together.'

Rennie had met Leanne, had heard the pissed-off way she spoke to Max. She'd wondered what they'd ever seen in each other. Leanne was attractive in that well-coiffed, fake nails, plenty of make-up kind of way and Max was as unpretentious and laid-back as you could get. Rennie imagined living with someone who had an attitude like that would make anyone want to walk out and slam a door every now and then, just to breathe some clean air. And she imagined Leanne would keep the drama going for as long as she needed to. 'What do you mean by "disappeared"?'

'He took off and didn't tell her where he was.'

Rennie's pulse picked up. 'How long was he gone?'

'The first time, it was just overnight. They'd had . . .'

'The *first* time? How many times did it happen?'

'Four or five, from memory. The final time, it was for a week.'

Rennie stared at her. This was Max they were talking about. Max who didn't let the sun go down on an argument. Who knew what it was like to be left alone and fearful. She pushed her plate away, the sweet, eggy smell of it making her nauseated now. 'And what, he just came back and they picked up where they left off?'

'I don't think it was as simple as that but yes, he came home, said he was sorry and they tried to work things out. They were unhappy for a long time. They fought a lot. Every time he took off, it was after a huge blue.'

Rennie didn't remember her parents' fights but she'd heard the stories and seen the scars on her mother's body. She shoved back her chair, wanting to move but stuck to the spot by disbelief and horror. 'He *hit* Leanne?'

Trish frowned. 'No.'

'You said a fight.'

Trish watched her a second. 'I meant a shouting match, not domestic abuse.'

Rennie ran a hand through her hair as she tried to make sense of what was whirling inside her. Relief and disbelief. Horror and confusion. Max had shouting matches? He'd disappeared before? There was a chance this wasn't an accident or violence, that he'd just gone somewhere and not told her? It should be good news but it didn't feel like it.

A rumble from the table made her look down. Her phone vibrating on the timber. A text from Naomi: *Spoke to H. No calls from M. Sorry. C u soon. X*

She looked at Trish. 'Naomi.'

'Anything?'

'No.'

Trish made a face. There was sympathy in it but she looked uncomfortable, too.

'What?' Rennie asked again.

She stirred her coffee slowly, as if she needed the time to make a decision. 'I saw the two of you having . . . well, words at the party last night and you were both a bit tense when you got here and, look, it's none of my business but I thought if you've been arguing, having problems, whatever . . .' She didn't finish.

'What are you saying? That he's gone somewhere because we had an argument?'

'It might be a reason.'

Rennie pressed her lips together with incensed denial. Max wouldn't leave over a ... a spat. It was ridiculous. 'We didn't have a *fight.* We don't have *problems.* We . . .' She stopped, doubt like a fist in her throat.

What the hell did she know about relationship problems? Before Max, she'd never spent enough time with anyone to have a problem. The only problems were that she didn't get close and she didn't stick around. Were they having problems and she didn't know?

She'd snapped at him after the road rage kid finally left. They'd snapped at each other later at the cafe. She remembered Max's words, the ones he tossed at her before she went to the kitchen. *Let's just file it with all the other stuff you haven't told me.*

She glanced up at Trish. She wasn't good at talking about herself - had spent most of her adult life revealing as little as she could - but maybe she needed a second opinion from someone who'd known Max longer than she had. Someone who knew how to hold a man for more than a few short years. 'What constitutes having problems?'

Trish seemed about to smile before a frown flitted across her forehead. 'I don't know, hon. Arguing a lot. If it was Pav we were talking about, I'd say throwing things.'

Rennie hesitated. 'We argued yesterday.'

'What about?'

'The kid in the car park. I suppose I should've been grateful he wanted to protect me but I didn't want that, it wasn't what. . .' *Look after yourself. Don't do anything stupid.* She'd wanted to shout her sister's standing order at him, surprised that after so long they were the first words on her lips in the driveway of the bottle shop. 'Then he carried on as though I was a basket case over it, like I couldn't handle it. And . . . and I was mad at him.'

'That's just shock.'

Not shock. She knew what that was like. 'I told him he was an idiot if he went to check on the car.'

'Not the most diplomatic way of putting it but that would be true.'

Rennie remembered his face when she'd said it. His words: *Is it what just happened or what happened before?* Oh, Christ, before. She turned her face to the counter, not wanting to share it with the cafe. 'Fuck.'

'Rennie, come on. That's nothing to worry about. It's hardly the kind of argument he'd walk out over. He and Leanne used to have real doozies.'

She shook her head. 'He asked me to marry him last night. Before the party.'

Trish's face softened and a small smile curled her lips. 'Oh, that's great. Congratulations, hon.'

'I said no.'

As Trish's smile faltered, something slid to the pit of Rennie's gut. 'It wasn't a flat-out rejection. It was, but . . .' They'd been lying among the discarded clothes on the floor, entwined, spent and a little sweaty, chuckling at the spontaneity of the passion. 'I didn't think he was serious.'

'A proposal is always serious.'

'He didn't get down on one knee and say, "Will you marry me?" It wasn't like that.'

'However it comes out, it's a man's pride at stake.'

'Except that... we always said we wouldn't get married. Like that movie about weddings and funerals - we'd agreed to *not* get married. He said he'd been burned once, it'd hurt too many people and he didn't want to do that again. Which was fine by me. More than fine. I saw what happened between my parents in the name of marriage and family and I've had to live with the consequences. I'll never put my name to a marriage licence.'

It was more than she'd ever said to Trish about her past and she guessed the momentary silence from her was the information being washed and diced and put into context.

'I'm sorry about your family,' Trish finally said. 'You never talk about them. I figured you had a reason.'

'There's nothing to be sorry for.' Trish had given her more than her family ever had.

'Have you told Max about them?'

'Bits. The more palatable bits.' And half-truths and watered-down versions. How do you tell a lover that violence and madness are in your genes? That your father murdered your mother. That you are capable of it, too. 'I wanted him to know that all the good things in my life happened when I came here.'

'Maybe he changed his mind about getting married.'

And not talk to her about it? Would he just propose and expect her to follow his lead? It didn't make sense. None of it did. And it was doing her head in. Okay, Rennie. He's missing - focus on something that'll help. 'Where did he go when he disappeared before? Did he ever tell you?' Maybe she could just go look there and deal with the fallout later.

'The first time, he slept in his car out at the point.'

'I looked this morning and he's not there. Where else did he go?'

Trish hesitated. 'How much has he told you about what happened with Leanne?'

She knew they'd married young: Max was twenty, Leanne, nineteen and pregnant. He'd told Rennie he gave up uni and took night shifts underground for the extra pay and that Leanne had hated being stuck with a baby in the backwater of Haven Bay. Max loved Hayden and had held on, trying to avoid the train wreck of their separation. He was in hospital recovering from the mine cave-in when Leanne decided it was over, leaving him and taking Hayden to live in Sydney - too far for Max to travel until he got out of rehab.

'How much do I need to know?' Rennie asked.

'It's just... if he hasn't told you.'

'He's missing, Trish. Just tell me.'

She took a breath. 'After he got out of rehab, he used to turn up at our place some nights and talk to Pav. The two of them would sit in the courtyard for hours, drinking and talking. I think it was some kind of confessional for Max. Maybe he needed a man who wouldn't judge, who had a few sins of his own.'

'And?'

Trish tucked an imaginary hair behind an ear, rubbed her lips together before she spoke. 'He had affairs. When he disappeared, he was with other women.'

Rennie didn't speak. Was struck dumb by the words. By their implication. By Trish's inference. She struggled to find voice. 'And you think he's . . . with another woman?'

'I don't know, hon.'

She wanted to stand up and yell that he wouldn't do that. But something stopped her. A spark of fear, a tap of doubt, her sister's voice. *We don't get a happy ending. We've seen too much shit. We're too fucked up. No one can love that.*

Max said he loved her and she'd believed him. Now she wondered if she'd wanted a better life so much she'd let herself forget the one that had shaped her. Had she been kidding herself for five years?

11

Rennie pushed her chair back and swiped up her mobile and keys. 'I need to go.'

Trish held onto her arm. 'You haven't eaten anything. You should try to have something.'

'I. . . can't. Not now. I just need to . . . go.'

'Then take something with you.' She signalled to the counter. 'Eliza, put a muffin in a bag for Rennie.'

'Would you like it heated, Rennie?' Eliza called.

Rennie waved a dismissive hand. 'Forget it.'

Trish followed her through the cafe, keeping her voice low. 'I'm so sorry to be the one to tell you, but in the circumstances, I thought you should know. It doesn't mean that's what's happening now. It might be something else entirely.'

Rennie stepped into the street, her squint in the glare feeling like a scowl. 'He's missing and so far every possibility has a horrible outcome.'

Eliza appeared in the doorway and held out a bag. 'Apple and cinnamon.'

Rennie took it to avoid further discussion, flicked her eyes back to Trish. 'Ask Pav who Max might stay with.'

Trish's face filled with regret and concern. 'Rennie, honey . . .'

'And ask Pav who Max stayed with the other times.' She didn't wait for a response, just headed for the car park with long, resolute strides, not sure what the hell to think now, just knowing that moving felt a whole lot better than sitting in Skiffs waiting for Trish to drop another bombshell.

What would she do if Pav came up with names? Ring and ask to speak to Max? If he answered, at least she'd know he wasn't dead or hurt. At least that'd be a change on the past.

At the lane as she stopped to check for traffic, she saw the man with the camera again. He was across the road, outside the real estate agency, looking back along the street towards the lake. The camera was hanging from his neck, a chunky thing with a fat lens that he held onto with a cupped hand, as though he was supporting its weight - or ready to click a photo.

Rennie turned the corner, glancing over her shoulder again. He was studying the display in the window now, properties and early Christmas decorations, his back to her. Old habits made her take a mental snapshot - average height, slight build, brown trousers, beige shirt, brimmed hat. She walked a few paces, took another glimpse, hoping to catch a reflection of his face but the sun was bright overhead and all she saw was the mirror image of the lane opposite and herself looking furtive as she headed away.

Out of sight of the street, she wove a path between the scattered vehicles in the car park, agitated with doubt and indecision. Should she tell the police Max had disappeared before? Would they contact Leanne for the details, follow up on the women he'd stayed with previously? It was years ago - would he still know them? Maybe there were others now. Maybe last night's proposal was a final test - rejection, and he was done. Across the tarmac, the uniform cop was still standing by the crime scene tape looking bored under his police-issue cap. Rennie thought of the splotch of blood he was guarding and the kid in the four-wheel drive and reminded herself what *had* shaped her.

Her life before she came here made violence the first and obvious conclusion. It didn't belong in Haven Bay but that didn't stop her mind making the leap. She almost wished Max had tired of her, that she could say she'd seen it coming and was satisfied that was the reason he'd disappeared. But she couldn't. And as she drew closer to the cop, knowing from experience that fast, instant action was sometimes all that would save you, she wondered what kind of response the police would have if they knew Max had gone missing before. Would they decide he wasn't worth their immediate attention?

At the bumper of her car, she called to the cop. 'Has the detective arrived?'

'Thirty minutes away.'

Half an hour of waiting, worrying, second-guessing, blaming. No, thanks. 'Tell him he'll need to call me.'

She drove out of the lot, stopped at the T-junction facing the lake, turned right and, for the second time that day, followed the road that led to Garrigurrang Point. The large houses that overlooked the lake were awake now: curtains and windows open, people about, cars on the move. This was Haven Bay's version of wealthy suburbia: six or seven streets that met the road at right angles, sloped straight up to the crest of the hill then back down out of sight, reconnecting on the south side like rungs in a ladder. The blocks were big, the homes angled for the best view, lots of glass and decking. Then the residences were gone, replaced by the close-packed bush of the conservation area. If the spit of land that was Garrigurrang Point really was a finger, the protected reserve would be the nail, its tall gums forming a canopy over dense native brush, huge hunks of sandstone heaved up by the earth and rough tracks that meandered down the incline to the green strip of the picnic grounds that sat at the very end of the point.

She stopped in the parking bay where she and Max ate fish and chips in winter and flicked her eyes around the view. Would he have come here? If Trish was right, if he'd disappeared willingly because he was upset or angry, *why* would he come here? He didn't have his car and it was a long way to walk in the dark. If someone else picked him up, same question: why come here? It wasn't the most private place, even at night. The sparkly lights on the opposite shore drew more than just Rennie and Max with their fish and chips. Most weekends there were at least a couple of cars with steamed-up windows. They'd fogged up their own a few times, scrambling into the back seat, giggling like kids. Like the kid she'd never been.

Had he done that with someone else? She clenched her teeth, told herself to concentrate on finding him, deal with the rest after she knew he was safe.

Getting out of the car, she started across the park. The afternoon had turned into one of those fairy floss cloud days, early summer warmth and the air still enough to hear the gulls crying as they wheeled out over the water. She kept to the road side of the grass, watching the ground. The metal clip on his watchband sprung open sometimes. If he'd been brought here forcefully, it might have fallen off.

She wasn't alone: there was a family finishing a hamburger lunch, four or five boys with bikes and a football. As she turned at the end and started back along the water's edge, she passed a boy and girl holding hands and talking quietly as they gazed out at the lake. Rennie and Max did those things out here as well. Picnics on the jetty, feeding the fish with crusts. Sailing club parties. Family days when his sister or parents were in town.

She lifted her gaze to the conservation area, squinting in the glare - they'd walked through there, too. A three- minute drive from the main street and you were in hushed bushland that felt like an eternity from anywhere.

It was the first place Max had taken her. Not on a date - he'd just convinced her it was sacrilegious to live in Haven Bay and not walk through it at least once. She'd only been here a month and it'd sounded like a line but she went because she wanted to know what it was like to be a local.

He parked up near the ridge where the tarred road ended and they walked the rutted tracks as far as they went, then the foot trails that led to the top of the hill. Clumps of long native grasses crowded the path so she could barely distinguish its beaten earth. 'If you see a snake, just stand still,' Max had called back to her and she'd almost turned and left him to it. At the highest point, he'd spread his arms and cried, 'Isn't great?' It just looked like a bunch of bush to her and she wondered if his Steve Irwin-style enthusiasm was an act for the new girl in town.

Then he led her off the trail through the tangle of scrub to a huge, flat rock ledge at the top of a steep drop on the south side of the finger. Down below was Garrigurrang Point Road and rocks and the shore, but he stretched an arm out towards the rippling, watery, deep green expanse that lay in front of them, told her the Awabakal people had stood right there, looking out to the long neck of channel on the opposite side that led to the mouth of the lake and the ocean beyond it. They'd called it Garrigurrang, meaning 'the sea'.

Not that Rennie had seen the ocean. After fifty years of conservation, the native growth was too thick for a clear view. Although, the enormous guns that had stood up here during World War II were testament to the vantage point it had offered back then. The gun emplacements were next on Max's tour: five sunken, circular, concrete pads where the weapons had sat, spread out in the bush like the footsteps of a giant elephant.

He showed her the dark, hollow cubes of concrete underneath that were the bunkers and ammunitions storage, explained how he and James and the other local kids had used the anti-aircraft command centre as a playground.

During the war, it'd been manned day and night to protect the seaplane base on the other side of the bay from the feared Japanese invasion. According to Max, the abandoned structure had later made an excellent fort, warship, dungeon and cubbyhouse.

He'd shown her the hawk's nest and the resident mother and baby koalas and the almost vertical short cut down to the road, pointing out the rock halfway down where he and James had carved their initials, back when they were too young to understand the concept of 'leave only footprints, take only photos'.

She'd realised well before they were back at the car that his enthusiasm wasn't an act. Max knew every square metre of the bay and the point and all that lay in between. The whole place had been one big backyard for him growing up. He loved it, had never lived anywhere else, couldn't fathom what Leanne had wanted to escape from. It hadn't taken much to talk Rennie around to its charms, although she didn't have his passion - only Max could pull that off without sounding like a nutcase. In five years, the place had managed to burrow its way through the stone wall of her heart like no other place had in her nomadic life.

After the night her mother had fled with Rennie and her sister, twelve months anywhere was a long stay. Pursuit and fear kept them on the move for years and 'home' was whatever caravan, on-site cabin or dingy flat they stored their backpacks in. Later, after her mother was dead and her father was serving his first sentence, Joanne upheld the rules, finding new schools, new jobs, new towns every six months or so. They never became attached - to places or people. They weren't staying; there was no point. When Rennie finished high school, they followed the work: the beaches and resorts in summer, the snow and mountains in winter.

Then their father, Anthony, was released and the hunt started again. For two years, they skipped out on employers and rent, running and hiding, lying and ducking to keep their trail hidden. When it was over and the cops finally believed their story and a judge put their father away again, they suddenly had years ahead of them without needing to run. Rennie was twenty-three, Jo was twenty-six and neither of them knew how to stay in one place. They moved and worked and partied - until Rennie was backhanded by a man she'd slept with and lashed out. Dr Foy called it an 'episode'. Jo said the bastard deserved it. Rennie worried about what was in her DNA.

Then they came here. Jo lasted three weeks. She wanted to head up the coast to somewhere bigger and brighter. Rennie didn't. There was no argument; they both knew it was coming: twenty-nine and thirty-two years of age was way past time for cutting the apron strings.

Rennie had planned to stay a year - long enough to fulfil her goal to sketch the bay through its seasons. She drew the wild southerlies and ferocious thunderstorms that battered the shore. And the lake when it was as still as a millpond and sailboats waited for a breath of wind; when it was chopped up and throwing windsurfers into the air. Then she did it all over again with paint and canvas. And she ran, worked at the cafe, made the tentative journey to friendship with Trish and Pav and Naomi, made love to Max and moved into his home. And for the first time in her life, she had one of her own.

She told Max she wouldn't stay. Told herself she'd eventually pick up and leave like she always had. She figured there'd be an argument or a drifting apart, and driving off into the sunset would be the obvious step. And when her father came out of prison the next time, there'd be no encumbrances. When she and Jo had word of his release, they'd hit the road again and get on with the life they'd been dished up, staying out of sight and trying to keep others out of his path.

It hadn't occurred to her that Max might love her, that there might never be a breaking point, that she wouldn't get restless. Or that her heart was capable of tenderness and compassion and forgiveness and trust. And love.

Almost back at the car, she aimed the key, watched the flash of amber lights as the locks disconnected and felt the pull of the place like a magnet under her feet. Sanity. Serenity. Home. She took a last, fruitless glance around the picnic area, pulled open the driver's door and told herself Max hadn't left. This was his home more than it ever was hers.

Rennie drove on around the Garrigurrang Point loop, along the south side of the finger, past the top end of the main street where there were houses instead of shops and onto the shores of Winsweep Bay, meeting up with the road she and Max went in on last night. She slowed to search the winding verge again, not expecting to find anything new, wondering if she missed something the last time.

She remembered losing her keys once and spending hours searching the house. The obvious places first: her handbag, the hook by the door, the old dresser. Then she looked in spots she might have left them in a distracted moment - pockets of clothing, the basket under the phone, her bedside table. She'd tried to think of logical explanations, hunted through kitchen drawers, the TV cabinet, the laundry bin. Widening the circle, she'd looked under the bed, in the studio, the garden. Finally, she'd pulled the place apart, forgetting logic and hunting through the bathroom, the pantry, the spare room, under the cushions on the sofa.

Max phoned at lunchtime, told her he'd discovered them tucked into the folds of his jumper. Rennie hadn't thought to call him. Her key ring was distinctive, a miniature hand weight, a weapon and a tool in one, and she hadn't imagined he'd mistake them for his own, but as soon as he'd told her, she realised how it'd happened. He'd tossed the jumper on the kitchen bench when he was getting organised for work, must have put it on her keys then taken both when he left.

Now, as she drove along the water's edge for the third time since she'd lost Max, she wondered about the keys. How she'd kept searching the same places, how she'd tried to find reasons to explain why they'd be somewhere she'd never put them. How all the time they were somewhere else, somewhere logical that she'd never considered possible.

Was that where Max was now?

12

Rennie had expected to see Naomi's car in the driveway and when the white dual cab came into view, hope and relief caught in her chest like a gasp - then she realised it was James's and she was driving Max's work truck. Beyond it, the front door was wide open. Was Max back? Was there news? Walking quickly to the porch, she heard TV voices and a brief clatter from the kitchen and her mind conjured the sight of Max in the next room, while instinct told her not to cross that bridge prematurely.

Hayden was slumped on the sofa, eyes glued to the flat screen, feet on the coffee table and a dirty plate balanced on a cushion. Further into the room, Naomi glanced up from the sink and sent her a thin smile.

It told Rennie all she needed to know. Max wasn't here and there was no news.

She did nothing for a second as her needy, wishful self crashed in on itself. Then she raised brows at Naomi, flicking her eyes at Hayden. Naomi shook her head. She hadn't told him. Rennie swallowed hard and tried for a smile. 'Hey, Hayden. How'd you sleep?'

His body didn't move as his eyes rolled condescendingly in her direction then back to the TV. Translation: what made you think your presence was recognised in Hayden World?

Rennie was tempted to bark that his father was missing, that he should pay some goddamn attention but she reined it in, looked to Naomi for an alternative approach, who shrugged, made a what-do-you-do face. 'Have you eaten? I didn't know what you had in the house so I brought a loaf of bread and some ham.'

Naomi was right. Calming down and improving her blood sugar level was probably a better way to start. She ignored Hayden as she passed between him and the TV and took in Naomi's tired face and the hand pressed to the small of her back. 'You look like you need to take a load off. I'll make something.'

'No need. I've already done it.' Naomi opened the fridge, pulled out a plate and slid it across the counter.

Rennie eyed the thick slices of multigrain and the lettuce fringing the crusts, not sure she could relax enough to force any of it through the tension in her throat. 'Thanks. And thanks for coming.'

'Let's sit at the table,' Naomi said, then lowered her voice to a whisper. 'So Hayden can't hear.'

Christ, there was more and unless it was a map to Max, Rennie wasn't sure she wanted to hear it, but she carried the plate to the table that overlooked the garden and the gums and the lake beyond, sat with her back to the rest of the room and waited until Naomi had settled her pregnant belly. 'What?'

'Brenda rang.'

Brenda was Max's mum, James's aunt - and maybe she did have a map to Max. 'Has she heard from Max?'

'No. I think she just rang for a chat.'

Brenda and Mike rang every weekend, talked to Max about the garden and his cooking exploits and the weather on the lake. It was so far removed from Rennie's parental experience that she'd listen to Max's end of the conversation with a mixture of scepticism and longing. 'What did you tell her?'

Naomi made a face, like she wasn't sure if she'd done the right thing. 'Well, I didn't want to start a panic, and I wasn't going to say anything at all, but then I wasn't sure if you'd told her already and I figured if she was starting one of her weekend ring-arounds, she might hear it from someone else. So I told her Max was missing.'

Rennie imagined Brenda at the breakfast bar in the house at Yamba, sun streaming in, the hiss of surf in the distance and her hand on her chest in shock. 'Was she okay?'

'She was all, "Oh my goodness" and "Oh dear", and she kept relaying the information to Mike in the background.' Rennie winced. Their visits to Haven Bay could be awkward, Brenda flushed with maternal warmth, Rennie decidedly uncomfortable with it. But to watch her and Mike laughing and fussing over Max was like a window to another kind of life. 'Did she have any ideas?'

'Not really. She seemed as baffled about it as we all are. But she was going off to make a few phone calls, see if anyone's heard from him.'

Was she baffled Max had disappeared or that he'd left another woman?

Naomi pulled the cling wrap from the plate and slid it closer to Rennie. 'Have something.'

She took a bite, forcing it down. 'How come you've got James's car? I thought he was going to the office.'

'He came with me.'

Rennie glanced into the empty yard, a sudden flare of possessiveness at the thought he might have turned his attention to her own private space in the studio. 'Where is he?'

'In the study looking through Max's stuff.'

She swung her head towards the hall, possessive on Max's behalf. She returned the sandwich to the plate and pushed her chair back. Slow down, she warned herself. James wasn't just a business partner. He and Max grew up together, shared a happy kinship all the way into adulthood, forging some kind of proprietary bond that Rennie had never understood. She'd always assumed it was her distrust of family and blood ties that was the real problem. She trusted Max. It didn't extend to relatives. Max could explain him all he liked but James's unreadable face had never changed her mind.

They had something in common today, Rennie reminded herself. He was worried about Max, too, so she should cut him some slack, and maybe he'd see something in the study she'd missed. She got to the door, expecting him to be standing in the room as she had, eyeing the shelves and desk, but he wasn't. He was in Max's swivel chair, parked in front of the computer, hand on the mouse, screen alight, making himself at home with a cup of coffee and a half eaten sandwich.

She couldn't keep the surge of possessiveness from her voice. 'What are you doing?'

His shoulders tensed for half a second before he turned. There was no greeting; he just spoke as though he'd been waiting for her to get there. 'Do you know Max's password?'

She folded her arms and asked again. 'What are you doing?'

He frowned a little, just a hint of what's-the-problem? 'I'm trying to get into his computer.'

'Our computer,' she corrected. 'Why?'

'I thought there might be something on there that would tell me . . . us where he went.'

As though there was forethought to it? 'You think the kid in the four-wheel drive sent him an email?'

He raised his eyebrows. 'You think a teenager in a four-wheel drive took him?'

'I don't know what's happened.'

He watched her for a second, maybe weighing up the edginess in her voice and the day they'd both had. 'Okay, look.' He rubbed a hand across the stubble on his chin, took a deep breath and let it out. 'I'm not sure what to think, either. I just thought it was worth a look.'

She'd been out to Garrigurrang Point twice for the same reason. 'Okay.'

'What's his password?'

'For the email?'

'That too, but I meant for his files.'

Rennie stared at the monitor and the screensaver photo of a sunset over the bay. 'There isn't a password.'

James swung the chair back around, gave the mouse a nudge and the picture was replaced with the desktop photo - another one of the bay taken from Garrigurrang as huge storm clouds gathered like a Hollywood version of an alien invasion. He held the arrow over the icon labelled Max's Stuff, double clicked and a password window popped up. 'Yeah, there is.'

When had Max put a password on his files?

'Any ideas?' James asked.

Was Max worried about her looking at his files? Or maybe he was worried about Hayden getting in and moving things around. He'd done it before. But if he was concerned, why hadn't he told her to do the same? 'No, no idea.'

'I've tried names and birthdays and combinations thereof. His, Hayden's, yours, his family's, mine. Are there any other names he might use?'

'Try Max-Renee.' She spelt the combination of upper and lower case letters that he used for internet security: MaXReneE.

James hit enter and an electronic beep sounded an invalid password. 'Are you sure of the capitals?'

'Yes.'

'Spell it again.'

She watched the keys as he tapped, lifted her eyes to the screen as the beep sounded again. 'I emailed a file to the office for him a while ago and there was no password.'

'When was that?'

'Maybe two weeks ago.' She watched James, thinking the time frame might make sense for him. Possibly there was work that required a password, something with privacy issues. He kept his eyes on the screen, his face expressionless as a muscle at the hinge of his jaw started a slow pumping. If something clicked, he wasn't talking about it.

'What about his email password?' he asked.

'That's the one I gave you.'

He tried it with the email and was refused entry. 'He must've changed it.'

Rennie slid her hands into the pockets of her jeans. It was good practice to change a password and Max had every right to alter it whenever he wanted but, as far as she knew, he'd used the same collection of letters for four years, since she'd moved in and contributed to the cost of the computer. She kept her emails separate, had several accounts, used a different password for each of them, none of them in her real name. She'd encouraged him to be more careful but he always claimed the chances of forgetting a new password were higher than the likelihood of someone hacking in.

Naomi's voice cut the silence. 'Have you found anything?'

'We can't get in,' Rennie told her.

Naomi stood at the door, her gaze moving from Rennie to James and staying there as though she was reading something in his face. Maybe Rennie was the only person who couldn't do it. She glanced at him and saw their silent exchange. Some kind of question from Naomi, an answer from James. Then Naomi smiled at Rennie. 'Come and eat your sandwich.'

She hesitated, trying to interpret what hadn't been said out loud. Was it: Do you need her help?/No, I'm fine? Or: Are you two all right in here?/No, get her out?

'Come on, you should eat. And we have to talk to Hayden.'

Maybe it was Trish's earlier bombshell making Rennie brace for more or the ghost of her past still crowding the corners of her mind or that she just didn't like to be excluded in her own home - but suspicion flared.

She turned to James. 'What are you looking for?'

13

James watched her a second, tipped his head slowly, pensively to one side. 'I don't know.'

It seemed like he'd taken the time to consider his answer, given her the best one he had, but there was something about it, something that made her gut tighten with doubt. Rennie glanced from Naomi's encouraging smile to James's concerned sincerity, feeling the silence stretch with her hesitation.

On the other side of the wall, the toilet flushed, a door banged and then Hayden was in the hallway, speaking before they saw him. 'When's Dad coming back?' He must have expected to see James in the study and seemed surprised when all three of them turned to look at him.

There was no time like the present, Rennie told herself. 'We should talk.'

Hayden rolled his eyes. 'I just want to know when Dad's coming back.'

'That's what we need to talk about.'

He heaved a sigh and slouched against the wall. 'What then?'

'In the living room.' She didn't want to do it crowded into the tiny study or with Hayden taking a stance in the hallway. And she needed the walk to shake off the previous moment and find some empathy for the kid.

Rennie took a seat on one side of the corner formed by the living room sofas. Hayden slouched on the other, as far from her as he could get. Naomi perched awkwardly on the coffee table between them, as though she didn't want to take sides.

Rennie ignored the look of practised boredom on Hayden's face and said, 'I don't know where Max is.'

His brief sneer replied, *Is that it?* 'So you don't know when he's getting back?'

Naomi shifted uncomfortably on the table.

Rennie started again. 'He disappeared from a party last night. I don't know where he is.'

'So he went somewhere. Big deal.'

Maybe to his fourteen-going-on-twenty-three logic, it was cool to go off without letting anyone know - after all, he'd jumped a train in the middle of the night. Or maybe he was too intent on pissing off Rennie to get the message. She continued, her voice a little firmer. 'When the party was over, he was gone. He hasn't come home and he hasn't rung.'

He shuffled himself a little more upright and lifted his chin. 'So, what are you saying? I've got to go to Cairns with Mum? I can't. The plane's already left.'

'No, Hayden. I'm trying to tell you your dad's missing. I don't know where he is.'

He didn't say anything, at least not for eight or nine seconds. It was sinking in, Rennie figured, like a puddle into a rock. She waited, expecting to see alarm or concern grow on his face. Instead, one side of his mouth turned up in a nasty smirk. 'What, he left you?'

Her skin turned cold, anger hardened in her gut and she wanted to deny it resolutely enough to shut down the doubt that was souring in the back of her throat.

'Hayden,' Naomi reproached quietly.

'Well, I would. She's a bitch.'

'*Hayden!*' Naomi snapped.

Rennie clenched her teeth. He's a kid. Don't let him get under your skin. Lay it out and move on. 'I've reported him missing with the police. I'm waiting to talk to a detective.'

'You called the cops?' He said it like it was an overreaction, like maybe his mother had called the police when he hadn't come home before. Maybe she'd called them last night when he was on the train instead of in bed.

Rennie tried to keep the bleedingly obvious tone out of her voice. 'We're worried about him. We're trying to find him.'

'He's just gone somewhere.' It was a barely veiled, *What the hell would you know?*

'Have you spoken to him?'

'No.'

'Do you know where he is?'

'No.'

She hesitated. 'Do you?'

He turned to Naomi and pulled a face that said Rennie was a total loser.

'Hayden,' Naomi said gently. 'Do you know where your dad is?'

Whether it was the gravity in her voice or the fact that it was Naomi who asked, he lost the scorn. 'No, I said. You believe me, don't you?'

He was attempting to get Naomi on side and Rennie didn't have the patience or the diplomacy for this kind of conversation. She shifted to the edge of the sofa, gritting her teeth as she tried to find better words than the ones running through her head. 'This is not about you, Hayden. There's a chance something's happened to Max.'

He swung his face around, ready to unleash another round of go-fuck-yourself but whatever he saw in her expression stopped it before it reached his lips. Comprehension slid through his eyes and suddenly his arrogance looked more like vulnerability. 'What do you mean?'

Naomi shot her a glance, another silent communique like the one she'd shared with James. This one Rennie could read: *go easy*.

'I'm worried he might be lost.' Be honest, Rennie. 'Or hurt.'

He watched her a second, then Naomi, then Rennie again. Uncertainty morphing to fear morphing to agitation. 'Nah. No way.' He sat up straight, his agitation morphing to something angrier. 'No way he got lost. He knows this place better than anyone. Better than Uncle James.' He narrowed his eyes at Rennie, his voice abruptly loud. 'He's probably not even here. He probably hitched a ride to the station and jumped a train. Probably to get away from *you*.'

Her chin jerked up as though he'd given her an uppercut. Today, after her sister's voice doing the rounds in her head, after Trish's revelations, his words stung. She stood and stalked to the bay window.

'That's not fair,' Naomi was saying. 'We don't know where he is. And he loves Renee. You know that.'

'Well, he's not lost,' Hayden insisted. He still had his brain stuck so far inside his teenage resentment that he was missing the point.

Rennie walked back to him, no desire to soften the blow this time. 'He might be hurt. One of the options here, Hayden, is that someone hurt him. That someone took him and hurt him. And you need to get over yourself so we can concentrate on finding him.'

As soon as the words were out, she wanted to snatch them back. Hayden was a brat, no two ways about it, but he was also the same kid who'd come here last night to see his dad. And there were tears in his eyes. Shit.

'No one would hurt my dad. You can't say that.'

'Hayden.' Naomi reached for his hand.

He pulled it away. 'He's gone somewhere, that's all.'

'Hayden, honey,' Naomi tried again.

'*She* probably made it all up so I'd have to go to fucking Cairns.'

Rennie watched as he turned his back on her, grappling for Naomi's sympathy, his blame game not biting now, just throwing up memories of herself at his age. No, a year older and with worse news: her mother's murder. She'd reacted with disbelief, too.

She couldn't believe her mother had been right. After all the years of telling her daughters he'd come, drilling them to flee at a moment's notice, waking them in the night for practice, climbing out windows in their pyjamas, going hell for leather to the allotted hiding place -

enough paranoia to make Rennie think her mother was the one with the mental problem - and he'd actually, finally, brutally done it.

In all the time they'd been on the run, the cops had turned up only once. It was early on and their father had unearthed them at a block of flats. Rennie and Joanne, both too young for high school, had fled like they'd been taught. He'd beaten their mother senseless, would probably have killed her then if a neighbour hadn't intervened. Their mother claimed he'd found them other times after that, not that Rennie ever saw him. Every now and then, their mother would turn up at school or walk in after work, say, 'He's here. Go pack your bag.' And she'd load them into the car, no goodbyes and nothing that wouldn't fit in their kit. Rennie once saw the slashed furniture in their on-site van before they left but that had been well before her mother became the suspicious, over-disciplined, unhinged person she was at the end. By then, Rennie had decided her father had forgotten them, that it was her mother who was crazy, who couldn't give up the chase.

Then he parked a car right outside their van one night. Joanne was working, making burgers at a takeaway. Rennie was given the whispered order: *Go!* She'd answered back - *For God's sake, Mum, we've only been here three months.* Her mother dragged her from the kitchen nook, pushed her towards the back of the van, angry, insistent. *Go! Now!* So she had, past the allotted safe spot, not stopping until the pent-up anger was run out of her. When she got back, the cops were there and Sergeant Evan Delaney sat her down in the back seat of a patrol car, knelt by the door and explained her father had been there. No, she had no father. Her mother was crazy; it was all in her mind, she'd told him. But the fatal knife wounds were real.

Rennie had fifteen years to prepare for it and she hadn't been able to believe it. What could she expect of Hayden - an indulged kid with two safe homes and parents who loved him?

She backed off as Hayden shot to his feet and made no attempt to stop him as he stomped across the room.

'I'm outta here!' he yelled.

'Hayden, wait!' Naomi called, going after him as the front door swung open and hit the wall.

'Let him go,' Rennie said.

'But. . .' As loud footsteps crossed the deck, Naomi looked anxious, holding onto her stomach as though she might follow if she didn't have the weight of an almost full-term baby to haul with her.

'If he can catch a train in the middle of the night, he can go for a walk in Haven Bay,' Rennie said. 'Let him work it off.'

Rennie wanted to join him. Not literally - pacing it out alongside Hayden would probably do both their heads in. But remembering her mother's late-night drills and the organised pick-up-and-run routine made her want to do something now. Anything except standing around feeling useless and uncertain. She thought of her mother tossing a sandwich or pack of chips into the back seat after she'd filled up with petrol on those get-the-hell-outta-there trips. *You should eat now. I don't know when we'll be stopping again.* Rennie walked to the dining table, picked up half of the sandwich Naomi had made, stood at the back windows looking out at Max's garden and forced herself to eat.

'Sorry that went so badly.' Naomi stood next to her, the rest of the sandwich on a plate in her hand. 'I don't think I helped much.'

'No, you were great. It would've been worse if you weren't here.'

'He doesn't mean what he said. He's just upset.'

'Don't be too sure about that.'

Naomi made a face - sympathy and comfort. 'How're you holding up?'

'I don't know. I'm worried more than anything. I think it's something bad. That kid in the car. But then . . .' She turned a little to see Naomi's face better. 'Trish told me Max disappeared a couple of times when he and Leanne were together.'

A small frown was followed by a gasp of memory. 'Oh God, I'd forgotten about that.' Then uneasy eyes met Rennie's as the significance hit home.

'We had an argument last night,' Rennie told her. 'Before the party and then at the party. Just a few nasty words but it was the last time I spoke to him.'

Rennie saw the torment on Naomi's face and knew not all of it was about Max. She hated to see people upset.

She didn't watch sad movies because she couldn't bear it, even on screen. Rennie had heard her go beyond the call of duty to find nice things to say to people who didn't deserve it or want it. Now, biting her lip, forcing a comforting smile, she looked desperate to say something reassuring but struggling to find a direction. 'It was a long time ago. He was different back then. Before the cave-in.'

And yet he was missing after they'd had an argument. 'I thought we were okay, that everything was fine but ... if he was unhappy . . .'

'Rennie, he loves you.'

Yesterday, she would have said, 'Well, yeah, obviously.' Today, she wasn't the same Renee Carter, the one she'd 'discovered' in Haven Bay. Today, she had voices in her head - Hayden's, Trish's, Joanne's. *Who can love that?* And her own voice was asking, *Does he?*

A sound from the study made her glance around, another question in mind. 'What's James looking for?'

'He said there was some work stuff he needed for next week, you know, in case Max . . . isn't back. Or needs some time off after . . . just if he needs some time off.'

Rennie frowned. 'That's not what James said.'

Naomi's eyes flicked briefly to Rennie's, too quickly for another of those unspoken conversations, long enough to reveal the discomfort in them.

'Naomi, what's he looking for?'

The shake of her head was almost imperceptible. 'I can't. . .'

Then James was at his wife's side, a proprietary hand on the mound of her stomach. 'Everything okay?'

'No, James. Max is missing,' Rennie snapped, mad at him because there was no one else.

'I meant with Hayden.'

'Oh, that was peachy. A real bonding moment. Did you find it?'

He hesitated, then glanced at Naomi.

'She didn't tell me what you were looking for but I want to know.'

'Rennie, I don't think . . .'

'If you know something, tell me. I just want to find Max.'

'You should tell her, James,' Naomi murmured.

He didn't say anything, simply watched Rennie for a long drawn-out moment. Not tense, not relaxed, just still and unreadable like always. The landline rang, shrill and urgent in the silence. She wanted to bolt across the room and grab it but she held her ground. There was something else and James knew what it was.

'Rennie, the phone,' Naomi said.

She moved then, blood pulsing in her ears as she grabbed it. 'Hello?'

'Renee Carter?'

'Yes.'

'This is Detective Phil Duncan. I'd like to talk to you about Max Tully.'

A hand flew to her throat. 'Have you found him?'

'No, I'm sorry. I have no news regarding his whereabouts. I'd like to ask you some questions, though. Where are you now?'

Naomi stood beside her as she gave directions from the main street. James stayed by the back windows, his gaze fixed on the view.

'Do you want us to stay while you talk to the police?' Naomi asked when she'd disconnected.

Rennie knew enough about cop stuff to guess the detective would want to talk to relatives and colleagues. James filled both categories. If he stayed, it might speed things up and, for better or worse, because facts were safer than assumptions, she wanted to hear what he had to say.

'Yeah. I think that would be best.'

14

'I was at my in-laws' place over at Coal Point for Sunday lunch, which was why I could get here so quickly,' Detective Phil Duncan told Rennie as he followed her into the living room.

Quickly? It was four o'clock. She found the blood at nine-thirty this morning. But it was his day off, she told herself, and he came anyway. 'Sorry your lunch was interrupted.'

He held up a palm. 'My mother-in-law is a lovely lady but her pork crackling could break teeth. I picked up a toasted sandwich at that cafe near the car park.'

She smiled a little, figured there'd be time to fill him in about her job later. Right now, there were more important things to talk about. She made the introductions to James and Naomi, explained the family and business connection. He shook hands with them both, made nice for a few moments.

'So what happens now?' Rennie cut in, impatient to get started.

'Do you mind if we sit?' He gestured to the sofa as though he was the host.

Actually, she wanted to pace the room, wring her hands, check the backyard again, but she nodded, took a seat on the sofa and waited while James and Naomi sat together and Detective Duncan eased his large frame onto the cushion next to her. She picked him as late forties, early fifties, short cropped hair with more salt than pepper, probably as tall as Max but twice his size. Not fat, not by a long way. Big-boned, broad-shouldered and meaty, the kind of man Rennie guessed wouldn't move fast but could take a hit like a punching bag. She glanced at his square, solid hands as he pulled a small notepad from the pocket of his shirt and figured he'd probably throw a fist the same way. He'd look like a standover man if it wasn't for the easy smile and the fluid, baby blue of his eyes.

'So,' Rennie started, 'the blood in the car park. Have the forensics been done down there yet?'

He nodded, took a moment to include James and Naomi. 'First up, the crime scene tech says it's definitely blood and he estimates it got there late last night or in the early hours of this morning.'

Rennie pressed her hands together and slid them between her knees. 'Max went out to the car park at around ten.' He patted the air with his palm, spoke with the tone of experience. 'It's important not to jump to conclusions. There's nothing to connect the blood to Mr Tully at this point.'

'But you took samples? You must think there's a connection.'

'The blood collection is done in case it turns out there was foul play involved in Mr Tully's disappearance. For the moment, though, the fact it's there doesn't prove it one way or the other.'

'But he's missing and . . .'

'Let him finish, Renee,' James said.

She shot him a glance. 'And there's blood in the last place he was known to be. Doesn't that suggest something?'

The detective nodded again, some kind of recognition that further explanation was required. 'There was also a brawl at the pub last night. I took a witness report this afternoon that suggests the fight continued in the car park and that a man was seen with blood on his face. I'll be following up further but at this stage it suggests there are at least two possible explanations for the blood.'

Rennie said nothing, not sure what to think. Detective Duncan had clearly done more than buy lunch and talk to a crime scene tech.

But if it wasn't Max's blood, if someone else had bled on the roadway, what did that mean? That the cops would be less likely to look for him? That Max had just walked away from the party? 'Can't you test it or something to see if it's Max's?'

'It sounds like they're doing everything they need to do, Rennie,' James said, his tone more patronising than soothing.

The detective smiled patiently. 'The sample will be sent off to test for blood grouping. If it doesn't match Mr Tully's, we can obviously rule out that it's his. On the other hand, if it matches, we still can't assume it's his, just that it's his blood type. Do you know what his is, Renee?'

'I can find out for you,' Janies offered.

'He's A,' Rennie said. Max was a regular blood donor. He called it reimbursement for the blood he'd received after the cave-in - and he always came back boasting as though his type was an exam result.

The nod from Duncan this time was apologetic. 'Unfortunately, thirty-eight per cent of the population is type A.'

Great. 'What about DNA? Wouldn't that show if it was his?'

'DNA takes a couple of weeks and it won't be done unless there's evidence of a crime.' He saw her frustration and held up one hand like a stop sign before she could say anything. 'There's no point for DNA yet. It won't find him and it's only used as evidence to help prove guilt in the event of foul play. While I'm here, though, it would be helpful if I could collect a DNA sample for our files. A toothbrush or hairbrush would be best.'

She glanced at James, not sure she wanted him adding any more supportive comments while she was out of the room.

'Before I leave will be fine. Can you tell me what happened last night, Renee?'

Rennie crossed one leg over the other and pulled in a long breath. 'I've explained it three times to three different police officers and I went into Toronto Police Station this morning and signed a missing persons report. What part of the story do you want me to repeat?'

She saw James shake his head, Naomi touch his knee and

expected the cop to reply with irritation, but Detective Duncan surprised her.

'I know this is frustrating and you'd probably prefer to have a search party out looking for Mr Tully but I'm coming in fresh here. I haven't seen the report you filed yet and I only spoke briefly with the constable you met this morning at the car park. It was more important that we got a canvass of the area going. It'll help me a lot if I can hear the story from you.'

Rennie wondered briefly if the hard man in him had to work on his concern or whether it was a naturally useful foil for his physique. Maybe he'd just seen enough people on a bad day to know staying calm got a better result. Either way, his tone took the edge off her anger - and it made sense for him to hear it firsthand. She closed her eyes for a second, tried to ease back on the impatience and think chronologically.

She told him about going to the party, the kid in the four-wheel drive, the altercation in the car park. About Angus McDonald hearing Max say he was going to check the car and the search they'd conducted in the dark. She tried to remember the questions the other cops had asked and included that information, too. She finished with everyone she'd phoned. Detective Duncan interrupted only once to confirm he'd written down the number plate of the four-wheel drive correctly. Other than that, he listened, took notes and held up his hand once to James when he tried to interrupt with his version of the search party.

When she was done, he turned to James and Naomi and went through their versions of the evening. Naomi spoke to Max a couple of times at the party, last saw him when they stood together during the speeches. He hadn't mentioned the road rage kid and didn't seem worried. James explained he was late. 'A little after ten, probably before ten-thirty,' was as close as he came to an arrival time. He didn't see Max at all; after the search he drove to the office in Toronto to look for him. The last time he saw him was at work on Friday afternoon.

Detective Duncan had been there three-quarters of an hour when he asked for a drink of water. As Rennie filled four glasses, Naomi propped herself on the other side of the counter.

'How are you doing?' she asked.

'I'm fine.' She'd had worse interviews with cops. 'I just wish he'd move on to something that isn't already written down somewhere.'

'I'm sure he'll get there.'

And Rennie was sure Naomi's only reference was the police information stall at the annual Haven Bay Fair.

The detective had moved to the back windows and was peering into the garden as James talked quietly beside him. Rennie watched their backs as she carried the drinks over, wondering what James needed to say out of earshot.

'Nice view you've got,' Duncan said as he took his glass.

She 'mmm'd' in reply, figuring he was using the opportunity to make some kind of assessment of where Max lived.

'James was telling me the house was his grandmother's.'

'She lived here for almost sixty years,' James added. 'She passed away a year or so after Max's accident. Apparently, she thought he'd never work again and changed her will a couple of months before she died so he'd have somewhere to live.'

Rennie looked quizzically at him. That's not how she'd heard it explained.

'What kind of accident was he in?' Duncan asked.

'Do you remember the mine collapse at Teralba?' James asked. 'Max was the guy they pulled out.'

The cop made a soft whistling sound. 'It took a while, if I remember.'

James nodded. 'Twenty-odd hours.'

'There was a fatality, wasn't there?'

'The other guy in Max's team. Dallas Brownston.'

'That's tough. He obviously worked again, if you two are in business.'

'Yeah, nothing much stops Max.' James said it as though it was a breeze, as though he just got out of the hole and got over it. Maybe it was pride in Max's accomplishment but Rennie knew it paid for a cop to understand history.

'He worked at it,' she said. 'He's still working at it. It hasn't been easy.'

'Yeah, of course,' James added.

'I'm sure,' the detective said. 'And it's great you're all here to help locate him. I've only got a few more things I'd like to go over and I'd prefer to do it with Renee and James separately, if that's okay with everyone.'

'Fine by me.' James propped his hands on his hips, ready to go with his important information.

Rennie crossed her arms. 'Sure.'

He took Rennie first, leading the way back to the sofas and smiling like they were buddies now. 'Mr Tully . . . Max . . . Do you mind if I call him Max?'

She shook her head, wishing he'd just get on with it.

'Can you tell me what kind of mood Max was in before the party?'

Finally new questions. Playful, she was going to say, remembering him grinning at the bedroom door. *Hey, honey, let me help you with those pesky buckles on your overalls.* Then she remembered it hadn't stayed that way. By the time they'd got out of their clothes and reached the floor, he was intense and focused, making love as though nothing else mattered. Then there was the just-throwing-it-out-there *Let's get married.* And the awkward, curt, joke-but-no-joke conversation that followed. She wanted to tell the detective Max didn't have a care in the world but would that make the cops look in the wrong places? 'He was tired. A little stressed, too, I guess.'

'What was he stressed about?'

'He'd had a long week and he'd brought work home. I assumed it was that.'

'What about in the car? How did he react to the other driver's aggression?'

'He was ticked off.'

'Uh-huh. Angry?'

'I suppose.'

'Did he drive faster to try to shake him off?'

'Are you planning to send him a speeding ticket?'

He laughed like she'd cracked a good one. 'Actually, Renee, I'm trying to establish what state of mind Max was in before he disappeared. Did he speed up?'

'No, he slowed down. Forced the kid to drive under the speed limit all the way to the main street.'

'Nice tactic. And the conversation in the car park. A kid in my face like that would make me want to deck the guy. How did Max handle it?'

'He was mad but he kept his cool. He did his best to stop it escalating.'

'Uh-huh. What about at the party? How was he once you two got there?'

Touchy. 'Fine.'

'Did he need a stiff drink?'

'He had a glass of champagne. Not what I'd call stiff.'

'Is that his usual choice of drink?'

'No. Beer and red wine, mostly.'

'Did he drink much at the party?'

'I don't know. I was busy. I work at the cafe and it was a birthday party for one of the owners. I was helping with the food.'

His eyebrows slid upwards. 'Oh, you work at Skiffs. Great toasted sandwiches.'

She nodded, like she gave a toss what he thought of his lunch.

'How much did you *see* Max drink?'

'Only that first glass of champagne. That was the last I spoke to him.'

'And how was he?'

'Well, not drunk, obviously.'

'Still angry?'

'He wanted to check on the car. I told him I didn't think it was a good idea.'

'Why not?'

'I thought the kid might be out there waiting for him. The fact he didn't come back says I might've been right, don't you think?'

He tipped his head from side to side, undecided. As he took a long, silent moment to sip at his water, Rennie glanced across the room at James and Naomi sitting quietly at the dining table. She got an encouraging smile from Naomi, a blank stare from James.

'I don't know what you and Max are like,' Detective Duncan said, 'but when my wife and I go out, I always get her to put my keys in her handbag. I know it annoys her but I can't stand them jangling around in my pocket. Is that what you and Max do?'

'Sometimes.'

'Did Max give you his keys last night?'

'No.'

'So he had his keys with him when he went out to the car?'

'I assume he did.'

'Does he carry just a car key or a bunch of keys, you know, house and office and whatever else?'

'A bunch. Why?'

'Just a thought.'

Rennie saw the give-nothing-away flatness in his eyes, the cop expression every detective she'd ever met had perfected and knew it was more than an errant thought. If Max had his wallet and keys, it wasn't a big leap for someone to find the doors they opened. 'Do you think I should have the locks changed?'

'If that would make you feel safer.'

His noncommittal response told her something else. He was asking about keys and gauging state of mind. Max had been stressed, drinking champagne before he left for the car park. Detective Duncan was assessing whether Max had left of his own accord. She searched for words to convince him that Max wouldn't leave but she had none - no promise not to, no deal struck between them. Only a rebuffed marriage proposal and resentful last words.

'Does Max have other family here in Haven Bay?'

Yes, there were other reasons Max wouldn't pick up and leave. 'It's just James and Naomi now but he's lived here his entire life. He's a fixture at the sailing club and the soccer club.' She smiled, hoping he understood what that meant.

'Okay, all I need now is the contact details of a few friends.'

Rennie felt the smile falter. 'Sure.' Trish and Pav were Max's closest friends. They were the first people he would turn to. But as James took her place on the sofa, she wondered what kind of help they'd offer. So far, Trish had sown seeds of doubt and Pav was party to Max's earlier indiscretions.

15

'It's a gorgeous afternoon. Let's sit on the deck,' Naomi said.

Rennie pulled her face away from the other end of the room and eyed the view through the windows as though she'd forgotten it was there. The lake was still and flat, the calm after a breezy afternoon. She knew nothing about sailing, didn't like the vulnerability she felt on the water, but Max would know with a glance the wind direction, the knots, the best tacking tactics. At this point, though, the only thing she wanted him to tell her was, 'Hey, babe. I'm home.'

Naomi hooked an arm through hers. 'Come on. You're doing everything you can. Some fresh air will help.'

Naomi sat at the barbecue table, while Rennie stood with a coffee mug, watching the talking heads through the windows. 'What should James tell me?'

Naomi squinted up at her. 'What do you mean?'

'Earlier, when the cop rang, you said, "You should tell her, James." Tell me what?'

She sipped tea with her eyes on the lake. 'I love the view from here.'

'Please, Naomi.'

Curling her hands around her mug as though the day was cold and she needed the warmth, she said, 'Something happened at work. I don't know the details.'

'What kind of something?'

'They had a big argument on Friday. I didn't know anything about it until this morning. James wasn't going to tell me but he's so worried about Max.'

'What were they arguing about?'

Her small smile was apologetic, anxious. 'Work stuff. I don't know the details.'

Inside, Detective Duncan's mouth was moving and James was nodding. 'Did something go wrong on a job?' There'd been stuff-ups before - wrong deliveries, billing mistakes - and cross words.

'James should explain it to you. I don't like to get involved in the business side of things.'

'I don't either but... is James worried about Max because of the argument?'

Naomi ran a hand down her throat, dropped it to her belly. 'I can't, Rennie. It's not for me to say. Please.'

Rennie lifted her eyes to the windows again, alarm growing in her gut. What the hell had happened? And why hadn't Max mentioned it? She didn't press Naomi further, figured anything she told her would be a watered-down version of whatever it was she didn't want to tell. Thinking back to Friday night, Rennie remembered Max was distracted. So was she, working on a huge canvas out in the studio. He was tired, said he planned to veg in front of the telly and he was asleep in bed when she came back in at midnight.

Rennie checked her watch, uneasy that James was taking longer with the cop than she had. When the two men finally stood, she walked back inside, looking expectantly from one to the other. James looked right back and said nothing.

'All I need now are those phones numbers and that DNA sample,' Detective Duncan told her. Okay, so he wasn't sharing. She'd tackle James when he was gone.

In the bathroom, she grabbed Max's toothbrush from the cup on the basin, held it for a second like it might send her a message. Christ, she was collecting DNA. She didn't want the cops to have his toothbrush. She wanted Max to come home and use it.

Detective Duncan had a plastic zip lock bag ready when she came back, held it open and asked her to drop the brush in. It was all nice and friendly, no crime scene gloves, no drama, no grave respect for the evidence. Just a friendly smile and a 'Ta.' He gave her his business card on the way out. 'Don't hesitate to call,' he said. 'And make sure you let me know if you hear from Max.'

She found James and Naomi on the deck. 'What took so long with the detective, James?'

He pushed his hands into the back pockets of his jeans and gazed at the water.

'I told her about the argument on Friday,' Naomi said. 'I thought you should be the one to explain it.'

'We should sit down,' he said.

Oh, Christ, it was bad.

They sat around the small, scuffed table in their usual places - Rennie facing Naomi, James in between. One empty seat.

'We've had some financial issues in the business,' James started. 'There's some money missing. A considerable amount.'

Rennie frowned. 'And?'

'I've been trying to trace it back through our accounts.'

'Is that what you were looking for on Max's computer?'

He shifted uncomfortably. 'I spoke to Max about it and he couldn't explain it.'

'So he was trying to trace it, too.'

James paused, took a breath. 'I'm concerned he had something to do with it.'

It took a couple of seconds for his meaning to sink in. 'You think Max *took* it?'

'I don't know. It's possible.'

'Possible?'

'Yes.'

Naomi put a hand on her arm.

'How much money is missing?' Rennie asked.

'Several hundred thousand.'

Her eyebrows rose as though they were on strings. 'How does someone take several hundred thousand without anyone noticing?'

James's smile was laced with amusement. 'We're not running a cafe, Renee. We deal with invoices for that kind of money all the time.'

She pressed her lips together, embarrassed by her ignorance, irritated at his condescension. 'Did you ask him if he took it?'

'Of course I asked him.'

'And?'

'That's what the argument was about.'

'He denied it, right?'

James nodded.

'Doesn't that tell you something?'

'It doesn't tell me where the money went.'

'Oh, come *on*. You can't seriously think Max stole money from MineLease? It's *his* business.'

'I don't know what to think.'

'For Christ's sake, James. He's your cousin. You grew up together. You know he wouldn't do something like that. Couldn't.'

James didn't answer, just let his eyes fall to his hands on the table.

She glanced at Naomi and saw only distress. What the hell? Was James feeling guilty for suspecting him or because he actually thought Max was capable of it? Rennie pushed her chair back, unnerved by James, unnerved by the whole damn day. Then completely thrown by the next thought that went through her mind. 'You think Max's disappearance has something to do with the money going missing, don't you?'

James's eyes were dark when he looked up.

'Oh Jesus. You think he took the money and ran.'

'I don't know what to think,' he said again.

She stood. 'Yeah, James, you do. This is Max we're talking about.'

'And he's a complicated man.'

'*Max* is complicated?'

'How long have you known him, Renee? Four, five years?'

She took a breath, ready with a rejoinder but swung away. What did it take to know a person? What did she know about making an assessment? She'd never trusted anyone but her sister before Max.

Rattled and edgy, she stalked away from them across the deck, leaning against a corner post as the clump of her footfall on the timber brought memories of Max - breakfasts out here and drinks in the evening. He'd carry bowls of food and icy glasses to the table, lounge on a chair with his feet propped on another and say, 'Wonder what the peasants are doing?'

She watched James across the lengthening afternoon shadows, wishing she could read what he was thinking. 'How much did you tell the cop?' she asked.

'I answered his questions.'

'Did you say there was money missing?'

'Yes, of course. He's asked to see my documentation.'

'Did you tell him you think Max took it?'

'I said it appeared that way.'

She clenched her teeth. 'Did he have anything to say about that?'

James seemed to bristle at her tone. 'He asked if I thought Max had . . .' he made quote marks in the air '. . . done a runner. I said, yes, I thought it was possible.'

For someone who claimed to be smart, he was a goddamn fool. Her voice was loud with exasperation. 'What if he hasn't, James? There was blood in the car park. It might be his. He might be hurt somewhere but the cops aren't going to be in a hurry to follow it up now. Not when they think it's more than likely he's taken a bunch of money and . . .' fingers in the air '. . . done a runner.'

James lifted his chin. 'I wasn't going to lie.'

Was he worried about the money or Max? 'You could've given Max the benefit of the doubt so they might look more places than your paper trail.'

'It's the police, Renee. I'm sure they know what they're doing.'

Her scoff did nothing to win his approval. He didn't speak for a long time, just stared at her with the same unreadable, impassive expression he always wore. Naomi glanced anxiously between them.

'We should go,' he said as he stood.

As Naomi braced herself for the upwards push of her belly, he strode ahead to the door and passed Rennie without meeting her eye. Naomi stopped to hug her, whispering in her hair, 'It'll be okay. They've just got their wires tangled. I'm sure that's all it is.'

Rennie followed them through the house, anger and uncertainty and dread loud and pulsing inside her. She closed the front door before they were on the driveway, took long resolute paces to the bedroom, filled with memories of other times in a different life when the same emotions had surged through her.

Like one of Pavlov's dogs, she reacted with her own brand of learned behaviour. She threw open the wardrobe, hauled the stepladder from under the hanging space, climbed high enough to reach the rear of the top shelf and dragged a backpack over the edge.

Unzipping, working fast, she found with her fingers the items she knew were in there: the change of clothes, the rolls of money, the rigid coldness of the weapon, the phone. That was what she wanted. She pulled it out, the charger still attached, plugged it into a socket by the bed and stood by the window as she waited for it to come to life, watching James's car disappear at the end of the street. She scrolled through the stored numbers. There were only a handful, just the names she wanted to keep with her - for speed dialling, for comfort, for police notification - but there were only three she needed to see right now: 'Jo' and 'Evan Delaney' and 'Max'.

She checked the driveway again and thought about running. Leaving and not looking back, the way she'd done it all her life. Never staying to finish anything, leaving when time was up. She'd learned it at her mother's side. Her father's existence, even in prison, kept the training close. Sometimes, lots of times, it'd been more excuse than reason. Sometimes she and Jo had left because they'd never learned how to stay.

The urge was pressing hard on her mind but she didn't *want* to run. Not yet. Not with a chance Max would be back. But she left the phone by the bed to charge and placed the backpack on the floor inside the wardrobe. They were just in case. In case she needed the numbers. In case she needed to run. And because she felt calmer knowing she was ready to go.

16

It was well after six-thirty now and the sun wouldn't set for an hour or so but the end of the day was already in the light that hung over the house. Long shadows stretched across the drive at the front and the edges had softened the shade around the lawn in the yard.

And Hayden had been gone for hours. She found his number in her mobile, typed a text: *Do u need a lift back? I can come get u.*

She hit send and stood by the back door, looking out along the carpet of lawn that rolled towards the lake. The lush hedges that marked the borders of the yard were given extra height by the gnarly, old fruit trees on one side and the pitched roof of the converted garage on the other. It screened them from their neighbours and anyone on the pathway who wasn't standing directly in front of the fence. Secluded, safe, blinkered from the rest of the world. Like her life here. Now, she wondered what she hadn't seen.

Shifting her eyes around the garden, settling her gaze on the veggie patch over near the studio, an involuntary smile started. 'Hey, M-'

She stopped before his name got further. She'd been going to announce that the first cucumber of the season was ready to pick. But he wasn't here to enjoy it. And his best friends thought it was possible he'd buggered off with someone else or left with a bag of stolen money, that he didn't care about his cucumbers. Christ, Rennie, they're *cucumbers.* She squeezed her eyes for a moment then pushed her mobile into a pocket and grabbed the handset for the landline.

Crossing to the fence first, she opened the gate and looked up and down the path again. Nothing had changed. She let herself into the studio, glancing quickly around the neatly stacked tins and canvasses. If James had been in here searching for a clue to the missing money, she'd know. She never left without returning everything to its allotted place. Max laughed about it, called her anal like it was an insult. But she knew what happened when stuff wasn't where it should be.

She was five or six when that lesson was burned into her psyche. She couldn't find a teddy bear one cold morning when they left in a hurry. The next time it was her favourite cap. After that, everything went back where it belonged and she kept only what would fit in her backpack. Later, when it was just her and Jo on the run, the military-style order their mother had instilled in them had let them know when he'd been there, sifting through their stuff - the warning to grab their kits and go.

Rennie spent years drooling in art stores at the big tablets of thick paper but had only ever bought cheap supermarket notepads, the kind that could be stuffed in a bag or left behind without regret.

She crossed the studio, flipped open the large sketchbook on one of the easels Max had made for her and ran a hand over the heavy paper. She didn't remember when she'd started drawing, just that she'd rarely been without pencil or paper. She sketched what she saw: hands, trees, park benches, beach, bush - and the swirls and shapes she saw in her head. There were never any lessons, just the sometimes calming, sometimes frenzied compulsion of it. Then she'd come to Haven Bay and Trish and Pav had unleashed it from its cage.

Not that it was their intention, they just wanted the cafe repainted and left her alone for a couple of hours with paint and brushes. Rennie had never painted anything, let alone a huge expanse of freshly undercoated wall. One long streak of gorgeous lime on pristine white and she couldn't stop. Without thinking, she kept dipping the brush and spreading the green, giving size and colour to the swirls she'd only ever drawn in pen and pencil. By the time they got back, she'd covered half a wall.

Embarrassed, she apologised, promising to paint over it. Trish and Pav insisted she keep going. It turned into a mural and they told everyone about the 'promising artist' working for them. Rennie thought it was a tad over the top until someone offered to pay her. That she could earn money by having a ball with paint and a brush still astonished her.

Rennie stood in front of the almost completed work in the middle of the room. It was as tall as she was, a commission for one of the customers at the cafe who'd wanted a 'wow factor' for the foyer of her home. She'd been working on it for a week. Max had leaned on the doorframe yesterday afternoon and said, 'Nice one, babe.' The rose pink and taupe was still wet on the overalls he'd peeled off her later. What were you thinking then, Max?

The impromptu passion wasn't out of place. He had a thing for her in her overalls and the bed in the studio had got some use more than a few times. But the mood yesterday was . . . different. Their spontaneity was usually lighthearted and fun, especially when there were large canvasses and wet paint to work around. She remembered the naughty-boy grin he'd had on his face when he came into the bedroom but it hadn't stayed there. As he'd covered her body with his and plunged urgently inside her, his expression became focused, driven, his eyes closed until the throaty groan of his release.

When they were done, she'd raised her eyebrows and said, 'Impressive.' He'd replied with a slow, deep kiss on her mouth. At the time, she'd figured he was thinking the same thing she was: that it was a pity they had to go, that they couldn't stay there all night. Now she wondered what else might have been in his thoughts. A final kiss? A lasting memory? A farewell fuck?

She picked up a tube of paint and hurled it at the wall. 'Where *are* you, Max?'

Her voice bounced off the studio walls and came back at her, angry, anxious, apprehensive. She wanted him to drag his arse home and explain himself. Make him mad as hell that she was doubting him, hear him say, 'Why the fuck would you think I'd leave you?'

She wanted to believe he wouldn't. She wanted to believe he loved her. She wanted to believe her life here was the real deal, not something she'd invented to fill a gaping hole in her heart. 'Just come back, Max,' she whispered.

The click of the side gate came like a reply. She lifted her head, heard a crunch of gravel. The path that ran beside the house.

Max?

She skipped around the end of the bed then hesitated at the half-open door. Why would he come around the back? He had keys - or at least he did last night. There was a shuffle on the pebbles, a skitter of stone on stone as feet stumbled. Outside, the yard was grey. She could only see the garden opposite but knew the narrow strip between the house and fence would be dimmer, shadowed by the house and the neighbour's garage. Max left pots and tools and big bags from the nursery down there - his organised chaos, not her fastidious order. Still, Max would know his way.

A clang as something fell. An 'oomph' of male voice.

Rennie glanced behind - not a lot of weapons in an art studio, unless she was happy to swing a can of paint or go for close-order combat with a scraper. Her eyes landed on a stainless-steel kettle. Five seconds later, she was gripping its handle and listening at the door.

Maybe it was Hayden. He had a key, too. She had no idea if he'd brought it with him last night, figured he was more likely to knock on the door and phone if he didn't get a response: Gen Y and unable to proceed without using a mobile first. But he might come around the back if he didn't want to speak to her.

She stood by the wall, pushed the door wider, poked her head briefly around the jamb. There was a lamp glowing deep inside the living room - too far away to illuminate beyond the deck. In the yard, the shrubs and flowers were unformed and colourless in the shadow.

Except by the doorway she stood in. Light spilled over the threshold and through the window beside her. If it wasn't Max or Hayden . . .

She slid a hand up the wall, flipped the switch and listened in the sudden gloom to the quick intake of a breath. Not hers. Out in the yard.

17

Best escape route was through the gate in the fence. With her back to the wall inside the doorway, she flicked her eyes to the gap in the hedge. A clear path from here to there, maybe a ten-second dash. She stuck an eye around the jamb again, just a brief glimpse, pulled her head back as alarm fired like sparks in her veins.

A person halfway across the lawn. Not Max or Hayden. Someone big and silent. She closed her eyes. Not him, Rennie. He was locked away. This was someone else, *something* else - and nothing about it made her want to stop and ask first. She tightened her fist on the kettle, decided surprise was her best chance. She took a breath and launched herself through the door.

She ran straight at him, kettle raised like a club.

'Fuck!'

It came at her loud and breathy. She swung, he ducked, stumbling to a knee.

'Jesus, Rennie!'

Oh, Christ. It was Pav. 'What are you doing?' she yelled.

'What are *you* doing?' He stayed on his haunches.

'*Me*? You're the one creeping around in the dark.'

'I'm not creeping. I was looking for you.'

'Shit, Pav. Why didn't you call out?' She swung the kettle in frustration, away from him this time, heart thumping.

He got to his feet, keeping his distance. 'The house was empty so I came to see if you were out here.'

'So you could scare the crap out of me?'

'No, look, sorry.' He ran a hand over his bald head. He was breathing as hard as she was. 'It was so quiet and when the light went out, I thought something might be wrong.'

He didn't mean a power failure. That kind of 'something wrong' didn't make you creep around. Max had disappeared and Pav jumped to the same conclusion she had: intruder. It should've made her uneasy to have her paranoia confirmed but what she felt was closer to reassurance. If Pav thought Max was with another woman, he wouldn't be worried about a bad guy.

'I thought the same thing when I heard the gate,' she told him. 'I figured Max wouldn't come around the back and he wouldn't be creeping across the yard. Sorry.'

'You're a scary woman when you decide to be.'

She smiled a little. 'More than you know.' The adrenaline was still surging through her as she walked back to the studio to lock up, shoulders and legs twitching with the same energy that had made her charge without hesitation. The same drive that put her father in prison. Scary didn't describe what she was capable of.

She flicked on the yard light, remembering Hayden as they walked to the house. His mobile went to message bank. As Pav let Trish in through the front, Rennie left Hayden a message: 'Can you call me?' She tapped it out in a text, too.

Trish still had post-party eyes plus takeaway from the cafe. She flicked dials on the oven, making worried and relieved noises as Pav told her how he and Rennie had freaked each other out.

'Cannelloni and salads, enough for four of us,' she said. 'We thought you might need some company. Where's Hayden?'

'You didn't see him on the way over here?'

'No,' Trish said. 'Where did he go?'

'I don't know. He's been gone a while. We . . . he . . . was upset when I told him Max was missing. He took off.'

She frowned. 'When was that?'

Rennie checked her watch. 'Three and a half, maybe four hours ago.'

Pav stood beside her at the counter. 'Have you tried calling him?'

'Yes and I've texted.' She picked up the landline, dialled and left a new message: 'Can you call, please? I'll come and get you, if you want. At least let me know where you are.' She heard the edge of anxiety in her voice that sounded like impatience, imagined the roll of his eyes as he listened to it.

'I think we need alcohol, Pav,' Trish said. She pulled the lid off a plastic container, pieced together a cracker with cheese and held it out. 'Eat something, Rennie.'

'Why does everyone want to feed me?'

'Because we need to do something. Here, eat - make me feel useful.'

Rennie smiled a little as she took the cracker. The bourbon and Coke Pav handed her went down a lot easier. She texted Hayden: *Pav and Trish r here. Pav can pick you up if you don't want me.*

'What now?' she asked them both.

'Have you tried his friends?' Trish suggested.

'I don't know who they are. Max keeps a handle on all of that.'

'Who does he talk about then?'

'He hardly talks to me at all. I usually let him have Max to himself and when they're not together he's in front of the TV. I get the feeling the kids around here don't consider him a local these days and tend to fob him off. I know he used to ride his bike around with a couple of boys - brothers, I think - but I haven't seen them in ages.'

'You mean the Beecher kids?' Trish waved her hands around her head. 'Crazy, curly blond hair.'

'That's them.'

'The family moved to Singleton about six months ago.'

'Well, he's not with them then.'

'I could ring some parents with children around his age,' Trish tried. 'See if anyone's seen him.'

Rennie knew what it was like to be the outsider kid and having anxious adults asking if anyone's seen little Johnny wasn't going to make him any more popular. 'It's eight o'clock and only just dark. Maybe we should give him a bit more time.'

'He knows his way around Haven Bay. I think we could wait a while,' Pav agreed.

Rennie nodded at him, at Trish, not entirely sure. About anything.

'Come on, let's sit.' Trish picked up the container of nibbles and Pav took Rennie's elbow, steering her over to the sofas.

'The detective wants to talk to you both about Max. I gave him your numbers.' Rennie sipped her drink, wishing the alcohol would hit a little harder.

'What did you tell him about the other times Max didn't come home?' Trish asked.

'I told him I've never known Max to disappear like this and that I don't know any reason he'd go off without telling me, which is the truth.' She had an itch of doubt and nothing to base it on except her own screwed-up history and she didn't want that colouring any decisions the cops might make. If Detective Duncan knew who she was, he might decide Max had good reason to do a runner.

'Maybe we shouldn't mention it either,' Trish said.

Rennie was grateful she wanted to protect Max but a story like that would come out. Leanne had been a local, too; someone would know her side of the story and Detective Duncan would wonder why they'd covered it up. 'I don't want you to lie.' She turned her head. 'You either, Pav. Is Max having an affair?'

He flicked eyes at Trish, reluctance and guilt in them.

'At this point, Pav, I don't care if he is. I just want to know *where* he is.'

He took a second as though considering how to phrase it. 'If he's having an affair, I don't know about it. If he's with a woman now, I don't know who it is.'

'But?'

'I didn't know before, either.'

'Trish said he told you.'

'He did but not until after Leanne left. When it was happening, he told me the same as he told her, that he stayed with a mate somewhere on the other side of the lake.' Rennie drained her glass and put it down hard on the coffee table. Okay, you want to know where he is, you've got to look everywhere, not just the obvious places. Cold, hard reality had kept her safe for years, no reason not to embrace it now. 'Did you make a list of who he might stay with?'

Trish put a hand on her knee. 'It doesn't mean that's where he is now.'

'No, but I need to cross that possibility off my list. Do you know who he stayed with before, Pav?'

'He never told me names but there's a woman who comes to the pub sometimes who knows him from before. I thought they must've had something going once. And a couple of months ago a woman at the sailing club, crew off one of the boats, came on to him pretty strong. I didn't think Max was interested but. . .' He shrugged.

'What crew? Do you know her name?'

'I'll make a few calls. The questions might get better answers if they don't come from you.'

She nodded. Max hadn't told her about the woman at the sailing club or the one at the pub. It didn't mean he was sleeping with either of them. It didn't mean he wasn't. She checked her watch. It was almost twenty-four hours since he'd left the party, and his son had been gone for more than four. 'It's eight-fifteen. I'll try Hayden again.'

'You text. I'll try him on the landline,' Pav said. He left a message, telling Hayden he wasn't in trouble, they just wanted to know he was okay.

Trish fed her another cracker. Pav topped up their drinks. At eight-thirty, Rennie checked her phone. The battery was fine, the volume was up, there was no text, no missed call.

'What about Naomi and James? Maybe he went to their place,' Trish suggested.

'They were both here when he stormed out. I figured they

would've rung if he'd turned up on their doorstep.' Rennie picked up the phone anyway.

'I'll give Rhonda Tapwell a call. Her kids know Hayden,' Trish said, getting up to find her own phone.

Pav pulled a mobile from a pocket and headed towards the hallway, saying, 'I'll phone Ed at the sailing club.'

'Naomi hasn't seen or heard from Hayden,' Rennie reported back to Trish and Pav. 'She said James went to the office again. She was going to call him to see if Hayden phoned.'

The three of them were gathered at the end of the kitchen counter, Trish and Pav looking as uneasy as Rennie felt.

'Rhonda Tapwell's kids haven't seen him in a couple of months,' Trish said. 'One of the boys looked up Hayden's Facebook page. His last post was on Friday morning.'

'Did he say anything about coming up here?' Rennie asked.

She shook her head. 'Apparently he was talking about school holidays and complaining about going to Cairns. I spoke to Jenny Penzo, too. Her son saw him a couple of weekends ago but not today. She was going to make a few calls and ask people to phone here if they knew anything.' Trish reached across the counter and pressed Rennie's hand to the cool marble top. 'They'd both heard about Max and sent their condolences.'

Condolences? As though he was dead? He wasn't dead. He was missing. Now Hayden was, too, and . . . 'Maybe Hayden's with Max.'

No one spoke for a moment. Three set of eyes flicked from face to face as the concept hung between them. 'What are you thinking?' Pav finally asked.

'I don't know. Maybe Max came back to get Hayden.'

'But he didn't know Hayden was coming,' Trish said.

'Hayden tried to call him from the train before he rang here,' Rennie told her. 'He must've left messages and texts. So if Max had his phone, he'd know Hayden was here.' Rennie remembered the thud on the back fence last night, the dislodged brick. Was it Max out there? 'Maybe he didn't want Hayden to worry about him.' Like she was worried.

Pav frowned. 'How would Max find him?'

Rennie shrugged. 'Maybe they've got a favourite spot. Maybe Hayden went there this afternoon and Max found him.'

'Why would he even look there? Wouldn't he expect Hayden to be here?'

She remembered his words from this afternoon. *He's just gone somewhere.* 'Maybe Hayden lied about not talking to him. Or they spoke after Hayden took off.'

'Max's mobile's been dead for hours,' Pav said.

Since mid-morning, Rennie had only got phone company recorded messages when she dialled his number. She shrugged again. 'If he's with someone, he could've borrowed theirs. He could've borrowed a car, too.' She remembered the mobile she had charging in the bedroom and a new thought crossed her mind. 'He could have another phone. He could have a whole other life.' Christ, he could have taken the money *and* left with another woman.

'Come on, Rennie.' Pav wrapped an arm across her shoulders.

'Don't do this to yourself,' Trish told her.

She was grateful for their support but they didn't know about the missing money and James's accusation and that the revelations of the day were adding up to a Max that Rennie didn't recognise. Guilt and dread pounded in her head as she pushed away from them. She had a life Max didn't know about, that no one in Haven Bay knew about. She'd always figured ordinary people with decent, nice lives didn't need to keep secrets, that it was just her and her screwed-up family. She'd been so intent on keeping her own skeletons locked up that she hadn't wondered if Max had any.

With a bad temper and affairs and stolen money.

Could he have taken money from the business?

It felt like a horrible, disloyal thought and she wanted to hear Trish and Pav's reassurance there was no way he'd do it but after today, she wasn't sure their reply wouldn't start with, 'Well, back before you knew him . . .'

And what about before he knew *her?* Would he believe it if she

disappeared one night and someone from her old life turned up and told him about her trail of destruction?

She walked to the dining table, clung to the back of a chair with a new scenario playing through her mind. Had Max taken the money and left with another woman to set up a new life while Hayden was in Cairns? Was he somewhere buying a new home, planning to pass the news on to his son when he was back and everything was in place? Had he got Rennie's frantic messages and Hayden's telling him he was on the train, ignoring her but coming back for his son?

She glanced up at the touch of a hand on her shoulder. Trish's reflection in the glass was tired and concerned. 'Rennie, honey, you're crossing bridges that aren't even built yet.'

She wanted to scoff at the cliche - there'd never been one that fitted her life. But she knew Trish was only trying to help. 'The problem is that any bridge that gets built from here leads to somewhere I don't want to go.'

'Rennie, stop.' Trish turned her around and gave her a stern stare. 'We're not going there, do you hear me? You need to stay positive. Don't make yourself crazy.'

Crazy like her mother. 'Yeah, you're right.'

'So we're going to have something to eat and wait to hear back from James. Then we make a decision about Hayden, okay?'

It was a plan. Plans were good.

Trish served up the cannelloni and Rennie pushed it around her plate until her phone cut short the stilted, anxious conversation. 'Rennie, it's Naomi. James found him.'

18

'Max? He found Max?' Rennie almost shouted.

'Hayden. Sorry, I'm sorry. I should've said.'

Rennie clutched a hand to her chest, relief and disappointment fighting for a place. 'Hayden,' she mouthed to Trish and Pav. 'Where was he?' she asked Naomi.

'Up at the old gun emplacements.'

'The gun emplacements?'

Trish's eyebrows shot up, Pav's narrowed to a frown. Their faces mirrored what Rennie was thinking. 'What the hell was he doing up there?'

'James said he was planning to spend the night.'

'Are you kidding me?'

'I guess he was upset about Max.'

Naomi was trying to shine a better light but it didn't work. His father was missing, he knew people were worried and he'd made it worse by hiding in the bush in the dark. Did the kid need glasses to see past the end of his own nose? 'Where are they now?'

'On their way to your place. I'd have him here but we haven't got a spare bed at the moment and the baby could come at any time now.'

'Yeah, of course. And he should be here.' This was his home. It didn't matter that Rennie didn't want to see him.

'Don't be mad at him.'

No chance of that - mad didn't cover it. 'We'll be fine.' She hung up and filled in Trish and Pav as she paced about waiting for James's car to pull into the driveway. When the lights flashed on the bay window, she watched from the open front door. James acknowledged Rennie with a brief uplift of his chin from behind the steering wheel. Hayden appeared on the passenger side, shoulders slumped with his standard don't- give-a-shit body language but - and possibly it was just wishful thinking - there seemed to be a little shamefaced head bowing in it as well. Perhaps James had a word or two with him in the car. She hoped so. It would be better coming from him.

Hayden kept his head down as he climbed the steps. 'Haven't you got something to say?' James called.

'Sorry.' It was more grunt than formed word and barely delivered before he'd shoved past Rennie. She watched him skulk down the hall and turn into his bedroom. Did he think that made it all right?

'I don't know if he would've lasted the whole night,' James said from the top of the stairs. 'The wind's come up again and it's pretty blowy at the point tonight.'

She'd been angry at James this afternoon - she still was - but he'd been a one-man search party for Hayden. 'Thanks for finding him. Do you want to come in? Trish and Pav are here.'

He glanced briefly at the glow in the bay window. 'No, thanks. I'll get going.'

She took in the dark circles under his eyes, the shadow of growth on his chin, the stress in the tightness of his mouth and nodded. It'd been a tough day for him, too. 'How did you know to look up at the point?'

'I called him.'

'I called him, too. About a hundred times. When Naomi said he was at the gun emplacements, I figured he didn't have reception. Ignoring me, obviously. And what, he just told you where he was?'

'No. That was a hunch. Max and I stayed up there once. I figured he'd heard the story.'

She'd never heard it. 'You stayed all night up there without telling anyone?'

'It wasn't last month, Rennie. We were kids.'

'Weren't your parents worried?' Her mother would have gone out of her mind.

James shrugged. 'Probably.'

Decent, nice lives in a decent, nice place. 'Well, I'm glad you remembered it. Thanks. I say that for Max, too. He'd be glad you were looking out for Hayden.' Something flickered through his eyes. Concern, disappointment, anger possibly. James had accused Max of leaving town with money from MineLease, maybe he didn't give a shit what his cousin thought at this stage.

'I told Hayden he has to stay here to help you,' he said.

'Gee, thanks.' She could do without Hayden's assistance. James's help was something she hadn't expected.

'I'll talk to you tomorrow. Max'll be all right. He's always all right.'

'I wish I knew that.'

James didn't say anything. No point, she knew what he meant. 'All right' wasn't the same as honest and trustworthy, wasn't the same as, 'He's coming back and everything will go back to the way it was.'

When James was gone, Rennie eyed Hayden's door - what was going through his mind was anyone's guess. She pushed it wide enough to see him on the bed, shoes smearing dirt on the doona, fingers tapping on his iPad. Pushing down her irritation, she tried to find something compassionate, something Max would want her to say. 'Are you okay?'

The narrowed eyes that found hers from across the room were the warning before his words. 'What the fuck do you care? You don't even like me.'

Okay, she knew nothing about dealing with children; she'd barely had a chance to be one herself. All she knew was that she was sick of being spoken to like that. She walked into the room, stood by the bed, her hands balled into fists. 'No, Hayden, I don't like you. You haven't given me a lot to work with. But that doesn't mean I'm cheering when you disappear or that I'm happy for you to sleep rough. I wouldn't wish that on anyone, especially Max's son. This is your home. That doesn't change because he isn't here.'

He looked at her as though she'd just shovelled a great load of horse shit. 'Sleeping out there would be better than being here with you.'

'No, it's not,' she said firmly. 'You don't have to like me, Hayden. You don't even have to talk to me. But believe me, here is better than out there.'

His sullen expression was replaced with a sneer, as though he'd found a hole in her argument. 'What the fuck would you know?'

'I know it's hard and damp and you can never get warm. And you need your head read if you think a concrete bunker at the point is better than what you've got here, even with me in it. Besides, I thought you would've stayed here just to spite me.' She turned, not interested in his response. 'By the way,' she said from the door, 'Trish and Pav are here. They brought cannelloni. There's a plate of it for you in the kitchen if you're hungry.'

'Can I have it in here?'

She watched him a second, not sure if it was a final attempt to piss her off or if he actually thought she might bring it to him with a napkin and a glass of milk. 'If you want it, you can eat it with the people who cared enough to bring it for you.'

Trish and Pav were still at the kitchen counter where she'd left them. 'He's fine,' she told them. 'Ticked off and smelling like he camped out in a cigarette factory but fine.'

'Do you want us to go?' Trish asked.

'God, no. Please stay for a while or I might have to disappear next.' She smiled but the irony made her want to throw something. She always knew she'd have to leave, had told Max right from the start she wouldn't stay. Now it was possible she was the only one who wanted to be here. She took the fresh bourbon and Coke Pav poured for her and gulped like she was dying of thirst.

It didn't take long for Hayden to appear, slouching and sullen as though he was the one who'd been put out.

When Trish wrapped him up in her arms, he pulled his hands from his pockets and held onto her shirt, taking a quick, surreptitious swipe at a tear on his face when she was done. Pav, who didn't shake hands in moments of high emotion, pulled Hayden into a bear hug and told him he had to let them know where he was until his dad got back.

Rennie watched, thankful for Hayden's sake they were there, content to watch how other people did it. Was it any wonder Hayden didn't like her? Standing at his door to ask if he was okay made her seem like a cold-hearted bitch by comparison.

Would she have been any different if her mother had showered her with hugs and gushes of endearment instead of 'Where have you been?' and 'What did you see?' Not maternal interest but covering their bases and instilling observation skills. Those lessons had kept Rennie and her sister alive and she was grateful for that but wondered sometimes if a little less survival training and a bit more affection might have taught her more.

Trish and Pav stayed another hour, keeping the conversation light and smoothing out Hayden's mood as he ate dinner off his lap on the sofa. Rennie felt it soothing her, too, the anger dissipating, the tension in her shoulders loosening a bit, the angst easing up enough for her to unlock her jaw and eat some cannelloni. But the late night followed by a long, anxious day had taken a toll on all of them and when Trish stifled a yawn, Rennie called her on it.

'You guys have been great but it's time you went home,' she told them.

'Are you sure?' Trish asked.

No, she wasn't. The house felt empty and unsettled without Max. 'We'll be okay.'

As she walked them to the car, she breathed in the cool, slightly salty night air, glad to be pacing further than the length of the living room, bracing herself for the next question of the day. 'Pav, did you talk to Ed at the sailing club?'

'It's okay, Rennie. I spoke to the skipper of the boat that woman crews on. He said she separated from her husband six months ago and has been enjoying the company of a few men at the club. Not exactly how he put it but he was pretty sure Max wasn't one of them.'

She nodded. One woman, one option she could cross off. Trish hugged her briefly. 'Try to get some sleep.'

'Do my best.'

'Your shift is covered tomorrow,' Pav said. 'But come in if you want. Pull up a chair or work your arse off. Whatever you need to do.'

She was pleased he understood the need to keep on the move. When he was stressed, he chopped and stirred, baked and sauteed, cooking multiple dishes at once. It'd push anyone else's blood pressure through the roof but he grew calmer and more focused as he worked. Rennie never understood why people recommended rest when you were anxious. How could putting your feet up make you feel better than working or making plans, or running away?

She waved goodbye and started up the curve of the driveway, the gloominess making the hairs on her neck tingle, glad she'd flipped on the powerful outdoor lamps that saturated the carport and front yard with great pools of light. It was Max's thing - he had lighting all around the house. Darkness brought back bad memories. She understood that more than ever after the last twenty-four hours. Wherever he was, she hoped he wasn't in the dark.

Up ahead in the carport, the floodlight mounted on the back wall made his big work vehicle almost glow in the harsh glare and as she approached, she frowned at a dark stripe on the driver's side. Passing the porch, she kept walking, watching the strip. It ran top to bottom as though something had been slipped into the edge of the doorframe. Then she saw it wasn't an object. It was a shadow. The driver's door hadn't caught properly and the bright, white beam behind it was casting a clean line of shadow on the rear passenger panel.

Rennie stood in front of it, her mind reeling back to the early afternoon when she'd driven in. Had she left the door like that? It wasn't like her but she'd seen James's twin cab out front and had thought Max might have been inside.

She gave the handle a light tug. It didn't move. The lock was partially latched, as though the door hadn't swung hard enough into the jamb - it was a heavy vehicle, it happened sometimes. Or when you were trying to do it quietly. A soft click to close, another to fully engage.

Had someone been in the car?

Rennie opened the door, ran her eyes over the interior by the light in the carport: front seats and foot wells, back seat and floor. There were no shoes, no spare clothes, no old receipts or food wrappers. It was Max's car but she rode in it and kept it like it was hers.

Getting in, she breathed deeply through her nose. No new smells, at least not that she could tell. And it was darker in here than it should be - the internal light hadn't come on. She pushed the overhead button and, as the fitting on the ceiling lit up, a chill scuttled across her shoulders. Not broken, turned off.

She glanced uneasily around, leaned past the gearstick, yanked open the glove box and snapped her hand back as though the contents were contaminated. She knew what it *should* look like in there, how she'd left it when she took out the notebook as she made calls from the car park this morning - neat stack of manuals, maps and papers on the left; a torch, a couple of pens and a small first-aid kit on the right. But it didn't. It looked like it'd been picked up and shaken.

Somebody had been through it.

Sometime in the hours she'd been home, someone had let themselves in, turned the automatic internal light off and searched the contents of the glove box.

She got out, closed the door quietly and looked up at the house. There had been people in and out all afternoon, she was out in the yard and the studio for twenty minutes or so at nightfall and it'd been dark for two hours. She turned around, eyeing the front yard. How hard would it be to push through the hedge and slip into the carport without being seen from the house? Not hard at all, even in broad daylight.

Wariness tightened in her gut. Instinct made her hurry to the house. Her mother's voice played in her head. *What did you see*? Rennie wound her mind back to the unexplained: the kid last night, the thud on the fence, the blood in the car park, the man with the camera.

As she let herself in, she remembered that frantic search for the keys Max had mistakenly taken and how the explanation had been obvious. And the ghost of her past whispered another possibility.

Inside, Hayden was sprawled on the sofa, the telly on again, a glazed look on his face. He didn't move as she grabbed her key ring from beside the TV. She stood at the front door, hit the auto lock, watching the rear lights flash and remembering Detective Duncan's question about Max having his car keys with him.

'Did you go out to the car this afternoon?' she asked Hayden.

He didn't bother to peel his gaze from the screen. 'No.'

'The driver's door wasn't closed properly and the automatic light had been turned off.'

'I said no.'

She walked quickly through the house, locked the back door, pulled the roller blinds down. Checked the windows in the study and the bathroom and Hayden's room. Went to her bedroom, shut the door, pulled the blind, picked up the phone from the backpack that she'd left charging by the bed and dialled. It was late, after ten now, but she'd called at worse times.

'Evan Delaney.' The voice was deep, gruff and slightly irritated.

'It's Katrina Hendelsen.'

There were seconds of silence. Maybe he was gathering his thoughts, maybe he getting out of bed, maybe he was clenching his teeth in dread. Whatever the reason for his pause, there was pleasure in his tone when he finally spoke. 'Katrina Hendelsen. That's a name I haven't heard in a long time. I'd ask how you are but it's late so I figure we'll get to that. Where are you?'

'Haven Bay.'

'It's, what, coming up to six years now?'

'Five.'

'Good for you. How's Joanne? Still cranky?'

She smiled, despite the question that was bitter in her mouth. 'Of course, she doesn't know any other way. She's up north. We haven't spoken in a while.' She wanted to get to the point but couldn't bring herself to start or to break the fond familiarity of the moment, feeling calmer just for speaking to someone who knew all her secrets.

Either he sensed her reluctance or he wasn't ready yet to hear the reason for her call. 'Still running?' he asked.

'Every day. You?'

'Only five or ten k now. I'm getting old, you know. You working?'

'At a cafe. And I paint.'

'Houses or pictures?'

'Pictures. Huge ones. People actually pay money for them.'

There was a quiet chuckle. 'You finally graduated from those dinky little notebooks, huh? I've still got one here, you know. Have you got a fella?'

She paused, closed her eyes. 'Yes.'

'You better tell me, Kat.'

'Where's my father?'

PART 2

DARKNESS

19

Max gasped. Shuddered as consciousness arrived. Then the pain hit like a torpedo. Searing, howling, shoot-me-and-get-it-over-with pain.

A cry pitched from his throat and the hollow echo that ricocheted back made panic buck inside him. Eyes bursting open, he blinked fast, hard. It didn't help. There was nothing there. Just black. Dense, suffocating black.

What the fuck? What the *fuck*? When had the roof come down? He hadn't heard it. He should have heard it. Last time . . . rumbling, cracking, thudding as it started to drop.

'Dallas.'

Raising his voice hurt. He was wrapped in hurt. So much of it he couldn't tell where it was coming from. Maybe he'd been crushed. Christ. Not that. Not again.

'Dallas?'

He tried to listen for him, for a sign it was about to fall on top of him. All he heard was the hiss of his own breath, rising dread turning it fast and uneven.

'Dallas!'

He twisted a foot, then the other. Both clear. So were his legs.

How long had he been out? How much air was left? Did he need oxygen?

He snapped an elbow out to grab for the self-rescuer at his belt and toppled sideways, the movement firing sharp, hot missiles. Ribs, neck, head. Something really wrong up there. He could feel the thickness of swelling on his face and his nose was throbbing. No air moving through it. Broken for sure.

Trying more gently for the breathing gear, he stretched out his fingers, felt upwards and sideways over his clothes and . . . No mask. No belt. Where the . . .?

And he was out. Gone. Consciousness snapped off like a light switch.

It came back slowly, a tide coming in. Then it was gone again, flip of a switch.

In like a tide, out like a light. Over and over. And over.

A pattern to it, he told himself in brief seconds of acuity. Hiss of breath first. Sharp pain in his hip next. A starburst pounding in his skull. Then a gasp of panic that made him want to get up and run, made him fling an arm, scrabble for . . .

Out like a light.

Next time, maybe it was ten more times, he didn't know, but he heard the hiss of breath. Don't move, he ordered himself, braced for the panic, gritting his teeth when it arrived, concentrating on the air he was pulling in and out of his lungs instead of the terror of being trapped, lost.

Breathe, Max.

Good.

Last time, Dallas had . . .

Last time . . .

Oh Christ, *last time.*

His agonised cry rebounded into the blackness. Pain, but not from injury. At least not a new one. And not one that could be pinned or stitched and worked off in rehab. Memory hurt like hell.

Dallas wasn't here. He was gone, crushed under rock years ago.

You were never going back, Max. What the fuck are you doing in a coal mine?

'I RETIRED EIGHTEEN MONTHS AGO,' Evan Delaney told Rennie. 'I can't get access to the files at this time of night but I'll make some calls in the morning. First thing, okay, Kat?'

She sat on the edge of the bed, the phone clamped to her ear, an arm wrapped tightly across her waist. She could make calls, too, but retired or not, he'd get the answers faster. 'How long will it take?'

'Depends. If he's still in maximum security at Goulburn, it'll be ten minutes. If he was released, it could take a while to find him. I'll probably have to track down a parole officer.'

Rennie had told Evan everything. The facts first, in chronological order, starting with the kid at the roundabout, finishing with the search of the car. Then she listed everything she'd discovered today: Max's other disappearances, the missing money, the women, the password protection on Max's computer files. Then she padded it out with her own fears, relieved to tell them to someone who didn't need an explanation, who wouldn't tell her not to be negative, who understood where she'd come from, what she'd done to survive it and the facts on the man behind it.

Evan had assumed, like Rennie, that Anthony Hendelsen was in prison, eleven years into his fifteen-year sentence for the attempted murder of his two daughters. He didn't *know*, though. There were processes for informing victims of a prisoner's release and Rennie and Jo had an arrangement, beyond Evan, to make sure they were notified. Release was unthinkable but Evan was out of the loop and it wasn't inconceivable that Anthony was on the street and had found them before news of his freedom had.

Age was a consideration for early parole and her father was sixty-three now. Not your average sixty-three, Rennie guessed. He'd been wiry and strong and tenacious his whole life, he'd run and sparred and lifted weights to stay that way - more than a decade with access to a prison gym wasn't going to reverse that.

'I always hoped he'd piss someone off and get knifed or he'd just rot and die in there. Christ, he could be walking the streets,' Rennie said.

Evan sounded the same as he always had - calm, solid, trustworthy. 'Don't pull the plug yet. It might not be what you think.'

'"Might" doesn't cut it right now.'

'Give me your phone numbers and just sit tight, Kat.'

She gave him both mobile numbers, the landline and two email addresses. 'And it's Renee Carter now. Friends call me Rennie.'

'Nice name. It suits you.'

'Thanks. I like it.'

She hung up, clenched her hands in her hair and felt panic take flight inside her like a large bird spreading its wings. Her father was a violent, disturbed, terrifying man. If he was out, there was every chance Max was bleeding, injured, maybe dead already. The thought made her want to cry out in rage and fear but it was something else that crushed the air from her lungs.

She didn't want to go back. She always knew she'd have to but, now it was here, she wasn't ready - for the dread, the running, the disconnection, the loneliness - and already it was tugging at her like a rip in the surf.

Her breath scraped and rasped in the silence of the bedroom. She clung to the edge of the bed, head bowed, teeth tight, inner voices screeching and berating as she fought the urge to howl out loud - for Max, for herself, for everything she'd found and loved and was suddenly too fragile to survive.

Get your backpack. We're leaving.

She'd heard the words countless times from her mother. Rennie had said them herself. Joanne would say them to her now. Even the possibility that their father was free was reason enough to hit the road.

She shoved the hair from her face, stood and dutifully went for the backpack. It was a lightweight, heavy-duty, black pack with padded straps, reinforced stitching, pockets and zips. Not the kind student travellers bought to lug around the world; that would mark her out as a tourist or visitor. It was small for blending in and moving fast - and she could live out of it if she had to. This afternoon, when she figured the memories were all that would come back, it'd been a comfort. Now the sight and the weight of it made her want to flinch. She knew what was inside and didn't want its lethal coldness in her hands again, didn't want to be the person who was capable of firing it.

She carried it from the wardrobe but didn't lay it on the bed like she'd planned. Just stood for a moment in the centre of the room. Max's room, Max's house. Her home. And thought about the last time she'd hauled it out in a hurry.

When she'd thrown it in her car and almost left him.

They'd argued. She couldn't remember why, just that there'd been yelling. He'd thrown a newspaper across the room, stomped out the back and it had rattled her: her response, not his. She'd felt a familiar heat rise, remembered what was in her DNA and did what she'd always done when it didn't feel right - grabbed the backpack and headed out the door.

Then Max was at the car, breathless, trying to jump into the passenger seat as she headed down the driveway. She slammed on the brakes, not wanting to run him over, surprised he'd made it around the house so fast with his bad hip.

'What are you doing?' she said.

'Going with you.'

'You don't know where I'm going.'

'It doesn't matter.' He clipped his seatbelt in and looked at her. 'So where *are* we going?'

In the silence of her reply, his eyes did a quick tour of the car, finding the backpack on the rear seat. It was the one and only bag she'd brought when she'd moved in and he realised its significance. 'You're leaving?'

'I always said I would.'

'Because we had an argument?'

'I won't argue.'

He didn't speak for a moment, as though her words were moving in slow motion across the space between them and he was waiting for them to arrive and sink in and make sense. 'Okay,' he finally said. 'Then we better get going.'

'What?'

'You said you were leaving - you didn't say I couldn't come. If we have to leave to sort this out, then let's get started.'

'There's nothing to be sorted.'

'Then come back inside.'

'No, Max, I'm going. I never lied about that.'

'Then explain it to me again. I get that you've never lived in one place for long, that someday you'll need to move on. I get that, I do. But why leave when it's good? Okay, we had a disagreement but it was three minutes of frustration in a year and a half of quality stuff. Superior, A-l relationship stuff, Rennie. I mean, if you're unhappy or bored, fine, go. It makes sense, I wouldn't want you to stay. But we're good together. Why would you leave that?'

'I don't want to . . . fight.'

'It's not a prerequisite.'

She'd smiled a little then. He could make her do that.

'Look,' he reached out and tucked a strand of hair behind her ear, 'I don't know what happened to you before we met and I'm not going to ask what you don't want to share. It was bad, I know that much, and I figure *this* . . .' he waved a hand around, taking in the pack in the back, 'has got something to do with that. I'm the last person to tell you what to do. I've fucked up just about everything that can be fucked up. I just know that the past doesn't have the right to stop you from enjoying what you have now.'

The memory of Max's words, his actions that day, made Rennie flick her eyes around the bedroom. 'It's not the bad old days. Not yet,' she said out loud to herself. 'I'm not Katrina Hendelsen. Not yet.'

20

Rennie propped the backpack against the wall by the bedroom door, then lifted her head at the noise coming from the living room. Tyres screeched and something crashed and exploded somewhere in Hollywood. You are Renee Carter tonight, she told herself. Responsible for Max's son.

She brushed her teeth and washed her face then went to the living room. 'It's late. I'm going to try to get some sleep,' she told Hayden. 'You should think about it, too.'

'I'm not going to bed,' he said as though she was threatening to make him.

'Okay. Can you leave the lamp on in the bay window when you do? In case Max comes home.'

His eyes flicked to the lamp and back to her, his tone softer when he answered. 'Yeah.'

It encouraged her to probe a little. 'Were you looking for him this afternoon?'

He shrugged, his eyes dropping from hers.

'Where did you go?'

'Around the bay. This fishing spot we go to sometimes.'

'Where?'

He looked up, his focus not quite making it to her face, as though he was prepared to have the conversation, not ready to admit it was with her. 'On the south side of the point. I didn't think anyone else would look there.'

'Did you find anything?'

He shook his head. 'I searched all around the rocks. I kept thinking his watch might've fallen off. You know how it's got that dodgy clasp?'

'Yeah, I looked for it, too. Is that why you went to the gun emplacements?'

'I didn't really think he'd be there. It's just that, well, it's right above the fishing spot and on the way back I figured . . .' The explanation trailed off to another shrug.

She imagined him up there doing the same thing she'd done - searching unlikely places because she'd already searched the likely ones. 'Did you get to all five of them?'

'Yeah.'

Then maybe he got mad and upset and felt sorry for himself, like she had out in the studio. If she was Trish or Naomi, she might offer some words of wisdom, maybe a bit of sympathy, but she was Rennie and Katrina and all she had was her own brand of empathy. 'We'll keep looking tomorrow.'

His eyes found hers then, something young and needy in them.

'Good thinking today,' she added, cringing at the echo of her mother's no-nonsense tone. Oh, that'd make him feel a whole lot better.

MAX FELT like he'd been crumpled on the gritty, unyielding surface for hours.

It could have been days.

Or minutes.

He blinked to be sure his lids were open. Pitch didn't describe the blackness. It was a substance in itself, filling his nose and mouth. One he'd lived in fear of for six and a half years. Twenty-two hours he'd spent in dark like this, pinned by rock, Dallas dying slowly at his side with nothing but Max's fingers to hold onto. Then he'd just laid there, waiting - for rescue or death.

He didn't know where he was now or how he got here or whether there was anyone who knew he'd gone. All he knew was that it was a different day and a different place and he wasn't dead yet.

Moving gingerly, he lifted fingers, ran them across his pockets, his wrist. No phone, no watch, nothing to shed light. He lowered them to the ground, felt the floor underneath him. Small stones, loose earth, not coarse dirt but soft like sand - and dry. He raised his other hand, met a hard, flat surface centimetres from his hip, going straight up. Rough. Not regular enough for concrete. Cut but not hacked up. Intact, not crumbly. Solid and immovable and stretching as far as his fingers could reach. He pressed his leg against it, felt it at his thigh and ankle. Still rigid and solid down there. Like the wall of a mine. Or a cliff face.

No, wherever he was, it was too silent and black to be outdoors.

A tunnel then? Or a cave? An underground air hole? Chamber? Dungeon?

Fuck.

A stone under his hip was the source of the sharp pain there - not crushed bones this time. He scooped it out then used fingertips to prod at his sore bits. There was rib damage, possibly a crack but nothing dislodged. His nose was a mess: swollen, tender, the nostrils crusted over. Blood, he assumed. He traced more dried blood up one side of his face to a gash that ran across his temple and into an eyebrow. Feeling gently across his scalp, he found the source of the starburst thumping at the spot where his skull met his vertebrae. He pressed it, felt pain explode and his stomach lurch with nausea - and froze, wondering if turning his head would sever his spinal cord.

What now? Stay here like a corpse, hoping someone came to get him? The Grim Reaper would, no doubt about that. Whether anyone else would, he had no clue. But he'd waited to die in the dark once before - he wasn't doing it again.

Breathing hard, clenching his teeth, he heaved himself upright, pressed his back into the wall and hoped the crazy spinning in his head was going to stop. He wiggled his toes then his fingers. Okay, that had hurt but it hadn't severed his spinal cord. Good start.

He took a careful breath and let it out on a shout. 'Oi!'

The effort stabbed at his ribs. The sound echoed back at him. Not the shy reverberation of a wide open space but a gutsy, rebounding repetition that told him he was somewhere large and enclosed. He picked up a pebble from under his palm, threw it straight ahead. It'd barely left his hand when it hit something and bounced back to the earth beside him. He stretched his legs out, pushing with the heels of his shoes, feeling only clear air. The other side was close; not close enough to touch.

He tried again with another small stone, throwing to his right. It was a second or more before he heard the missile land with a soft tink. The same to the left. One more time, he tossed straight up. A small tap was followed by a drop to the floor. Further than the surface opposite, not so far as left or right.

All right, closest first. He held his neck as he lifted his spine from the wall, shifted butt then feet, a little at a time, pain drilling in his head, until his shoes touched something. He patted across the surface with a hand. Same as the other wall - hard, solid, immovable.

Two sides of a narrow, hollow space. Which meant. . .

He was in a hole? An old mine shaft, maybe. He'd fallen in here? Headfirst? Like Alice in fucking Wonderland?

What were you doing, Max, to be stupid enough to fall down a goddamn hole?

He looked right then left, as though the blackness on either side might tell him. All it said was that if he went one way, an escape hatch could be two metres in the other direction and he'd never know.

No guts, no glory, Max.

He paused, took a breath and rolled to his left for no other reason than to protect the damaged ribs on his right. Pain ricocheting around his skull, he kept the wall within touching distance. He'd been in enough coal mines to know the giveaways - wire on the walls, mesh for ventilation control, timber supports, roof and rib bolts. A disused mine, even an ancient one, would have supports and/or bolts.

When he stopped, he was breathing as though he'd run five k. There was no way of knowing how far he'd gone - not as far as he'd like, possibly only a few body lengths - but enough to find the evidence if it was here. And it wasn't. This wasn't a coal mine.

So he hadn't smashed his head falling down a mine shaft.

Had he even fallen? Was he already injured when he got here? Maybe he'd cracked his head some other way, in a fight or a car accident, and he'd stumbled about concussed and confused and ended up here. Which meant if there was a way in, there was a way out, right? And maybe it was dark because it was the middle of the night. Maybe if he just sat here for a while, the sun would come up and he'd see his way out.

He rested against the wall, swallowed on the harsh dryness in his mouth and rubbed at his forehead, trying to coax out the memory of how he got here. But there was nothing. His recall was as black as the space before him. No faces, no places, no conversations. The only thing he got was an urgent, pressing sense that there was something he needed to do.

He squeezed his eyes tight. What was it?

Nothing. No idea at all.

Then what did he remember?

Dallas.

Not his big, stupid grin or his gravelly, you-know-you- want-to laugh. But the weak, breathy sound of his voice in the dying moments of his life. *Have a good life, Max. I don't mean a good time. We've done that already. I wish I'd thought about it before now. It's got to be ... I don't know. Worthwhile. Just don't fuck it up.*

Max dug his hands into the earth beneath him, squeezing on the sharp pebbles until they cut into his palms, not sure he wanted to remember now.

I don't give a shit where you are, Max.

Thanks, Leanne. Thanks a whole hell of a lot.

She wasn't going to come looking for him. He was gone a week last time and she'd welcomed him home like he'd ruined her holiday. Well, what had he expected? He drank too much, he stayed out late, he put his hand up for night shifts. Everything she told him not to do. He'd tried to make it work - seriously tried - but it didn't change the fact they should never have married. That they were a summer romance that'd run too long, that hauling rocks out of a hole paid the bills but would never satisfy him. That saying 'I do' for the sake of an unplanned pregnancy didn't make it 'I can'. Maybe this time, she'd just go to Sydney like she was always threatening.

Oh God. Hayden, he thought. And a great wave of sadness crashed through Max's pain.

He didn't want to lose Hayden, didn't want him growing up with a weekend dad, wanted his son to have a family like he had. And now he remembered Leanne had already taken his son. She didn't have to worry about finding a job before she buggered off - she'd met some arsehole dentist with a fucking mansion while Max was digging mines. All she had to do was drop by his hospital bed on her way out of town. *I don't love you. I don't even like you anymore. And I don't want to look after you when you get out of here. I've already wasted enough of my life in Haven Bay.*

A week after promising Dallas he wouldn't fuck it up, he had. He was Max Tully. It was what he did.

And now he'd done it again. He must have. He was in a goddamn hole with blood oozing from his head and there was something . . . something big and important he had to . . . and he couldn't remember what it was.

21

Rennie's night was long and restless. Plenty of tossing and turning, plenty of ugly thoughts, plenty of memories to reinforce them. Enough to make Rennie flick the bedside lamp on in the quiet, early hours, pull the gun from her pack and clean it.

It was a Glock 17, the world's most reliable semiautomatic handgun - a lethal piece of equipment but useless if it wasn't in good working order. Joanne had given it to her the day she finished her treatment with Dr Foy, a replacement for the one the cops had removed from her. A graduation present, Jo called it. It'd repulsed and reassured her and after twelve months of discussing security and stability and dealing with her fears, she'd wanted to sample life unarmed but couldn't bring herself to hit the road without it. Lessons of a lifetime versus three times a week for a year.

She'd cleaned it regularly at the start, kept it oiled and the clip empty to save the springs. Then not so often, then not at all. She wasn't sure if it was complacency or a sense of security. But at this point, neither was appropriate. She fitted it back together, tested the slide, dry-fired, loaded the clip, inserted it and left the chamber empty.

Before dawn, Rennie stood in the bay window, peppermint tea warming her palms as she watched the sun come up for a second morning in a row, anxious, wired and a little ticked off.

It might not be what you think, Evan had said. She hoped to God he was right about her father but after hours of trying to pull all the threads together, none of the possible scenarios fit.

If the kid from the four-wheel drive had gone back to the car park and assaulted Max, it explained the blood and not much else. Not the thud on the fence or the overturned brick or the search of the glove box. And how did the missing money come into it?

Some of the pieces held together if Max had left her: his previous disappearances, the password protection on the computer, the missing money, the women, maybe even the unfinished text message. But what about the blood, the fence and brick, and the glove box. She could reason that the blood wasn't Max's and that Max himself had been at the back fence and had later riffled through the glove box except. . . what would he have been looking for? Pen and paper to write down his escape route?

The father-released-from-prison option didn't come together neatly, either. The unfinished text message, the blood, the fence and brick, and the glove box made sense. Even the guy with the camera worked - she had no idea what her father looked like now, but the photographer with the brimmed hat had been small, wiry and carrying enough years. That still left the missing money and the password protection. What did they have to do with her father?

And how long was it going to take Evan to get back to her?

She wandered aimlessly through the house, tidied the sofa cushions where Hayden had been sitting, washed and dried the dishes he'd left. She was sick of searching the house for clues to Max but in the end, she found herself standing in front of his side of the wardrobe again.

She tucked errant clothes into drawers, straightened shirts on hangers, sorted and refolded. She wiped down his junk shelf with a rag and flipped through the papers again. There were receipts for new shoes and a phone charger, she saw the car insurance was due next week and smiled at a photo of the two of them. She fingered through the ashtray, spilling coins, paperclips, rubber bands and tacks. She couldn't locate a mate for a single cuff link but found the plastic cap for a USB thumb drive and replaced it. As she was scooping the contents back in, the landline rang.

She dived across the room. 'Evan?'

'Rennie, it's Brenda. Did Max come home?'

She closed her eyes. On the odd occasion Rennie spoke to Max's parents on the phone, she felt clumsy and cautious with her words, not sure of the right response to their enthusiasm, rattled and uncomfortable with their warmth, conscious of not saying anything to damage it. 'No. Not yet. I take it you haven't heard from him, either.'

'No. I've called everyone I can think of. Annette in Perth, Aunty Roz, Aunty Cath and Uncle Grant in Wangi . . .' Rennie listened as Max's mum reeled off a long list of relatives and family friends, school and sports buddies who lived close and far. She must have been on the phone for hours. 'I expect they'll let me know if they hear anything but I'll do another ring-around as soon as I've had my breakfast.' She sounded concerned but also efficient and practical, as though it was just a matter of tracking him down so they could stop worrying.

Rennie figured that was about to change. 'I spoke to a detective yesterday afternoon.'

She heard a quick intake of breath then a new current of alarm in Brenda's voice. 'Wait a minute, I'll get Mike.' There was crackling and rustling before Brenda's muffled voice called to Max's dad. 'Mike, I've got Renee. You need to hear this.'

Five seconds later, his brisk voice was on the line. 'I'm listening.'

'The police are involved,' Brenda said into the phone and Rennie guessed Mike had picked up a handset in another room. 'Rennie's been talking to a detective. Go on, Rennie.'

She hesitated, not sure how much to tell or how to phrase it. Habit made her want to cut straight to the chase, concern about upsetting them urged restraint. She told them that when a 'couple of drops of blood' had been found in the car park, the police decided to get more involved.

'Did they find that kid from the four-wheel drive?' Mike was obviously making the same connections Rennie had.

'They hadn't when I spoke to the detective,' Rennie told him.

'So he's gone to ground then? That tells us something, the little bastard.'

'*Mike*.' Brenda's voice was a slap on the wrist.

'I don't think they'd even looked for him yesterday,' Rennie explained. 'And the detective wasn't convinced the kid had anything to do with it.'

There was a scoffing noise from Mike. 'That makes no sense.'

Rennie closed her eyes, wishing she could agree with him. 'Apparently there was a fight at the pub on Saturday night so there's nothing to connect the blood to Max at this stage. He said he has to consider a range of possibilities when someone goes missing.'

'Like what?' Mike asked.

'Like Max leaving of his own accord.'

'No,' Brenda breathed.

'James was here when the detective came around. He told him there were some financial issues with the business. He thought it was possible Max might've taken some money.'

'Oh, for goodness sake,' Brenda snapped.

'*James* said that?' Mike's tone was incredulous.

'Yes.'

'How much?' he asked.

'I don't know. Thousands. Something to do with invoices.'

'James is the damn accountant in the partnership,' Mike growled. 'And he shouldn't be making accusations about his cousin when Max isn't around to defend himself.'

'Max doesn't need that kind of money, anyway.' Brenda said it as though she typed up his weekly budget. 'He got that insurance payout from the mine and he owns the house.'

Rennie wanted to cheer their wholesale support, relieved they hadn't for a second considered Max might take the money. But it wasn't the only possibility as to why he'd disappeared.

'Give me the detective's number - I'll see what I can do,' Mike said.

When he hung up the second handset, Rennie figured the conversation was over but Brenda had stayed on the line. 'You must be worried sick, Rennie. We are, too, of course but, well . . . how are *you* holding up?'

The switch in focus and the unexpected concern made something tighten in Rennie's chest. 'I'm okay, thanks. And yes, I am worried. Quite worried.' She winced at her stilted words, wishing she knew how to match Brenda's warmth. For both their sakes.

'You didn't have a quarrel, did you?'

What could Rennie tell her? They'd had sex on the floor, he'd proposed, she'd rejected him and they'd snapped at each other at Trish's birthday party. It was Max's *mother* and, put like that, she'd think it was no wonder he'd gone. 'No. Nothing like that.'

'It's just that when he was married he needed a bit of time out once or twice and forgot to let Leanne know where he was.'

Rennie had always been amused at the spin Brenda put on stories about her children. They didn't put on weight; they filled out comfortably. They didn't drink too much at Christmas dinner; they were merry and entertaining. This time, Max hadn't walked out on Leanne; he'd needed time out. He hadn't made her worry; he'd forgotten to call. Turning an awkward truth into something more palatable - and it made her wonder about Brenda and Mike's insistence that Max hadn't taken the money. 'I don't think he'd forget to tell me where he was,' Rennie said, wishing it sounded more convincing.

'No, I'm sure he wouldn't, dear. How's Hayden coping? He must be terribly upset.'

That was probably the nicest way to describe him. 'Yes, he is. He's had a couple of late nights. I'm hoping he sleeps for a while this morning.'

'That would be best. He's still so young. Do you want us to come down? Mike's got a committee meeting tomorrow morning but I could catch the train and be there this evening and he could drive down later.'

Was that what other people did in a crisis? Have family turn up en masse? She was touched by the offer but Rennie didn't want to be dealing with anxious parents and watching her words while she fretted about Max. And if her father was out of prison, she certainly didn't want them anywhere near. 'No, please, I don't think that's necessary. He's only been gone a day and a half, he could be back anytime.'

'Well, if you're sure, but don't hesitate to call if you change your mind. I'll be thinking of you, dear.'

Rennie held onto the phone as though it might keep Brenda's generosity in the room with her for a while longer - at a manageable distance. It felt inclusive and slightly intrusive, sincere and implausible, nice and unnerving. Come on, Evan, *ring*.

She moved restlessly about the house, not searching now but staying busy, feeling as though the adrenaline that'd been pooling inside her since Saturday night would start leaking out her pores if she didn't get rid of it. If she went for a run, she could take another look around for signs of Max, do a little reconnaissance at the same time.

She pulled on shoes, tied her hair back, zipped both mobile phones into the pockets of her running pants and checked Hayden was still asleep. Five minutes later, she'd locked the doors behind her and was turning left at the lake's edge, the water smooth and deep green like an enormous sheet of opaque glass. She thought again about Max's detour on the way to the party - was it the lure of the sunset or a last look before he left?

Shaking it off, she focused on more reassuring things: the beat of her stride, the rhythm of her breath.

Rennie was born with a built-in capacity to run. As a small, skinny kid, she'd done everything at a trot - going to the car, to the shops, down the road, around the park. It drove Joanne crazy. Her mother had watched with distaste, seeing only her father's genes in it. She'd finished a couple of school cross-country events so far ahead of the pack she thought she'd taken a wrong turn. A teacher once accused her of cheating, others got stars in their eyes about rep teams and trophies, but Rennie was never in one place long enough to achieve any of that.

Evan and his kids were training for a fun run when Rennie and Joanne stayed with them. Up early and out on the road before school every day. It was all bullshit, as far as Jo was concerned, but Rennie was desperate to be part of it. Evan taught her how to breathe better and move more efficiently and after the first week bought her decent shoes and she'd never stopped. It made her feel cleansed and spent and strong. Plenty of times it'd kept her sane.

At the roundabout where the four-wheel drive had cut them off, the grassy path at the water's edge narrowed to nothing. Rennie stepped onto the roadway, feeling the hard surface in her shins, and ran on the outside edge of the two-lane strip of bitumen, facing any oncoming traffic, the short drop to the water at her side.

The kid had tailgated them along this stretch, swerving into the lane that was now her running track. She alternated her gaze between the road and the water, searching for anything that looked like it had come from Max - watch, wallet, shoe, a scrap of the fabric from his clothes. The only way something like that would get there was if he'd been scrambling around the rocks or his belongings had been thrown from a car. It fit her father-released scenario and the one with the kid in the four-wheel drive. Not the version where Max had left her.

As her eyes moved in a side-to-side pattern and her legs counted the rhythm for her breath, she thought of other roads she'd run with awareness. It was one of the lessons her mother had drilled into her: know what belongs and what doesn't - the homes, the cars, the faces. Familiarity was a useful tool when you were hiding from a ghost.

Her father's pursuit started before Rennie was old enough to remember. Her earliest recollections were of arriving in caravan parks in the dead of night, sleeping on the back seat of a car and the large knife under her mother's pillow.

She knew virtually nothing about her father's life until after the murder. Evan Delaney was part of the investigation and eventually answered her questions. Her parents had met in the army: Donna was a training officer and Anthony was SAS, an expert killer who was kicked out when he developed tendencies for paranoia. That he was nuts was no surprise and the training explained a lot - why Donna gave up calling the police, why she never believed he'd disappeared, why even a whiff of something out of place and she'd pack up and run. The fact she'd survived as long as she did was evidence of her own survival skills, the ones she'd drilled into her daughters.

The first time around, Anthony was convicted of manslaughter. Donna was stabbed to death with her own knife, a fact his solicitor said was proof Anthony hadn't met her with intent to murder and was, in fact, protecting himself. That he didn't need a knife to kill wasn't mentioned. He got six years non-parole. After his release, it took him just six months to find Rennie and Joanne.

They had a head start, warned by their solicitor that he was out. Rennie used to think it might have been easier on all of them if her father had simply gunned them down in the street, but the SAS training had screwed up his brain and the furtive, clandestine nature of it all was part of his game.

Why a game in the first place? It was simple, insane logic that made sense only to Anthony Hendelsen. His wife and daughters left him so they had to die. Killing Donna was only part of the assignment.

The first sign of him after he was out of prison was a note pushed under their door: *Daddy's back.* They knew the drill and headed up the coast, keeping their eyes wide open for two fraught years. He left plenty more messages - caravans searched, tyres slashed, a cafe Rennie worked in was smashed up, a one-night stand of Joanne's was beaten to a pulp.

One evening, he waited for them in a caravan park. No time to get to the car, barely enough time to run. Joanne was slower. Rennie doubled back. He brought his own blade this time and struck first, slicing her across the ribs. She made sure it didn't happen again. She shot him twice - once in the shoulder, a second time in the thigh, trembling too much with adrenaline and fury to be more accurate. But it was enough to bring him down, swearing all kinds of wrath and retribution.

Rennie still remembered the rage that'd filled her up in those minutes he lay on the ground. Not a mindless, reckless, do-or-die insanity that lawyers convince juries of. It was certain, single-minded, unwavering vengeance. As he screamed threats, she'd walked the distance between them, ready to shoot him in the face and watch him die. It didn't happen like that, though. The cops were there by then, called by a neighbour when the shouting started and their drawn weapons and urgent, uncompromising shouts were enough to pull her back before she turned into her father.

Rennie shook the memory off as she looked down the length of the main street. If she went down there, she could join the path on the northern side of the bay, be home in fifteen minutes. But she wasn't ready to stop yet, couldn't burn off the anxiety while the past was stoking its fire. She continued along the road to Garrigurrang Point, heading in the opposite direction to yesterday, glancing up at the steep short cut to the gun emplacements and out to the rocks where two stout men had lines out. She rounded the tip of the finger, ran along the grass at the water's edge, eyeing the shore and the single parked car, then followed the path that meandered through the caravan park, a stretch of gums, wealthy suburbia and on to the barbecue area at the northern end of the main street.

He'd already seen her by the time she recognised him leaning on the passenger door of a car. He had a large takeaway coffee from Skiffs and something in a white bag. As she got closer, she made out the grease stains on the paper and figured Detective Phil Duncan had a thing for toasted sandwiches. He pushed off the vehicle as she slowed to a stop in front of him, uneasiness replacing the anxiety she'd run off.

'How you doing, Renee?'

She watched him as she caught her breath. She didn't see good news in his face. Or bad news. 'Were you looking for me? Have you found Max?'

22

Max thrashed through broken, confused dreams then woke with his head on fire and vomited. His skull throbbed, his ears rang and there was fresh oozing from the wound on his temple. He'd sat through enough first-aid courses at the mine to know the signs of concussion: headaches, dizziness, disorientation, vomiting. He should probably rest but the solid, soundless darkness felt too much like the nightmare that had terrified him for years.

Crawling, stopping, crawling a bit more, he kept going the way he'd started. It took all his concentration and energy, which was just fine. If he kept remembering, there was a chance he'd suffocate on his own self-pity.

When he couldn't hold his weight on his hands anymore, he collapsed, wheezing and gasping. Dirt scratched at his skin where his shirt rode up, creeping under the waistband of his trousers. It was in his hair, in the blood caked on his face, in his ears. It felt like it was in his mouth, too, but it wasn't sand, it was thirst. Dry and cracked on his lips, raspy and swollen in his mouth. Not like the thirst you got on a stinking hot day or from running around a soccer pitch. Not the kind of thirst that an ordinary drink would quench. A glass of water wouldn't touch it. He'd need a swimming pool. He tried to coax his saliva glands into action, felt his tongue stick to the roof of his mouth, the sharp dryness at the back of his throat. Make that two swimming pools.

In a cup or a mug?

Was she kidding? *Do I look like a cup kind of guy?*

The new girl's expression didn't change but her eyes said *one of those guys*. Except he wasn't one of them; he was jaded and worn and down on himself. Nothing like he used to be when he *was* the guy who'd flirt with the waitress at the cafe. Not that it mattered - she looked like she wouldn't take crap from anyone.

So a mug?

Thanks.

She came back with a cappuccino and serve of raisin toast. 'There was a mix-up with an order. You look like the kind of guy who could do with some extra breakfast.' No hint of a smile, something not so hard-arsed in her eyes, though.

Max, he told her.

Renee, she said. From around and about, wherever that was. *Bit of a gypsy, never stay anywhere too long.*

She didn't look like a gypsy, at least not the crystal ball kind in the old movies. No make-up, no jewellery, no headscarf. Her thick, messy hair was simply twisted into a bump at the back of her head and held in place with a pencil.

I won't stay, Max. I never stay. I don't know how.

He opened his eyes, awake now, the smell of dirt in his nostrils and a vague sense of nausea in his gut but the darkness kept the dream afloat in his mind.

He might never have paid her much attention if he hadn't been slouched at the end of the counter every day, waiting for the court and the lawyers and the psychologists to decide how much his life was worth. How much the tonne of rock that fell on him was responsible for the state he was in. Was the stress caused by twenty-two hours in darkness or the realisation he'd failed as a husband and father? Was the grief related to the death of his friend or the end of his marriage? Was his anxiety the result of a shattered pelvis or losing custody of his child? He couldn't move forwards or backwards until they came to a decision. So he sat in Skiffs, morning after morning, drinking coffee and feeling like shit. He was only lucky that Pav and Trish didn't own a pub.

Renee was a distraction. She didn't know about his boring, endless bloody saga, didn't treat him like he was broken, cut him only as much slack as every other man who fronted up to the counter for a morning coffee fix and bloke banter. So he watched her working. Fast, efficient, a memory for faces and orders, a tad prickly. Then he just watched. It was obvious she was fit, even if he hadn't seen her running by the lake. A little underweight for his liking. Plain - not as in a euphemism for ugly, more like an attempt to avoid standing out. And there was a stillness about her, some sort of combination of avoiding attention and containing her energy.

It was the eyes that got him, though. They were constantly moving: alert, observant, a little wary. When she settled them on him, it felt like X-ray vision with a bullshit detector.

Max moved his parched tongue around his mouth, rolled it over his dry lips, shifted to let the dirt trickle out from under the collar of his shirt. He should keep moving but he didn't want Rennie to go. He held onto the vision of her in his mind, working the coffee machine, handing over change, watching the customers, that first smile.

Not the polite one she used for customers but a small, private curl of her lips that was directed straight at Max and went all the way to her eyes. It'd made his sad, old heart go pitter-patter.

He lifted his ear from the dirt. Was she down here, too?

'Rennie?'

He spoke it as though she might be there beside him, the word bouncing back as a single repetition coming from further down the hollow space. Would she hear that? How big was this place? He filled his lungs and exhaled on her name.

'Rennieeee!'

He waited for it to finish reverberating then listened into the new silence. He knew there'd been more than a secret smile between them. He couldn't remember what or when, he just knew. The same as he knew he had to keep going. That he had to get out and . . . do . . . finish . . . something.

He heaved himself to all fours again, arms shaking with the effort. Hands first, now knees. Good. Three more, he told himself, and he could lie down. Hands then knees then a palm to the wall - the last part for reassurance that he wasn't completely lost. Six. Now seven, now . . .

The end of the wall was so unexpected that Max snatched his hand back as if it'd been bitten. He sat on his haunches, eyes blinking in the blackness, not sure what to do for a moment. Maybe it was the edge of the world and if he leaned too far forwards, he'd tip into everlasting space.

'Pull it together, you idiot,' he said out loud. No company like your own.

He slid a palm to the edge. Okay, it was a corner. A little chopped up but it felt like a right angle. An elbow in the tunnel? He shuffled forwards, one arm out searching blindly for the opposite side but as his fingertips left the wall behind, a flash of panic made him lurch back, clinging to it like a rock climber. If he left it, he might never find it again. Might flail about in his nightmare for all eternity.

'Right, then. Do the pebble trick.'

He pitched a few around, heard a combination of taps, clatters and 'pffts' on dry earth.

'Great. A T-junction. Two tunnels. Max Tully, master of the fuck-up - pick a corridor. And don't forget: the exit is down only one of them.' He tried to laugh but the fear welling in his chest made it sound like he was choking. What if the exit wasn't down either of them? What if it was back the way he came? What if there was a jug of water waiting for him and he'd gone the other way?

What if . . . this whole damn thing was in his mind?

Had the knock on the temple jettisoned him into some kind of altered state? Was he stumbling through a maze symbolising all the stupid, reckless choices in his life? Fuck. He rested his elbows on bent knees and sucked at the air.

Then another concept slithered through his mind. What if it wasn't him that was crazy? What if someone had beaten him up and dumped him in here? He lifted his head. What if they were down here with night-vision goggles and a camera? Max Tully filling in tonight for Jodie Foster in *Silence of the Lambs*.

The darkness seemed suddenly smaller and more sinister. He scooped up handfuls of dirt, flung them about in every direction. 'Hey! *Hey.*' Pebbles pinged and bounced as his shout rolled off into the distance.

Fuck, Max. Calm down.

He rubbed at his forehead, trying to massage his memory for something recent. All he got were snapshots: Rennie laughing, slapping paint on a canvas, naked in his bed; James grinning with a beer, frowning at his computer; Pav, Trish, Naomi, Mum, Dad, Gran. A slide show of frozen moments of his life as his memories flew backwards.

Okay, what about forwards? What if he started at the last solid memory and hit play?

Rennie at the cafe, then what?

Rennie moving to the backyard flat...

Gran died the year before when Max was living in the flat, still going to rehab and doing handyman jobs around the house while he kept an eye on her. Except that afternoon, he didn't stop in for a cuppa, didn't have the energy to stay upbeat after the physio so he slipped down the yard and crawled into bed. The house was dark when he woke.

He found her in her chair, knitting still entwined in her old, knobby fingers. It was the second time in nine months that he'd held a lifeless hand and the sadness and loss and regret got mixed up with all the other sadness and loss and regret that was piled up inside him.

She left the house to Max in her will. His mum told him it wasn't the last-minute whim of an elderly lady: he'd looked after her and not only in the few months before she died. Max had loved her, he'd lost everything and Gran had wanted to give something back. It didn't stop him feeling bad about it, though, especially when the news caused a few rumblings - his sister, Annette, and his two cousins, James and Lorna, had all expected to get a cut. Max had thought about selling and splitting the money but in the end, he'd just moved in. Not because he'd made any kind of decision - he had no job, no savings and nowhere else to go.

Rennie was asking about rentals in town, so he offered her the flat and she relocated from the caravan park while he was renovating. The compensation money from the accident had come in so he was mulling over his future while he knocked out walls and banged in nails. Good therapy, the psychologist reckoned. The exercise didn't hurt, either.

He hardly saw Rennie the first couple of weeks then he figured out her routine. Early shift, afternoon run; late shift, morning run. After that, he managed to need a breather just as she came through the gate, sweating and panting hard: morning run, coffee break; afternoon run, a cold beer.

She was different away from Skiffs. Not so much attitude and a little more guarded but she'd stop for a chat, sometimes a glass of wine in the evening, sometimes two and a takeaway. She didn't ask for answers he was unwilling to give and when he got the gist she was sidestepping his questions, he returned the favour and kept them to himself. Besides, he liked the mystery of her and not just where she'd been and what she'd done with her life. It was as though she was wearing someone else's skin and there was another person entirely on the inside.

One evening, as the sun turned pink over the lake, he kissed her. She didn't push him away, didn't shut it down but when it was done, she stood and said, 'I've got some things I have to do. I'll see you later.'

He kicked himself. She didn't want him - why would she? But the next evening, he waited as usual on the half built deck like a lovesick schoolboy. When she turned up, it wasn't from a run and she had a cold bottle of chardonnay that she held out to him.

'Sorry about disappearing last night,' she said. 'I needed to do a bit of thinking.'

'And did you?'

'Yes.'

'What did you think?'

'That we should sleep together.'

He managed to catch his jaw before it hit his shoes. 'Right, well. Good thought.'

'Glad you like it.'

Okay, it was a trick. Had to be. Let's sleep together but not yet. Let's wait until we know each other better - a week, a month, until you go insane thinking about it. 'Did you have a time frame on that?'

She answered with a kiss. Followed it with, 'You doing anything now?'

He took her to the bedroom. There was no small talk, no awkward silence, no hesitation: she'd made the decision and wasn't wasting time second-guessing it. She lost her clothes in under a minute and they were lost in each other for what felt like a lifetime. He saw the scar on her rib cage but didn't want to break the mood by asking. And he got a glimpse at what was behind her outer layer. It was some kind of energy source that was bold and passionate and tender all at the same time.

He made like a guy, of course, and fell asleep while she was curled around him in the stillness afterwards. When he opened his eyes, she was dressed and about to leave.

'Sorry to wake you,' she whispered from the edge of the bed.

'I thought we were going to sleep together.'

'You slept.'

'What about you?'

'I don't do the staying-over bit well. I'll see you tomorrow.' She planted a kiss on his forehead and left.

Max ran a dry tongue across his cracked lips now, not sure why the memory made him uneasy. Any memory at this point was good and that one was crystal clear and beat everything else he'd thought since he'd woken up in a black hole. That night had been spectacular, even her farewell kiss with a promise for tomorrow. He'd wanted her back, hadn't slept for thinking of it, but that wasn't the sensation that lingered with him now.

All he felt was the hope that she'd finally left like she always said she would.

23

Detective Duncan nursed his coffee cup and answered Rennie's question with a shake of his head. 'No, no news, sorry. I'm here following up on those names you gave me yesterday.' He raised the paper bag in his hand. 'And stopped to pick up breakfast.'

Rennie put her hands on her hips - easier to recover her breath, better than clenching her fists. 'Have you found the kid in the four-wheel drive?'

He cocked his head at a picnic table. 'Why don't we pull up a seat? I can have my breakfast while we talk.'

She followed him over and perched on the edge of the bench. Detective Duncan squared up to the table and laid out his paper bag and coffee cup like it was dinner. She propped an elbow on the timber top and waited while he tore his package down the middle, releasing cheesy, toasty smells into the air between them.

'So did you find the kid?' she prompted but he'd filled his mouth with a huge bite of sandwich. She hoped Pav had spread the bread with a thick smear of urgency.

He finally wiped his lips with a napkin. 'You said you didn't know the driver of the car that tailgated you on Saturday night.'

'Yes.'

'Did Max?'

'No.'

'He said that?'

She frowned. 'Not specifically. I mean he didn't say either way but there was no recognition from either of them. Why?'

'Do you know the name Dellacourt?'

'No. Is that the kid's name?'

He lifted the sipping lid off his cup, took a moment to test the temperature with his lips before drinking through the foam on top. 'We traced the registration number you gave me yesterday. It belongs to a silver four-wheel drive Subaru owned by a Mrs Helen Dellacourt of Adamstown.' Adamstown was a suburb of Newcastle, a long way from Haven Bay. 'It was stolen?'

'No. Her son was driving it. We've spoken to him and he says he was at a party out this way until three am.'

'Convenient. Did he admit to the road rage?'

'He claimed a vehicle had cut him off in a roundabout, that he'd continued on to the shops and when he saw the driver in the car park, he stopped and exchanged words about the incident.'

'And you believe that?'

'I checked his story about the party and the parents at the house are vouching for him until two-thirty. The rest of it is pretty lame but, at this point, I only need to establish him as the driver of the four-wheel drive you reported and his version of what happened does that. His presence at the party also puts him out of the picture for coming back to the car park when Max was there at around ten pm.'

Rennie looked away from him, swallowing hard. The kid in the four-wheel drive was the easy answer.

'I did some checking back at the station last night,' the detective said. 'You didn't mention Max had a record for assault.'

She swung her head back. 'He doesn't.'

'Seven years ago, he was charged after a pub brawl in Toronto.'

The skin on her bare arms prickled as though an icy breeze had blown up and circled her. Detective Duncan kept his clear, blue eyes on her face, his sandwich cooling in his hand as she tried to make sense of it. 'So he was one of a bunch charged after a fight in a pub. He probably threw a few punches to defend himself.'

'Not according to the report. Only two were charged. The other guy got a hundred and twenty stitches after Max threw him through a plate glass window.'

Something pitched in her gut and her chest heaved as though it was two minutes since she'd stopped running, instead of ten.

'How's Max's temper these days?' Detective Duncan asked.

Rennie stood up and put a couple of steps between herself and the cop.

'We got the results back on the blood in the car park, by the way. It was type A. Thirty-eight per cent of the population. So it could be Max's or it could be someone else's. It might have nothing to do with him. On the other hand, he might have caused it.'

'What difference does it make? He's missing.'

'I'm just saying there's more than one possibility for how it got there.'

Rennie's father had spilled plenty of blood. Should she tell him? If he knew about Anthony Hendelsen, would he start a ground search for Max? And what if it turned out Anthony was still in prison and he did some checking on Katrina Hendelsen? 'But it's not just the blood. Our car was searched yesterday.'

A small line appeared between his brows. 'Someone broke into your car?'

'I don't know how they got in. I thought I locked it when I came home in the afternoon. When I went out to it last night, the driver's door wasn't closed properly and I realised someone had gone through the glove box.'

'The glove box?'

'Yes. The contents had been shoved about.'

'Anything else shoved about?'

'No, but the automatic internal light had been switched off. I'm assuming whoever did it turned the light off so they wouldn't be seen.'

'Was the car in a garage?'

'No, a carport.'

He nodded as he took a bite of toastie and pushed the food to one side of his mouth. 'So someone broke into your car and you only thought to tell me this now?' he said through his food.

'Well, yeah.' She heard the irritation in her voice. 'I didn't discover it until late last night.'

'We've been talking here for a while.'

'And you've been eating breakfast while you took the long way around to tell me you don't think the kid went back for Max.'

He took a sip of coffee, nodded his head, like maybe she had a point, maybe she didn't. 'You said Max had his keys with him when he went out to the car park?'

'Yes.'

'So it's possible he used his keys to open the car so he could get something from the glove box?'

Why would he sneak around his own house? It made no sense, but she hesitated before answering. 'If someone assaulted him, they'd have his keys.' When he said nothing, she added, 'There's no reason for Max to do that.'

Detective Duncan drained his coffee cup, folded the paper over the second half of his sandwich and stepped over the bench seat. 'In my job, Renee, we see all sorts of things for all sorts of reasons.'

RENNIE RAN HOME, her stride out of rhythm, her breath uneven - like her brain as she tried to digest the detective's words. He didn't think Max was missing, he thought he was hiding. James had told him about the missing money and Detective Phil Duncan thought he'd figured Max out.

Christ, she'd lived with Max for four years, had been sleeping with him for almost five, and she thought she knew him. And now she wasn't sure what she knew.

He'd been charged with assault? He'd thrown a man through a window in a brawl?

Rennie had worked in bars, she'd seen all-in fights. There was no finesse about them. They were out of control groups of men, testosterone and alcohol fuelled and, depending on the participants, exceedingly dangerous. Max could've been caught up in one. He drank with mates, they got rowdy at times; that was usually how trouble started. Was he physically capable of throwing someone through a window? Seven years ago, when he was fit from working in the mines and sailing and soccer, sure. Probably even now, despite the permanent damage to his hip from the cave-in - he was still strong. Would he have the aggression it took? Before he disappeared, she would have said no. She would have said it was ridiculous, that his dislike of all things antagonistic was one of the reasons she'd stayed.

But Detective Duncan was a cop. It wasn't rumour or suggestion. He'd looked up the file, he knew the gory details. A man needed a hundred and twenty stitches and Max was the cause.

Something edgy and uneasy stirred inside her. If she'd known about an assault charge five years ago, she never would have stepped out of the cafe with him, would have served him coffee and given him a wide berth. She'd wanted nothing to do with violence or volatility or the threat of it.

If she'd found out later, would she have met him again? Would she have slept with him? Would she have stayed?

She sprinted the short cut behind the houses in her street, sweat trickling down her back, anger spurring her on. Had she been so desperate for something else, something better, that she'd latched onto the first man who was gentle with her? And all this time, there was violence in his soul. Like her father.

She stopped beyond the back fence, breathing hard. She'd always known he was hurt inside, never imagined he could be hurtful. When she'd met him, Max had sat in Skiffs every day like a man who'd had the life sucked out of him and was waiting for a refill. She'd heard about the mine accident and his friend dying and his wife leaving, figured the damage had been done to him not the other way around. He talked about never letting the sun go down on an argument, he tended the garden like a lover, he could be gentle and funny. But a man needed a lot of stitches because of Max. He'd left his wife and child to worry about his safety while he screwed other women.

He also had black spells. Nights when he woke with a gasp and wandered restlessly, angrily for hours. When Leanne berated him on the phone, he'd retreat to the back deck in tense silence, arms folded and fists clenched. Some days he'd dig in the garden until he was exhausted, heaving a pick or driving a shovel into the earth as though it was a beast that needed slaying.

Rennie thought about the blood in the car park and Detective Duncan's words and wondered if whatever Max tried to hold back had finally escaped. She stalked to the water, watched the still, glassy surface of the lake, and asked herself, Who the hell was Max Tully?

24

Rennie ran to the back door, wanting to keep going all the way through the house and out the other side. In all the years before Haven Bay, moving on had been her fallback position, her automatic plan B, her comfort zone. She'd never planned to stay, had been here longer than she should have. Years longer.

The backpack was where she'd left it by the bedroom door and as she picked it up, the weight of the Glock and the memory of other guns pulled her up.

Of all people, she had no right to a flinching, knee-jerk reaction to Max's assault charge. She'd shot her own father, would have killed him if she'd had the chance, and she'd terrified a man who'd made the mistake of hitting her.

The 'episode'. She was in Falls Creek on the Victorian ski slopes working two jobs: a cafe during the day, a bar at night. He was a rich businessman, liked the apres skiing more than the outdoor kind. She slept with him twice. The third time she went to his apartment he'd had too much alcohol and something you don't buy over a counter. There was a nasty conversation; she told him he was an arsehole. The backhander sent her sprawling. It cut her lip, made her nose bleed and opened a door on the fury inside her. Not calm and full of vengeance that time. It was as if an angry, injured wild animal had been let off its leash.

She remembered roaring so hard it hurt her throat and lashing out at whatever was in reach: chairs, glassware, kitchen appliances, lamps. She'd found her pack and the gun and shot out a light fitting when he told her she wouldn't use it, backing him into a corner and onto the floor until he cowered at her feet. It went on long enough for the cops to turn up and bash on the door. She threw the gun across the room and raised her hands over her head as they came through.

The rental was trashed, the guy was a blubbering mess and she was taken away in handcuffs, unable to speak. It was the only time her father did anything to help her - his record and her past were enough for a judge to order counselling instead of gaol time. That had changed everything, given her a chance to become Rennie, someone closer to the person she used to dream about. But it didn't remove what was inside her. DNA couldn't be talked around. Or cut out.

Would Max have taken her to Garrigurrang that first time if he'd known all that? Would he have offered her the flat if he knew what was in her backpack and what she was capable of? Would he have slept with her? Would he have let her go the day she tried to leave if she'd told him what was in the bag he'd carried inside?

She didn't know how he'd respond if she did, only knew it was part of the reason she never had. And if he did find out, she'd want a chance to explain that her actions were consequences, that it wasn't who she tried to be.

Of all people, she should give him a chance to explain. And if he wasn't here . . .

She threw open his side of the wardrobe again, looking for clues - and not just to where he'd gone.

She sifted through the sheaf of papers on the shelf again, opened drawers, reached behind the underwear and socks she'd tidied earlier. At the back, under it all, was an envelope. Sliding it out, lifting the flap, she found two photos. Old ones of her. In the first, she was standing beside a huge canvas that had taken months to finish; in the second, she was bundled in scarf and coat standing on the jetty at the point. She'd seen both of them before as digital shots on the computer but didn't know he'd printed them out. Was it a sign of endearment that he'd kept them or indifference that they'd been left in the back of the wardrobe?

In the bottom drawer, among old jumpers, she found a half-empty packet of cigarettes. How long had it been there? Max had given up smoking before she met him. Had he started again and kept it secret?

On the upper shelves, there were odd socks, a blond wig he'd worn to a fancy-dress party, winter gloves and the holey remains of his old school rep soccer jersey. Stuff he'd kept, stuff he'd treasured, stuff he hadn't bothered to throw away.

She closed the doors, checked Hayden was still in his room and asleep, then stood in the study and scanned the shelves. She'd been looking for notes before, now she paid attention to the myriad photos. Some were in frames, most were propped against books and folders and taped to the edges of the shelves. Hayden, Brenda and Mike, group shots from Christmases and birthdays, old ones from his sailing and soccer days. And Rennie - with him, with others, on her own. If he'd stopped loving her, he hadn't bothered to remove the evidence. He hadn't thrown out his odd socks, either.

She pushed fingers through her hair in frustration. She'd hoped to find some kind of evidence that would explain him but his study, like his wardrobe, only said he was disorganised, messy and busy. Maybe it said he was happy, too. Or lazy. She wasn't sure.

Wasn't sure of a lot of things she been certain of two days ago.

What the hell was taking Evan so long?

She paced the living room, watching the time, questions and dread roaring around her head like a car on a track. She needed to move. She took both mobiles and the landline handset to the bathroom and showered. Then dressed. Then put on washing, made coffee, de-crumbed the toaster, wiped out the fridge, glad Hayden was sleeping through her agitation. She wanted to leave, wanted to stay, wanted to know what the hell was going on. Finally she carried all three phones out to the flat, set up a new canvas, lined up colour and brushes but couldn't start, couldn't concentrate. Running was easy; it took no thought at all.

Then a phone rang. The mobile from the backpack.

'Evan, where is he?'

'Kat, take it easy. It's not that simple.'

'How hard can it be? He's either in a cell or he's not.' She listened impatiently as Evan took a breath.

'I made a few calls. I've got some details but not everything. It's going to take some time.'

'Well, is he at Goulburn or not?'

'Your father was moved out of maximum security there a year ago.'

'Where to?'

'A minimum security centre outside Sydney.'

'Oh, Jesus. He escaped.'

'No. He was released five months ago.'

25

Rennie said nothing, her fingers tight on the phone, her other hand curled into a fist.

'I'm trying to get hold of a parole officer to find out where he's living,' Evan told her.

Anywhere outside prison walls was bad. 'Oh, Christ. Oh, fuck. Why weren't we told? *Why weren't we told?*'

'I don't have an answer for that yet. You're not the easiest person to find. I can only assume that had something to do with it.'

No, this wasn't her doing. She wasn't stupid enough not to plan for this. Prisoner release notification was meant to be sent to her and Jo's solicitor. He knew how to contact them; they both checked for correspondence. Had he forgotten the urgency? Forgotten *them*? Anger rose like bile from her gut. She wanted to shout and rant and yell obscenities. At the system, at the world, at her fucking life. Experience reminded her it was a waste of time and energy - and that her life had always been screwed. 'I have to warn Jo.'

'It might not be what you think. He's been in prison a long time.'

'Long enough to nurture his fucking obsession.' And this time he had gunshot scars to keep him warm at night.

'I'm going to put in a call to the detective investigating your case. He might be able to speed things up.'

She thought about Detective Duncan and his breakfast. 'I'm not sure speed is a priority for him.'

'You know you can come here, Kat.'

'You think I should leave?'

'I don't know what you should do. We don't know where he is yet. I only know what you're like.'

She closed her eyes. 'The kind of person who wished her father would rot and die.'

'Katrina...'

'No, it's okay. I know who I am. I just hoped Haven Bay might've changed me. Call on this number when you find out where he is.'

Rennie stood tense and still as something old and hardened and programmed for survival opened a door inside her and stepped through. Before any kind of independent thought kicked in, she'd checked the yard, locked the studio and was moving quickly to the house.

The father scenario made sense. Max's unfinished text message, the blood in the car park, the thud on the fence, the search of the glove box, the man with the camera. Was that what he looked like now - old and wiry - or had he hooked someone into it with him? She wondered about the blood, about how it had got there. Maybe Anthony had seen her with Max earlier and wanted him out of the picture, or maybe he'd spoken to him when he went back to the car park and it had gone badly. Then what? Had he bundled him in another vehicle and dumped him? Where? Where would he take him?

By the time she reached the back door, guilt was pulsing in her throat and images of Max were flashing in her head. What state was he in? Battered? Cut? Dead? Oh God, was he dead?

The thought threw her momentum off course and she paced the length of the windows and back again, filled with frantic, shameful remonstrations.

She'd thought her past wouldn't find her here.

She was going to be gone by the time he was out.

She'd hoped Anthony Hendelsen would die before that happened.

When the hell did she ever get what she wanted?

She clenched her fists, raked them through her hair, stalked and turned and stalked some more. She shouldn't have stayed past the first year. She'd left too big a footprint. She'd endangered the only man she'd ever loved. Max hadn't deceived her; she'd set him up.

A knock at the door killed the angst like a switch. Her head snapped up and a pulse of fear shot through her. Think, Rennie. It was a light rat-a-tat-tat not an angry thump. And not her father's style to knock on a door. She ran quietly to the bay window anyway, keeping out of sight as she looked onto the porch. She saw Naomi first, her pregnant belly straining against the fabric of a long shirt, James beside her watching the street as though he might see Max coming. She wished they weren't here but felt more glad than she should to see them.

She glanced briefly at the houses along the road. Would she know if her father was watching? Covert had once been his middle name. All the years Rennie had been on the run, she'd seen him only four times and never in broad daylight. Monday morning on a front doorstep was as safe as anywhere.

She swung open the entry and saw Naomi's good morning smile turn to alarm. 'Rennie, what's wrong? Have you heard something about Max?'

What could she tell them? That he might be dead and it was her fault? 'No. I . . . Come in.' She didn't say more, just ushered them in and locked the door.

Naomi was hovering in the living room waiting for her. 'Is it the police? Did you speak to them again?'

For a moment, Rennie thought she meant Evan. 'No. Yes. I saw Detective Duncan this morning.'

'Was it bad news?'

Her conversation with Detective Duncan felt like a lifetime ago and right now all she could think about was calling Joanne, but the apprehension on Naomi's face made her circle her thoughts back to the early morning conversation. 'No news. He found the kid from the four-wheel drive but he was at a party all night. Detective Duncan doesn't think he had anything to do with Max going missing.'

'I thought it was unlikely.' James was propped against the kitchen counter, arms folded across his chest as though he'd been proved right.

Rennie remembered the missing funds and shuffled through the possible scenarios again. The kid-gone-crazy version was gone. There were still the father-out-of- prison and Max-taking-the-money options. Neither fitted perfectly, she reminded herself. There was a chance he'd left her, that she hadn't killed him. Shitty options.

'It's something, though,' Naomi said, reaching for Rennie's hands.

'I'm . . . tired. And worried. I . . .' Her eyes dropped to Naomi's fingers on hers, stilled by the friendship in them. It was something new for her in a moment of alarm. She gave them a quick, thankful squeeze. 'Why are you here? Have you got news?'

'No. We wanted to keep you company, see if there's anything more we can do to help. Didn't we, James?'

'I thought I might have another go at Max's computer before I take the financial details into the police.' He cocked his head, a concession. 'Maybe I can find something that will sort it out.'

He didn't look convinced but at least he was trying. 'Can I make you a coffee?' Naomi asked.

Rennie could drink a bucket of it, was more than grateful to have someone ask, but the callous survivor in her remembered there were reasons she didn't have friends in the old days. It was harder to leave when she cared. When they cared. 'Maybe later. I need to make a call.'

She shut herself in the bedroom and found her sister's number in the mobile. She hadn't spoken to Joanne in almost a year. The last time was on Rennie's birthday and the conversation ended with the same pissed-off question she'd been asking Rennie since they parted company five years ago.

Why are you still there?

They'd kept up the regular email check-in, the couple of lines to let each other know they were still breathing but neither had called. Rennie guessed Jo felt the same as she did - no desire to go over it again.

A male voice answered. 'Simone Carter's phone.'

There were sounds in the background: people talking, somewhere busy and noisy. A cafe was her guess. 'Can I speak to Simone?'

The man raised his voice without covering the mouthpiece. 'Hey, Simone, can you take a call?'

'Who is it?' There was no mistaking the irritated edge to Jo's voice.

'It's her sister,' Rennie said without waiting for the question.

'I didn't know you had a sister,' the voice called.

There was no answer, just the sound of the phone being carried about, footsteps, a quieter place. 'Katrina?'

Rennie kept her voice low so it wouldn't carry to the living room. 'Yeah, Jo, it's me.'

'What's wrong?'

'Hey, how are you,' would have been nice after so long but Rennie wondered whether she'd do it any differently if Jo called out of the blue. 'He's out.'

Three seconds of silence then Jo got straight to the point. 'When?'

'Five months ago. Evan's trying to find him.'

'You called Delaney?'

'Last night.'

'What happened?'

Rennie told her about Max, the blood, the man with the camera and the car being searched, all the time hearing her voice slip into the blunt rhythm she heard in her sister's, feeling a familiar toughness creeping around the edges of her thoughts.

'Where are you now?'

'Haven Bay.'

'Why the fuck are you still there?'

And there it was. 'I can't leave.'

'Of course you can. You pick up your pack and walk out the door.'

'I can't. Not yet. There's more to it. It might not be Anthony.'

'Do you want to wait to find out?'

Did she want to see her father? Under no circumstances - ever. 'Max might've left. Or maybe Anthony only hurt him. Either way, I need to find out.'

'No, Kat. You need to stay alive.'

Her sister's rapid-fire responses were making it hard to think. She stalked across the room, stood to one side of the window and looked into the street. 'This is my fault. I need to fix it.'

'No, this is not your fault. It's Anthony Hendelsen's fault. It's always been his fault. He's got a bottomless pit of shit to answer for. It's not yours to fix. Your job is to *survive* him.'

It'd been their mother's mantra. She'd brought them up on it, made it a war cry. Rennie and Jo had recited it to each other when she'd gone and told themselves it was their right, their revenge, to live.

Except it wasn't just her and Jo anymore and Max deserved to survive him, too. 'I have to find Max. Even if it's too late. Even if he's . . .' She squeezed her eyes. 'And Max's son is here.'

'He'll be safer if you're not there.'

'I can't leave him on his own.'

'How old is he?'

'Fourteen.'

'Christ, he's old enough to look after himself. Think what we were doing at fourteen.'

'I wouldn't wish that on him.'

'He's not your kid, Kat.'

The volume of her voice slid up as she spoke. 'I've got a life here, Jo. It's more than just somewhere to live. I can't pick up and leave.'

'Then you made a mistake staying.'

Had she? Was it a mistake to find Max? 'It's different now. *I'm* different. I'm not her.'

'Who?'

'Katrina. I'm not Katrina Hendelsen. I'm Renee Carter and I can't leave.'

'Jesus, Kat. You think whatever name you use is going to make a difference to *him*?'

She was right, Rennie knew it. And she knew it didn't matter. 'It makes a difference to *me*. As soon as I walk out that door, I'm her again. A hand-to-mouth callous bitch whose only goddamn role in life is to survive. I don't want to be her. I want to be the person I am here and if I leave, I can't come back. I can't waltz into town when it's all blown over and say, "Gee, sorry I couldn't hang around to find Max." I *love* Max and I need to find him.'

Rennie heard hard breathy sounds through the phone and the beat of muffled footsteps. She guessed her sister was pacing angrily.

'Rennie?' It was Naomi calling quietly from the other side of the door.

How much had she heard? Rennie put a hand over the phone before she answered. 'Yes?'

Naomi talked as she eased her way in. 'Sorry to interrupt but I made the coffee.' She was carrying a large plate with a mug and two thick slices of toast. 'Trish sent a fruit loaf from the cafe for you this morning. She said it was the closest she could come to French toast, whatever that means. Anyway, I spread it with butter, I hope that's okay.'

Yes, Rennie thought, it was perfect. And no, it wasn't a mistake to be here. 'It's great. Thank you.'

'Are you okay in here?' Naomi asked. 'I wasn't listening - I just thought you sounded upset.'

Upset, pissed off, terrified, thankful.

'Is it the police?' Naomi asked.

Rennie answered without thinking. 'No. It's my sister.'

'I didn't know you had a sister. It's nice she's keeping in touch while Max is . . . well, while we're looking for him. Is she close enough to come and stay? It might be a comfort to have some of your own family with you. Anyway, I'll let you get back to her. Oh, and by the way, Hayden's awake.' She touched Rennie's arm as she passed, smiled back at her from the door.

Rennie wanted to laugh at the disparity of the moment - tough-arsed Joanne in her ear, Naomi at the door worried about her food intake. When she'd gone, Rennie closed her eyes, trying to find a middle ground.

'Katrina? Who was there?' Jo asked.

'A friend.'

'What did she want?'

'She brought me coffee and toast and asked if I was okay.'

There was silence from Jo for a long moment. Rennie hoped she was getting the message - that what she had here was worth holding onto.

'What did you mean, Max might've left?' Joanne eventually asked.

The explanation wasn't pretty but she wanted Jo to know she wasn't being completely reckless by staying, so she explained how Max had disappeared before, the password protection on his computer files, the money missing from MineLease, James's and the detective's version of what had happened.

'Jesus, Katrina. Are you sure you want to find this guy? Not exactly what you were looking for in happy Haven Bay, is it?'

She clenched her jaw. 'I need to make sure.'

'Have you still got the Glock?'

'Yes.'

'Keep it with you. And don't let some sucker in a fairytale make decisions for you.'

26

'How'd you get the scar?' Max wasn't sure if he was conscious or out again, whether he'd said the words aloud or just remembered them. He was sprawled in the dirt again, dreaming about lying in a puddle and soaking up water through his pores like a human sponge. But he'd turned the corner in the tunnel and it felt like progress.

'It's a demarcation line,' Rennie answered him. It was in his mind, he knew it was, but the moment played like a movie across the darkness in front of his eyes.

It was the second time she'd been in his bed. Two days after the first, the afternoon sun streaming through the curtains, both of them naked and a little breathless. She was on her side, a hand resting at her hip, the bent arm framing the fine, pink curve of scar that resembled an upside-down smile on her rib cage.

'What does it demarcate?' he asked.

'The end of one chapter and the beginning of another.'

'Was it a good new chapter?'

'The one after it is better. So far.'

Him? Here? This was a better chapter? 'What kind of book is it?'

A cynical half-smile. 'A horror story.'

Grit scratched at the pads of his fingers as they shifted across the fabric of his shirt, imitating the way he'd caressed the slight bump of her healed tissue, feeling the ladder of her ribs underneath.

'Was it surgery?' Maybe she'd been sick and the chapter before her was rehab.

'No.'

He made another pass over it, enjoying the warmth of her flesh, the soft swell of her breast, trying to imagine how someone got sliced there. 'Was it an accident?'

'No.' She lifted his hand away.

In the darkness of the tunnel, his fingers fell slack. Like he had then, he wanted to know what happened but sensed a full-on assault might make her pick up her clothes and leave. 'It must've hurt,' he heard himself say.

'It wasn't as bad as it could've been.'

'How many stitches?'

'Thirteen.'

He raised his eyebrows, impressed - one stitched-up survivor to another.

She gave a brief, grim smile of agreement, reached down and pulled the sheet to her breast.

It was a big hint but he couldn't resist. 'What happened?' He saw her again, rolling onto her back, watching the ceiling as she spoke.

'Please don't ask. I don't like to think about it.' She'd turned her head on the pillow and her face was so close he could feel the breath from her lips as she talked. He wished he could feel it again. 'We're the same, Max,' she told him. 'We both survived, we both want to find something better. Telling our ugly stories won't change them; it'll only bring them into the present with us. If you want to talk about yours, I'll listen but you need to know I won't tell you mine. I don't want you thinking about it when you see me naked. I don't want to see it in your eyes when I'm in your bed. All you need to know is that if the scar wasn't there, I wouldn't be here. I would've made different choices, been a different person. That's what I want you to think about when you run your hand over it.'

It didn't explain anything, only added more question marks to the ones already floating around her like an aura. But it had let him off the hook. She knew about the mine accident and that his wife and son had left him. He hadn't told her he'd been an arsehole, that he was reckless and thoughtless, that he hurt people and damaged himself.

He tugged at the sheet, pressed his lips to the pink ridge on her ribs then rested his cheek on her breast. 'I'm glad you came here.'

'I want a different life, Max, a chance to live better stories. Can we just tell each other those?' She pushed fingers into his hair, pulled a little, making him lift his face. 'Is that enough for you? I need to know if it isn't.'

Enough? She was already more than he'd hoped for. 'Yes.'

Her pupils moved back and forth between his for a moment, her bullshit detector switched to high. She must have found what she was looking for because the corners of her mouth turned up just a smidge - approval, relief, empathy.

'What would you do if it wasn't okay?' he asked.

'Leave.'

At least he knew she wasn't going to beat around the bush. 'Now?'

'I told you when I took the flat I wouldn't stay. I never stay. There'd be no reason to stay if it wasn't enough for you.'

'But *now*? Immediately? With me naked and kissing you?'

Amusement joined the mix in her smile. 'You think that'd be enough to make me stay a few minutes more?'

'I was thinking it'd take more than a few minutes.' A lot more. Months. Years.

'Again? Already?'

'I'm ready when you are.'

They were talking about different things but it didn't matter. He remembered now that she'd eventually stayed all night, moved in sometime after that. Win-win for Max. And the intriguing mystery of her had never dulled. The more he knew of her, the more she seemed like a different species of person, someone who'd grown up in another culture - or planet. She was obsessively tidy, she never cried, she didn't yell when she was mad. She'd never grown a plant or dug in a garden, sleeping in was a concept she didn't understand, she made decisions like there was only one option and she didn't like owning stuff. When she moved into the house, she brought all her belongings in one small bag.

'Where's the rest of it?' he'd asked.

'This is it,' she said as though there were other people who carried their entire lives in a backpack.

She'd eventually put on a little weight, filling the spaces between her ribs, and conceded to owning a few more possessions: three pairs of shoes, a dress, the painting gear. Layers of her were slowly eased away to reveal new, delicate ones underneath - and he'd been fascinated and intrigued by each one.

Not now, though. As he leaned against the wall, trying to gather his strength to crawl again, he wasn't charmed or captivated or entertained by her mystery.

He didn't know why but he was fearful of it.

RENNIE THREW the phone at the bed, angry with her sister. Maybe Joanne was right, maybe she was a sucker. Maybe this whole thing was going to turn out badly whichever version proved right. But she was wrong about the fairytale. Rennie hadn't come to Haven Bay pretty and defenceless, Max wasn't a rich prince and he wasn't here to save her.

And surviving her father wasn't enough anymore.

She needed to find Max for her own sake, possibly for his sake - whatever it meant, whatever the outcome. If he'd left her, then she'd mark it up as another shit chapter in her life and move on. If it was Anthony . . .

She stalked to the window and stared angrily into the street. If her father had killed Max, she'd embrace her DNA, turn the tables on Anthony and hunt him down - and this time, she wouldn't miss.

27

The priority now was to *find* Max. Rennie had kept secrets to protect herself and now it was possible those secrets had hurt him. It was time she 'fessed up so James and Detective Duncan started looking in a few more places.

Rennie took a couple of seconds to down some of the coffee Naomi had delivered, listening to the sounds in the house as she fortified herself. The TV was on, which meant Hayden was more than just awake. At least she could count on him to be preoccupied while she prostrated herself before Naomi and James.

Hayden graced her with a silent glance when she passed between him and the telly. Naomi was on her own at the window, two fists kneading the small of her back.

'Are you okay?' Rennie asked.

'My back's a bit achy today, that's all. What about you? Is your sister coming to stay?'

'No. She's not the staying kind. Where's James?'

'In the study having another go at Max's password.'

The spark of irritation she usually felt for James flared but she wasn't entirely sure he deserved it this morning. He'd accused Max of fraud yet he'd also found Hayden and he was trying to help.

He was shutting a drawer in the desk when she stepped into the study and he looked up at her as though he was running out of ideas. 'Still no luck. Have you had any thoughts on the password?'

'I'm not sure you need a password. I think it could be something else.'

His mouth made a quick, downwards curl of doubt. 'I know you don't want to believe me but the money *is* missing.'

'It's possible this isn't about him. It's possible his disappearance is about *me*.'

James's pupils found hers, the eyelids tensing as though he was attempting to read her subtext before deciding how to respond.

'We need to talk,' she told him. 'Naomi, too.'

'I'm coming,' Naomi called quietly from the hallway. She appeared with a steaming mug that she passed to James. 'Here, James. I made you some tea.'

Without a glance at Naomi, James set the mug on the mousepad, swung the desk chair to face Rennie and folded his arms across his chest, waiting for an explanation.

She wasn't sure how to start. It was a long story and she didn't want to take all day about it or tell more than they needed to know. And she didn't want Hayden hearing it. She reached around Naomi, swung the door and shut the three of them into the tiny room. Naomi leaned against the jamb and Rennie backed up against a filing cabinet but with James's shoes overhanging the base of the swivel chair, there was barely a metre of floor space between them. The atmosphere felt instantly close and tense.

'What is it we need to talk about?' James asked, more impatient than curious.

It was brutal and shocking however she told it; there was no point trying to soften it. 'My father murdered my mother when I was fifteen. His goal was to kill my sister and me, too. He almost achieved it when I was twenty- three. He's been in prison since then. I've just found out he was released five months ago. It's possible he came here looking for me and found Max first.'

While James watched her with a flat, unreadable expression,

Naomi's hand flew to her mouth. 'Oh, God, Rennie. I'm so sorry about your mother. Oh, Rennie, I . . .' Her voice trailed off, not finishing the sentence. Or maybe it was the thought she didn't want to follow through.

'Why would your father be looking for you now?' James asked.

'Obsession. Revenge. I shot him twice. He promised he'd find me.'

'Oh, Rennie. Your own father.' Naomi reached out and clasped her arm.

'It wasn't your average family, Naomi. Nothing like what you have here.' She glanced at Naomi's swollen belly and wondered if she'd have a chance to see the child inside.

James bypassed the sentiment. 'What do you mean *found* Max?'

Rennie swallowed hard, aware of the closeness of the bodies in the room and the family ties that bound them. 'I don't know. The blood in the car park . . . it's possible my father hurt Max. Maybe he saw him with me and wanted him out of the way or ... or he spoke to him, asked about me and they got into a fight.'

His pupils did tiny side-to-side flicks as he thought. 'Wouldn't Max know not to talk to him?'

'No.'

'But if he knew your father might turn up one day?'

'He didn't. He doesn't know anything about my family.'

His eyebrows came together in reproach. 'Jesus, Rennie. Don't you think he had a right to know?'

Yeah, in hindsight. 'I changed my name. The whole point of that is not to tell anyone. And my father wasn't due out for another four years. I thought I had plenty of time to break the news about my screwed-up gene pool.' Or leave before it showed up.

Silence filled the room, sucking the oxygen out of it. Rennie wished she could open the door, let a draught in, do something other than stand and stare James down.

Naomi shifted her feet and pushed fists into the small of her back.

Rennie held out a supporting arm. 'Do you need to sit down?'

'It might help.'

Rennie shuffled sideways to let her closer to the desk. James rolled the chair back a tad, clearing a space on the desk. Hadn't he noticed the size of her?

'It might work better if you gave her your seat,' Rennie suggested pointedly.

He stared at her a moment, then stood and made way. Geez, what would he be like after the baby arrived?

'Is it just the blood?' James asked as Naomi was still lowering herself into the chair. 'Because Phil Duncan seemed satisfied the fight at the pub would explain that.'

Of course he wouldn't take her word for it. 'If it was just the blood, I wouldn't be telling you any of this.' She held up a thumb to start counting off the other elements. 'I heard someone behind the back fence after you left on Saturday night.' She raised her index finger. 'There was a man in the main street yesterday taking photos of the cafe. I haven't seen my father for a long time but the age and size seemed about right.' Middle finger. 'And our car was searched yesterday when it was sitting in the carport. I discovered it last night after Pav and Trish left.'

James angled his face away, running his eyes across the shelves above Max's desk as though the connection between the pieces might be up there. 'What are the police saying?' he finally asked.

'I haven't spoken to Detective Duncan about my father yet. Like I said, I just heard about his release myself. That's who I intend to speak to next.'

'So you didn't hear it from the cops?'

'No.'

He waited a couple of seconds, maybe hoping she'd fill the silence with details but she figured he had enough. When she didn't, he moved on. 'What did your father do exactly?'

'He'd find us and watch us. Sometimes he'd break in and search our stuff. Sometimes he'd let us know he was there, make threats.'

'So if most of what he did was watch and make threats, it's a bit of a stretch to think he's done something to Max. *If* he's here.' He was searching for rationality, as though Anthony Hendelsen's behaviour made sense.

'He murdered my mother with a large knife. A fair clue that watching and threatening wasn't his main game. He beat people up, he trashed places. He sliced me open before I shot him and promised he'd find me and make me pay. And he's just spent more than a decade in maximum security. He's not going to come out of a place like that all nice and reformed. *If* he's here.'

He patted at the air with both hands like he was tamping down her sudden anger. 'I'm just trying to understand, Rennie. We're both on the same side here.'

'Are we, James? You've been trying to prove Max did the dirty on both of us.'

'Okay, you're right, I'm sorry. We should consider every possibility at this stage. So, if I can ask a question without upsetting you, how do you think he would he find you if he's been in prison for years?'

She ignored the condescension - arguing wasn't going to find Max. 'There are plenty of ways to locate someone if you've got time and you know how to look.'

Anthony watched them long enough as kids to learn their mother's habits. It was difficult to be unpredictable when she had two young daughters who needed to be fed and educated, and most people are happy to answer questions when you show a photo of two little girls and say you just want to see them. The second time around, he got good at calculating where'd they'd go to find work - when your skills are limited to pulling beers and serving coffee, it cuts down the search area. He'd enlisted some prison mates and used private investigators, too, still spinning the missing daughters tale.

James's eyes slid away from Rennie to the shelves again, maybe deciding how plausible it was. 'So if your father's here, you're at risk, too,' he said, his attention back on her.

'Yes.'

Naomi's hand flew to her lips. 'Oh, Rennie, I didn't think of that.'

'You should leave for a while. At least until Max turns up,' James said as though the decision was made. 'Naomi said you were talking to your sister before. Could you stay with her for a while?'

Rennie felt one side of her mouth curl up at the concept that

Joanne and James had something in common. 'No. I'm not leaving until I know where he is.'

'There are other people looking for him, Renee.'

But they might look in the wrong places. 'No, I think you're right about the "if", James. I don't *know* that my father is here. So I'm . . .'

The door jerked against Rennie's back as Hayden called from the other side. 'Uncle James? Are you in there?'

She pulled the door and the sight of him felt like a replay of yesterday, except his face when he saw the three of them turned to apprehension instead of resentment.

'Have you found Dad?'

'No, honey,' Naomi told him.

'Then why are you all in here?'

'We've been talking,' Rennie said.

He eyed her suspiciously. 'So I wouldn't hear?'

'Yes, so you wouldn't hear.'

Hayden looked about to demand to be told what was being said but his attitude faltered as he moved his eyes between their faces. When he looked back at Rennie, there was uneasiness and determination in them. 'When are we going to look for Dad? You said last night we'd go look for him.'

She'd forgotten but he obviously hadn't. He'd changed out of his PJs, put on shoes and had a cap in his hand. Right now, she needed to talk to Detective Duncan and she didn't plan to wait for the cop to take his time coming to the house - and Hayden in tow wasn't going to work. She glanced across the room, saw Naomi with a fist pushed into her spine again. She needed a hot water bottle not a sullen teenager. 'James, can you . . .?'

He shook his head before she'd finished, directing his words at Hayden. 'Sorry, mate, I've got to go into the office and hunt down some stuff that might help find your dad.' Or the money he'd taken. James was right - Hayden didn't need to have anything to do with that process.

Could she leave him here, with the doors locked and instructions to stay put? Would Hayden do what he was told? She hesitated on the edge of asking him. There was surliness and a little fear in the way he waited for an answer - and a plea. Not the supplication of a spoilt kid wanting his fourteen-year-old needs met. It was something new. A plea to let him *do* something, to give him a job and a chance to help his father.

Well, shit, Rennie understood that kind of thinking. She understood, too, about being fourteen and frightened - and that moving and acting and making decisions burned off the adrenaline that fear poured into your system. And maybe she was a sucker for a kid with sad eyes. 'Okay. But I have to talk to the cops first.'

'Then we look for him after that?'

She wasn't letting him do any searching if Anthony was here. 'Yes.'

28

Detective Duncan was in his car when he answered his mobile. Rennie told him she'd meet him at the station. He didn't ask why.

She didn't want to waste time so while Naomi fussed in the kitchen, cleaning up the toast and coffee makings, she moved quickly through the house checking the locks, Joanne's words ringing in her ears. *Have you still got the Glock?*

She couldn't take a loaded pistol - any kind of pistol - to a police station. Carrying it in the car was a risk, too, with a nosy, unpredictable teenager aboard. So she pushed her pack into the back of the wardrobe, out of sight but easier to grab than from the top shelf.

Naomi was waiting for her by James's car when she came out. 'It's not what you think,' she whispered as she hugged Rennie. 'It'll be okay. I know it will. It has to be.' She held Rennie's hand against her belly. 'Squirt needs both Aunty Rennie and Uncle Max to be here.'

The mound of baby under Rennie's palm felt firm and full and warm. She had little to offer a child beyond babysitting but she wanted to be there anyway - for herself, if not for the baby. As she held the door for Naomi, her gaze wandered to the car's rear seat where a large, cardboard box filled the space. She read the label on top. 'Oh, you've got the cot at last.'

'Better late than never, huh?' Naomi laughed. 'James finally picked it up yesterday. It's only been waiting at the store for a month.' She cocked her head at the back seat. 'I just hope it gets assembled before the baby arrives.'

And again: What would he be like after the baby arrived?

'Let me know what the police say,' James told her across the roof of the car.

'Let me know how you go, too,' she returned firmly.

As they left, she eyed Hayden warily as he headed towards the carport, remembering last night's disappearing act. If Anthony Hendelsen was in Haven Bay, Hayden needed to stay close.

'Listen, Hayden,' she said as she caught up with him at the back of Max's car. 'You need to do what I tell you, okay?'

His blink was intentionally slow, the resentment clear.

'Don't give me that.'

'What?'

Possibly there was some tried-and-true method for making a teenager do what you want but she had no idea what it was, only that a threat in the right place would get the job done. 'Okay, fine. This is how it's going to go. There are things I need to do and you're going to have to wait while I do them. You stuff me around for five minutes and I put you on the first train to Yamba and you can see this out with your grandparents, you got that?' His face screwed up with the beginnings of an indignant retort. She didn't wait for it. 'You got that?'

'Geez, what the . . .?'

'Do you understand?'

'*Yes.* All right. Whatever.' The last word was tossed over his shoulder as he opened the passenger door. That was fine; she didn't need him to be polite, just obedient.

Brood was what he did as she drove out of Haven Bay, slumped in his seat, face turned to the passenger side window. The silence gave her a chance to think through her options with Detective Duncan - a past like hers took some explaining and the fact she hadn't been honest from the start might be the least of her problems. Whichever way the conversation went, it was going to have its rough moments, no getting out of that. She just wanted to make sure that at the end of it, the cops understood they needed to look for Max. She turned onto the highway and stepped on the accelerator.

Maybe it was the speed that gave Hayden some extra nerve. 'Why have you always got the shits?' he said.

She raised her eyebrows. 'Me?'

'Duh.'

She turned away to chuckle silently. 'My older sister set a bad example. What's your excuse?'

'I haven't got the shits all time.'

'No? What do you call it then?'

He didn't answer so she flicked a look at him across the car and grinned a little. Oh yeah, he had the shits now.

By the time they'd parked and walked to the door at the police station, Hayden's mood seemed more sombre than ticked off. The gravity of his father's situation was hard to miss from there.

Detective Duncan's blue eyes scanned her flatly as he crossed the foyer to meet them, different to the breakfast- munching distraction by the lake, not so relaxed as yesterday. Had Evan spoken to him already? How much would she need to explain? He covered his expression with a smile. 'Renee, how you doing?'

She nodded. 'This is Hayden, Max's son.'

The cop held out a hand, spoke firmly and earnestly to him. 'I'm Detective Phil Duncan, Hayden. I'm trying to locate your dad. It'd be a big help if one of my detectives could have a chat with you. Would you mind doing that?'

The kid grasped his hand awkwardly and stood a little taller. 'Yes. I mean no, I don't mind.'

'Great.' He said it as though the kid was joining the investigative team.

Rennie had been worried about what to do with Hayden while she was here, not wanting him to hear what she had to tell, not sure about leaving him alone in the waiting area to get bored and frustrated. Now she followed with a degree of relief as the detective took Hayden into a large office and introduced him to a twenty-something cop with a crew cut, a huge tattoo growing out of a sleeve and a gun in a holster at the waist of his jeans.

'I'm having a Coke, you want one?' the young officer asked as he led Hayden out the door. Rennie wasn't sure if the cop would impress him or scare the hell out of him - either would be fine.

'We can talk over here, Renee,' Detective Duncan told her as he steered his way around a collection of workstations, rolling out a chair at a desk, pointing at another one for her. 'I got a call from a friend of yours this morning. An Evan Delaney. Except he knows you as Katrina.' He kept the smile on his face as he waited for her to sit, a friendly, how-about-that kind of thing. When he spoke again, his voice had found some steel. 'I'm wondering why you didn't give me that name yesterday, Renee.'

She felt the defensiveness before she spoke. 'My name *is* Renee Carter and yesterday I didn't think it had anything to do with Max's disappearance.'

He nodded, like he'd give her that one. He pulled a file from the top of a stack and opened it. 'Katrina Hendelsen, right?'

'Yes.'

'Interesting name, as it turns out. I whacked it into the computer after I got off the phone from your mate Evan and, I've got to admit, I was surprised.' He tapped a printout, raised his eyebrows as though it was an incredible coincidence. 'Mother died from knife wounds inflicted by father; father serves six for manslaughter; currently serving fifteen for attempted murder of two daughters, one of whom shot him twice.' He lifted his eyes. 'That would be you, right?'

She fixed her gaze on him and clenched her jaw at his casual recounting of the facts.

'Katrina Hendelsen has a long list of charges against her name. I can see why you might want to change it.'

This is for Max, Rennie told herself.

• • •

He was counting. Twenty-two hands-knees-slap on the wall, twenty-three hands-knees-slap on the wall. No reason other than a need for some kind of order. Maybe when he wrote a book about it, he could say he'd crawled three hundred and seventy-six hands-knees-slaps in an easterly direction. Of course, he wouldn't know if it was easterly until he got out. In which case, the book was on hold.

He stopped, rubbed his knees, eased onto his back. Either he was running a temperature or the ground was cooler here. He scooped up a handful of surface dirt, let it slip through his fingers. Did it again with a little more focus. It wasn't wet, not even damp, but it seemed a tad sticky. He touched the wall - dry and cool like it'd always been. He listened for the trickle of water. Nothing. He sniffed at the air. His nose wasn't working too well but maybe, just maybe, it smelled a bit. . . dank.

His pulse tapped with newfound energy, his throat swallowed deeply, painfully in anticipation. Please be a river of fresh flowing water. One that would quench his thirst and wash him out of this goddamn place. He got to his knees, ignoring the pain in his head, testing the floor and the wall with each hands-knees-slap. Six shuffles and he hit a damp patch. He patted at the ground, edging forwardss, his trousers turning wet where his kneecaps pressed into the dirt.

Sludgy then muddy then . . . aahhh.

Cold, liquid water.

The puddle was too small to lie in. Just a narrow indentation where the floor of the tunnel met the wall. He grazed his cheek on the rock as he tried to get his lips to it. Fuck, *fuck*.

The wall. The wall was *wet*. He flattened a hand on it, found a thin trail of wetness, followed it upwards, the surface underneath slimy and slightly furry. Moisture oozed between his fingers, dribbled over the webbing and down the backs of his hands. His mouth was tingling as he put a palm on either side of the trail but as he leaned in, stuck out his tongue, he felt the solid mass of the rock face looming above him and hesitated.

What if it was a toxic leak? He was in an underground tunnel; he had no idea what was above it. A dump site, chemical storage. He rested his cheek on the cool, trickling flow, need and craving making it hard to draw breath. The real question was, could he crawl away without drinking? He turned his face and touched his lips to the slick trail.

There was barely enough water to move around the inside of his cheeks but he slurped and sucked, the sound loud in the hollow silence. Oh, yeah, you've come a long way, Max Tully. Once voted Most Likely to Succeed, now alone in a dark tunnel and licking a wall to stay alive.

A million years ago, he'd been the it-kid in high school - rep soccer, rep sailing, good marks, lots of friends, no real effort. Got into uni no problem. He was going to be a mine engineer - design the holes, not dig them. He took it all for granted, never considering that the good things in life might not always be there just waiting to be claimed. Then a little unprotected fun in the back of his car and he screwed up his own dream run.

He'd figured just once without a condom, how unlucky could they be? Then he'd figured it was his fault, he should do the right thing, marry Leanne and become a family - they could fall in love afterwards and live happily ever after. Then he'd figured six months off uni to earn a little money down the mines and he'd go back to the books. Easy.

Except Leanne couldn't get a full-time position after Hayden was born and it cost money to pay rent and feed a family. And they didn't fall in love and they weren't happy and there was never enough cash for him to go back to uni. Then he and Dallas, looking for a quick, extra buck, swapped a night shift with another mine team and the roof came down and any chance to retrieve his golden days was gone.

All his life, he'd wanted without thinking. The first half he'd got everything he'd reached for. Maybe if he'd had to work harder or if he'd missed out a few times in those years, he might have learned to think when he wanted more.

29

Max clawed at the earth at the base of the seepage, scooping out a bigger gathering hole, his tongue dry again before the water was deep enough to drink. Then he got on his haunches and lapped like a dog.

'You'll do anything if you're desperate enough.'

You got that right, Pav, Max told him silently, mud clinging to his tongue and coating his teeth. Different time, different place and Max was still disgusting himself.

The two of them had been in Pav's courtyard, slouching in garden chairs, watching the lights over the lake and drinking themselves into philosophers. Max was out of rehab, back in Gran's flat without Leanne and Hayden, limping, depressed, edging his way towards alcoholism, trying to find excuses for doing things the clever schoolboy in him would never have thought he was capable of.

'Does it make it okay if you're desperate?' Max had asked cynically.

Pav had shrugged. 'It just makes it a fact.'

Except Max hadn't been desperate, he'd been angry. Not a yelling, shouting thing, although sometimes it came out as that. There'd been a fire inside him, smouldering, hissing, hot coals slowly cauterising him from within. He hadn't known how to staunch it - or maybe he had and didn't want to think about it. Either way, it'd fuelled him, made him reckless and thoughtless and self-centred. He'd cheated on his wife, he'd put a man in hospital, he'd cried for himself while his best friend lay cold beside him.

'Could you drink your own piss?' he'd asked Pav, tired of thinking about his own low acts.

'If I had to.'

Well, Pav, just to let you know - when you're dying of thirst, you won't have any piss. Or a cup to catch it in. 'I wouldn't kill anyone.'

'What if someone was trying to kill you?'

'Okay, then I wouldn't murder anyone.'

Pav looked unconvinced. 'You can't know that.'

Max remembered raising an eyebrow at him over the rim of his bourbon glass. 'You'd be okay with murder?'

'I know what it's like to be desperate.'

'Doing it is one thing. Being okay with it is another.'

Another Pav shrug. 'I've done bad things and lived with myself.'

'Yeah but did you kill someone?'

Pav looked at him for a long, silent moment. Not like he was trying to remember whether he'd committed a murder, because who'd forget that? More like he was deciding how to answer. Or maybe he'd had too much vodka to come up with an explanation. As he took a breath, there was a voice from the door.

'Pav.' Trish said it quietly, some kind of private warning. Pav glanced up and back down at his drink. She was in her dressing-gown, short, red hair standing up in patches, eyes bleary. She'd been in bed and got up to put an end to the philosophy session. Max wondered how long she'd been standing there. 'You've had enough to drink. Come to bed.'

'It's all right, Trish. I'll be there soon,' Pav told her gently, waiting until she'd slid the door closed before looking at Max. 'She doesn't like me talking about it. She still worries it could find us here.'

It had taken Max a few drunk, baffled seconds to understand Pav's meaning. 'What could find you here?'

'The past. The world is a small place now.' The shrug again. 'Trish worries.' He stood up, capped off the bourbon and vodka. 'Come on, you've had enough, too.'

Max pushed himself out of his chair, unsteady but not ready to finish. 'What, wait. You killed someone?'

'I did a desperate thing. It's in the past. I left it there. It's where it belongs. You should learn to do it as well.'

Max followed him to the door and as Pav fumbled the latch with his bottle-laden hands, asked him softly, 'Does Trish know what happened?'

'Yes. And she'll kill both of us if you ask her about it.' The door slid open but instead of stepping through, Pav turned and looked him hard in the eyes. 'No more, Max. No more questions and no more self-pity. You've done enough of that. It's time you learned to live with yourself.'

Max leaned away from the puddle of water, spitting, trying not to retch. He'd tried to take Pav's advice, wanting to leave the past behind and live the way he'd promised Dallas. And he'd found Rennie. He didn't know what she'd been through, just recognised the hidden scars of a past left behind. He wasn't sure he deserved to find love but he wanted to be worthy of it. She'd been hurt, manipulated, frightened, damaged, he'd figured that much. She deserved better and he'd wanted to be the one to give her it to her.

So what had he done?

He was alone in a black hole, injured, concussed. He had a track record. People around him got hurt - he got hurt - when he wanted without thinking.

Had he hurt Rennie too?

Had he wanted more?

Was that what he'd done?

THE EDGINESS RENNIE had felt when she'd spoken to Joanne bubbled under her skin again. She wanted to tell the detective to quit pissing around and make his point so they could move on. But she'd known it would go something like this. If she was going to help Max, she'd have to sift through the garbage of her life first. Even knowing that, the diversion was worth a try. 'My record has nothing to do with Max. He's never heard of Katrina Hendelsen.'

'Let's see.' He kept reading from the file as if she hadn't spoken. 'We've got, and in no particular order, resisting arrest, theft of a motor vehicle, a vagrancy charge, use of false identification, defaulting on rent. And then there's the illegal possession of a firearm, illegal *use* of a firearm, assault and court-ordered counselling.' He glanced up. 'That's pretty serious stuff, Renee. We generally like to know that kind of information when we're conducting an investigation. It would've been better coming from you.'

If that was the only point he was trying to make, it wasn't so bad. She could do contrite. 'I'm sorry I didn't tell you. I wasn't trying to be deceptive. I just didn't think it had anything to do with Max disappearing. I still don't. It's my father I'm worried about.'

'So I hear.' He leaned back in his chair and crossed his arms. 'You want to tell me about that?'

She gave him the potted version: SAS, delusions, the hunt-and-scare campaign, the murder, the attempted murder, the vow to find her. 'Anthony Hendelsen is a resourceful and violent man. He's out of prison so there's every chance he's responsible for whatever's happened to Max.'

He nodded. 'When did you learn he'd been released?'

'This morning when Evan rang.'

'But you rang Evan last night to find out where your father was.'

'When I realised the car had been searched I started to wonder. It's the kind of thing my father would do. Then there's the man I saw taking photos outside the cafe yesterday. And the blood, of course.'

'And you didn't know your father had been released prior to that?'

'No.'

'You weren't notified by Corrective Services?'

'No.'

He watched her, let the moment draw out. She knew it was a ploy to make her say more. She should have left it at that but her defensiveness was working overtime and she fell right in. 'I can't explain that. Our solicitor is listed as the family representative on the Victims Register. He knows the situation with my father. I don't know if he wasn't contacted or he hasn't followed through.'

'You said our solicitor?'

'Yes.'

'That would be you and your sister, Joanne Hendelsen?'

Wariness made her slow to answer. 'Yes.'

'Did she change her name, too?'

'Yes.'

'So what does she go by now?' It was said with a grin, like it was all a bit of fun picking a new name.

She should have kept her mouth shut. 'Simone Carter.'

He jotted it down. 'She live around here, too?'

'No.'

'Where is she then?'

Rennie hesitated. 'Up the coast.'

'Queensland?'

She watched his genial smile, trying to figure out where he was heading. He probably used his chummy cop front for both victims and bad guys - reassuring for the frightened, a false sense of security for the guilty. Problem was, she wasn't sure which category he'd put her in and didn't know whether the curiosity about Jo was to settle her down or whether he had a genuine interest in the other Hendelsen daughter. 'I'm not sure. She moves around a lot.'

'Have you got a number for her?'

'She's got nothing to do with this.'

'I'd still like a number, Renee.'

The resolve in his voice made her heart thump. Her instinct was to say nothing and keep her sister out of it but this morning, Detective Duncan thought Max used his own keys to get into the glove box, had implied he was hiding, not missing. He'd been told money had disappeared from MineLease and now it turned out Max's girlfriend hadn't been completely honest, that she and her sister had long police records involving theft and deceit and illegal weapons.

She took a breath, trying to calm the alarm that was rising inside her. If he thought Jo had any relevance to his investigation, he was shuffling around the wrong pieces of the puzzle. If she resisted his questions, would he jump to the conclusion that past guilt made them the most likely suspects? That Rennie and Jo were somehow involved?

'Look, Detective Duncan, my sister and I broke the law, I'm not denying that. But we're not criminals. Neither of us has done anything wrong in six years. Check the record. We just want to live like other people while we can.'

'It can cost a lot of money to live like other people.'

He wasn't smiling so much now and Rennie felt her agitation bump up a notch. She was meant to be helping Max, now there were three of them in trouble. Would she make matters worse if she tried to explain again? If she didn't convince him about her father, it could get a whole lot worse. 'Okay, I'm not stupid. I see where you're going with this but you're on the wrong track. I don't know anything about the money James mentioned. All I know is my father is out of gaol and you should be looking for him.'

'I think we should consider that for a moment, Renee. Max didn't come home on Saturday night. It's now Monday lunchtime - let's call it a day and a half later - and you're only now talking to me about your violent, ex-con father who's been out of prison for five months. I'm wondering why it took so long for you to have a conversation with me about that.'

'I didn't know he was out of prison.'

'I'm not convinced that's the truth.'

She said nothing, not sure what he was accusing her of, worried she'd make it worse.

He watched her a long time. Waiting, gauging, judging, she guessed, maybe trying to figure out what exactly was going on. There was no smile when he finally spoke.

'Fraud is a serious crime, Renee.' He edged forwards, softened his eyes with sympathy. 'I know you know about being in trouble. That makes it harder when someone you love does something wrong. You want to protect them, try to keep them out of it. I've seen it over and over and it's tough. And here's the thing.' He laid a hand on the table, palm up. 'I'm not sure what's happening here. At this point, I'm willing to believe you have nothing to do with the money. You say you're on the straight and narrow now and maybe you just want him to come to his senses and hand the money back. I understand it if you want to buy him some time, try to redirect the investigation for a while. Maybe you've talked to him, maybe you haven't. I don't know. But either way, it makes you an accessory, Renee. And for someone like you, with your record, protecting a criminal won't look good.'

Realisation hit like a thump to the back of the head. He thought the story about her father was bullshit. Fuck. She stood up.

He followed suit. 'You need to think about yourself here.'

'No.' For the first time in her screwed-up life, it wasn't herself she needed to think about. 'I need to find Max.' She hauled her bag off the floor and turned to leave.

'It's not too late to help yourself, Renee.'

She took a second to glare at him. 'You are so far off base you may as well take a bloody holiday.'

'I still need your sister's phone number.'

'Try investigating.'

30

She found Hayden in the next office still talking to the cop with the tatt, both of them on the visitor side of the desk with cans of Coke. Two heads lifted as she swung through the door.

'We're leaving, Hayden.'

He glanced at the cop like he was his new best friend. Maybe she should let him stay. He'd be out of the way and safe here, regardless of what the cops thought of her. 'You can stay if you like but I'm leaving now.'

He slumped his shoulders as he stood, as though she'd told him to hurry up or there'd be no ice-cream. Maybe he didn't want to look under the thumb to the cool cop or maybe he was still too much of a kid to do more than protest at a parental instruction. As he followed, she wondered if she should even be giving him orders. She'd kept herself safe for years but this was Max's son; she wasn't sure she should be responsible for him, too.

In the car, she pulled quickly into the traffic, heading towards the lake instead of the highway, putting distance between her and the police before she called Jo. 'What did that cop ask you about?' she asked Hayden.

'Dad.' It was sarcasm, not an answer.

She clenched her teeth, out of patience for his crap. '*What* did he ask?'

'A bunch of stuff.'

She shot him an irate glance.

'How often I stay with him, what Dad does when I'm here, how he gets on with Mum, where I go to school. Stuff.'

Hayden went to a private school, paid for by Leanne's dentist husband. Rennie knew it made Max feel as though he couldn't provide for his son. She wondered whether Hayden knew it, too - and whether the cop would interpret that as motive for wanting money. 'Did he ask about me?'

'Yeah.'

'What did you say?' She saw his shrug. 'Hey, it's no secret what you think of me. I don't care what you said. I just want to know what they're working with.'

He crossed his arms defensively. 'I said you had the shits all the time.'

Hardly a crime. 'Was that it?'

'I said you did good French toast,' he mumbled.

She raised an eyebrow. 'You like my French toast?'

'It's all right.'

A small smile pulled at her lips. Let's see what Detective Duncan and Cool Cop make of that. She stopped beside the park that fronted the water in Toronto. Across the road, the cafe strip was doing a good trade in the sunshine, people sitting under awnings eating lunch, drinking coffee. 'I've got to make a call. Stay here,' she told Hayden.

She stood at the rear bumper, squinting in the glare and eyeing the passing traffic as she waited for Joanne to pick up.

'Katrina.' She must have found the quiet spot again.

'Yeah. I'm ringing to warn you. The cops have your name.'

'What the fuck . . .?'

'I'm sorry, it's my fault. I should've kept my mouth shut but I was worried about Max.'

'What did you say?'

'It doesn't matter now. The detective got my name from Evan, did a search on Katrina Hendelsen and it's all turned to shit. He thinks Max's done a runner with the money and I'm either involved or protecting him - because, hey, I've got a record and can't be trusted.'

'Renee?'

Her head snapped around. Hayden was standing at the kerb, watching her across the dual cab's rear tray. Could he not do as he was told just once?

'Can I get something to eat?' He hooked a thumb at the takeaway joint across the road.

She glanced up and down the street. 'Yeah, okay, be quick.'

'Can I have some money?'

He's a kid, she told herself. Kids need money. She found her bag on the back seat, pulled a couple of notes and passed them to him through the car. 'Grab me a cappuccino, too.'

She needed food but caffeine was what she wanted. As he walked across the road, she called, 'Make sure it's got a lid.'

He rolled his eyes.

'Who's with you?' Joanne asked.

'Hayden, Max's son.'

'Fuck.' Exasperation not criticism. 'What are the cops saying about Anthony?'

'The detective thinks it's bullshit. He thinks I'm trying to mislead his investigation to give Max time to sort things out. Told me I'd be done as an accessory to Max's crimes, whatever he thinks they are.'

'You've got to leave, Kat. I've got a car, I can meet you halfway between here and there. We can go north again, way north. You can't get caught up in it.'

She already was, but maybe Jo was right. Maybe staying would make it worse for Max. As long as she was here, Detective Duncan would be searching in all the wrong places. Looking up records, mashing them together, jumping to conclusions. If she left, would he realise he was wrong or would he think she'd gone into hiding? Christ, if she left, she'd never know what happened to Max. And regardless of the outcome, she needed that or the last four years were worth nothing. 'I can't. Not before I find Max.'

'Fuck, Kat. If it's Anthony, he'll be back for you.'

'I know.'

'Kat...'

'I *know,* Jo. If it's Anthony, he won't stop until I've paid for his bullet holes. But it's different this time. I've got baggage and I can't leave it behind. I need to know what's happened to Max and if Anthony wants to come and find me, then I'll take the risk.'

'No. We don't do it that way, Katrina. You don't stand a chance if you let him close.'

'It's not "we" anymore. I've got a different life now and different decisions to make and I want more than just survival. I'm staying.'

In the silence that followed, she imagined her sister shaking a fist, clamping down on angry words but her voice was matter-of-fact when she spoke. 'Okay, fine. If you want to do it like this, throw away everything we've fought for on some arsehole who promised love and devotion, who might turn out to be a lying, stealing, cheating bastard, then you're no better than the rest of the goddamn family.'

Rennie held the phone to her ear long after Jo broke the connection, the breath knocked out of her. Was she as crazy as her parents? Their blood was in her veins and it carried something that made them hang onto violence and hate when they should have let go. Was that what she was doing? Hanging on?

'When are we leaving?'

As Rennie glanced around, she saw Hayden beside her with a cardboard tray of food but what registered were the chocolate colour of his eyes, the wavy hair and full lips - and, for a heart-stopping half a second, he was Max. Long enough to make the air in her lungs catch. Long enough to feel like a kick in the face when her brain recognised the younger version.

'What?' There was fear in his voice.

'Nothing. It's... nothing.'

'*What*?' His face was pale and the drinks on his tray were tipping sideways.

'You looked like Max then. It... freaked me out a little. That's all.'

He watched her as though he was deciding if she was telling the truth. 'I look like Dad?'

'Yeah. Same eyes, same mouth.'

He smiled briefly - pleasure and sadness. She understood both, wished she could tell him it would be okay. She took the coffee from the tray and he held out the hot chips. 'You want one?'

Greasy food was the last thing the stress in her gut needed but she knew a peace offering when she saw it. 'Thanks.' She pulled a tomato sauce-covered one, took a bite and screwed up her face. 'Vinegar, too? Man, you really do take after your father.'

'Only way to eat 'em.'

'Are you kidding? They're hot chips. They're meant to be crisp, not soggy and smothered.'

'I s'pose you like them with just salt.' He was backing around the front of the car, his you're-an-idiot tone not having quite the same impact with half a grin.

'Like God meant them to be.'

'Yeah, right. Like God makes hot chips.'

'Get in the car.'

She took a gulp of coffee, the smell of steamy, oily chips and vinegar wafting around her while he buckled up. He alternated between shoving wedges of potato into his mouth and dragging his tongue around his greasy fingers. She drove, trying to ignore his feeding noises, feeling unfocused and agitated. Rennie and her sister had been bound to each other their entire lives and for all of Rennie's thirty-four years, Joanne had been angry and tough and sharp-edged, but her support had been unconditional. Their relationship was the one decent thing their family had created and Jo had just kicked it in the head and cut her adrift.

You're alone now, Rennie. No one to ride with, no one at your back, no one to haul you out.

And no idea where to look for Max. She kept her eyes on the road, going nowhere in particular, driving familiar streets while her mind tried to reel in the options she was left with. Anthony Hendelsen or lying and stealing.

If it was her father, Max could be anywhere. Anthony could have confronted him then driven him out of Haven Bay and dumped him God knows where - alive or dead. He could have tied Max up and locked him away as bait for his daughter. Or it might have happened another way, a fight, like she'd thought earlier. Anthony could have needed to get his handiwork out of the car park fast, unloading him nearby but out of sight. Maybe Max was concussed and wandered off, managing to find his way to somewhere he recognised and got no further.

'What are we doing here?' Hayden asked.

Rennie eyed the front entrance to MineLease. She'd been on autopilot and arrived without thinking. Sometimes she had a late lunch with Max, driving over after her shift, eating at their favourite cafe down by the water or sitting in the park. Hayden's chips and vinegar reminded her of the taste of Max's goodbye kiss on some of those occasions.

There was money missing from the business. James had accused Max of taking it. Rennie wasn't sure if she didn't believe him or just didn't want to - but if she was staying to find Max, she had to look everywhere. 'It could be worth checking while we're in Toronto.'

'He's not here. Uncle James said.'

'No, but there might be something else worth finding.'

31

You don't need to run, Max. There's no time limit on recovery, the psychologist had kept telling him. He had a time limit now, though. On his life. Dehydration would kill him if nothing else got him first and if he stayed here sucking at the trickle on the wall, he'd die of thirst with water on his tongue.

His head ached but the dizziness had eased up a bit so he struggled to his feet, waited for his brain to clear and lurched forward. No hands-knees-slap now, no number to remember for the *How I Survived* book, just one foot in front of the other. Maybe if he'd finished his degree he could work out an equation around the probabilities of survival without water while finding his way out of a pitch-black maze.

James might know. He was good at numbers. Max would ask him if he got out. *When* he got out. Inviting James to join him in the business was one of the few good decisions he'd made. There was no wanting and grabbing there. It was a chance for both of them.

When the compo money came in, he was surprised how quickly the idea for the company formed and took hold. Max wasn't an engineer but he knew mines and mine machinery and way back in his golden days, his plan had been to run his own business one day.

James had never been down a mine back then but he knew about budgets and balance sheets, profit and loss. He was in a job he hated and sick of living in Sydney and Max figured the offer somehow made up for keeping Gran's house.

James listened to the plan in his usual pokerfaced way and took a week and a half to think about it, making phone calls, doing projections and coming back with a yes. Naomi was the unknown factor. Max knew how Leanne had felt trapped in Haven Bay and didn't want it to be like that for Naomi. He wanted it to be worthwhile for everyone. There was no need to worry, though. She'd grown up on the opposite shore where it was more populated and a little faster but it was still the lake and she loved being back and closer to her family.

Max stopped, leaned against the wall and breathed hard. He meant to just rest for a few seconds but woozy, nauseated and with a pulse thumping in the wound on his temple, he slid to the floor. Concussion was a bitch.

'You bastard,' James grinned inside Max's head.

'You loser,' Max said to the darkness.

He'd missed James when he went to Sydney. They'd spent their entire lives together to that point - all except for the first two hours of Max's existence. Their mothers were sisters, pregnant together, due a week apart but Max arrived early and James a day late. The family joke was that the DNA gods got confused when both Thompson girls fronted up for delivery on the same night and got the genes mixed up. James and Max shared the same dark hair and eyes but James was tall and bulky with the body of a sportsman and zero coordination or interest. Max, on the other hand, struggled to keep weight on, scraped in at one hundred and eighty centimetres and before the cave-in, could carve up a soccer pitch and sail the wind off most boaties on the lake.

They both got the family competitiveness, though. Max loved to win in sport and James liked to prove he was smart. It pissed some people off but Max understood where it came from - James was a big, strong klutz; he had to get one up somehow.

When they were at school, the jocks didn't appreciate it and it was usually Max who sorted it out. He'd straddled most of the school cliques: the sports guys, the cool group, the smart kids, the theatre arts and music dudes. He was too upbeat for the grunge factor but they never bothered James. Max got in a scrap once or twice in his cousin's defence but mostly all it took was a few words and an all-inclusive laugh that reassured the muscle heads they weren't the butt of a joke.

It was years later, when Max was married and the fire was spitting and steaming inside him, that coming to James's defence turned nasty.

'How stupid *are* you?'

James said it loud enough to be heard over the crowd lined up at the bar. Max had no idea what it was in reference to, only saw the body it was directed at: big and tough with the nose of a brawler. It didn't start there - twenty minutes later, after the bloke stewed for a while and found some friends, there was some shouting and shoving before the first punch was thrown. As usual, James did nothing to defend himself. Didn't apologise, didn't back off, didn't flinch - and was sat on his arse. Not that Max stopped to help him up. His old role of Cousin Protector was reignited by the anger in his gut and he jumped into the fray.

He wasn't friendless in there. The mates he was drinking with joined in, mostly trying to break it up. But it was Max who ended up shoving the insulted bastard hard enough to topple over a table and straight through a plate-glass window. The cops were called, the ring-leader needed a hundred and twenty stitches and both he and Max were charged with assault. It was Max's first offence and he got off with a good behaviour bond. The other guy's fingerprints matched those from a long list of robberies and he got five years.

Toronto homes were probably safer with him in prison but the arsehole's family played it like it was Max's fault the guy did time, that he wasn't going to be around for his young kids and pregnant girlfriend. Leanne carried on like he'd blotted her reputation in the community. James nursed a black eye and swollen jaw and told Max he hadn't asked for a brawl on his behalf.

'You're the fucking loser,' Max told himself in the darkness, the adolescent, misplaced aggression still capable of filling him with shame.

And as he fingered the clotted, drying blood on his face, he asked out loud: 'What did you do this time, Max?'

HAYDEN SCUFFED his shoes along the footpath all the way to the front entrance of the MineLease office. Some kind of protest, Rennie figured, and a welcome change to his swearing and snarling.

MineLease was in a weatherboard cottage, once a modest home, now converted to the workplace of like-minded private enterprises. It was owned by a mine engineering consultancy that rented space to a company specialising in mine safety practices and Max and James's equipment leasing business. On either side of a central hallway, rooms had been adapted to accommodate small offices and storage. There was a large, shared meeting room in the rear and the backyard was used for parking. Rennie stopped inside the front door, where Amanda, the office coordinator, did administration for all of them in what had once been a sunroom.

'Amanda, hi.'

The sound of Rennie's voice made Amanda's head snap up and a hand fly to her throat. 'Oh God, Rennie. James said you still can't find him. Oh.' Her eyes flicked to the teenager following Rennie in. 'Hayden. How're you doing, mate?'

He answered with a shrug. Amanda glanced at Rennie, worry and sympathy in her face. 'Any news?'

'No. I thought I'd take a look in his office, see if there's ... I don't know, something that might make sense.'

Amanda spoke as she rounded her desk. 'James said he went through it yesterday and couldn't find anything.'

'It's worth another try, just to tick that box. Has James left for the police station yet?' She didn't want him looking over her shoulder.

Amanda shrugged. 'I don't know where he went. He dropped in a couple of hours ago and left again. Do you want me to call him?'

Maybe he hadn't needed to search for anything. Maybe the financial records were printed and collated and ready for the police after his argument with Max on Friday. Or maybe he was still driving around looking for Max. 'No, I don't need to speak to him. I'll just take a look in Max's office.'

Amanda turned a smile on Hayden. 'Hey, I just bought mud cake muffins. They're out in the kitchen. You want one?' It sounded like a ploy to keep him occupied. Rennie was grateful - she'd do better on her own - but he'd just had chips and a milkshake.

'Those little ones with the swirly icing?' he asked.

'Yep.'

'Sure. Can I make a hot chocolate from the coffee machine?'

'If you like. Make me a cup of tea while you're at it, huh?'

He pointed at her, squinted an eye. 'Milk and one sugar, right?'

'Yes, thank you.'

Rennie raised surprised eyebrows - did he plan to take a doggy bag and when had he started making drinks for anyone but himself? As he disappeared into the hallway, she said, 'He's just eaten.'

'He's fourteen.' Amanda had two boys in high school so Rennie guessed she knew all about teenage food intake. And she probably knew more about the three businesses here than anyone else.

'How did Max seem last week?'

'He seemed . . . fine.'

'But?'

'It's not my job to say anything.'

'Sure, I understand, but Max is missing.'

She clasped and unclasped her hands. 'This is an old house, the walls are thin and noise travels. I don't eavesdrop but sitting at my desk I hear stuff, you know?'

'Of course.'

'Well,' she hesitated a second longer. 'There was something going on between Max and James all week. They had some kind of row early on. Monday afternoon, I think. One of them must've shut the door before it started but I could hear them. No actual words, just angry, raised voices. And they were at it for ages. Not shouting all the time but there was obviously some serious discussion. Gerard left for the day while it was still going on and made a face as he walked past reception.'

Naomi had said the argument was on Friday and James hadn't corrected her. Was there more than one? 'Did something happen on Friday?'

'I don't know. I had a half day and went home at lunchtime.'

'You said "all week". What else happened?'

'There were a couple more closed-door conferences and they were both just really tense. James, in particular. I mean, he can be moody and a bit sharp when he decides to be but it wasn't that. It was like he was trying hard to look normal, smiling and all, and underneath he was fuming. And Max, well, he's always laid-back, as you know, and even he looked stressed.'

Flashes of memory played through Rennie's mind. The love-making before the party, the proposal and argument, Max's snapped words the last time he spoke to her. She thought back to earlier in the week. She'd painted in the studio every evening, trying to finish the 'wow factor' commission. At least three nights, he was in bed and asleep by the time she got in. One night, Wednesday maybe, he had a drink with Pav. Once, possibly the early hours of Thursday, he'd flicked on all the lights in the living room and prowled the house. It's what he did when the nightmares woke him. They usually roused her, too, when he gasped awake and she'd make a sleepy trip to the bathroom. Sometimes she'd make him a cup of tea before she went back to bed; sometimes she'd fold herself around him and try to soothe his memories with the heat and rhythm of her body. But she didn't remember getting up last week, just his restless pacing. Had she been tired enough to sleep through his nightmare or had something else made him get up and walk the floor?

'Was there a problem on a job?' Maybe there'd been something else going on before the argument on Friday.

Amanda's shoulders did a quick up and down. 'Nothing that's crossed my desk. But both of them were in and out of the office a lot after the argument so I suppose there could've been and they were trying to pacify a client.'

Rennie remembered James had said he'd been trying to trace the missing money back through the accounts. Maybe there'd been an argument on Monday when he'd discovered the shortfall, some kind of dispute over how they were running the business, then another one on Friday when he'd accused Max of taking it. 'Naomi said James worked late last week.'

'Did he? He was gone most days when I left but that doesn't mean he didn't come back. Come to think of it, I cleared away a couple of empty wineglasses on the sink before Gerard's conference on Thursday morning. They might have been his.'

Drinking as he pored over the figures?

From the other end of the cottage, the coffee maker gurgled. If Hayden's earlier snack was anything to go by, he wouldn't take long to down a hot chocolate and a couple of muffins. 'Right, well, thanks, Amanda.'

She headed down the hall, wondering about Amanda's version of events. What did it mean? What did any of it mean? What could she draw from a second-hand account of an argument and a work schedule in an office she knew nothing about?

32

The waiting room between MineLease's two small offices was a tiny space taken up with filing cabinets, a couple of chairs and magazines with glossy photos of extremely large machinery.

It was months since Rennie had been in Max's office and when she opened his door, the sight of his silent, cluttered space made her heart stop. He was everywhere - hard hat and earmuffs hanging on a rack, high-vis work trousers and shirt draped over a chair, steel-capped boots dropped carelessly under it. There was a pushbike and helmet, an orange kayak propped against a wall, a wetsuit draped over it like an empty skin. A bookcase was stacked with folders and fat manuals and his desk looked like nothing had been filed since last Christmas. And there was his uniquely Max scent: fresh and salty, slightly woody, a little coffee and hot food mingled in. It filled her nostrils, making her chest tighten and her tear ducts tingle. Made her want to wail his name.

Do something that will help, she told herself.

She went to his desk, found Post-It notes everywhere: stuck to the sides of the computer screen, in lines down the tabletop, on the edges of the shelves. There were photos, too, taped and pinned and propped. Not duplicates of the ones at home but the same themes: family, friends, Hayden and Rennie. His monitor and keyboard were angled to one side, a blotter with large, tear-off sheets positioned in front of his chair. A thick diary lay closed next to it.

Rennie opened it where a pen was stuck between the pages: Friday, three days ago. The hours were marked down the margin, Max's shorthand on corresponding lines. At ten am: *Teralba at Teralba.* Midday said *Simmo.* Pete's name was written across the bottom of the page with another name and mobile number underneath - the replacement crew for Sunday sailing, she guessed. At three pm, there was a single, underlined word: *James.* A meeting that'd turned into an argument?

She flipped back through the week and found more of the same two- and three-word cryptic notes. She shut the book and moved onto the Post-Its. Three clinging to the monitor were curled at the edges and looked like they'd been there as long as Max had: his sister's number in Perth, his parents' address in Yamba, Hayden's school details. On the desk, there was a reminder to pick up photos, to buy milk, to call Hayden for his birthday. There were dates that had passed and for weeks ahead. Four of them reminded him to 'call Rennie'. It told her he knew he was forgetful, that he cared, that he tried to keep in touch, that he never cleaned his damn desk. And if he was having an affair or planning to leave, there was no trace of it here.

'Did you find anything?'

It was Hayden, licking the fingers of one hand, a frothy mug in the other. She almost suggested he wait with Amanda then remembered he'd spent a lot of time here over the years hanging out in the office during school holidays. And he wanted to search. 'Why don't you take a look?'

While Hayden read the Post-Its, she hovered over the blotter, trying to make sense of the scrawls and doodles. A line had been drawn from top to bottom dividing the page in two. On one side were squares and loops and odd shapes, on the other, notes were jotted in columns. It looked like company names and there were dates and other groups of numbers.

'You see anything?' she asked Hayden.

'A lot of sticky notes.'

'Gee, I missed that.' She caught his brief grin in profile.

'Did you look on his computer?' he asked.

'Not yet. You want to fire it up?'

'Sure.'

Mention of the computer seemed to inject some enthusiasm into him. He ducked around her, flicked the monitor on, rolled the chair into place. She let him at it as she pulled open the desk drawers: in the top one there were pens, rulers, paperclips, electrical leads and a thousand multicoloured, sticky Post-It pads. His stockpile. Spare notebooks were stacked in the next one, with a cardboard file sitting on the top. There was a single sheet of paper inside, lists of numbers running down one side. Some of them were calendar dates for this year. Others were long groups of numbers like she'd seen on the blotter. She pulled the page and checked them against the ones on the desk. All six were the same.

'It wants a password,' Hayden said.

Rennie glanced at the screen and back to the numbers on the page. Passwords? 'Try this.'

Hayden typed as she read out a series of numbers.

'No.'

'Try it with these spaces.' She read it again.

'No.'

They went through them all, in case Max was changing his password and writing it down so he wouldn't forget. Nothing. She pushed a hand through her hair and let out a gust of air. Maybe the numbers weren't anything to do with the computer. Maybe they were code numbers and service dates for machinery. Maybe he'd bought lottery tickets. Maybe she was grasping at straws.

'Okay, we're getting nowhere here.' She went to drop the page into the folder again, changed her mind, folded it and pushed it into her back pocket. She had no idea what it was but she was sick of leaving empty-handed.

On the way out, she eyed James's closed door. She knew his office was identical to Max's, minus the clutter, but he'd pulled together the financial records in there. Maybe there was a copy, maybe his computer wasn't password protected. She tried the knob. Locked. There was no deadlock, just a handle and strike plate. She could open it without damaging it. It'd barely leave a scratch.

'Take your mug out to the kitchen,' she told Hayden quietly.

As he turned, Amanda appeared in the hallway. 'How're you guys doing down here? Found anything?'

Rennie stepped away from James's door. 'It's hard to tell.'

'Anything I can help you with?'

'Yes. Do you know if Max and James always use passwords on their computers?'

'I don't know about James. I've never used his computer. He either emails me with work or drops off hard copies at the desk. Max doesn't. Anything he forgets to drop off, I go into his office and look it up on his computer.'

'Right. Thanks.'

Amanda waited as though there might be more. There wasn't, just Rennie's burning desire to help herself to the contents of James's office.

Hayden followed her to the car in silence, which she was more than grateful for. She wanted to ask Max what the hell it all meant. The argument, the numbers, the passwords, the blood. The only thing she knew was that the answers weren't going to be good news. She pulled on her belt, started the engine, then just sat.

'What?' Hayden asked.

'I'm running out of ideas.'

'*Now* can we check his fishing spots?'

Yeah, there were still places to look. 'Okay, let's do that.'

Taking the highway back to Haven Bay, Hayden directed her to a small, rocky cove further south than the curve of Winsweep Bay she'd run this morning. She stood at the edge of the road and knew they wouldn't find anything. It made no sense for Max to be here - dumped, stumbled or otherwise. Too close to houses, too far from Skiffs, in the opposite direction to home. She let Hayden wander around the rocks anyway, understanding the need to keep looking, tilting her face and squinting in the bright sunlight, the promise of a hot summer filling her with apprehension. Was Max seeing this, too? Was he somewhere exposed, sunburnt and dehydrated? Injured and disoriented? Or were his eyes closed and his body cold?

Or was he lying in a soft bed with another woman, ordering room service with stolen money?

They stopped at two more fishing spots and Rennie watched Hayden clamber about, feeling the jitters and short temper of too much coffee and not enough food. 'Let's go to Skiffs. I need to eat,' she finally told him.

It was after two when they got there and the lunchtime crowd had been and gone. Pav had probably started to close down the kitchen but maybe he'd fix her a sandwich. Maybe she'd beat him around the head if he didn't.

'He's not here,' Eliza told her, a couple of cappuccinos in hand as she passed them on the way to a table.

Trish appeared from the kitchen, embracing Hayden first then whispering in Rennie's ear as she hugged her. 'You look shattered.'

Rennie wondered how much Trish knew - whether Naomi had revealed her secrets over the phone or the counter, whether Detective Duncan had asked incriminating questions. She was tired of keeping up the mystery now, of pretending to be someone else. 'You're probably going to hear some things about me. They're not pleasant but...'

Trish held up a hand. 'Don't. It's okay. Naomi called.'

Rennie nodded. 'Have you spoken to the police yet?'

'Detective Duncan was in this morning.'

'You're probably wishing you'd asked for a resume five years ago.'

'I'm wishing I'd been a better friend. You might've had someone you could talk to.'

There were good reasons Rennie loved her. 'You're the first friend I ever had. I didn't want to scare you off.'

'I don't scare easily.' She said it firmly, a message - and more than a hint of the resilience that must have kept her safe around the world. 'Now, fill me in on Max.'

'I've got to eat first. Is the kitchen closed already?'

Trish waved Rennie and Hayden to stools at the counter. 'No, Shannon's here. She should have enough to throw a sandwich together. What about you, Hayden?'

'He's already eaten. A lot,' Rennie said.

'Have you got any ravioli?' he asked, leaning over the counter as he hoisted himself into the tall seat beside her.

'No, but you can have a toasted cheese and tomato sandwich.'

'Great.'

'Thanks,' Rennie corrected him. He rolled his eyes. Trish ruffled his hair before calling the order into the kitchen. Shannon worked alternate weekends for Pav and three nights a week at a restaurant in Newcastle. Rennie couldn't remember the last time she'd been in during the week. 'Why is Shannon here?' she asked Trish.

'Pav had to go out.'

Rennie raised her eyebrows. Was he searching for Max, too? 'In the middle of the day? Did he swap bodies with someone who takes a break?'

Trish laughed a little. 'He's been having problems with a supplier. He's trying to sort something out.'

'The Serbian guy?'

Trish cocked her head, pulled a face that said she wasn't impressed.

The lean, heavily accented sales rep had started dropping by to see Pav a couple of months ago. Pav would come out of the kitchen, sit at a table with him, drink coffee and talk in one of the eight or so languages that could roll off his tongue. He'd told Rennie the guy sold good condiments but whenever he'd been in, Pav would launch into one of his stressed cooking frenzies. He was in on Saturday morning when he was prepping food for the party and his cook-off got the job done faster. 'What's the problem with him?'

'Pav knows him. It's a long story. Let me see how your lunch is going.'

Eliza slipped into Trish's place behind the counter. 'You're probably too preoccupied for inquiries about paintings but a man rang a couple of times asking about you.'

Caution stiffened Rennie's spine. 'What man? Did he leave a name?'

Eliza flicked a startled glance at the hand Rennie had clasped around her wrist. 'He didn't want to leave a name. He said something about admiring your work and wanted to talk to you.'

Anthony had shown photos of his daughters at shops and real estate agents and caravan parks, played the concerned, desperate father looking for his kids. Sounding convincing about her paintings wasn't a stretch. 'What did you tell him?'

33

'That you don't give your details out over the phone,' Eliza told her. 'And you wouldn't be in for a few days.'

Good girl. 'Was that all?'

'The second time he rang, he asked if you had a studio or showroom somewhere.'

'And?'

'I told him you worked from home. And no, I didn't give him your address.'

'Did he ask for it?'

'Yes.'

Rennie interlocked her fingers, squeezed tight, fighting the urge to get up and walk straight to the car.

'Here you go.' As Trish slid plates across the counter, Eliza ducked away to serve a customer at the register and Hayden groaned like he hadn't eaten for days. Rennie just eyed her food, heart pounding beneath her ribs, and waited for Eliza to finish serving.

'The man on the phone, Eliza, what did he sound like?'

She shrugged. 'I don't know. He seemed really nice.'

'Who?' Trish asked.

'I meant age,' Rennie pressed. 'Could you pick what sort of age he was?'

'He was on the phone. It's hard to tell. What difference does it make if he wants to buy a painting?'

'Have you sold a painting?' Trish asked.

Rennie gripped the edge of the counter, frustration and fear and low blood sugar making her want to shout at them. 'It might have something to do with Max.' Beside her, Hayden turned his head. 'Did he sound young or old?' she asked.

The mention of Max made Eliza focus. 'Well, his voice was kind of gravelly. Yeah, I'd say he was an older guy.'

Rennie wasn't sure what a twenty-year-old considered as an 'older guy' but the man with the camera in the street yesterday was well past forty. 'When did you take the calls?'

'The first one was yesterday afternoon just before we closed up and then he rang again today.' She checked her watch. 'Maybe an hour and a half ago. I remember because we were really busy and I was trying to get him off the phone.'

Rennie did the sums. Max disappeared on Saturday night and the first call was around three pm Sunday, almost eighteen hours later. Her father could have left and come back. Hurt Max in the car park, taken him far away and returned for her.

'What's going on, Rennie?' Trish asked.

'I'm not sure.' She didn't *know* it was her father - there was no way of confirming it from a couple of phone calls - but she wasn't prepared to take any chances. She glanced at Hayden still chewing on his sandwich and wondered about leaving him here. He would slow her down, however this panned out. But if her father had seen him with her, if he'd already hurt Max for the same reason, Hayden was safer where she could keep an eye on him. 'Come on, we've got to go.'

'I haven't finished,' Hayden complained.

'And you haven't eaten anything,' Trish said.

Rennie took a large bite from the corner of her sandwich then pushed the plate across the counter. 'I'll take it with me. Can you wrap it up?'

'Rennie, what is it?' Trish tried again.

'It's what I didn't tell you about. I'll call you later.' She waited impatiently as the sandwich was pushed into a bag. Hayden didn't bother with wrapping, eating as he followed her to the car.

'I thought you were hungry,' he said as he clipped himself into his belt.

'I can eat on the way.'

'Where are we going?'

'Home.' She needed the backpack. And the gun.

THE LANDSCAPE WAS THE SAME. Still dense black and silent, still dry and sandy under his hands. The only difference was the pain. It was worse. Deeper, dragging, clawing its way into every part of his body. Max knew it wasn't just his wounds now but blood loss, dehydration, shock, maybe infection, too. He wanted to curl up in a ball and sleep forever; he wanted to grab the agony by the throat and call it a fucking arsehole. What he did was grit his teeth and crawl slowly, exhaustingly forward, hoping it was taking him somewhere and that he'd get there before he died.

The memories kept his mind focused on something other than the pain and the darkness. He tried to open his mind to them like a door, whistle for their attention, beckon them in with the scoop of a hand and the promise of an endless glass of water. There was no rush in response, though. They trickled in one by one, as though somewhere out of sight they'd got into chronological order and were coming back in an organised, unhurried fashion. When Rennie's gun sauntered in, it made his heart thump all over again.

He'd found it the weekend after she almost left him. That event in itself had scared the hell out of him. The argument was short and firey, out of character for Rennie but nothing like the yelling matches he'd had with Leanne, then five minutes after he'd stormed out to the deck, he'd heard the old garage door wrench up and her car start. Even though he was well past his running days, he found enough pace to reach the bottom of the driveway as she did, almost getting dragged under a wheel as he jumped in beside her. She'd seemed more resigned than angry when they talked, as though she'd been waiting for the moment it would turn to shit.

He'd wanted to stagger about with relief when she agreed to stay. Instead he carried her backpack inside so she couldn't change her mind and make a dash with it. There was barely anything in it but it was as heavy as if she'd grabbed Gran's antique silver candlesticks on the way out. She took it from him when they reached the bedroom and shut it in the wardrobe before she let him kiss her.

He'd wondered for days afterwards what was in there, enough to make him go and look when she was working the next weekend. The pack was back on the top shelf and weighed down by a single object that distended the soft base.

He couldn't remember now if he'd felt guilty about doing it, just recalled the curiosity that made him unzip the bag like a kid uncovering a treasure. He'd spent a lot of time wondering about her life, concocting episodes that might explain her various layers. What he found made him scratch the lot.

A gun. What the fuck?

Shock made him fumble and drop it, cringing, expecting it to go off. It was black and mean looking, with moving parts and an empty hole in the grip where the canister for the bullets went. He tried to fight the image of it in her hands but the bold, tough, wary parts of her slid together in his mind and yeah, a gun could make sense - if she'd needed to protect herself or someone else or . . .

Looking for answers, he went through the contents of the backpack. There was an empty clip and loose ammunition in a pocket, fat rolls of cash in a plastic bag, a mobile phone and charger, a zip lock bag with someone else's birth certificate pressed against one side of the clear plastic. He'd got up and paced around, wringing his hands, not wanting to connect the dots that were on his bedroom floor. Then he opened the zip lock and the first thing he saw was the photo. One of the kids in it was definitely Rennie around the age of nine or ten. The woman was similar enough to suggest it was her mother and he guessed the other girl was her sister, Simone. He'd seen her once at the cafe when Rennie first started there and met her, very briefly, at the house after Rennie moved in.

He'd come home early from work. Both of them seemed startled when he walked in, as though they'd been caught out at something. He tried a bit of friendly 'So what brings you here?' chitchat but Simone looked him up and down with such tough-arsed scrutiny that he almost felt like apologising. She went out to her car after that and he watched discreetly from the bay window as Rennie talked with her in the driveway. Simone was a taller, darker, pissed-off version of Rennie. There was no endearing sisterly familiarity between them; they were tense and edgy together and he thought maybe there'd been an argument. They hugged before Simone got in the car, though. A sudden, taut clinch that said more for the intensity of their relationship than love and tenderness.

Max almost returned the photo without flipping it over. The writing on the back was old-style cursive: *Katrina, Mum, Joanne, Feb. 1989.* He turned it back and forth a couple of times, thinking he must've been wrong. But he wasn't. It was Rennie and she'd once been called Katrina or Joanne. He checked the birth certificate again - it was for a Katrina Nicole Hendelsen; mother Donna, father Anthony, born in 1978. Same year, same month as Rennie.

There was more in the plastic bag, leftovers from a childhood: a blue ribbon from a cross country race, a medallion for swimming, but an old driver's licence and the School Certificate confirmed the other name.

Max's heart pounded and his hands trembled. There could be a lot of explanations for Rennie changing her name, plenty of reasons why she hadn't told him. But she had a gun in the wardrobe - and none of the dots told him whether it was Katrina Hendelsen or Renee Carter who needed it.

He shoved the backpack on the shelf again, went to the yard and dug up a storm. He was mad: that she had it, that he'd found it, that he'd been so far off base about her. That the story she hadn't told him was ugly and dangerous and she'd brought the remains of it to his house. He considered undercover cop, witness protection, on the run.

He thought about things she'd said: she didn't know how to stay, this chapter was better than the two before it, the book of her life was a horror story. And his anger became fearful and apprehensive. For her. For himself - because he didn't know how to protect her.

And as he hacked at the soil, he knew that was what he wanted to do - keep her safe so she didn't need a gun. Whatever the hell had happened in her past had made her tough and wary. It also made her twitch and gasp in her sleep, quietly anxious at times, slow to make friends. It'd carved deep scars that were hidden under the layers of the person she was now - and she looked at him as though she understood his damage, the way only someone who'd lived it could.

Max took a breather in the dark, tried to move his thoughts on from the gun. He didn't get a whole lot further.

The contents of her backpack and his deception in rummaging through it had weighed on his mind but it didn't stop him going back the next weekend, hauling it out, plugging in the mobile phone and going through the contacts list. There were only four numbers. The name 'Jo' seemed to confirm his theory that the Joanne in the picture was the Simone he'd been introduced to. His name was there, which was comforting. There were two others: Evan Delaney and Nathan Bruce-Allen. He returned everything and went online.

Bruce-Allen was easy to find. He was a defence lawyer at a Sydney firm called Bruce-Allen & Beckeritch. According to the website, they handled anything from drink-driving charges and hearings with sporting tribunals to extradition proceedings and murder trials. He didn't call, realised they weren't going to tell him anything about a client, if that's why their number was on Rennie's phone.

Evan Delaney was a little harder to locate but Max eventually found him mentioned in newspaper articles. He was a police detective, quoted in stories about grisly murders. With a bit more digging, he discovered that before rising to detective ranks, he'd been a country cop around New South Wales.

He googled Rennie's name, too: Hendelsen and variations with Katrina, Joanne, Donna and Anthony. Mostly he found websites in some Scandinavian language that didn't help even when he hit translate. He signed up to a search engine for archived newspapers and magazines but she'd lived all over and after three hours of trundling through national dailies and regional rags, Rennie came home from work and he had nothing except a raft of unanswered questions and the same possibilities of undercover cop, witness protection and bad girl on the run.

Max took up the crawling again, trying to figure it out, wondering if he'd already discovered the answers and couldn't remember.

He doubted she was an undercover cop, not because she wasn't up to it. She spent her time working in a cafe in Haven Bay - what was there to investigate?

Witness protection fitted. The contents of the zip lock bag might be the last scraps of her old self. Maybe whoever she was being protected from was still walking the streets or she doubted how well she could be concealed.

On the run was his least favourite possibility. She could be hiding from the police and he didn't want her involved in something that could send her to prison. On the other hand, if it was bad guys, bad enough that she needed to change her name and carry a gun, what could he do to protect her?

He paused, panting and aching, apprehension and misgiving heaving in his chest. Had whatever she was running from found her? Had it found him, too?

Was he meant to protect Rennie? Was that what he needed to do that he couldn't remember?

34

Rennie took a roundabout route home, scanning the few cars that passed, thinking about her father and wondering what the hell to do. She only knew how to run. Staying was new territory.

'Pass me some food,' she told Hayden.

He handed her half a sandwich and she chewed as she tried to pull thoughts together. If the caller asked for her address, he didn't know where she lived - at least he didn't ninety-odd minutes ago. But the question indicated more than that. If he'd been watching her in Haven Bay, following her home wouldn't have been difficult. Which meant he probably hadn't been here long, more than likely only a few days. Then how did Max get caught up in it?

She'd worked Thursday, Friday and . . . Max had dropped into Skiffs for lunch on Saturday. She remembered now; there were markets at the park in the morning and everyone who visited the stalls seemed to want a coffee, too. She hadn't had time to stop and talk and Max had gone to the kitchen to see Pav. Had he even eaten? She couldn't recall him sitting at a table, only that she'd walked him out when he left. She'd kissed him goodbye on the footpath, a quick crush of lips before she hit the coffee machine again. Had her father been out there? Was that where he'd seen Max? Had he hung around hoping to find them again and struck it lucky when they turned up at the party?

Rennie parked in the carport, anxious to get inside and feel the security of a gun in her hands, but a well- rehearsed caution slowed her up. She checked both sides of the house, glanced up and down the street from the porch, examined the base plate of the lock for tampering before she inserted the key and swung the door wide. It was cool and dim in the hallway, only silence coming from the rest of the house but she hesitated, years of suspicion and wariness telling her to take it slow.

Hayden moved to walk around her and she stuck out an arm. 'Wait,' she murmured.

'I need to go to the bathroom.'

'Be a big boy and hold on.'

He folded his arms but didn't challenge the order.

Moving quietly into the hall, she tipped her head into the living room. It was empty but a sense of intrusion tickled at the hairs on her neck. She let her eyes roam around the room: bay window, sofas, kitchen, table, glass at the back. The only sign of disturbance was on the lounge, the scatter cushions tossed to one side, the foam upholstery askew. She couldn't remember what state they were in when they left and, not for the first time, she wished Hayden had picked another occasion to run away from his mother and throw himself at the furniture.

She crossed the hall and as she stood in the bedroom doorway, fear scuttled up her spine. Both wardrobe doors were ajar. She wanted to charge across the room and grab the gun from the backpack but she kept the urge in check. She could be cornered over there. Or Hayden reached before she could get to him. She swung her head to him on the porch. If she took him with her, they could both be trapped in the bedroom before she could get her finger on the trigger.

Sweep the house first, she told herself. Slipping back to the front entry, she picked up the doorstopper - a large and rusted nut and bolt

Max had found in a mine somewhere - and gripped it by its narrower end. Not a bullet but it would drop a man if she swung it well. Hayden lost the folded arms and stood a little more anxiously.

'What is it?' he asked.

'Stand inside the door and don't move,' she told him.

Blood hissed in her ears as she made her way quickly, noiselessly down the narrow corridor, listening as she went. She pushed Hayden's door until it touched the wall. It was empty but the room looked like it'd been ransacked - how much he'd done himself, she couldn't tell. The bathroom was clear. In the study, she ran her eyes over the cluttered space. Stuff had been shoved about: the mousepad, the keyboard, a pile of paper. The line of Post-Its along the shelf edge was broken in several places where notes had dropped to the table-top. Two drawers in the filing cabinet were half open, the bottom one in the desk wasn't quite shut.

Breathing hard, trying to contain the urgency building in her, Rennie went to the back windows, checked the door - locked - scanned the yard. Nothing moved, nothing looked out of place.

But someone had been here.

It was her father. It had to be.

After he'd called the cafe. Sometime in the last two hours.

Rennie clenched her teeth and squeezed her eyes shut. The familiar hum of dread rose in volume but anger was louder. Fuck. Fuck him. He'd been in her house. Her *home.* His filthy hands had touched her belongings. Max's things. Their lives.

'*Bastard.*'

'Who?'

Hayden was at the far end of the room, not in the hallway where she'd told him to stay. There was no belligerence or cynicism from him now, just alarm and the vulnerability of an untried boy. Christ, he was a kid. He knew nothing about real danger or survival.

She took off fast, almost jogging down the hall to the bedroom, reached the wardrobe in long strides, threw the doors wide and saw why they'd been ajar. Her pack wasn't pushed to the back where she'd left it. It was in front of the drawers, tipped on its side, obstructing the opening. Rennie snatched it up, the zip gaping open and the weight telling her the full story. She upended it on the bed anyway and pushed her hands through the tangle of contents. It was gone.

The gun was gone.

'What?' Hayden had followed her as far as the bedroom door, hovering there as though he wasn't sure whether to come or go, the tight, higher pitch of his single word conveying some comprehension of the moment.

Except he wouldn't understand what it meant and Rennie didn't want to. She wanted to stay here and find Max. But Hayden was Max's son - and he couldn't stay. Not with her father capable of walking through the door.

'We need to leave,' she told him, returning the contents of her backpack with angry thrusts.

'Is that money?'

She picked up the plastic bag with the two thick rolls of cash and stuffed it into her pack. 'Yes. Go do what you need to do in the bathroom, then get your bag and a warm top and long pants.'

He frowned, a little annoyance in it now. 'What for?'

'We're leaving.'

'But we just got here.'

Slow it down, she told herself. He hasn't done this before, doesn't know how it works and panic won't help. 'Someone's been in the house, Hayden. It's not safe for us here.'

He glanced down the hallway as if he expected to see a figure standing at the other end. 'How do you know?'

'He . . . they've been through the rooms.' She zipped the pack.

'Did they take anything?'

'Yes.' She cast a brief look at the wardrobe - both sides had been searched. The papers on Max's shelf were scattered, the contents of the ashtray tipped out.

'They didn't take that money,' Hayden said.

'No.' She closed the wardrobes and walked over to him.

'Are you going to call the cops?'

'Later. We should get out first.'

Hayden stood in the doorway, not moving, not talking, just watching her like he was waiting for something more.

'Come on, Hayden. *Move.*' She pulled a breath as he left, memories flashing through her mind - of herself when she was younger than him, running for her bag, more scared of her mother's wrath than the father who was lying in wait. If they were going to escape him, Hayden needed to do what he was told and she needed to be patient with him. Skills neither of them was proficient in.

She walked the length of the living room while she waited for him, wanting to check the studio, knowing there wasn't time. He was in the hallway again when she returned to the front entry, something determined in his eyes.

'Where are we going?' he asked.

'I haven't made that decision yet.'

'What about Dad?'

It was a fair question. She didn't know how to answer it. 'We can talk about it in the car.' She opened the door.

'No.' Hayden stood in the shaft of light that flooded into the corridor, arms folded once more.

She wanted to shunt him through the door like her mother would have. 'There isn't time to stand around and discuss it. We get out, then we talk.' She turned to leave.

He wasn't finished. 'So what if someone broke in? They've gone already and they didn't even take your money. Big deal. We can call the cops.'

The bright afternoon at her back made her feel exposed.

She peered briefly around the empty neighbourhood then swung the door back to its lock. 'It wasn't a robbery, Hayden. The person who did it was looking for something. He might come back and we don't want to be here if he does.'

He watched her a second. 'Who was it?'

'Someone looking for me.'

She saw the deep breath of defiance as he pointed a finger in her face. 'Then you go. I'm waiting for Dad.'

She batted it away, raising her voice. 'Max isn't coming back here.

Wherever he is, he's not going to wander up the front steps and let himself in. But the arsehole who was here might and you have no idea what that will bring.'

'You can't make me go.'

She wished she didn't have to. She wished he'd toe the line for five goddamn minutes. 'Cut the petulant kiddie bullshit, Hayden. You're fourteen. Time to grow up. Something's happened to your dad. He's not lost and he hasn't left. It's something else. Something bad. And we're in danger if we stay here.'

'What would *you* know about danger? You're just a fucking waitress. You make fucking coffee for a living. What would you know about *anything*?'

Rennie had hoped to scare him. Standing here like this sure as hell scared *her*. She swung away from him, slammed the flat of her hand into the wall. 'Jesus Christ, Hayden!' She pushed past him into the living room, stomped across the room, barking through clenched teeth, 'This was never meant to happen here.' She picked up a cushion from the floor, threw it at the wall, cried out at the empty space in front of her. Fury and frustration and fear made her turn back to him, made words spill out of her as she marched towards him.

'Don't presume to *know* me. I am not a nice person. I've done bad things. But the man who was here is worse. He's *my* father and he's spent a long time wanting to hurt me. He'll hurt you, too. He might have already hurt Max. What I know, Hayden, will keep you alive. What I know . . .'

She stopped, realising she'd backed him into the hallway, that his eyes were wide, his mouth slack and that she'd said far more than she'd intended with a rage that shouldn't have been aimed at him. She rubbed a hand over her face and forced air into her lungs. Hayden watched her with something new and a little unnerved in his eyes.

35

'I'm sorry, I . . .' Rennie started then realised there was nothing she wanted to explain. 'Can we just get in the damn car?'

Hayden didn't say anything this time, just picked up his bag and waited as she pulled the front door. Squinting in the glare, she scanned left and right along the street then led the way to the carport, trying to contain the emotions that had surged to the surface.

'Bag on the back seat,' she told him as she threw her own pack in. She reversed out of the driveway, glad to have the dual cab's turbo engine underneath her, and drove before she knew where she was going, glancing towards the point but turning the other way, instinct taking her away from Haven Bay.

Hayden spoke for the first time when she pulled onto the highway. 'Where are we going?'

'North.' It was the only direction that made sense. With Hayden's mother in Cairns, Sydney was pointless. His grandparents were up the coast in Yamba - it was a long way, at least eight hours' drive and it was already three-thirty in the afternoon, but she could put him on a train for part of the journey. Getting him far away from Haven Bay was what counted. Joanne was up north somewhere, too. Rennie wasn't sure where or whether she wanted to go there but it was an option. One of them.

Making the turn onto the expressway, she worked the car into fifth gear and pushed the speed to a little over the limit. She kept her hands firm on the wheel, watching the traffic behind, the steady drone of the diesel engine and the beat from the radio becoming the background noise to the tense silence between them. Familiar and not, she thought. She'd left places with Jo a hundred times and it was always fraught with urgency and unfinished business. She'd never done it with anyone but her sister, let alone a dissenting kid who hated her.

How had she got to this? What the hell had gone wrong? She'd just wanted a life for a while. Someone to love. Had she wanted too much? Not been good enough or generous enough or grateful enough? Or was it some kind of cosmic fucking joke to let her have it then snatch it away before her time was up?

To take Max and make him pay for *her* sins?

She wanted to shout and cuss and shake her fists. But Hayden had witnessed her fury once already. She tightened her fingers until they hurt, clenched her teeth until her jaw ached, told herself to pay attention and not crash the car and save her father the job of killing them.

She heard Hayden through the ringing in her ears. 'What?'

'It's your phone.'

It took a second to hear it. The in-car system was trilling softly. Both phones were buried too deep in her backpack to hear which one it was. Max, please be Max. She hit the button on the dash. 'Hello?'

'Katrina?' Reception was bad; the voice difficult to hear. She wanted it to be Evan but she wasn't sure.

'Yes?' she answered warily, keeping her eyes on the road as Hayden's head shot around.

'It's Evan.'

'He found me. He's been in the house.'

There was silence over the speaker long enough to make her wonder if the connection had dropped out. 'No, Kat. He's in a hospital.'

'Where?'

'Sydney.'

'Then he got out and he came up here. He was in my house this afternoon.'

'It wasn't him. He's sick.'

'Bullshit. You know what he's like.'

'I spoke to someone. They went to his room.'

She hesitated, blood pounding in her head. 'Then they saw the wrong person.'

'Katrina, listen to me. I spoke to his parole officer. He's not going anywhere. He's got a brain tumour. It's advanced. He's dying.'

The words felt like a slap across her face. Her arms went slack, her foot eased off the accelerator, her heart crashed against her ribs. Her father was *dying*? He would be gone from the face of the earth? He would never hunt her again?

'Katrina? Are you there?'

'Are you sure? Absolutely sure?'

'Yes. It's over, Kat. For good this time.'

A tremor started in her gut, spread to her chest, thighs, arms, hands. A car sped by, its horn blaring.

Evan's voice was loud with concern. 'Where are you?'

In speeding traffic with a kid in the car and gorge rising in her throat. 'I can't talk.' She hung up, heard another angry blast as she swung off the expressway onto the narrow verge. Dirt scattered as she hit the brake. She had the door open before the car had finished rocking to its stop.

'Stay here,' she told Hayden and got out, the suck of wind tugging at her hair and clothes as a truck roared past. She lurched around the front of the car, heading for the guardrail, gripping it with both hands, staring into a steep, wooded drop as she gasped for breath. She waited for her stomach to empty itself but nothing came. Nothing but fat, hot tears that filled her eyes and fell like raindrops into the gully beneath her. It was over. Finished. It felt like skin had been torn from her.

Over the noise of the traffic, she heard a crunch on the rubble, looked up and saw Hayden standing by the car. 'I told you to stay put,' she barked.

He opened his mouth, closed it again, glanced uneasily at the traffic. 'That guy's on the phone again.' He held up the mobile.

She wasn't sure her legs would work. 'Toss it here and keep an eye on the road.' She caught the mobile. 'Evan, sorry. I had to pull off the road.'

'Who's the boy?'

'Max's son.'

'You took him with you?'

'Someone broke into the house. I thought he was in danger.'

'Where are you now?'

'On the expressway. It's not a good spot. I've got to go.'

'Where are you going?'

'I don't know.' She hung up and stared into the bush. Someone had been in the house, found her gun and taken it - and it wasn't her father.

PART 3

SECRETS

36

Rennie paced the dirt beside the expressway, careless of the vehicles thundering past. She was running out of versions. Father-on-the-loose was over, never to rear its bloody head again. Now she was left with only one - that Max had taken the money and left her.

Was it Max at the house? Had he used his key like Detective Duncan thought? Had he come back for something? For them? Was it bad timing that they'd been out or had he planned it that way?

If he'd found the Glock, he'd found everything else - the cash, the ID, the photo. What would he make of it? And why take the gun - so she didn't turn it on him when she learned the truth?

Or was he in trouble? Had he taken the money after all and figured a weapon might come in handy?

What have you done, Max?

She glanced at the car. Hayden was in the passenger seat again, his head down. They were almost an hour from Haven Bay, seven from his grandparents. If she stuck him on a train, he'd probably get off at the next station and head straight back.

She paced some more, thinking about Yamba and Jo and heading far north. If Max had left her, was there any point in going back to Haven Bay? It wasn't her home without him.

A huge road train roared just metres from her, making the earth shake and blowing grit so hard it stung her face. Whatever she was going to do, she needed to get away from here. As she slipped into the driver's seat, she saw her backpack between Hayden's knees, two plastic bags on his lap. '*Hayden!*'

He looked up without a hint of guilt but it wasn't his attitude that snagged her attention.

'What the f . . .?' She snatched up the bag with the zip lock. It held the few items she kept to identify herself: birth certificate, an old driver's licence, Evan's phone number in case her mobile died. There was a blue ribbon from a school carnival, a bronze medallion for swimming, her School Certificate. And the photo: Katrina, Joanne and their mother, Donna. It was taken in a park somewhere, the colour so faded it was almost sepia - Joanne with two fingers behind her mum's head, Donna grinning and Katrina pulling a stupid face. Evidence that one day in their lives they'd been happy.

Rennie knew what was in the bag to the last item, except now as she looked there was something else. Another photo.

She'd seen it before but not in her backpack. On the computer at home. Her and Max in the backyard by the vegetable garden, his gran's cottage behind them and a gorgeous blue sky overhead. She pulled it out.

'Where did you get this?' she snapped at Hayden.

'From the backpack.'

'No. *This!*' She shoved the picture in front of his face.

'It's not mine. I found it in there.'

She flipped it over. One line in Max's messy scrawl: 'If you leave, can I come too?'

Rennie stared at the words, her heart beating hard.

And she knew. Without a doubt.

Max hadn't left her.

She had no idea how long the photo had been in her bag. Possibly a year. Possibly he'd put it there this afternoon as he was taking the gun. It didn't matter. The only thing that mattered was the message on the back.

Max wasn't a complicated man. He didn't wax and wane over ideas and needs. He didn't suffer pangs of indecision, he didn't agonise over what to do. He lived and loved. He lamented loss, he tried to do the right thing, he had nightmares and he was scared of the dark.

He didn't change his mind.

If the photo had been there for a year, the sentiment hadn't changed.

If he'd put the photo there today, he was sending her a message.

Either way, he was telling her something. That he knew about Katrina and he loved Rennie anyway.

And it told her she'd never needed to search for clues to who he was. That she was a goddamn fool to have doubted him. She hadn't stayed all this time because she was complacent. She'd stayed because she could trust him. Because there'd never been a reason to leave. Because he loved her. Whatever the hell had happened, whatever the hell he'd done, he was the one to trust.

And now she had to find him.

She started the big engine and pulled into the high speed traffic.

'How much money is it?' Hayden asked.

Three minutes ago, she would have told him it was none of his damn business. Right now, she couldn't think of anything to tell him but the truth. 'A couple of thousand.'

'Whoa.'

'Put it back. The other bag, too.'

He did and zipped the pack. 'Why did that guy call you Katrina?'

He'd probably seen and heard enough in the last couple of hours to have a right to know more. 'It used to be my name.'

'Does Dad know you changed it?'

'No.'

He paused. She wasn't going to pre-empt him.

'Who was the guy on the phone?'

'A cop. Retired cop. A friend.'

'Who's dying?'

'My father.'

The next pause was longer. Comparing fathers or digesting the information.

'Is that why you went psycho back there? 'Cause he's dying?'

Yeah, it probably looked psycho. 'Yes. Is that all?'

'S'pose.'

'Good. I have to think.'

There was an exit ramp in five k. She had to decide what to do with Hayden by the time they reached it. Someone had been in the house and her Glock was gone. If it was Max, the only problem was whether he knew how to use it. If it wasn't, someone else had a lethal weapon - and the question was, why take it? Just in case or because they planned to use it? There was no way of knowing without knowing why they were there.

She pictured the study, the toppled notes, the open drawers in the filing cabinet. It'd been searched. Maybe if she could figure out what else was missing, she could work out where to look for Max. She remembered the password protection on the computer, the lists of numbers in his Toronto office. She dropped a hand to her back pocket. The page from his drawer was still there.

Hayden was slumped in his seat now, watching the scenery fly past. He knew more about computers than she did. He stuffed about on the one at home for hours some visits, whole days during school holidays. Maybe he could get past Max's security. The person with her gun was a risk but they'd broken in when no one was home and searched the place. Why would they go back?

'How much do you know about hacking into computers?' she asked.

'A bit.' His expression was a little cagey. She figured that meant more than a bit.

Two k to the turn-off. If he was going to help, it had to be on her terms.

'We have to talk, Hayden. Can we do it without an argument?'

A shrug.

It would have to do. 'I made a mistake. I thought I knew what'd happened to Max and who'd broken into the house. It's not what I thought but something's going on. I don't know what it is but I think the answer, or at least part of it, might be at the house. I'm going back there. I think you can help but you can only come if you promise to do what I tell you.'

'Why?'

'Because whoever broke into the house has a gun.'

'How do you know?'

'It was in my backpack and now it's gone.'

'You had a gun?'

'Yes.'

He gave her a long, hard look. 'Were you a cop, too?'

She raised an eyebrow, wondering what scenarios he'd invented for her. 'No.'

'Then why've you got a gun?'

'People like me need a weapon. Are you going to do what I tell you?' He looked like he wasn't sure he wanted to go anywhere with her. 'You don't have to come. I can take you to a station and you can get a train to your grandparents' house.'

'No. I want to help find Dad.'

'Then you do what I say.'

'Okay. What's at the house?'

'The computer.'

FRESH PANIC HAD PUSHED Max hard, scrabbling in the darkness, calling out to Rennie, hoping and dreading she was down here with him. Had her past come after her? Had she lured violence to Haven Bay? Fear and anger felt the same.

He didn't have the energy to sustain the pace, though, and now he could barely shuffle one knee in front of the other. He couldn't save himself, let alone the woman he loved. Falling against the wall, clenching his fists around the dry sand under his hands, he felt a stone and threw it. Frustration, futility, a final fit of pique.

The tap was close. Very close - and different from the sound that came off the rock. Sharper, tinnier. He stretched out a hand, edging forwards. Fingertips, then his whole hand touched the cool, rough and smooth surface of a brick wall - and something stirred in his memory.

He used the brickwork to drag himself to his feet, patting high, low, wide. It was built into the tunnel, curved where it met the roof, mortar bulging like ooze between the rectangular blocks.

Squeezing his eyes tight, he tried to hold the memory his mind was catching on. What was it? He relaxed his face, fought for slow, even breaths, pleading with the memory to keep still long enough for him to get a hold. It was ... in the dark, running, shouting.

'James!' Max was calling. He was a kid, the sound of his thudding feet and crazy laughter echoing around him. He had a torch in his hand but it didn't work. It didn't matter: he only had to go in a straight line. *'James! Slow down!'* The tips of his fingers were stinging as he trailed them along the rock, making sure he didn't run right into it.

A rock wall? The same one? How many could there be?

He skidded around the corner, trotted through the doorway, climbing up and out into bright sunlight that hurt his eyes, flopping to the ground, laughing and panting, exhilarated by the speed and the darkness and the thrill.

'You're a fucking dickhead, Max.' James was above him, sweating and mad.

'What? It wasn't me. The torch ran out of juice.'

'Bullshit. You did it on purpose.'

Max hitched himself up. 'What's wrong? The torch has carked it before.'

'We were bloody miles in.' James was stalking about in front of him. 'You think you're so fucking clever. Fucking clever and fucking funny. And you're not. You're a dickhead and you can just piss off.'

They were both dickheads back then, hormone-addled teenage boys. Max remembered his adolescent 'gotcha' chuckle at realising his cousin was scared of the dark. And his pathetic shout as James was flouncing into the trees: *'You piss off!'*

Max shook his head. Ironic, wasn't it, that Max was the one who ended up with the darkness phobia. And why was he remembering that? There was no brick wall in that memory. The torch had died, they'd . . .

Wait, another time. He saw it hovering behind his eyes, squinted to encourage it.

A blink of light. On then off.

'Yeah, okay, hilarious, Max. You can you turn the bloody thing back on now.' It was Pav.

'No, mate, seriously. The torch is dead.'

'Let me see it.'

'You can see it all you like if you've got more batteries.'

Pav fumbled along Max's arm before he found the lamp in his hand. Max listened to a couple of thumps, a metallic unscrewing and rescrewing, a bit of rattling and a stream of Polish.

'You been eating many carrots lately?' Max asked.

'They'd need to be grown in nuclear waste.'

'Ah . . . why?'

'So our eyes would glow in the dark.'

'Now there's a good look. How about a phone instead?' Max pulled his mobile from his back pocket, tapped the screen and a dull glow lit up his hand. 'Better than a Swiss army knife.' He turned it around to show Pav and saw the brickwork behind his head in the gloom. Mortar oozing between cheap, red blocks of clay.

Like the ones under his hands.

Was he *there*? 'Oh, fuck.'

He knew the place. He and James would've run through it the day the torch failed. Several kilometres of brickwork erected when the council got worried about insurance and kids getting lost. A long, long way when he had to do it on his hands and knees and in pain.

Sinking to his butt again, he leaned against the cool, lumpy surface and tried not to think about the distance. Told himself it was easy now, just a straight line to the exit.

Unless the council had put in more brick walls. It was years since he'd been down here. That day with Pav was probably the last time.

He and Trish had only been in town a few months and Max was doing his, 'Let *me* show *you* the bay'.

At the time, he thought Pav was a nice guy with a who-gives-a-shit attitude, a laugh like a clap of thunder and a cool accent. Later, he was a mate, the kind you need when your life turns to hell. He didn't judge, didn't tell him it would get better, didn't try to fix anything. Just listened and nodded and said that's the way it goes sometimes. Maybe it was something Polish or European, from a place where death and devastation had cut a regular swathe over the centuries, where people grew up understanding about horror and survival and picking through wreckage for the things you need to start over.

Max pushed himself to his hands and knees, found the wall to his left and started up again. Christ, it hurt. His palms and kneecaps were sore, his back ached and his arms trembled - and they were just the new pains on the list. He didn't want to think about the others. They were telling him he was thirsty and sick and weak. Too weak. That he'd die if he didn't find his way out soon. Maybe he'd die even if he did.

37

Rennie drove fast, anxious to get back and figure it out. This was new for her - going back instead of moving on, covering old ground instead of finding a new one. And it made her apprehensive, not knowing what was ahead and how to play it.

She worked through the fragments of the puzzle, laying them out in her head like a deck of cards. The blood in the car park, the thump on the back fence, the half-finished text message, the tampering in the glove box, the password protection, the phone calls to the cafe - shuffling and sifting them, unsure which facts were related to Max and which weren't. Possibly all of them, maybe none.

The blood worried her the most. There was a chance it wasn't his, but if he was injured, what would the early summer heat do to him? It was coming up to forty-four hours since he'd been gone - almost two days - and it had been windy yesterday, the temperature in the high twenties this afternoon. She thought about blood loss, concussion, dehydration, infection, internal bleeding. How long would he last? Was he dead already?

Her mind kept coming back to the search of the house and the glove box. It had to be connected to Max's disappearance.

Technically, it wasn't a break-in. No locks or windows were broken. The metal plate on the front door wasn't scratched. Did Max use his key? Had he given it to someone - or had someone taken it? She let that thought sit for a moment.

Yes, it was possible someone from out of town had assaulted Max in the car park, taken his key ring, waited around to go through the car and the house when no one was looking. She wanted it to be that, an unknown, unnamed person who'd picked Max for no other reason than he was in the dark car park on his own. But doubt niggled and experience made her uneasy.

It wasn't a robbery, either, at least not the standard TV/stereo/computer kind. And who stole keys then just riffled through wardrobes and drawers? Not your average assailant after money and/or goods. Her father had done it like that. Reconnaissance, scare tactics, a sick private joke. But it wasn't that. Someone was looking for something.

Did they know Max? Was that how he let them get close enough to take his keys?

Or did it happen another way? Were they lifted from him at Trish's birthday celebration?

If that was how it worked, it was someone who Max knew, maybe someone they both knew. And that idea made her blood heat and her jaw tighten. That was *her* life, it didn't belong here.

The sun was starting to drop and shadows were lengthening as she pulled into the carport. Her father was out of the picture but caution still felt appropriate. Someone had her semiautomatic pistol.

She told Hayden to wait in the car while she checked both sides of the house. It was to test him as much as it was for security and she hoped he'd disobey so she could be loud and clear about his boundaries.

When she got back, he'd opened the door but was still sitting inside. She told him to wait on the porch while she checked the house and made a quick, quiet inspection of the rooms. As far as she could tell, no one had been there since they'd left. She stood by the study door and waved Hayden in. He sat in front of the monitor and said, 'What am I looking for?'

'First up, we need to get into Max's files. He put a password on them. It's not the one we use for emails. James couldn't get past it.'

'Uncle James is crap on the computer.'

'Well, let's see how good you are.'

She stood behind him, eyeing the Post-Its still in place above the desk. She collected the ones that'd dropped to the table, wondering if they were selected or had fallen while the room was combed. The ones in her hand were as vague as the ones on the ledge. Scrawled words, numbers, dates, names. She scanned the shelf: phone books, business how-to's, mining equipment manuals and chunky folders. Five folders in all and they weren't lined up neatly.

The first held records of his renovations on the house. The next was a history of his medical expenses. She flipped quickly through the rest - personal loan records, child support, copies of Hayden's school reports. Surprisingly orderly. Nothing of interest to anyone but Max.

She yanked on the drawer that was ajar in the filing cabinet. Hanging files, lots of them. She fingered urgently through the coloured tabs: Insurance, Legals, Warranties, Car - surprised at Max's organisation, no idea why they'd been searched. What interest were they to anyone? She gritted her teeth, swore under her breath.

'Did you find something?' Hayden asked.

'No.' She slammed the drawer.

'What?'

Exactly. What the hell was she looking for? How would she know if she found it? Or whether it'd been taken? She pushed her hands through her hair, saw the apprehension on Hayden's face. 'Keep working. I'm going to . . .' *kick something* '. . . go out there.'

She stalked the living room, needing space to release some stress without being watched. Lack of sleep and food were taking their toll. Her eyes stung, her brain was fading and her stomach felt like it was caving in. She swung the fridge open, tore a handful of grapes from their stalks, pulled a bottle of something fizzy from the door. Two minutes later, the cold drink had woken her up and the sugar hit had cleared her head.

Okay, maybe she was going about it the wrong way. Whoever had been here had searched the study and the wardrobe. Maybe they'd looked other places. Figuring out where might tell her more. She turned her gaze to the back windows, watching the yard in the late afternoon light.

'I'm going out to the studio,' she called. 'Don't leave the house.'

She took a large frypan with her - as good a weapon as any at short notice and safer to wield than a knife in the close quarters of the studio. She jogged quickly across the lawn, pausing to listen before opening the door. It was dim inside but bright enough to see she was alone and that the big easel in the middle of the floor had been bumped off its usual spot. Not by much, maybe only the span of a large foot, but she was particular about it, liked it centred under the skylight and its new angle told her someone had been moving carelessly about.

Heart beating hard, she moved through the room, scanning for more signs of intrusion. Nothing among the stacked canvasses, the tins of paint, the bed. Nothing until she got to the back of the room, where Max's overflow from the study was in cardboard document boxes against the wall. One stack of four was now two of two. A cardboard lid had been lifted and not replaced.

Rennie glanced over her shoulder to the door, unnerved, thinking it through. Whoever had come in had made a hurried path through the room, knocking the easel and going through the boxes. Or at least checking under the lids. Were they after paperwork or something that would fit in a document box? Whatever it was, it was about Max, not her.

She went back to the house and began a sweep through the rooms, wondering about the intruder's state of mind as they'd moved about. A jar out of place on the old dresser, the sofa cushions untidy. It wasn't angry, there was no destruction, barely more than a few items shifted about. Maybe it was casual, a stroll in someone else's space, opening drawers, touching their stuff, like her father had done.

Or was it hurried? A brief, rushed search, the fear of being found making them careless.

In Hayden's room, the bed and floor were a jumble of blankets and clothes. It was a fair guess that was his doing. She doubted he'd considered folding anything or using a coat hanger, which meant someone else had left the wardrobe door and top drawer in the dresser open. They held nothing of value - neither did the cupboards in the bathroom - but someone had thought they might.

In her own bedroom, she swung the wardrobe doors wide again and cast an eye over the disarray. Study, bedrooms, bathroom. Was it random or logical? Had they looked in the obvious places first or did they start in one spot and move systematically through the house?

And why look in every room? What could potentially be kept in all those places?

Not files or folders. Who kept those in a bathroom? Jewellery maybe, except they didn't have any. Tissues, pens, condoms, candles. No. Something . . .

She took a wide-angle view of their wardrobe. Okay, don't get specific.

Her eyes moved slowly up and down her sparse belongings, then over Max's stuff. The underwear she'd folded and sorted had been shunted about in the drawer but it wasn't socks and jocks being hunted down. Something that would fit under or among the clothing. She stared at the shelf above. What was there before?

She thought back to this morning when she'd tidied Max's belongings, made some order out of his clutter, trying to find some trace of who he was. It was like that game she'd played as a kid - name every item on the table and you win. She'd been good at it, trained by her mother to take note of what she saw. So think.

She went through it in sections, closing her eyes and listing items in her mind then checking them off with what she saw in the wardrobe now. His stuff on the shelf: all present. The paperwork: nothing she recalled was missing. The spilled contents of the ashtray: she'd forgotten the rubber bands. Had she left anything else out?

She went over it again: rubber bands, single cuff link, coins, paper clips, tacks. They were all there, all except...

The USB drive. Small, black, shiny. She'd found its plastic cap and replaced it.

She sifted through the stuff on his shelf, lifting and sliding and relocating until she'd covered the whole surface. Then she searched the carpet, among his shoes, around her own.

The USB drive wasn't there.

MAX RESTED MORE than he crawled. No keeping tabs with the wall, just shunting his hands forwards and dragging his knees in behind.

Pav held court in his memory now: the time they were down here, the deep roll of his laughter rebounding around the walls. Nights in his courtyard, the vodka and bourbon, Trish's brief visits to deposit food and retrieve empty plates, not unhappy to have the house to herself. Good times, not the ones when Max had beaten himself up and drowned what was left.

And then Rennie was with them, making it four. Barbecues on Max's new deck, cold nights gathered around the fire in the brazier, celebrating Rennie's first paintings, toasting someone's birthday with champagne at the water's edge, Hayden's party and Pav tossing a protesting, laughing teenager over his shoulder just because he'd dared him to.

'Remember I told you once I'd done a desperate thing?' Pav said.

They were sitting on Max's deck. The living room lights were glowing on the timber, the studio windows in the yard ablaze. It wasn't cold enough for the fire, not warm enough for T-shirts. When was it?

'Careful, mate,' Max said. 'Trish might have to kill us if you talk about it.'

Pav's smile was brief, forced. 'Turns out Trish was right. It found us here.'

'What found you here?'

He took a gulp of his vodka, rested his elbows on his knees and nursed the drink in the space between. 'I took something from someone and he wants it back.'

'What'd you take?'

'Money.'

Max paused as his eyebrows rose and fell. 'How much?'

'Not that much considering the amount that'd been flowing in and out. But I worked out where it was coming from, saw something I wasn't meant to and then it wasn't safe to stay. Trish was with me. We'd just started up and I wanted to get her away so I took, you know, fistfuls. I stuffed what I could in my pockets and down my shirt. I hit a guy, knocked him out. I think I broke his jaw. I locked him in a storeroom and . . .' he shrugged, '. . . walked out with the money. Right past them, like I was going for a smoke.'

'Shit.'

'Yeah.'

'Where was it?'

'Serbia. Actually, it was Yugoslavia back then. We got on the first train going over the border and didn't book a room until we were in Norway.'

'Norway?'

'Fucking cold place.'

'So what's the problem now?'

He swallowed another mouthful of vodka. 'The guy I took the money from came out here after the Bosnian War. He's got an import business, brings in all kinds of food. A sales rep came to see me just by chance. He's from over there, too. He recognised me, told his boss and now he wants his money back.'

'Have you got it?'

The look Pav gave him said it all. 'I run a cafe in Haven Bay. It's not a thriving metropolis. If Trish didn't own the house, we couldn't afford to stay.'

'What are you going to do?'

He pulled a breath in through his nose, blew it out through parted lips, took his time coming up with an answer. 'Ask you for a loan.'

38

'I'm in!'

Rennie heard Hayden's shout from the bedroom and ran to the study. He was standing, both fists in the air like a boxer after a victory. She grinned. He held up a hand for a high five and she let him have it, the clash of their palms both harder than she expected and weirdly fraternal after their hostility.

'Well done.' She made for the chair but he wasn't ready to give it up.

'I went through a bazillion combinations,' he said, sitting down, grabbing the mouse. 'All Dad's nicknames and made-up words and places he goes and types of boats he's sailed and . . .'

'And what was it?'

'It's right there.' He pointed at the row of Post-Its. 'I was just trying anything and I saw that: Dallas Worthwhile. First letter capitals, no space between.'

Rennie found the words on a note above the monitor.

'Worthwhile wasn't Dallas's last name, though,' Hayden was saying. 'It was Brownston.'

'Dallas Brownston?' She knew the name, couldn't remember the context.

'He was in the mine accident with Dad. He's my godfather. *Was* my godfather.'

Rennie frowned at the screen then up at the Post-It. He'd used his dead mate's name for a password? 'Worthwhile?'

Hayden shrugged like it was nuts but hey, that was Dad. No, it was more than that. Rennie straightened up, remembering now. When she was first sleeping with Max, he'd scared the crap out of her half-a-dozen times roaring out of nightmares. She'd joined him on the deck after a bad one, sat under a blanket in the glow of the floodlights and said nothing as he talked about Dallas - daft things they'd done, trips they'd taken, pranks, sailing, soccer. She'd wondered why he was thinking about it all at three o'clock in the morning. Then he told her about their last conversation, under the rock, in the dark. He didn't look at her, didn't move, barely spoke loud enough to hear. He'd used that word: *worthwhile.* Had said it over and over. *I want to be worthwhile. I'm not sure how to be worthwhile. I only seem to know how to fuck up.*

Rennie remembered how useless she'd felt. An arm's length away without a clue how to touch him. She didn't know what he'd fucked up, only that he'd been fucked over - by his wife, by the coal company, by the insurance, by fate. She had no skills for providing empathy or reassurance so she just slid closer, draped the blanket around his shoulders and kissed his neck, hoped he understood that even after so short a time, worthwhile was an understatement.

'So what are we looking for now?' Hayden asked, hands poised above the keyboard.

Max. She was looking for Max. She wanted him back. Hoped to God he hadn't decided to join his friend Dallas.

She squatted beside Hayden. James thought Max took the money from the business and had tried to get into the computer to confirm it or find it or trace it - she wasn't sure which; she just wondered what Max would hide behind the password *DallasWorthwhile.* Maybe there was something in there that'd been transferred from or to a USB thumb drive. Something that was important to someone else. 'I don't know. Let's just see what's there.'

There were the usual operating programs, music logs, game downloads, a couple of movies. Folders of photos. He had three cameras, different sizes for different occasions. Had he taken pictures someone wasn't happy about? Easy to store on a thumb drive. 'Open that one.' She pointed, Hayden double-clicked.

A large file unrolled, almost a thousand shots. She squinted at the first thumbnails. It would take ages to go through them. If he knew he had sensitive photos, if he was concerned enough to add a password, would he bury them in a bunch of other photos? What better place? Shit. 'Let's have a look at all the files first. We can go back to the pictures later if we need to.'

There were other folders with quirky, Max-style titles: *Jobs n Stuff* for work contracts, *The Go Tos* for client contact lists, *Show Me The Money* for invoices, *Work It Baby* for what seemed to be work he'd brought home. Rennie touched the screen with the tip of a finger. 'WTF - what's that one?'

'What the fuck,' Hayden said. It wasn't an exclamation or a question and there was no attitude behind it.

'Huh?'

'That's what it means,' he said. 'W-T-F, What The Fuck.'

For a computer folder? 'Open it.'

An index appeared on the screen. Nothing obvious.

'Let's have a look.'

Hayden worked his way down the list, opening and closing the files. There were invoices, lists of figures, bank statements for Mine-Lease accounts and a single written document.

Rennie stood up, keeping her eyes on the screen as fear and uncertainty pounded in her chest.

'What is it?' Hayden asked.

It was details of money and transactions, dates and accounts. Was this what James was looking for?

'Shit.' She paced the few steps across the small room. She didn't know anything about running a business or engineering a fraud. Her crimes were for protection, escape, survival, not about deceit or sleight of hand.

Hayden watched as she stalked back, waiting for the next instruction. It wasn't Max, she told herself. He hadn't taken the money; his password was *DallasWorthwhile.* And a voice in her head reminded her he'd also assaulted a man, disappeared for days and cheated on his wife. What else had he done?

She tightened her jaw. 'Right, Hayden. Go back to the invoices.'

He put all six of them on the screen. They were bills that had come in during the past twelve months, varying amounts, the final one the largest by far and dated last week.

Rennie kneeled beside him again, did some quick addition. 'There's more than half a million dollars billed here.' It seemed like a lot of money but as James had kindly reminded her, MineLease dealt in huge pieces of equipment.

'They're all from the same company. Does that matter?' Hayden asked.

'I don't know. Pull up the figures.'

'The ones from the bank or the other ones?'

She frowned. 'A couple of each.'

It took a few minutes of squinting back and forth before she realised what she was seeing. The bank statements were scans of original paper copies, the kind financial institutions send in the mail. The lists of figures seemed to be from the same statements but cut and pasted from electronic versions, perhaps from online banking. Why the two? Maybe the scans were verification. Maybe the online versions were for use in another document. Maybe she didn't have a clue. In the list of figures, some of the dates, account numbers and transaction amounts were marked in bold.

'Open that one again.' She pointed to a file titled *watsNys,* the written document. The first time, she'd just skimmed the page - now she took a minute to read.

It wasn't an official report - that much was clear. It read like notes jotted down as they came to mind. There were company names, job codes, a couple of towns up the coast were mentioned - Coffs Harbour, Forster, Byron Bay - the name S Baskin, sometimes Sondra

Baskin, was there a few times. And some of the numbers were in bold.

'Can you put a page of the figures in a separate window so we can compare the highlighted numbers?'

Hayden shifted documents around until *watsNys* was side by side with a page of figures. The numbers in bold were the same. Dates, account numbers and dollar amounts.

Rennie pulled the page from her pocket, the one she'd taken from Max's office. Dates, amounts, accounts. Another matching set - this one in Max's handwriting. There'd been a fourth set on his desk blotter.

Was it the money he and James had argued about?

James said he traced the money through their accounts and showed it to Max last week. He must have put this together, written the page of notes and given it all to Max.

She thought about the argument Amanda had heard and the one James told her about. Had James discovered the money missing on Monday, spent the week digging through the accounts, put this together then accused Max of taking it on Friday?

Hayden tapped the screen, his finger on a date. 'That's my birthday.'

August 26. It'd fallen on a Sunday this year and Rennie remembered how excited Max was to have him here - it was a long time since he'd celebrated his son's birthday on the actual day. He'd put on a barbecue, blown up balloons and invited the usual suspects. They ate a mountain of fresh prawns and chicken kebabs and potato salad. Trish brought a mud cake and they sang a Happy Birthday that put the local bird population into flight.

Rennie slipped the mouse out from under Hayden's palm, clicked on other files. There were no invoices with that date but it was highlighted in the bank records and corresponded with a payment from a MineLease account. Not to a client. A resort in Coffs Harbour was paid six hundred and thirty-five dollars.

A bewildered 'huh' escaped her lips.

'What are you looking at?' Hayden asked.

'Someone stayed in Coffs Harbour that weekend. Coffs Harbour is mentioned in the notes.'

'Dad didn't. He was here. He had a party for me.'

'Mmm.' What was important about the date?

'Remember? Dad and Pete and me went swimming and nearly froze our arses off. And Pav didn't get there until really late and Trish yelled at him for like an hour. And Aunty Naomi spewed in the garden. It was awesome.' Rennie raised amused eyebrows at his version of events. He'd seemed offhand and blase about it afterwards but maybe he was more impressed than she'd given him credit for. She thought about the party again. The lake swim was the penalty for losing the team prawn-shelling competition and left the three of them shivering and almost blue. Naomi's dash to the shrubbery came after five long months of morning sickness and she'd just wiped her mouth and laughed, 'Well, there goes breakfast again.' It was dark by the time Pav rocked up with beer and apologies. Rennie couldn't recall where he'd been, somewhere up the coast, from memory. Trish was worried that he hadn't phoned then stood in the living room and shouted loud enough to make everyone on the deck turn their backs and pull faces about the awkward domestic moment.

Rennie stared at the bank records. August 26. Coffs Harbour was north of here. Pav . . . was up the coast the day of Hayden's party.

He wasn't at Skiffs today when the house was searched.

He'd scared the hell out of her creeping around the dark yard last night - the evening the glove box was searched.

Something cold slithered down her spine. If she was another kind of person, the kind she'd tried to be when she came to Haven Bay, she might cringe at the concept of suspecting someone she cared for. But she wasn't. She understood firsthand that the crime statistics were right: the people closest to you were the most dangerous. And Pav was no angel. He had an array of scars on his hands and forearms and they weren't all from kitchen work. She'd seen them before on other people. Tough men with bikes and guns and worse crimes than hers. You got them from fistfights and knives and brawls. There'd been trouble in Yugoslavia before he and Trish fled that neither of them talked about. And there was an angry, dark side to him that kept the staff at bay when it was exposed.

She flicked her eyes over the screen, checking the dates against a calendar. A Friday in April, a Tuesday in June, a Thursday, a Monday - random days going back a year. She checked the amounts - they were all outgoing payments, some by internet transfer, some by credit card, large and small.

'Which one next?' Hayden asked.

'Wait.' She dropped a hand to his shoulder to hold him in place. 'Let me think.' Pav was at the cafe six days a week but it didn't mean he hadn't spent or moved the funds. And he could have searched the house and car. He wasn't at work this afternoon and he'd never explained *why* he was creeping around last night.

Was he looking for the USB thumb drive? Had he heard from Max and was helping to cover his tracks?

Or was he involved with the money? He and Trish were tight for funds sometimes. Had things got too tight and Max helped them out with money from the business, money he hadn't told James about?

Yesterday, Trish said Max and Pav talked for hours after he got out of rehab. He'd told Pav about the affairs. It was some kind of confessional with a man who had a few sins of his own, Trish had called it. What else had they talked about? And what *were* Pav's sins?

Words came to mind: blackmail, cover-up, debts.

HIS SKIN WAS HOT, his heart thumped like it'd been switched to high and he leaned again the wall like a sick dog. How far had he gone? His body said all the way to China. His brain said not nearly far enough.

Gritting his teeth, he shifted an arm forwards and the other buckled under him. His cheek scraped across rock as he fell. His ribs twisted, his lungs spasmed. He would've sobbed if he had the energy. Unashamedly, without restraint, howling with the recognition of death barrelling towards him.

His body was spent but his brain was still rolling out the memories. Not in a rush like it might if his life was flashing before his eyes, just in a slow, determined forwards progression as though it wanted to catch up before his lights went out.

It'd meant a lot to him that Pav asked for a loan, that he thought he could without ruining the friendship. Max would've given him the money if he had it but almost everything was in MineLease - he worried about leaving debts these days, the kind of thing he never thought about before the cave-in.

The conversation with James about withdrawing a portion of his profit share didn't go well. It was six months earlier than they'd budgeted for and it prompted one of those weird James moments when you'd swear he was hearing it in another language and needed to get in a translator. His face went blank and his lips almost disappeared in the effort of whatever he was stewing on.

Max had folded his arms and waited it out, then listened to James huff and puff about how a business wasn't a piggy bank, that it was irresponsible to just take money willy-nilly. Max had refrained from commenting on the 'willy-nilly' - who the hell said that? - and let him go on about schedules and structures and forecasting. If Max took funds now, they could end up needing them down the track and surely he knew things were a little tight this year and his time would be better spent bringing in clients and not thinking about what he could waste money on.

Max had seen enough of James's patronising benders to know it was best to just let him get it off his chest but this one pissed Max off. He didn't want the money for himself. Not that James had asked. He'd just let fly like Max was the lazy, incompetent half to the partnership.

He'd stewed on it for a while then got on the computer to have a look at the figures for himself. Maybe the business could afford to help Pav some of the way.

James lived up to the tight-arse reputation of his accounting profession, which was one of the reasons Max had brought him in. He kept the invoicing up to date, chased the slow payers, produced regular financial statements for review, kept an eye on the budget and made sure they didn't get ahead of themselves. They had several accounts and James shifted funds around, keeping sufficient available to cover automatic deductions and making the most of interest schedules. At first Max couldn't track it properly and was tempted to ask James to explain it but, still stinging from their earlier discussion, decided against admitting his ignorance.

It took a while but he eventually got the gist and James was right: there was profit, just not as much as Max had calculated. He told Pav he could loan him a portion of the debt - enough to satisfy his 'supplier' in the short term, maybe let him set up some kind of payback scheme. The guy had done without the money for twenty years, surely he could wait a while longer.

'He's not that kind of guy,' Pav had said. It was another session in the courtyard and not one of the good ones. Pav was agitated, obviously worried, drinking a little too quickly. 'He doesn't need the money. He wants it because I took it.'

'What kind of idiot leaves thousands of dollars lying around a cafe, anyway?'

'It wasn't cafe money. It came in the back door.'

Max frowned dubiously.

'Girls and drugs, Max. They were bad people and they did bad things. What I saw that night was enough to make me get the hell out fast.'

'It sounds like *The Godfather*.'

'Every country has its own version.'

'And that guy's here?'

'Yeah, and he brought friends.'

39

Rennie ran her eyes across the files on the screen again. 'WTF' held bank records and invoices. Not confidential information. James would have them, there'd be copies at the office, other places too. Why would someone want to steal them?

Maybe that wasn't what was on the USB thumb drive. She shook her head. There were more cards in the deck she was dealing now but which ones were being played? 'Let's go back to the photos.'

'Okay.'

She watched as Hayden clicked and shifted, the files that'd overlayed each other disappearing one by one - bullet points, figures, invoices, bank statements.

'Wait,' she said again.

'What?'

She eyed the contents list. 'I'm not sure.'

Starting at the top, she ran her finger down the screen. The bank statements were called *bstats,* the copies were *figs,* the invoices were numbered *Invl* through to *Inv6.*

The last one in the column was *watsNys.* She tapped it. 'What does that mean?'

'You want me to open it again?'

'No. We know what's in it but ... I thought the letters must've stood for something, an abbreviation for a client, maybe. But there's nothing like that in there. It's notes about dates and bank stuff. Thoughts written down, a couple of questions. "W-a-t-s" could be short for something. But why the capital N? And what does "y-s" stand for?'

The room fell silent as though her question had hit mute on the volume control. Hayden scratched his head. Rennie heard the bump of a pulse in her ears.

'The "N" could be "and",' he suggested. 'You know, like shoes 'n' socks. Dad used it on another folder - *Jobs n Stuff*?

'Okay, it could be wats *and* ys.' She'd said 'wats' like 'fats'. 'Or maybe it's *whats.*'

'Whats and y-s.'

'Y-s sounds like wise. As in smart.'

'Or whys, as in why not,' Hayden said.

'Whats and whys. Notes about what and why?'

'Yeah, that'd be Dad.' He grinned at her like she'd just passed an online exam.

She didn't smile back. Hayden was right; the title had Max written all over it. The whole file did. The numbered documents, ordered like the records in the folders above the desk. The quirky 'WTF' and *watsNys.*

Rennie stood up, her heart thumping as cards shuffled about inside her mind. James said he'd traced the missing money back through the business accounts after he noticed it missing. They argued when he accused Max of taking it. She'd assumed the WTF file was James's research, that he'd given it to Max as proof that couldn't be denied.

But what if it hadn't happened like that?

What if they argued when *Max* noticed a problem - *you're the accountant, why didn't you see it*? What if Max did some research, jotted down numbers and notes on his blotter, opened a file and wrote it all down then went to James and said, 'What the fuck is this about?'

Hayden tipped his face up. 'What is it?'

She didn't answer, just kept moving the cards around.

Yesterday and this morning, James had sat in here trying to break Max's password. He'd said he was hoping to find a trail to the money but maybe when Max didn't come home, James decided to get rid of Max's incriminating file.

She pulled in a sharp breath. Max was missing and his business partner, his *cousin*, had wasted precious time looking for files instead of searching for Max.

'What?' Hayden asked again.

'I think . . .' She saw the hope on his face and swung away. James was his uncle and she wasn't sure she could keep venom out of an explanation. Behind her, Hayden's chair clattered and as she turned back, it was James she thought of. As she'd seen him from the doorway this morning - closing the bottom drawer in the desk. Had he searched it? Where else did he look? The folders on the shelf? The filing cabinet?

Had he come back and searched some more?

'Maybe Uncle James can figure it out.' Hayden pulled a phone from his pocket. 'I'm going to ring and tell him I broke Dad's password.'

Rennie snapped out a hand like a stop sign. 'No, wait.' The surprise in his face made her hesitate, reminding her James and Max were cousins. They grew up together, worked together, shared blood. Normal people, normal family. Not hers. Hers had skewed her judgement, made suspicion her first, instinctive response.

Did she have it wrong? Was she jumping to conclusions? For all she knew, James could give quirky names to computer documents, too. It might run in the family like a gene. Like uncontrolled fury ran in hers. She reminded herself James had driven around looking for Max in the early hours of Sunday morning, went to the office after that and out to the plant the next day. He'd found Hayden up at the point.

He'd also accused Max of fraud.

Hayden's voice was suddenly loud and angry and in her face.

'*What?* What is it? He's *my* dad. You're not even married to him. I should know what's going on.'

She was tempted to explain her suspicions, get another opinion but he was a kid and James was his uncle - his instinct was as skewed as hers. 'I don't know anything, Hayden. I don't know what the bank stuff is all about. I'm just making guesses and . . .'

Her mobile rang, the sound like a buzz-saw in the tension between them. She checked the caller ID as she grabbed the phone from the desk. The name on the screen set off alarm bells in her head.

James.

And whatever doubt she'd felt in the second before was instantly overridden by gut instinct. She didn't know what had happened between him and Max, had no proof of anything, but right now suspicion felt like the safest option.

She hung up without answering.

'Who was it?' Hayden asked.

He was already mad at her. Explaining wouldn't encourage him to do what he was told, and experience was telling her he might need to. 'I don't know. I didn't recognise the number.'

'It might've been Dad.'

'I don't. . .'

Another ringtone. Hayden's.

'Hey, Uncle James. I broke Dad's password on the computer.'

The tinny, indistinct voice spilling from the earpiece made Rennie's legs itch to move. Old habits but she needed to stay this time. She glanced around the study as Hayden listened, trying to find something that would tell her what had gone on here. Today, yesterday. When Max had installed the password.

Hayden answered a question. 'Yeah, I can get into his files. I already did.'

The sheet of paper from her pocket was on the desk. Rennie could see the columns of numbers on it. Dates, accounts, dollars. She heard her own voice from half an hour ago. *There's more than half a million dollars billed here.* James and Max argued about the money.

Several hundred thousand was a lot of money. *Angry, raised voices,* Amanda had said of the argument on Monday. What about Friday? How angry were they then?

There was blood in the car park.

'She's here, too.' Hayden paused. 'Yeah, we looked through them together.'

James was worried about the money. He'd been here twice trying to get into Max's computer. Had he been to the office and the plant for the same reason?

'Oh, and someone broke into the house.' Pause. 'No, nothing was broken.' Pause. 'Well . . .' He glanced at Rennie. The gun?

She gave an emphatic shake of her head.

'Renee's still checking. Do you think it's got something to do with Dad?'

She could hear James talking, didn't care what he was saying - only what he'd been up to this afternoon. He left the office a couple of hours before Rennie and Hayden were there and they didn't get home until three. Plenty of time to let himself in and work his way through the rooms. Had Max given him a key to the house sometime? Maybe he didn't need to steal Max's.

Hayden spoke again. 'Nah. We got in the car and drove for a bit then she talked to some cop and we came back again. That's when I broke Dad's password.' Pause. 'We've been trying to work out what some of the stuff is about. Maybe you can figure it out.'

Rennie's head snapped around. No, she didn't want him here. Not until she understood what was going on. She felt as though she was playing more than one game with the deck of cards now. Didn't know if Max's disappearance was about the money or something else. Whether the two things were related or separate. Whether Max was assaulted by someone random and James had used the opportunity to retrieve the evidence, maybe blame Max while he was at it. Or whether James had . . .

'Hang on a minute. I'll put her on.' Hayden held the phone out to her. 'He wants to talk to you.'

She stared at the phone, heard her sister: *We don't make contact, we don't let him close.* She slid a finger over the 'End call' button as she took it. 'Yes. Hello. James?' She shrugged, held the phone out. 'We got cut off.'

She remembered other calls then. The frantic ring-around when Hayden was missing. Naomi told her James was at the office. Was he? Or was he searching the glove box?

She thought about how she'd phoned Hayden a dozen times, how he wouldn't pick up, how ticked off she'd been that he'd chosen to talk to James instead. 'Last night, when you were up at the point, did James tell you where he was calling from?'

'No.'

'How long did it take him to get there after he spoke to you?' It was at least twenty-five minutes from MineLease in Toronto to the gun emplacements at Garrigurrang Point. Around eight minutes if he'd gone no further than her carport. Somewhere in between if he was on his way home.

'I don't know. About two minutes.'

Rennie hesitated. 'What do you mean two minutes? As in hardly any time at all or it was actually *two minutes*?'

'I wasn't timing him.'

'Yeah, but which one?'

'Like I said - two minutes. I hung up, climbed up to the bunker, got my stuff, went up top and he was there. Two minutes.'

'It'd take more than two minutes to walk from the gate.'

'He didn't come from there. He used the track that goes down to the park.'

'He walked up from the park?' That would take even longer. Ten minutes, longer in the dark.

'No, he drove up the walking trail.'

Rennie blinked. 'Did he take you out that way?'

'Yeah, he said the gate was locked.'

'How long did it take to get down to the road?'

He shrugged. 'Couple of minutes.'

Her heart beat hard. Cards shifted about in her head. Facts and guesses.

Two minutes up, two minutes down. He must have already been at Garrigurrang Point when he called Hayden. If he was looking for him, the obvious way in was through the gate at the top. He'd have to drive up, realise it was locked, decide not to walk in, drive back down to the park, find the trail in the dark and then call.

Why do it that way? He didn't know for sure Hayden was up there. It was a hunch based on some story about him and Max camping out. He'd spent the day driving back and forth to the plant, to the office, home and who knew where else. Why not phone when he found the gate locked instead of hunting around for the walking trail before calling? Unless . . .

He was already up there in the bush.

More cards. More shifting.

Arguing at the office. Blood in the car park. Trying to get into Max's computer. James told the police about the missing money. He said he agreed with Detective Duncan's suggestion that Max might have *done a runner*.

Why tell him that if Max could come back and explain it? Unless . . .

He knew Max wasn't coming back.

'Oh, shit.' She pushed past Hayden into the hallway, moving on instinct.

'*What*?' Hayden called.

She pulled up in the corridor.

Hayden grabbed her arm. 'Tell me!'

Tell him what? What did she *know*? That James's hunch was spot on and he found his nephew first try.

He might have been on his way home. He might have figured Garrigurrang was worth a go, guessed the gate would be locked on a Sunday night, was familiar with the only other accessible entry and called before hustling up there. Yeah, it was possible she was making a quantum leap and coming up with the wrong answer. But precaution and instinct had kept her alive for a long time.

'Where did you look for Max up at the point?'

Hayden let a sigh out through clenched teeth.

'Come on, Hayden. You know as much as I do. I'm guessing and throwing darts. I don't know what that stuff is on the computer. I just want somewhere else to look.'

'At the big rock and the gun emplacements.'

'What else is up there?'

'Just bush.'

She rolled her eyes away, thinking. 'You said something before . . . about going up to the bunker then up to the top.'

'Yeah.'

'What's below the bunker?'

'The entrance to the tunnels.'

'There are tunnels there?'

'Yes.'

'You looked for Max in them?'

'No, I couldn't get in.'

'Where do they go?'

'Between the gun emplacements. One goes all the way through to the old seaplane base at Rathmines but it's been bricked up for years.'

'But the others are open? You can walk around in them?'

'Not really. There are padlocked gates across the entrances now but Dad says they got in there all the time when they were kids.'

'Who's "they"?'

'Dad and Uncle James.'

40

The memories were lethargic and a little disjointed now, as if they were trudging up an enormous mountain to reach his awareness. Max didn't know whether the ones that were surfacing were close to the end of the chronological queue but he hoped there were a few more to go because these weren't the kind he wanted to be left with for all eternity.

He and Pav were drinking, Pav sorting through ideas to raise some cash, Max encouraging him to talk to a lawyer or the cops, try to work something out that wouldn't bite back later.

After everything Pav had done to get him through his own shit, Max wanted to return the favour so he pored over the spreadsheets again, trying to follow James's system, looking for ways to move enough cash around to pull some profit out.

Panting like a dog, memory still inching on, Max remembered studying the list of clients and invoices and bank statements - and the rush of heat when he saw how it was done. He'd shoved his chair back, hands tingling with adrenaline. It was so simple.

It took a few days to pull it together, bringing it all home and going through it some more while Rennie worked the weekend.

Then he made his first bid.

. . .

WAS MAX IN A TUNNEL? Beneath the earth at Garrigurrang Point?

Rennie stared at Hayden as the questions fired in her mind. How did he get there? And why?

There were too many cards on the table now. Two or three decks set out and splayed and shuffled until she couldn't tell one from another.

Was Max hiding out up there like he had as a kid? From who? Or what?

Why was James up there last night? Had he been to see Max? Was his hunch about Max, not Hayden?

And what the hell did Pav have to do with it? Was it something the three of them were involved in? Or was it Max and Pav together and James found out? Or Pav and James, one trying to break into computers, the other searching the house?

There were more questions than Rennie could hope to answer by standing in the hallway. 'Come on.' She turned and headed for the living room.

'Where are we going?' Hayden asked, following.

'To the point.'

She pulled the drawer on the buffet and hutch, found the torch and some extra batteries. It wasn't dark yet but it wouldn't be long.

'I've already looked up there.'

In the kitchen, she filled a water bottle, found boxes of juice, a handful of snack bars, dug out a smaller torch and handed it to Hayden. 'We should look again.' Moving through the room, she grabbed her backpack from the floor, shoved the supplies inside, pushed her mobile into the pocket of her jeans and continued into the bedroom.

Hayden stood in the doorway as she kicked off her shoes and laced on runners. 'But. . .'

'I don't know, Hayden. I don't know what the files are about and I don't know why Max would be up at the point.' She was crossing the room again, talking as she moved into the hallway. 'All I know is we've run out of places to look and sitting here, reading numbers on a screen won't find him.' And Detective Duncan wouldn't rush to the point if she rang him with another theory on what had happened to Max. Not when all she had was guesswork and suspicion. Not when it came from her.

He followed her to the bathroom. 'Maybe we should wait for Uncle James. He said he was on his way.'

Rennie pulled a small first-aid kit from a cabinet and stuffed it into her pack. 'No.' There was a chance James was trying to help Max. There was a chance he wasn't. But he was family and she wasn't taking any risks.

'I could wait for him.'

If James was on his way, she didn't have time for another discussion with Hayden so she squared up to him. She only had a centimetre or two on him but figured the words would be enough. 'Someone found my bag at the back of a wardrobe, went through the contents, left a large amount of money behind and took my gun. No one does that unless they're prepared to use it. They've already let themselves into the house once. I will not let you stay here.'

A tremor of fear passed through his eyes. Good. It was better than cockiness and resentment.

'You made a promise in the car. Now it's time you came good on it. Do what I tell you, okay?'

His Adam's apple slid up and down as he swallowed hard. 'Okay.'

'No more questions. Your job is to keep your eyes open and your brain in gear. Have you got that?' Her mother's words. Rennie never expected to use them on another child.

He nodded.

'Good. Let's go.'

Flicking lights on over the porch and driveway, banishing the creeping grey of twilight, Rennie scanned up and down the street before leading Hayden out to the carport. She heaved up the door to the dilapidated garage and stepped into its musty, oily air. Her old hatchback was there, the one she'd bought for a pittance after Joanne left Haven Bay in the car they'd shared, but she didn't plan to drive it.

It was the tools on the workbench she was after. They were Max's tools and it took some ferreting about to find what she wanted. When she was done, she shoved a couple of screwdrivers, a hacksaw, short crowbar and mallet into the backpack and threw bolt cutters onto the back seat with it.

She drove with the headlights on, taking a lingering look over the lake, wondering if it'd be her last opportunity, hoping there was some other explanation than the one taking shape in her imagination.

One that involved spilt blood and broken trust, family and friends.

Money, assault. James, Pav.

She didn't want it to be that. For Max's sake. For her own. Even for Hayden's.

He didn't speak in the car, just stared out the window, face turned away, hands clenched into fists on his thighs. She prayed it wasn't resistance.

She took the main street and turned into Garrigurrang Road, following it out to the last street before the reserve, taking the hill up to the gate. It was probably locked but she knew the way to the gun emplacements from there and it was closer to the road - less distance to run, if it came to that. She stopped beside the track, killed the lights but not the engine.

'You know the gun emplacement near the track, the one with the big bunker?' she asked Hayden.

'Yeah.'

'Go there and I'll meet you in about five minutes.' It seemed the best place to start: easy to find in the encroaching darkness and if Max had come here at night, willingly or otherwise, the closest one seemed the obvious choice.

'What are you doing?'

'I'm going to park the car and run back. I can do it faster on my own.'

He nodded, didn't move.

'Stay off the path where you can. If you need the torch, hold it down low and try to minimise the glow. And stay out of sight when you get there. If the gate is open, don't go into the tunnel. Just wait for me. If it takes me longer than five minutes, stay put. Don't wander around.'

He frowned. 'Aren't we just looking for Dad?'

She'd sounded like her mother reeling off hasty, urgent instructions. She eased it back a bit. 'We are. Let's just do it safely.'

She watched him to where the rutted tracks began to rise. What was left of the light was fading quickly now and he'd probably need the torch by the time he got to the top of the hill. She drove a few blocks, turned right then right again, hiding Max's work car between neighbourhood vehicles. It might be overcautious but caution had kept her alive.

The tools weighed the pack down so she dumped everything of its original contents except the cash and the second mobile - she hoped she wouldn't need either but if Max was up here in a tunnel, she might have to leave in a hurry again, with or without him, and there might not be time to go back to the car. Then she hitched it onto her back and took off at a jog, torch in one hand, boltcutters slung over the other shoulder.

The sky was a deep grey when she reached the end of the four-wheel drive track, the glow from street lamps was well behind her and she could barely make out the ground under her feet. The gate was locked but it was to keep out vehicles, not humans, and she stepped around it, flicking on the torch as her shoes sank into long native grass. She played the beam briefly around. Dense bush filled the space on either side of a narrow walking trail. A soft whisper of wind in the brush was all she heard over her puffing breath.

Treading carefully on the uneven path, she passed the first gun emplacement, its position only obvious by the large gap in the bush further off the trail. A minute later, she saw the second clearing off to the right, not far from the track, the torch beam bouncing over tree trunks and tangled branches and sprays of sharp spikes.

She stepped high through the scrub until she was standing on the edge of a low wall that ran around a sunken, cracked and overgrown circular pad of concrete. It was about six metres across, half a metre deep and made her wonder briefly about the size of the gun that'd sat there more than sixty years ago. There was no sign of Hayden.

It was probably four years since she'd last had a tour of the installations with Max, so as her feet crunched around the outside, she kept the torch trained on the edge, not sure where to find the opening to the bunker underneath.

'Renee. Over here.' Hayden's voice was a whispered shout from around the other side. 'The steps are over here.'

'You okay?' she asked when she reached him.

'Yep.' He seemed more pleased to see her than ever before. She felt the same way.

The entry was little more than a hatch: three steep downwards steps one way, four the other, leading into an underground cube of concrete, not high enough to stand completely upright. The floor was covered in a thin layer of mush - soil and leaf mulch washed in through the single opening on one wall, high and narrow enough to be designed for eyes only. The air was cool despite the warmth earlier in the day and smelled of damp cement and rotting leaves. The dank, confined space made the dread sing in her gut.

'Where's the tunnel?' Rennie asked.

'This way.' Hayden's voice echoed softly off the hard surfaces as he shone his torch down another set of steps hidden by the ones they'd come in on.

Thick layers of spider webs lined the ceiling and corners and she ducked her head more than necessary to avoid them, the short walkway just wide enough for her shoulders, the bolt cutters scraping on the mortar.

Six steps straight down, coming out in another chamber, smaller than the first, rectangular in shape. Hayden's torch beam moved jerkily across the walls. There was nothing here but shadows and a doorway in the centre of the concrete opposite.

She hesitated, heart beating hard, breath short. Why would Max be in there? It didn't make any sense. He'd been buried alive in a coal mine; he still woke in the night sweating and edgy from the memory.

He would never in his right mind go in a place like that. It was no wonder he never talked about the tunnels.

Rennie didn't want to go in there, either. Claustrophobia had never been a problem but this place would test anyone's nerve. And a tunnel felt like a trap waiting to happen. But she came here to look for Max; she wasn't leaving until she had.

She crossed the floor, aiming her torch at the metal gate that covered the opening. It looked like a panel from a prison cell - thick, square bars running top to bottom. In the void beyond was a wide tunnel cut into rock, graffiti on both sides as far as she could see. Past that, the beam was engulfed by solid black. There could be a monster sleeping down there and she wouldn't know. Maybe there was.

Running the beam over the gate, she saw it was secured on one side with hinges held by flush-set rivets - no chance of moving them. The other was attached with a heavy-duty slide bolt and padlock. The bars were raw galvanising, aged to a dull, pitted grey. The padlock was smooth and clean and unscratched.

New.

41

Death might take a while but unconsciousness felt close. Max wanted to switch the memories off and find an old one that might keep him warm at the end but then he'd never know why he died in a hole. So he watched them stagger on, hoping there was something to come that wouldn't send him to hell.

James was his usual arrogant self. He tried the patronising blow-off but Max had already figured out why there wasn't enough money to help Pav. He'd calculated they were short at least... How much? He couldn't. . . Oh, yeah, five hundred thousand plus 'expenses' on company credit. He took a punt on the affair. Turned out James, his self-righteous, socially inept cousin, had bedded and lost his fucking heart to the uptight, straitlaced, cold fish financial controller of one of their biggest clients.

The argument ran for days, went well past business issues and made Max groan and writhe on the dirt with the memory. James needed the money to support his new life. He was going to stay until the baby was born because he wanted to see it. Like some kind of amoral moron, he had no guilt. Didn't care that Max was his cousin, that Naomi's life would be ruined, that she was carrying his child. It all made sense to James: the only reason he went into the business was because everyone told him Max needed him; Naomi was an attractive woman, she'd find someone else; Max would fall on his feet, he always did.

When Max saw Pav again, he wanted to purge himself of it, regurgitate every word his cousin had said. He'd spent years flagellating himself for ruining his own marriage and James was doing it without a second thought. But Pav was rattled by his own problems so all Max told him was that he could give him ten thousand. He'd take it from the remains of MineLease; it was finished anyway. Tainted and foul. Max had been broke before and Pav's supplier was making nasty threats - Pav needed it more.

RENNIE PRESSED her face to the bars and yelled. 'Max!'

The sound reverberated in front and behind, down the tunnel and around the bunker. There was just silence in its wake.

Hayden stood beside her, hands clenching the metal rods like a prison inmate. '*Dad? It's me, Dad. It's Hayden.*' He shouted it as though Max had extra reason to answer if he knew it was Hayden. When there was no reply, he tried again. *'Dad! Are you in there, Dad*?'

'He might be too far away to hear us,' she told him, unhitching her pack. Or injured or unconscious. Or dead. 'Can you hold my torch? Shine both of them on the lock.'

'The padlock is on the outside.' The low ceiling amplified Hayden's murmur. 'How could he lock himself in?'

The slide bolt and padlock were attached to the wall, probably impossible to reach with a key from inside the tunnel. 'Maybe he didn't. Maybe somebody else locked him in.'

His face was little more than a shadow in the low light but she saw the reluctant comprehension in it and the uneasiness that followed. Hefting the bolt cutters in both hands, she wished Hayden had gone to Cairns, that he didn't have to understand anything more than an argument with his mum and a phone call with his dad.

The padlock was huge: the lock casing was as large as the palm of her hand and the shackle as thick as her pinkie. She opened the cutters to their full width, set the mouth against the curved metal and knew before she tried that the tool was too small for the job. She heaved anyway and the cutting edge slipped straight off. She got closer, changed her angle, teeth clenched, arms shaking with the effort.

Nothing. Not even an indentation on the shackle.

'Let me have a go,' Hayden said.

His muscles were no bigger than hers but she handed him the tool, held the torches, watched him go through the same process with as much success.

'Shit!' He smashed a foot on the gate in frustration.

The reverb hummed on her eardrums. 'Okay, let's try this.'

Pulling the hacksaw from her pack, she set to work on the metal but it was old and blunt and would exhaust them both before it cut through anything. As Hayden took his turn, filling the chamber with the shish-shish of sawing noises, she propped her torch on the floor underneath him and paced.

'We could call Uncle James. He keeps tools in his car,' Hayden said, the hacksaw now dangling from his hand.

What should she tell the kid? That his uncle might be the one with her gun? That a man he loved couldn't be trusted? She didn't want another argument or to give him a reason to disobey, not when they were finally working together. 'Not yet.'

She found the crowbar in her pack and tried it on the padlock. It didn't move, didn't bend, but the tension felt taut and strong. She got her weight over it and tried again, sweat beading on her face and gathering under her arms. 'Put the torch down and give me a hand,' she told Hayden. They spread their hands along it, heads almost touching. He grunted. 'Keep going,' she ground out, willing it, wanting it, needing it to . . .

With a crack, the shackle snapped, the crowbar clattered to the concrete and they toppled into each other.

Hayden whooped.

Rennie laughed out loud as she reached for the gate. It didn't move: the slide bolt had bent. 'No, no.' She shook the bars, spun away, stalked the length of the chamber, anger building and burning inside her.

What the hell was she doing down here? It was a waste of time and energy. There were a hundred places Max could be. A thousand. Whatever had happened, there was no way he would have gone into that tunnel voluntarily. Not even in the middle of a bright day with all his friends and a swathe of floodlights. She doubted he'd do it bound, gagged and at gunpoint. He'd have to be out cold and dragged in.

She crouched in a corner as Hayden bent his head over the slide bolt with a torch. Why would Max be brought here? Where it was difficult to reach, hard to manoeuvre around and only five minutes from the main street?

'It's bent pretty bad. It won't move,' Hayden said.

She stared at the blackness beyond the bars. It was dark and dank, isolated by bushland, a metre underground and silenced by thick layers of concrete. Why not here?

She stood decisively, drained, sweaty, pissed off - by the gate, by the last forty-eight hours, by the thought that someone might have dumped Max in a place that would scare him to death.

'Let's just see.' She dragged the mallet from her pack, fronted up to the bars, pulled her arms back and swung. The high-pitched crash shattered the air and as she smashed again and again, it became a continuous roll of sound, no distinction between the thunder of the hammer and the replay that bounced and rebounded and ricocheted around her and through her. When the bolt slid free, she stepped away, breathless and shaken, skin and muscle vibrating, urgent intent pressing hard.

'Yesss!' Hayden swung the gate open and took a step over the threshold.

She grabbed his arm. 'Wait.'

'But Dad might be in there.'

'Right, so let's not rush in and stumble about in the dark. It might be how he got in there in the first place.'

He looked at her over his shoulder. 'Like he went in and someone locked the gates on him by accident?'

No, there was no chance of that. Given a moment to think about it, Hayden would figure that out but right now, she guessed he was still working on a happy ending. 'I don't know. Maybe. But let's make sure that doesn't happen now. Tell me what it's like in there.'

'I've never been in. I only know what Dad told me.'

'Did he say how the tunnels work? Is it one long passage that goes by each bunker or are they linked pathways?'

'I don't know but there's definitely more than one. He said the soldiers that were stationed up here gave them names. Newcastle Street, Rathmines Road, Haven Bay Hall, like that. They carved them into the walls like street signs so they'd know where they were even when it was dark.'

Her eyes flicked to the ceiling, imagining the gun emplacements on top. They were scattered through the bush, probably two kilometres between them if she walked a zigzag line to connect them all. How many kilometres of tunnel were underground? How far would someone drag him? Which bunker had they started at?

'Okay. It's just me going in, Hayden.'

A flash of anger. 'But I want to find Dad.'

She turned the torch so it shone between them. 'I know you do so I'm going to be honest with you. He's been missing for two days; if he's in there, he might be in a bad way.'

'I can help him.'

'He might be dead, Hayden.'

His face snapped away but she caught the sheen of a tear. It was better than what would be there if he saw Max's lifeless body in the filth of a tunnel. Rennie had seen her mother before a cop had thought to drag the teenage daughter away. Lying in the doorway of the caravan they'd rented, on her side, her skin grey, drained of colour by the knife wound in her belly, the one responsible for the blood that covered her dress and pooled in a lake around her torso. She had other memories of her mother but for a long, long time that was all she saw when she thought of her.

Rennie laid a hand on Hayden's arm. 'You don't want to see that. It's a bad memory to be left with.'

He glanced back, not meeting her eyes. 'What about you?'

'I've seen lots of things. One more won't make much difference,' she lied.

'Have you done this sort of thing before?'

'What sort of thing?'

'Rescuing people?'

He'd seen her pack equipment, use tools, bark orders, must have been trying to find an explanation - and she wished suddenly she was a better person for him, like the one he was trying to invent. Someone to give him hope. 'I saved my sister once.' She shrugged, tried a smile but it fell from her face as his question found its mark. 'Mostly I just saved myself. I never had anyone else who needed me. Who *I* needed. Now I need to find Max more than anything I've ever done.'

Her throat tightened and her eyes stung and she angled the torch down the tunnel again so Hayden wouldn't see the shine in her own eyes. 'I know how to find my way in the dark, I've done that before,' she told him. 'I need you to make sure I'm safe in there. Can you do that?' Could she trust him?

'I'll wait here for you, make sure no one locks you in.'

'Thanks, I definitely don't want to be locked in but it's not safe for you in here.'

'No one can see me.'

He had to understand. 'Listen, Hayden. I think someone hurt your dad and I think it's someone who knows us. It might be the person who took my gun or there might be more than one person involved. And they might come up here looking for us. Do you understand what I'm telling you?'

He opened his mouth to speak, then just nodded.

'If you stay in here, there's no way to get out if someone else comes down. So you need to go up top. Hide in the bush. Close enough to see me when I come out, far enough in so you won't be seen if someone shows up. Okay?'

Another nod.

'Don't make any calls and don't answer any. There'll be no reception in there so it won't be me and I'm the only person you need to be talking to. If someone turns up, stay out of sight. If they go into the bunker, call the cops.'

'What if it's Uncle James?'

'No one, Hayden. Even if it's someone you trust.' She saw the flash of uncertainty in his eyes. 'I know you don't want to hear that but I'm going into a hole with only one exit. Until we know what's going on, the only people we can trust are you and me.' She watched his face for a sign of dissent. He licked his lips and rubbed them together as he watched her back. What was *he* looking for? 'We need to get moving.' She grabbed her backpack, dug out a snack bar and box of juice and handed it to him. 'Try not to run the batteries down on the torch.'

He didn't move.

'Come on, Hayden.' Was he scared or debating her instructions?

It happened quickly. He was in her arms before she realised, ducking his head, pressing his cheek to her shoulder. A gruff, awkward, boy-type hug. It was so unexpected, so out of character that for a few seconds she didn't know how to respond. Just held one hand above his back, waiting for him to pull away. But he didn't, so she let it land, giving him a pat, then pressing him closer, holding him briefly, tightly to her.

'We'll find him, Hayden. I won't stop looking.'

He stepped away, knuckling a hand across his mouth, keeping his face averted.

'I'll see you soon,' she said. 'Brain in gear, okay?'

42

She stayed by the opening until the light from Hayden's torch faded from the ammunitions bunker then aimed hers straight ahead at the darkness, clenching her teeth on the dread filling her chest.

Don't be dead, Max. Be conscious enough to hear and answer back.

'Max!'

Her voice reverberated away, sucked into the depths of whatever lay ahead. She listened in the following silence. All she heard was the pulse pounding in her ears.

She put the mallet in her pack, left the other tools in the bunker, then hitched her bag onto her back, glad the tunnel was high enough to stand upright. Ten steps in and she saw the elbow in the wall ahead, the engraving and the arrow pointing in the direction she'd come: *No. 4, Bennett's Bunker.* So the gun emplacement closest to the road was near the end, not the beginning. Would the maze get more complicated the further she went in?

Stepping into the mouth of the new tunnel, she called again and sensed the space ahead of her. Narrow and never-ending. As she walked, graffiti moved past her on both sides like a cartoon reel in slow motion. Wartime scratchings and more recent: *MT was here; Jack Akkers, Corporal, 1943; Fuck you.* There was paint slapped about and sprayed on, the signature blocky letters of street artists; crude drawings; a devil's face, its red lines dripping like blood. None of it did anything to slow her breathing.

The air felt still and stale with the slightly sweet stink of something rotting. She moved the torch beam up and down, side to side, anxious to find the source of the smell before she walked into it. She was thinking bats and rats when she saw it. A brief, faint glint on the dirt near her feet. She moved quickly, focusing the beam on ... a piece of...

It was Max's watch.

THERE'D BEEN NOISES. Intermittent distant echoes that'd found their way through the dark passageways like whispers. He'd tried shouting but there was no volume to his voice anymore or enough fluid left inside him to make tears.

He closed his eyes, his mind reeling and spinning, turning inwards and backwards to the ever slowing march of his past, praying he could stay alive long enough for the source of the sounds to find him.

Rennie. Working, painting, stressing about the big job. He barely saw her for days, which he was grateful for. He was ashamed and disgusted with James, worried about Naomi, anxious for Pav. Rennie's bullshit detector would pick it up and he didn't want her involved. She'd wanted better stories in her life - this one didn't qualify.

It was the end of the week when Max started making demands. He got nowhere trying to reason with James and the shouting came back to him in dizzying, nauseating bursts. His cousin was going to leave a fucking mess and Max couldn't bring himself to just watch it happen. He told James he had to admit the affair to Naomi, give her a chance to get things in place before the baby came and gather her family for support. He told him he could take the profit to date, Max's share too, but the rest had to go back in the accounts - there were bills to be paid and business loans to close and Max wasn't going into debt for his cousin's mid-life crisis. If he didn't see the dollars in the bank, he'd go to the police. Funny how the 'you're my cousin' argument made sense to James when there was a chance he might lose something.

Max got drunk in front of the TV that night, watching the Friday night soccer and trying to bolster himself for the next episode. He felt the disjointed numbness of it now, not sure if it was memory or his brain cells checking out.

Saturday he . . . Had he spoken to Rennie before she left for the breakfast shift? He could only remember fortifying himself with painkillers so she wouldn't notice how bad his hangover was when he went see Pav at Skiffs later. Max cornered him in the kitchen, made him swear not to meet the supplier on his own. He needed cops or, at the very least, a friend who knew how to swing a fist. It was stupid bravado but it was all he could think of.

And Dallas. He thought of Dallas a lot.

None of it - Pav, James, Naomi, Rennie, the whole mixed-up ugly mess - felt worthwhile, not even the fact that he wasn't the arsehole in the equation this time. He just wanted . . .

Pain sliced through him. Knife-edge sharp. Icy, burning. It made his ears ring and his brain hiss with static and his pulse pound in his throat.

RENNIE SCOOPED the watch into her hand, heart racing, the light jumping and leaping across every surface as she searched the darkness for him.

'Max! It's Rennie. *Maaax!*' The echo seemed to roll on for a whole minute. How the hell would she hear him? She waited for the sound to die and tried again, speaking slowly through the reverb. 'Make a sound if you can hear me.' As she strained for a reply, the stench seemed to intensify. Whatever it was must be close. She crept forward, beam down, and stopped.

There were indentations in the earth on the tunnel floor. It looked like scuff marks made by shoes and the pressure of large body parts, hips and butt. Then in the centre, where the surface was hard packed from fifty years of foot traffic, was a puddle shape and the unmistakable residue of old vomit. 'Oh God, Max.'

Urgency and fear pushed her forward, moving fast, keeping the light trained ahead. The graffiti grew more sparse, as though only the strongest and bravest made it this far. Christ, she hoped not.

She'd gone about three hundred metres when she saw the opening in the right-hand wall. Shining the torch around the corner, she saw only more rock wall and a long, dark tunnel. There were engravings on each face of the corner. She was standing in *Wangi Wangi Way,* the new passage was *East Street.* Which way did you go, Max?

Calling as she ran straight ahead, she reached another locked gate, turned around and headed back to the T-junction, the pack thumping on her back as she turned the corner and followed it. A dark, damp strip on the wall made her pause - water leaking in from above that reminded her Max had been missing for almost forty-eight hours and losing more fluids by retching. Then another junction: *Rathmines Row* carved into the rock. The tunnel to the seaplane base at Rathmines? Hayden said it was bricked up.

'Max!'

She waited, turned left, heard a noise and stopped as the hairs on the back of her neck sat up.

'Max?'

The echo died, the silence enfolded her. She waited. Five seconds. Ten. Fifteen. There it was. Not a voice, not human. A brief, dull . . . scrape. It sounded like something dragged fleetingly across the rock. And again.

She fought the urge to cry his name and listened, swinging her head one way then the other, not sure which direction it came from. She didn't shout this time. 'I can hear you. Do it again if you can.' Another scrape and another, and adrenaline fired like electrodes. 'I'm coming!' She spun, headed the other way, feet pounding, light careering around the walls as she searched ahead.

A shape in the darkness at the furthest reach of her torch beam. Low down, hard up against the left-side wall.

'Max? Is that you?'

It didn't move. It didn't look like Max. It didn't look like anything living. And she started to slow up, unsure, unnerved, dread rushing through her veins.

SHE'D BROUGHT her bold game. It was in her voice. Firm, determined, hard-edged. It sounded fucking fabulous. Max let the stone drop from his fingers, glad she'd finally heard him, wishing she'd hurry up and get there. Wishing he'd curled in his foetal position facing in the other direction so he could see more than just the glow of light getting bigger and brighter. But man, after total darkness, he couldn't bring himself to blink.

'Max?'

There was hesitance in her tone. Maybe she thought he was dead. Maybe he was. He tried to swallow but his throat was like sandpaper. He nudged his head a little.

'Max.' A scatter of dirt and she was there, fingers on his shoulder, then crawling around his feet then her face in his. Oh God, her face. He thought he'd never see it again. He wanted to smile but only one side of his mouth twitched. She cupped his jaw in her hands and kissed him, pressed soft lips to his forehead, cheek, ear. She smelt of sweat and heat and fresh air and coffee and he wished he could get an arm around her, find enough voice to tell her he loved her.

'Don't try to talk. I've got water. Just hang on a second more.'

Then cool, wet, heavenly water was on his lips, his tongue, filling his mouth, trickling a magical course down his throat. He coughed, gagging on it, swallowing on compulsion.

'Slow down. There's plenty. It's going to be okay. You'll be okay. I'm going to get you out. I'm . . .' She was crying. For a few short moments, her shoulders shuddered, her lips trembled and a single fat tear slipped over an eyelid leaving a clean trail in the smudges on her cheek. Then she pulled it together, pushed the heel of a hand across her face. 'I'm going to get you home.'

He couldn't take his eyes off her. All wild hair and fierce resolve - and his guilt at bringing her down here joined the rest of the pain in his body. 'I'm sorry, sorry. I thought you'd leave.' It was more croak than formed words.

She cradled his head in her elbow. 'Shhh, it's okay. Try to drink some more.'

The water cleared his throat a little. 'Tunnels?'

'Yes, you're in the tunnels under the gun emplacements up at the point.' She fingered the crusted wound on his temple. 'Where are you hurt?'

'Right there.'

'Sorry. Where else?'

Her hands moved over him, feeling his arms, his pelvis, his legs. 'Neck hurts. Cracked ribs.'

'How's your hip?'

'Still there. Seems to work.'

'I found your watch back at the entrance. How did you get here?'

'Walked, crawled, dragged.'

'So you can walk?'

'Not if I don't have to.'

She picked up the torch, shone it one way then the other, uneasiness in her eyes when she looked back at him. 'I'm sorry, baby, but you're going to have to. We can't stay here. It's not safe.'

He wasn't sure what the problem was. 'Can't you call someone?'

'There is no one else. It's just me. You and me. I don't know why you're here but I think I figured some of it out and we need to leave before anyone else realises and comes to check. Can you sit up?'

She wasn't really asking, was already hauling him up against the wall. He tipped his head against it, closed his eyes on the spinning inside his skull, trying to process what she'd told him. Just Rennie. She'd found him on her own. She'd figured something out. Did she know what had happened?

She got his feet sorted, wrapped his arm around her neck,

squatted underneath it like a weightlifter. 'I can't carry you, Max. You've got to help, okay?'

'I've lost some weight recently.'

'Yeah, you look terrific.'

'Not as good as you.'

Her face softened for a moment, her mouth lifting at one side. 'We've both had better days. Use the wall for support. Here we go.'

He breathed hard against the nausea, the dizziness, glad his legs still worked and he didn't fall on his face again.

'Great. You're doing great,' she told him.

'I'm glad you found me.'

'I'm glad you kept breathing.'

While he rested against the wall and drank some more, she swung a pack onto her back and lit up the passage with the torch. It looked like hell down here. It *was* hell but it was better with a light on.

'Right, let's go.'

Half carrying him, staying close to the rock so he could hold on, she hauled him in the direction she'd come. The entrance was back there? 'How close was I?'

'Close?'

'To the bunker?'

'I don't know where the next one is. I came in through the second gun emplacement, number four, the one closest to the track. I found your watch back there. I think it's where you started. How many entrances have you been to?'

'I never found one. I took a punt, ended up here.' He closed his eyes. 'Shoulda gone the other way.'

'No. You did good, Max. I only heard about this place an hour ago. If you'd gone the other way, someone else might've found you first.'

She didn't want anyone else to find him? 'I could've got out.'

'No, Max. You were locked in.' She stopped, shone the light into an adjoining tunnel. 'Do you need a break?'

'Need a holiday.' He leaned against the sharp edge of the corner, sucking at the air, letting her words roll through his mind. Locked in. As in not meant to get out. As in left to die?

'Sorry, babe, but we need to keep moving.' She took his weight again.

'Who locked me in?'

'I thought you'd know.'

'I thought I was down the mine again. I thought a lot of things. I wanted to keep you out of it.'

43

It was Saturday afternoon in Max's memory and the promise of another shit-storm on its way had terrified him. Life as he knew it, as he'd encouraged and nurtured and harvested, was about to be hit by a road train. He'd dug over the garden, needing the release, not knowing what else he could do. Then he'd watched Rennie paint for a while before Trish's party, her overalls splattered in colour, her lean arms strong and sinewy, her hair piled up on her head like a crazed halo. Whatever she'd been through, she'd survived and come here and loved him. And it frightened him that she'd see the fallout and leave - like she always said she would.

Maybe it was better if she did. She didn't say it but he knew she loved him. Deep down in that place buried beneath all her layers. Maybe leaving would do less damage than staying and sifting through remains with him.

Maybe she had left.

Maybe she came back.

Maybe . . .

. . .

'DID I KISS YOU GOODBYE?' Max remembered the party now. The kid in the car park, the sharp words with Rennie, the dread that James would turn up and play happy father-to- be. 'I can't remember leaving the party.' Rennie had stopped talking a few metres back. Possibly she was just tired but he'd felt her spine stiffen and her pace falter when he told her he'd wanted to keep her out of it. What did she know? 'Can we rest now?'

She wouldn't let him sit. She propped him against the wall and gave him juice this time. It tasted awful in his dry mouth but the sugar hit was sensational. It loosened his chest, made it easier to breathe, made him feel as though he could hold the weight of his own spine.

'Where did I go after the party?' he asked when they were moving again.

'I don't know. You left on your own around ten o'clock. Someone said you went to check the car in the car park. No one saw you again. Is that where you went?'

Was it? He focused on the torch beam illuminating the arched ceiling of the tunnel, the rough-cut rock, the hardened track down the centre of the floor, the nothingness beyond it. He remembered standing on the footpath and writing a text to Rennie, receiving another one before he'd finished typing. And the glow of street lamps on the black tar of the car park, his shoes as he stepped in and out of the light. Vehicles were scattered about the wide-open space. A bunch near the dark centre, a few more spread out over by the pub, lights from its neon signs mirrored in their duco, music rocking behind the pub doors. 'I didn't go to check the car. I got a text message.'

'Who from?'

'I don't...' *We need to talk.* 'I went to meet someone.'

'In the car park?'

'Yeah.'

'Who?'

He slowed as a damp trail on the wall passed under his palm. The place he'd grazed his tongue on the rock. 'It was... Over by the pub.'

'Who did you talk to?'

They were boxed in by cars, a bunch of them parked side by side and nose to nose. *Who the fuck do you think you are?* The voice slipped into his memory as though it'd fallen through a crack. Deep and agitated. 'It was all turning to shit,' Max told her. 'He wouldn't listen. He wouldn't let me explain. I told him ... I said . . .' What?

'It was a man you talked to?'

'Yeah. It was a man.'

She didn't ask anything more. Maybe she knew something he didn't. Maybe it *had* turned to shit since he'd been down here. He wasn't unhappy to stop thinking about it. His head hurt and his neck throbbed and he thought he might puke the juice back up if he didn't concentrate on keeping it down.

When she stopped again, there was an edge to her voice that hadn't been there before. 'You should drink some more.' She held out the juice.

'Water this time.' He watched as she opened the backpack again, saw packets of food and a first-aid kit as she shuffled things around. 'How did you know I was in here?'

'I didn't. Hayden told me about the tunnels.'

'Hayden's here?'

'He's waiting up top for us.'

Hayden and Rennie together? Why was Hayden in Haven Bay? 'How long have I been down here?'

'I don't know when you got here but you've been gone two days.'

Christ, it felt like longer. Like a lifetime. 'Why didn't you bring someone to help?'

She didn't answer right away, just took the water bottle from him, wiped the top and poured some into her own mouth. 'I don't know who we can trust, Max. We should get moving again. Hayden's on his own up there.'

The way she said it made fear spark inside him - for his son, for his friends, for what might have happened while he was in his hole. 'Tell me what's going on, Rennie?'

She wrapped a supporting arm around him and hauled him on as she talked. 'I'm not sure. Bits and pieces don't add up. This afternoon, Hayden told me James was up here yesterday. In his car. He drove it up the walking trail. He said he was looking for Hayden but Hayden reckoned he was already here.'

Max stumbled on for a few seconds in silence. Why was James looking for Hayden? And if he was up here, why didn't he check the tunnels? 'So . . . you thought James didn't search the point properly?'

'I'm not sure what James has been doing. He told the police you'd taken money. The cops asked all the wrong questions - about you, about me, about my family - and decided you'd left of your own accord.'

She watched him as they hobbled along, as though she was waiting for a reaction. He didn't have one, he couldn't put it all together.

'Hayden broke the password on your computer,' she finally said. 'The one at home. We found the WTF files.'

WTF. He remembered that. By the time he started the file, the scrawled notes and bank statements were piling up and he was mad as hell. It should've been WTFJ. What the fuck, James? He decided not to confront his cousin until he'd collated all the figures and he could argue them inside out. He wasn't going to give James a chance to mount another patronising, you-don't-understand-the-accounting argument. Maybe the mafia-style shit Pav was dealing with had infected him but when he discovered James in his office one morning, Max got a little paranoid that his cousin would try to cover it up before he could confront him. So Max stored it all on a USB, deleted the documents on his office computer and put a password on everything.

'It's the money missing from the business, isn't it?' Rennie asked.

'Yes.'

'Do you know where the money is?'

'Some of it.'

She stopped, swore quietly as she pressed him into an elbow in the tunnel. 'I think someone who knows where it is put you down here and hoped you'd die and it would all go away.'

His pulse thumped in his ears, pounded on the back of his skull. Pav said desperate people did desperate things. *You're going to ruin everything, you arsehole.* The voice again. Close range, spat in his face through gritted teeth. The lights over the car park, the music from the pub, the salty tang of the lake in the night air.

'Is that what happened, Max?' Her eyes were huge and burning with something he didn't understand. 'Who was in the car park with you?'

He pushed thumbs into his eyes, tried to see it again. 'The text said we had to talk. I met him in the car park. I said, Right, I'm here. So talk. He ... he shoved a finger in my chest. He wouldn't listen. I told him . . . fuck, I don't know what I told him.'

She pressed her lips together, aimed the torch up ahead. A rectangle of lighter gloom appeared like a ghost. The exit. He wanted to run to it like he had that day with James, push through the bunker, throw himself into the light and breathe clean air. All he managed was a grunt of extra effort.

'There's something you need to know before we head down there.' Rennie spoke fast, not looking at him. 'Someone broke into the house and took my gun.'

He had a hundred questions but only one that mattered right now. 'Where's Hayden?'

She wedged a shoulder under his armpit. 'He's hiding in the bush. He'll be okay if he stays there.'

Christ, a gun. The bush wasn't bulletproof. As though she sensed his urgency, she lifted their pace, adjusting the throw of the torch so it didn't shine directly into the bunker beyond, her words staccatoed as she hustled him onwards. 'Listen, Max. I'm going up top first to scout around, make sure we're still alone. I've only got one torch so I'll have to leave you in the dark again.'

'No. Just get me up there and call the police.'

'The cops will take too long. We need to get off the point.'

'Don't leave me here.'

'You can barely walk. If someone's up there, I can't get you anywhere in a hurry.'

'But. . .' He held onto her, thinking, not thinking, trying not to scare away the memory that was pushing at the edges of his mind.

A group of cars, a figure standing in their shadow, hunched and taut. Max had folded his arms over his chest. *So talk.*

Who the fuck do you think you are? A finger in his chest.

A push back. *I'm trying to do the right thing.*

Rennie stopped him a few metres from the bunker doorway, pressed him close to the wall. 'Who was in the car park with you, Max?'

I'll give you half.

'He shoved me against the car.'

'Who did?'

'He had something in his hand.'

'Max.' She shook his arms. 'Was it James or Pav?'

It wasn't a guess, not like she had a list of his mates and was going to work her way down from the top until a name clicked. It was a choice: James or Pav. One or the other. 'What are you saying?'

'James came late to the party. Pav could've left and come back. Both had time to break into the house today.'

'No, Rennie . . .'

'Trust me, Max. The most dangerous people are the ones who say they love you.' She pulled a mallet from her bag. 'Wait here.'

She didn't give him a chance to protest, just ran the final reaches of the tunnel, the tool firm in her hand. He wanted to follow, to beg her to take him, to be careful. Could only lurch a few steps forwards as she stood with a shoulder to the opening and flicked the torch beam around the small chamber on the other side. She then moved quickly to the opposite wall and disappeared from sight.

44

His eyes clung to her torchlight until the darkness returned, sudden and complete. After the frantic, breathless urgency since she'd found him, the silent, solid black felt like a shroud. He gritted his teeth, forced the air to move slowly through his nostrils. And the crack in his memory opened like a crevasse.

Walking through the car park, the music from the pub, surrounded by cars. The cussing, the finger jammed in his chest, a scuffle, the shock as Max hit the chassis.

'It's my turn.'

'You don't get turns. You work hard and do the right thing and be grateful for every day you're not dead in a hole.'

'I told you I'd give you half.'

'It's not yours to give. And I don't want half. *I want you to fix it.'* The door thrown open. *'So get in the damn car and make it happen before I do it for you.'*

Hand fisted around a fat set of keys. *'You arsehole. You got Gran's house. You owe me.'*

Max saw the last of it in slow motion. The arm coming from out wide, the brief surprise, the thunder in his head, the crunch of his nose as it tore sideways, the edge of the doorframe in his vision.

He jerked as though it'd hit him again. 'Rennie. Wait!'

RENNIE SAW James half a second before the gun. It wasn't aimed at her, it was swinging through the air towards her.

'You bastard!' she yelled as she dived. She wasn't fast enough and hard metal clipped her low on the skull with a loud crack. Not as bad as the blow he'd intended but it still made stars explode behind her eyes as she hit the earth, her brain swinging like a pendulum.

She rolled, hoping it was away from him, and as she rose warily to a crouch, she saw the torch on the ground out of reach and the mallet in the triangle of light that stretched away to the bush beyond. She thought briefly of Hayden, kept her eyes moving upwards for James.

He was a couple of metres away, hands at his sides, the pistol held loosely in one. A black Glock. Hers. He wasn't following through and coming at her with more. He seemed startled that she hadn't dropped at his feet with the first blow.

'You fucking bastard,' she spat at him.

He licked his lips and shuffled his feet. 'Jesus, Renee. Sorry. You scared the shit out of me.' He said it with an apologetic grin, as though he'd bopped her on the head without realising who it was.

She didn't answer, just watched him as she got to her feet, looking for warning signs in his body language.

'What are you doing here?' He sounded puzzled and concerned, like he had since Max disappeared and, for a fraction of a second, the doubt that had descended listening to Max's fractured memory made her wonder again if she had it wrong - but her gun was in his hand. More than enough reason to hold back the torrent of abuse and accusation that was on her tongue.

'What are *you* doing here?' she growled back at him.

'Hayden said you were at the point. I thought you might've found something.'

Had Hayden spoken to him after he'd left her? 'Is that why you brought the gun?'

He lifted it, loose in his hand. 'It seemed wise, after all your talk about your father. You never know who might be around.'

She watched the way he handled it: the grip nestled into his palm, the fingers tentative, as though he'd hefted it before but was nervous about the trigger. More than likely he'd never held a gun before this afternoon but YouTube could teach you to cook and kill. There were plenty of demonstrations on loading and firing. In ten minutes, he'd know the Glock had no safety, that all it needed was a strong, steady finger.

She glanced quickly around. Running was her first instinct and, if she was fast, chances were the recoil and panic would make him miss but she had no idea where Hayden was and didn't want him hit by strays. And Max was in the bunker, just a few metres below James.

'Who were you expecting?' she asked, wondering if Pav was on his way.

'Not Max, that's for sure. He's long gone, Renee. He's taken the money and left with another woman.' He cocked his head, pity in his smile. 'Yeah, that's right. I didn't tell you before. I thought it was too much for you to take in but it's true. Max's been having an affair for months, screwing around behind your back. Now he and his fuck buddy have screwed us both.'

Fuck buddy? Did he think a cruder picture would make her more inclined to believe it? She was tempted to shout that she'd found Max, that she'd seen the file and knew it was all bullshit. But she wasn't sure what she knew.

Max said there'd been an argument, it had turned to shit, there was no way to fix it. Was it Max or James trying to fix it? Was it even James who was in the car park? Did it matter now? He was here with her gun, trying to convince her Max was gone. That in itself said plenty. And however Max got here, whether James dragged him into the tunnel, put on the lock or just left him in there to die, Max didn't deserve it - whatever he'd done.

'Then why did you come?' she asked him.

'It's not safe at the point in the dark, Renee. With Max out of the picture, someone needs to look out for you now.'

Rennie was torn between laughing at him and smashing a fist into his face, then she saw it from James's perspective. He must have watched her climb from the bunker on her own. He didn't know she'd found Max, didn't know she'd got past the padlock. Maybe he thought Max was dead and rotting, instead of living, breathing proof. He'd brought the gun in case he needed to shut her up, probably had the key to the gate in his pocket so he could lock her in the tunnel with Max. But maybe he figured he didn't have to. He wasn't her father - murder wasn't his sport. Perhaps it was only a last resort.

She decided to follow his lead. 'If you want to look out for me, you can put the damn gun away and help me search up here.' She pointed towards the path and the emplacement on the other side of it. 'You take the one over there and I'll try that one.' She swung her arm, aiming at Number Five, the bunker closest to the road.

'Sure.' He didn't move.

Almost behind him, at the edge of the torch's triangle of light, there was a movement. If it was Pav, she didn't want to let on she'd seen him. Making a show of looking around the clearing, she skimmed her eyes along the beam on the ground and a pulse of fear shot through her. It was Hayden. Out of the bush - still, silent and watching them.

She'd told him to hide, she'd told him to trust no one. But she was the bitch who slept with his father, James was the uncle he loved and Hayden didn't know about the blood already spilt.

'I've already looked here,' she prompted James. 'We need to check the others.' And get him the hell away from Max.

He still didn't move. 'What exactly are we looking for, Renee? I searched up here yesterday. All the gates are locked. Max isn't here.'

Hayden's shadow shifted in the light and from the corner of her eye she saw his head lift. Did he think she'd got it wrong? That she was on her own because she hadn't found Max? She needed to remind him of the facts.

'You searched a lot of places, didn't you? You didn't find him at the house, either. You got the USB thumb drive, though. And my pistol.'

A brief, lopsided sneer passed over James's mouth, as though now that she'd mentioned the USB, he may as well give up the concerned-cousin act. 'The gun was a bonus, I'll admit. Certainly gave me a new perspective on you.' He took a second to glance at the weapon in his hand, huffing a short, nasty laugh. Rennie wanted to let him know his perspective was a complete screw-up but hesitated as the shape in the torchlight moved.

'And all this time, I thought you were some worn-out, hard-luck case Max felt sorry for.' As James continued, Hayden slipped quietly back into the bushes. 'You got that silent, wary thing down pat. I figured you were a fragile rape victim or beaten down by some abusive husband. Figured you must've been a good fuck for Max to keep you around for so long. Then today I find out you're a criminal. Phil Duncan said you shot your own father. Now that was a surprise. Is it any wonder I took your gun? Didn't want you getting pissed off and pointing it at me.'

Rennie let the insults ride - she didn't give a shit what James thought of her. She was more interested in where this new version of him had come from. His standard poker-faced arrogance was still in place but there was something edgy and spiteful in it. She didn't think it was a performance, not like the feigned innocence - and it seemed closer to real emotion than anything she'd ever seen from him. Had it always been there, hidden behind his mask of impassiveness, emerging in the stress of the moment? Or had he found it when he left his cousin to die?

And was that deed his worst or just the lid coming off? Whatever the answer, she wasn't taking any chances. She wanted to get Max out of the bunker, out of the bush and to medical help - and James sure as hell wasn't going to step aside and let her do it. 'Yeah, well, you don't need to point a gun at me. I just want to look for Max. Are you helping or not?'

'Sure. You go over there, I'll check here.'

'I told you, I've been down there.'

'I'll check again. Have you got a problem with that?'

'It's a waste of time. The gate's locked.'

He pulled a small torch from the back pocket of his jeans, flicked open a bright, narrow beam of light that he aimed towards the edge of the gun emplacement like a lightsabre. 'I'd like to see for myself.'

Alarm pitched her closer to him. '*No*.'

James hesitated, eyes narrowed. She wanted to take it back, say something that would draw him away but it was too late. He shone the light along the perimeter of the sunken circle and, as it hit the opening, fear bloomed inside her.

She'd left Max in the tunnel but he was scared of the dark and as good at following instructions as Hayden. Had he found his way to the steps? Had he heard, or was he waiting, deafened by thick concrete, half-a-dozen steps from the cousin who wanted him out of the way?

She moved closer, a hand outstretched, hoping her voice was loud enough to carry to the bunker. 'James, come on. You're wasting time.'

He looked back at her, the lightsabre illuminating the entrance, the gun firm in his fist and pointing at her. 'Come with me, Renee. We can check it together.'

Down there, with Max, where he could shoot them both?

45

Every instinct was telling Rennie to run. Her legs were twitching, her lungs were sucking in oxygen, her brain was calculating the shortest route to cover. She'd been trained to stay out of sight, to avoid attention, evade the confrontation. It had kept her alive. Now she needed to keep someone else alive.

'I found Max, you bastard!' She shouted the words, letting anger give it volume - a warning to Max, the truth to Hayden.

James's head swung to the steps that led underground and for a moment he was stalled, staring open-mouthed at the narrow, downwards passage. Rennie didn't know if it was realisation or indecision or a lack of any kind of training to act fast. But she seized on his hesitation, trying to redirect his attention, making each word an indictment.

'He's *dead*. You killed him. For money. You fucking bastard.'

It snapped him out of his shock and he met her glare, fury and fear barely contained behind the taut expression on his face. 'You should've left, Renee. It would've been okay if you'd just left.' He lifted the gun - no wavering, no apprehension. A decision made.

And as she eyed the barrel of her own weapon, realising she was too close for the recoil to keep her safe, a massive wave of stored-up, deep-seated, enraged energy crashed through her. She'd spent years keeping out of reach of her blood-lusting father and now she was free of him, she'd walked into the sights of an arrogant, egotistical, greedy beginner. He'd committed a crime and he was holding a gun as though that was all it took to be a killer. She'd seen him in action, though, knew he was slow to react, was making decisions on the run, was still stunned by what he'd done - and he'd underestimated her. Which was more than she'd ever had on her side. She knew more about decision-making and calculating risks and acting on instinct than he could ever imagine. And she was not getting shot by a fucking amateur.

She smiled as though she had something contemptuous to add, then ran. Fast, hard, in a wide angle away from him, putting distance between them, tracking sideways through his vision, making it harder for him to take aim.

The cover of bush was ten metres away across unlit, uneven dirt that was underlayed with tree roots and rocks, strewn with stones and fallen branches. Unable to see any detail in the dark, she stepped high, pumped her arms, hoping she didn't fall before he shot her.

The blast roared in her ears, vibrated through her chest, made her legs reach further, faster. As she hit the bush, sharp foliage tearing at her face and arms, another explosion thundered around her. She heard the bawl of her voice without feeling it leave her throat, the thud of her hip as it hit the earth, the crunch of teeth as her jaw met the ground. It seemed like seconds before the pain arrived, spearing through her leg.

She didn't stop. Gasping, panicking, no idea how far she was from the clearing, she scrabbled backwards on her butt, dragging herself through the scrub, left leg like a dead weight, memories of other gunshots filling her with terror. Her spine thumped a tree trunk. A huge, old gum that she scuttled around, pressing herself into, breath fast and erratic, body shuddering, eyes squeezed tight. She shouldn't be here. He was too close. Close was bad. It was all bad.

Fingers shaking, she felt along the length of her jeans for the damage, unable to see in the dark. No slick wetness, no tear in the fabric. The arsehole hadn't shot her. She'd done something, though. Reaching underneath, she felt the stinging tear in the flesh down her shin, the blood starting to ooze, the hard knot of swelling already starting to form on the bone. Christ, had she broken it?

'Renee!' James's voice rose in the darkness. 'You can't get far in the dark.'

Squeezing her eyes on the pain, pulling air in through her nose, she moved her toes, her foot, rotated the ankle, flexed the knee. It hurt like hell and she'd probably need stitches but everything was working and that was all that counted.

'Renee,' James called again. 'I don't want to hurt you. It's not what you think. It was an accident and I panicked.'

Yeah, but a padlock on a gate was calculated. And he'd just fired two shots at her. However it'd started in the car park, it was now premeditated and lethal. She rolled the cuff of her jeans down, listened to the sound of James's feet thudding on the dirt in the clearing, wondering where Hayden was.

Then light filled the night, glowing upwards into the sky and shining through the bush, making sharp, black shadows of the scrub. She ducked, tipped her head around the tree trunk, searching for the source. James's dual cab was on the path, its headlights on high beam. Instinct sounded like the barked voice of her sister, telling her she had a chance if she ran now, if she just kept crashing through the bush until she'd disappeared.

'We had a fight, Renee. Max took the money. I was trying to stop him leaving,' James called. He was moving around the clearing, not heading for the gun emplacement but searching the perimeter. He thought Max was dead. He hadn't seen Hayden. He wanted her.

'He was having an affair, Renee.'

No. She didn't believe that.

'We can work this out.'

Nothing ever worked out. It was always screwed up. Screwed up and brutal.

'He didn't love you. He was leaving you.'

Why the fuck are you still there?

Using the tree for support, she pushed herself to her feet, tested the strength of her injured leg, wincing at the sting as the wound opened.

'Renee!' It was a bellow this time, the reasoning replaced by frustration and impatience.

The next words she heard made her run.

MAX GRITTED HIS TEETH, straightened his legs and rose up out of the bunker into clean night air, tasting the sweetness of it, squinting in harsh light, blinded by two days of darkness. He could hear James but couldn't see a damn thing. His cousin was somewhere close - not close enough to spit in his face. The bastard was shouting for Rennie. She'd run, Max guessed that much. He hoped to God James hadn't shot her.

Max had got sick of waiting in the dark, had dragged himself to the turn in the stairs when he'd heard Rennie cry, '*No*.' He took it as a warning and ducked back around the wall. A second later, torchlight flashed across the narrow passageway and she was shouting and the stairwell was alight and James's voice was above him, speaking then swearing then the gun shots booming inside the bunker, rolling around the concrete walls.

It knocked the air from his lungs. Not the noise but the image in his head of Rennie bleeding, shot, dead. Here to find him, killed because she had. Her gun, James's hand, Max's fault.

Then James was yelling her name and Max hauled himself up, holding his ribs, clinging to the walls, listening to the lies being bawled into the bush. Part of him wanted to shout the truth so she'd know. Part of him wanted her to believe it so she'd run for her life.

His eyes finally found James in the glare. He was standing on the other side of the clearing, head down as though listening for her. He seemed larger, aggressive, menacing in the light from the car. Maybe it was the eerie, elongated shadow that stretched from his feet. Maybe it was the gun in his hand. Max's legs were trembling and his heart raced just from climbing a few steps but it didn't lessen the urge to beat the crap out of him.

The snap from the bush was loud enough to carry all the way to him. James heard it too, lifted his head, turned his face. It came from the south, closer to the gun emplacement. Rennie and Hayden were both out there.

'Renee!' James bellowed.

Without thinking, without any idea how to play it, Max ground out the first words that came to him. 'Don't. Go. Near. Her.'

James stopped as though he'd hit a post. He stared across the clearing like a man watching his life pass before his eyes. 'Max?'

'Yeah, you fuck.' The effort to raise his voice tore at his ribs.

'Jesus, Max, are you okay?'

'I'm still breathing, no thanks to you.'

'Oh, man. I thought you were dead.' He made it sound like relief but he stayed where he was, keeping his distance, one hand upturned in appeal, the other still gripping Rennie's gun.

'Bullshit. You dragged me into the tunnels and locked me in.'

'No, I came back to get you and the locks were there. Somebody else put them on. The rangers must have done it.'

'It's too late, James. You took the money and you left me to die. You just shot at Rennie.'

His cousin's elongated shadow made an exaggeration of the shrug. 'What are you going do about it, Max? You going to wrestle the gun off me? You can hardly stand. I won't need to shoot you. I can just push you down the stairs.'

Maybe that's what he was planning. 'It won't get you what you want. Rennie knows everything. She found me, she knows about the fraud, your affair with Sondra, leaving Naomi, the fight in the car park.' She didn't but if she was still in the bush, he wanted her to. 'And she's gone. She's probably down at the street already, phoning the cops.' Where Max hoped she was, running for her life.

James swung the gun in a stiff-armed arc, not to fire a shot but with some kind of pent-up, frustrated fury. 'This is *your* fault, Max. You should've let it go.' Walking now with a jolting, angry pace, the volume of his voice rose with each step. 'I told you I'd give you half. But you had to be a righteous prick, didn't you? Had to pretend like you've never done anything wrong in your whole fucking life. And you got Gran's house. You owe me.'

Max sensed the hollow air of the bunker at his back, remembered his feet were planted on the top stair and moved two steps into the clearing, trying to hide the fact he could barely support himself.

Still metres away, James raised the gun, aimed it at Max. The sight made his brain recoil. It was James, the cousin he'd rushed to defend his entire life, now ready to kill him in cold blood. Shock and fear and fatigue made his legs threaten to give out but he thought of Rennie and Hayden and managed to keep upright and focused. Because if James killed him now, the bastard wouldn't let them go home and fix dinner. There wasn't much Max could do, he was too weak to charge him; buying time was all he had - and thirty-five years' experience of James trying to best him. He injected as much scepticism and scorn into his tone as he could. 'You going to kill me?'

A sneer pulled James's mouth into an upturned curve and his stalking became a swagger. 'You think I won't?'

It was just like when they were kids, except this time it was James with the strength and Max using his brains. 'You haven't got the guts to do it like this.' It was a taunt, not a challenge.

And James bought it. 'You think you're so fucking . . .' Max heard the same soft rustle that halted James mid sentence. He turned and his heart stopped.

'Leave him alone!' Hayden cried.

His son, his lovely son.

46

Hayden was at the edge of the clearing, face crumpled, fists clenched, glancing back and forth between his father and uncle.

'Jesus Christ, Hayden,' James shouted before Max could find voice. As his cousin turned, the gun shifted aim.

'James, don't. It's *Hayden!*' Max yelled.

The weapon swung back, James wavering, rattled.

'What the fuck is wrong with you?' Max spat.

'This is your fault. You did this. If you'd shut up and let me do it like I planned, your kid wouldn't be here. I wouldn't have had to put you in that fucking tunnel.'

Max wanted to argue the point on so many levels, he wanted to put his body between Hayden and the gun, he wanted to smack James in the teeth, but he sensed the edge of the cliff his cousin was on. A step in one direction and logic was a lost cause. He abandoned the goading and lowered his voice, hoped there was still enough of the man James used to be to coax him back.

'Are you going to kill both of us? In cold blood? Hayden's fourteen.'

James's hand shook as he ran it over his hair and the film of sweat on his face shone like plastic in the light from the car. His eyes flicked tensely to Hayden and back.

Max tried again, forcing a lighter, cousin-to-cousin tone. 'Come on, James. This is insane.'

'Hayden,' James called. 'Your dad needs help. Come and give him a hand.' The gun hadn't moved and his hand hadn't loosened its hold. He wasn't being benevolent, he was drawing his targets closer.

'Stay there,' Max told Hayden.

His son held his ground but his voice was doubtful, urgent. 'Dad, you look pretty bad.'

'Get over there,' James ordered. 'He's bleeding. He can hardly stand. He needs you.'

'No, Hayden. Go. *Now,*' Max tried to yell it but he couldn't push the sound from his damaged chest. It was weak and tremulous and made Hayden hesitate.

'Get the fuck over there or I'll shoot him,' James yelled. 'You've got three seconds. One . . .'

'Leave now, Hayden.'

'Two . . .'

Then Hayden was at his side, crying, holding him, trying to shield him and Max's heart swelled with love and pride and disgust with himself. He'd fucked up again. He should have let James have the damn money; he should have given him the whole fucking business. He should have bought a goddamn going-away present for him and his girlfriend.

Now his son was going to die and he would, too. And probably Rennie.

'What now, James?' he asked, no pretence in the loathing in his voice.

'Shut up!' James was breathing hard, pacing side to side. Rethinking or working himself up to it?

'Don't do it, James.'

The plea seemed to make up his mind. James straightened his gun arm, took a single step towards them. Another two and the barrel of the gun would be on Max's sternum. 'Get down the steps.'

Max pushed Hayden behind him. 'You don't need to do this. Take the money. I don't care. Just walk away.'

'It's too late for that.'

'We won't say anything. I'll make sure Rennie doesn't.'

James's explosion of laughter echoed into the bushes. 'You think she's going to do anything you tell her? You think she's some goddamn angel, don't you? She's a criminal, Max. Did you know that? You think she loved you? You think you got it all worked out? She was using you. She changed her name so the cops wouldn't find her. She's been spreading her legs and keeping you happy and laughing at you the whole time. Work hard, do the right thing and be thankful you're not in a fucking hole. You self-righteous prick. Get in the bunker. Both of you.'

'Not Hayden. Let him go. Leave him and Rennie out of it. Whatever shit you've got stored up, whatever the problem you've got with me, it's between us. So let's sort it out. You and me. Here and now. It's not too late for that.'

'The cops are looking for you. You're fucking covered in blood.'

'I'll tell them someone mugged me and dumped me up here. That Rennie and Hayden found me.'

'I keep telling you, Max, it's *too late.*' He spoke slowly, like he was explaining it to a five-year-old. 'They know the money is gone and it works better for me if they think you took it. Don't you see that? I can make it look like I topped myself. They won't even look for me. Then Naomi gets to be the grieving widow with the baby and you're the bastard responsible for the whole fucking mess.'

A beat passed as Max took in what he'd said. He knew James and Sondra had planned to leave the country, he'd got that much out of him when he accused him of taking the money. He was waiting on passports, expensive ones with new names. That's why he hadn't just left, why he'd panicked. He'd wanted everything - the money, the lover, the new life in the US. Max had tried to stop it, had tried to make James own up to his deceit but he'd just given his cousin a better way to hide it.

'You don't need to hurt Hayden for that. Let him go. Let Rennie go.'

James smiled like it was funny, like it was some kind of in-joke. 'Max the hero. Always making me look like the loser in the family. Laughing at me behind my back. Jesus, you cheat on your wife and put a man in the hospital but everyone forgets about it when you come up out of that mine. The company even gives you money just for breathing. Not this time. Now you're a sucker. The cops think you stole the money. Your friends will, too. Oh yeah, and Rennie knows all about it. She asked for a share to keep quiet. She fucked me, too, to seal the deal. All the sweeter now I can tell you, don't you think?'

James took a moment to be a cocky bastard, letting the gun swing from his fingers as he spread his arms in some kind of see-who's-clever-now.

Max saw the opportunity, knew he might not get another one. He shoved Hayden sideways and lunged for his cousin. James barely moved as he made contact. Christ, he had nothing more than anger and instinct and hope that it would be enough. As Hayden shuffled with indecision at the periphery of his vision, Max found the underside of James's gun arm and shoved upwards.

RENNIE BURST from the scrub as James pushed back, ramming the heel of his other hand at Max's ribs.

Life on the run hadn't taught her to fight - no one stood a chance if it got to that with her father. But she knew how to put a person down for long enough to run and that's all she needed to scoop up Max and haul him and Hayden out of sight.

She came in from behind James, watching the semiautomatic arc skywards, still clutched firmly in his hand. Dropping a shoulder as she reached him, she opened her arms and launched herself. Pushing off the ground with her good leg, wrapping herself around his thighs, driving at the back of his knees. She felt both legs buckle and his weight tip slightly back before pitching forwards. Then she was falling with him, thrusting down, making sure he got all the way to the dirt. Until now, he'd been slow to react, thinking and deciding before acting, and as air burst from his lungs on impact, as she lifted her head in search of the gun, she wondered how much of a fighter he was when the tables were turned.

He landed face first, his free arm underneath him, the gun arm outstretched on the ground above his head, the weapon still in his palm. He was tall and bulky, he had long arms and legs and from where she'd landed with her shoulder jammed into the back of his thighs, he seemed mountainous and the gun a long way away. But he moved like a big man, too, as though the messages took a long time to reach the muscle, and he was dazed and caught unawares. As he started to roll backwards, releasing his free arm first, she moved faster, off him, slipping in the dirt as she pushed to her feet, clawing forward, trying to get to the pistol before he came to his senses. Before he aimed and fired.

She met his eyes briefly - saw them narrowed with anger, then flaring with surprise and recognition. He thrust sideways and she dived - for his hand, his wrist, his forearm, anything she could reach that would stop the message she saw in his face reaching his finger on the trigger. She didn't know where he planned to aim, figured it was probably at her, figured the bullet would hit before she got to his arm.

The blast was deafening. She didn't hear her own scream, felt his body underneath her as she fell, assumed the pain would come later and kept stretching, reaching for the weapon while she could, flung upwards again from the recoil. She thought the shouting was about her, some kind of panicked, desperate yelling, until Hayden's high-pitched voice sliced through it.

'*Dad!*'

47

Rennie lifted her head, saw Max on the ground in front of Hayden, curled in a ball, both hands clutched to his side. Blood was shiny and bright in the glare from the headlights, seeping through his fingers, spreading across his shirt, staining the waistband of his dirty jeans, spilling on the earth.

His howl of pain finally reached her. And Hayden's terrified shriek - and she remembered her own screams. And Jo's. And her father's bellows and the cops shouting and the arsehole who hit her. And the sirens that took her mother away. A cacophony of sound that filled her up and blurred her vision and fired adrenaline and rage into every cell.

Then James was shunting her back, trying again to turn the gun on her. She rose to her knees, lifted her elbow and slammed the tip of the bone into his cheek. She was wiry, smaller than him by more than a head, with the fine, lean arms of a runner. The blow didn't knock him out but it threw his face to one side. She flung herself across his chest, arms outstretched, still too far away to reach the gun so she dropped her chin, opened her mouth, found the thick flesh high up on the outside of his chest and closed her teeth on it.

His scream was shrill and she knew if he'd had any kind of experience or training, he would have followed through with the pistol and knocked her senseless. But the pain made him panic. He dropped the weapon, swung his hand instead, pushing at her forehead, trying to get her off him, squealing like a goddamn kid. She wanted to bite right through, make him bleed and hurt and wail some more but she let go, the gun in her sights.

He was faster. With his large palm on the crown of her head, he shoved her, the force of it crunching in her neck. And he kept coming, rolling, heaving her off him. He might have been slow to act but he was strong enough to lift her up and dump her on the hard-packed earth beside him, the impact rattling through her joints.

Maybe he finally realised his physical advantage, maybe it was some kind of male instinct or maybe he'd watched a lot of movies but he got over her, on his knees, and swung like a boxer. A big, round-house thing, lots of backswing, a huge fist - and plenty of time to see it coming. Cringing as she spilled away from him, pushing to her feet, she turned, lifted her uninjured shin and drove the toe of her shoe deep into his gut.

It was her big hit, the one learned at her mother's side, the one designed to drop a man and run like hell. The swing was strong and aggressive. She felt ribs and soft gut. It might have knocked him down if she'd waited to see.

She might have had time to haul Max off the ground with Hayden's help. It's what instinct told her to do but something else took over.

It came from deep inside. The same thing that drove her father. Illogical, hate-filled, red-hot and consuming. She'd been ashamed and fearful and haunted by it. Now she welcomed it, breathed in the rage and hurt and loss and madness - and directed it at James's gasping, tipping body.

She struck out with her foot again. In the ribs as he hit the deck. Breaking his nose as he lifted his head. She wanted to hurt him and stuff him in a tunnel. Make him pay for what he'd done to Max. To Hayden. To her. For deceiving her, for making her want to run. For all the times she had. For the arseholes who'd threatened her and terrified her and made her bleed.

She slammed down hard, aiming for a shoulder joint and he grabbed her leg, dragging her off balance, pulling her to her knees, hands grabbing for her throat.

'Stop! Just stop! Fucking stop!'

Hayden's voice was full of fury. The gun trembled slightly in his hands but he held it straight and double fisted like a TV cop.

Rennie wasn't sure if he was pointing it at her or James. It didn't matter. The sight of the crying, terrified, angry teenager with her semiautomatic less than a large step away was more frightening than when James had aimed it at her. And as though a pause button had been hit, her rage and insane bitterness froze - not erased, not rewound, just held in check like her fingers entwined in James's collar.

'Hayden, no,' she said, not letting James go, the consequences of any sudden move by either of them playing through her mind.

'He was going to kill Dad.'

'No, I wasn't. I wasn't going to use the gun,' James said slowly, clearly. 'I just wanted him to understand. It was Rennie who made it go off.'

'Bullshit. Fucking bullshit. I saw you. You were pointing it right at him. At us.' The pistol swayed and jerked. *'You were gonna fucking do it!'*

Rennie flinched, saw James do the same. She released her grip on him and eased away. If Hayden fired, she didn't want to be too close.

Max's voice reached them, a whisper from beyond their angry clutch, weak with pain, tremulous with fear. 'Hayden. Put it down.'

Rennie saw it then, what was coming, how it would end, and she wanted something different for Hayden.

For Max. For herself.

It was too late for a happy final chapter, however this finished. But it could be better than the one where Hayden pulls the trigger. Where he kills his uncle and has to live with what he's capable of.

'Hayden, put the gun down.' She pushed her butt along the dirt, sliding away from James. He must have figured he was safer with her closer and snapped his hand out, grabbing her wrist.

It made Hayden jump, the gun with it. 'No! He'll hurt you. He tried to shoot you before. I saw him.'

'Then give the gun to me.'

'Don't give her the gun,' James said. 'Didn't you see her? She'll kill me.'

Hayden didn't answer, his eyes flicking between Rennie and James, breathing in short, shallow gasps.

Fear and impatience filled her words with her mother's tone. 'You promised to do what I told you, Hayden. Now I'm telling you to give me the gun.'

'But my dad . . .' His face crumpled as fresh tears streamed down his cheeks. The gun wavered. James's hand tightened on her arm.

Rennie understood her mother now, how the desire to protect grew with sharp edges. But Hayden didn't respond to orders and she hoped she'd learned enough from Max to give him something better than her own mother had.

'You've already saved your dad, Hayden. You got into the computer, you showed me where to find him, you kept your brain in gear and you got the gun away from James. You've done great. You should be proud of yourself. Now you need to do something else to help your dad. You need to call the police and an ambulance, okay? Detective Duncan won't believe me. It has to be you.'

Hayden licked his lips, swallowed hard. Kept the gun where it was.

'I'll hold the gun on him, Hayden. I'll make sure he looks at it long and hard. He won't hurt anyone else.'

Another swallow, another moment of thought. 'Let go of Rennie,' Hayden shouted.

James lifted both arms in the air like a footballer showing his hands to the ref. 'You don't have to give her the gun. I won't do anything.'

Rennie shoved him hard with the flat of a shoe as she backed away. 'Don't listen to him, Hayden.' Pain shot through her shin as she stood. A quick glance down and she saw blood had soaked the lower half of her jeans and was leaking over the white of her runner. A flick of eyes towards Max told her he was conscious, holding his side and watching them with an agony that wasn't caused only by injury. She wanted to rush to him, get him to a damn hospital but she limped to Hayden's side, aware the danger wasn't over yet.

'Come on, mate,' James tried again, a touch more agitation in his voice. '*She* tried to kill *me.* Don't give her the gun. She shot her own father, for God's sake. She'll shoot me, too. She won't even think twice about it.'

Hayden didn't move. The weapon trembled in his hands, tears glistened on his face. Over the last two days, she'd yelled at him and gone a little crazy. She kept a gun and running money, had told him she needed them because she wasn't a good person. She *had* shot her father. Plenty of reason for Hayden to listen to his uncle. Still plenty of opportunity for the moment to turn bad. A three-way tussle for a loaded gun was very bad.

She wanted to find a way to make him trust her, to tell him his uncle was worse, that blood ties could be deadly but she didn't need to. As she put a hand on his shoulder, he turned and passed her the weapon. Just like that, like he'd been waiting for her to get there.

'You shouldn't have done that, Hayden,' James started. 'She's . . .'

'Don't speak to him!' she yelled, pulling Hayden behind her.

Relieved to have the weight of the Glock in her hand at last, she curled her fingers around the grip, straightened her arm and pointed it at James. 'Go to your dad, Hayden. You need to put pressure on the bullet wound. Use the palm of your hand and push hard. It'll hurt but you need to do it, okay?'

'Okay,' he said quietly.

She pulled her phone from her back pocket and held it out to him. 'Use the other hand to call an ambulance. Wound first then the ambulance, okay? Now go.'

He skidded softly across the dirt. Rennie kept her eyes on James, his attention now where she wanted to be - with Max. She listened, relieved to hear Max's soft murmur, not unhappy for his groans, knowing it meant Hayden was doing his job properly. But as she watched James focus on his cousin and nephew, his eyes narrowed and his lips tightened, resentment and contempt contorting his face until it was hard and callous - and the pause on her anger released. Not wild and uncontrolled now but taut, sharp, hot.

She spoke loud enough for James's ears only. 'You want to revise your perspective of me now?'

He swung his head and met her eyes. The alarm she saw in them made her smile with satisfaction.

'Look, Renee . . .'

'Don't. There's nothing you can say that won't piss me off.'

He closed his mouth.

'My father was going to kill my sister and she's a pain in the arse. You tried to kill Max and I love him.' It was a slight movement but she made sure he didn't miss it, slipping her index finger inside the trigger guard. 'He was my *father* and I shot him. You're just a greedy, condescending arsehole.'

He sucked in a breath.

For five seconds, she weighed it up. It would be loud and messy. She'd seen it before, had been brought up expecting to do it. The concept frightened her and soothed her. James had shot Max, had almost killed him before that. He had a lot to answer for - and there were no cops here to stop her.

For five seconds more her heart thumped and her index finger tingled with adrenaline.

And then she thought some more. About Max and what he'd want. About Hayden and the way he'd handed her the gun. About her life here and what she'd just fought for. About Naomi and her baby, Trish and Pav, Brenda and Mike - their faces when they looked at her if she pulled the trigger.

She thought about Katrina and Renee, too. The two people inside her. The one she wanted to be and the one thrust on her. She'd been both tonight, had needed to be - to love Max enough to stay, to be hardened enough to save him. Katrina would pull the trigger and bury the shame where it couldn't be found until she was back-handed across the face. Rennie hadn't been tested yet.

Both of them had her father's blood running through their veins.

As the seconds stretched, as Hayden spoke urgently on the phone, a bead of sweat gathered on James's temple, trickled down his cheek and dropped off his chin.

He'd done enough damage. Tonight, two nights ago, for weeks and it wouldn't end here. Did she want to add to it? She had a home here. A life, people to love.

'An ambulance is coming,' Hayden called.

'Good work,' she told him.

'Dad keeps saying he doesn't mind being shot. He keeps talking about Dallas. I think he's delirious or something. Is that bad?'

Rennie smiled a little. He didn't want to join his friend; he wanted his approval. 'No, I think it means he's okay.'

She held James's gaze for a moment more then removed her finger from the trigger, replaced it on the guard. Not for Max or Hayden, not for Naomi, not even for herself. But because she didn't need the cops to stop her. Maybe she never had.

'You need to make another call, Hayden. Phone Detective Duncan and tell him we found your dad. His number's in my message bank. Tell him he was wrong. Tell him to get his arse up here. And tell him there's no time to stop for a toasted sandwich.'

48

Rennie opened her eyes to the soft morning light, listening to the whisper of Max's breath, enjoying the warmth of him at her back, the weight of his hand on her hip, like she'd dreamed every night he was gone.

Six of them in all - two in the tunnels at the point, four more in hospital. It was good to have him back. Despite the gunshot wound, severe dehydration was the worst of his injuries but there was also blood loss, shock, infection, a hairline fracture to his skull, six stitches to his scalp, whiplash, two broken ribs, concussion and amnesia. It was better than dead.

Slipping out from under the sheets, she pulled on clothes and moved quietly to Max's side of the bed. A wad of gauze didn't quite cover the patch of shaved head where the sutures were still in place. The yellowing bruises looked as though they were leaking out from underneath, oozing across his eye and down his cheek.

She brushed her lips across his hair, not wanting to wake him, filling her lungs with his sleepy, slightly antiseptic hospital smell before she left. In the hallway, she heard the shower running, guessed it was either Mike or Brenda up, tiptoed across the floor and poked her face into the living room.

In the half-light, she could see Hayden sprawled on the sofa bed, sheets twisted around him as though they were tying him down, the TV remote just out of reach. The kid had been smacked in the face with cold, hard reality but some things never changed.

He'd held it together with anger and adrenaline until Max was taken into surgery, then he'd sat in a chair and cried so hard and for so long that Rennie finally joined him. In the following days, Rennie saw how the terrifying hours up at the point had changed him in ways that made her wonder about herself after her mother's murder. It hadn't made him any neater or more polite or less moody but the resentment was gone. There was fear in his eyes still, a little wariness in the way he moved at times and something more respectful when he spoke to Rennie. She was grateful for that, if nothing else.

The evening after Hayden gave his official statement to the police, his mother and Brenda tried hard to talk him into going up to Cairns to join his stepfamily.

'What do *you* think I should do?' he'd eventually asked Rennie.

She didn't know what he'd wanted from her, possibly just a vote either way but Brenda looked at her as though she expected support.

Rennie disappointed her. 'You should do whatever you need to do.'

'I want to stay here with Dad.'

'Then stay.'

'But it's all so upsetting here,' Brenda insisted. 'I don't think being around all this is good for a young boy.'

'He's not a boy anymore.'

Hayden had watched Rennie for a good few seconds, as though weighing and measuring what was assembled inside him now. 'Yeah, I'm going to stay, Gran.' He said it without a hint of antagonism. Something else new.

Rennie heard the soft purr of a car in the driveway and let herself out.

'You ready for this?' Joanne asked as Rennie buckled herself in.

'No, but let's do it anyway.'

Joanne had arrived in Haven Bay while the police floodlights were still blazing over Garrigurrang Point. When she'd heard the locals babbling about the gunshots, she'd put two and two together and gone looking for her sister. It took another hour to track them all down at the hospital.

'I thought you were staying out of it,' Rennie had said when Jo finally found her nursing a freshly stitched shin.

'You thought wrong.'

'I told you it wasn't Anthony.'

'I told you it didn't matter who the hell it was.'

'I didn't get that text.'

'You shouldn't have needed a text.'

In the days that followed, Jo's tough, familiar support felt like a brick wall. Rennie had spent so long being envious of what other families had that she'd forgotten what her sister's presence was like. Now she understood that nice people with nice lives didn't always make nice families and that the unrelenting, unbending bond she had with Joanne was strong enough for anything she'd ever need.

They'd talked only briefly about Anthony. Short, curt phrases from daughters who'd wished their father dead. Disbelief, cynicism, resentment. And now, as Joanne drove, Rennie wondered if relief would come when they saw for themselves.

They stopped for breakfast ten minutes from the hospice. Jo ate like she had something to prove. Rennie drank two cups of strong coffee and worried she wouldn't be able to keep it down.

She didn't know what to expect. She hadn't seen her father in eleven years, barely knew him before that, remembered little more of his face than the rage-fuelled figure from the night she shot him and his angry, unrepentant expression in court.

He was in bed with a clean, white sheet tucked neatly across his chest. The arms folded over the top looked like candy canes in red-and-white pyjamas.

Rennie stood beside Jo just inside the doorway, the dread that'd been gathering pounding loud and clear in her ears. She stared at his face, trying to find something of the brutality that'd existed behind it for so many years. His eyes were closed, his mouth ajar and the lines etched into the pale, slack skin could have been carved by hammer and chisel.

Joanne broke the silence with a harsh voice. 'Anthony Hendelsen.'

His lids fluttered and as his eyes tracked slowly around the room towards them, his lips moving as though warming up for speech. Rennie's stomach clenched with irrational, involuntary fear. There was no need. His pupils were unfocused, his voice when it eventually made its way from his throat was a gurgling rasp of cough.

Jo shifted beside her. It was just a transfer of weight from one foot to another but it seemed to mirror what Rennie felt inside. No cascade of emotion. No wrath, no sense of just deserts. No pity, either. Just an internal nod of realisation - that he wasn't going anywhere. That he was all but dead.

Maybe it would hit harder later, maybe when he was finally gone she'd shout with rage. For now, though, there were no words she needed to say or hear. Nothing would explain it, nothing could excuse it, nothing would change it. All she needed to know was that it was over.

'Bastard.' Joanne's voice was quieter this time, tight with rancour and disgust.

'We've got what we came for. Let's go,' Rennie said.

They were halfway back to Haven Bay before either of them could string whole sentences together. Then they talked about futures they'd never planned: choosing somewhere to live, taking out a six-month lease, buying furniture.

'I'm going to get myself an industrial-strength vacuum cleaner,' Joanne declared as though it'd been a lifelong ambition.

'I'm going to buy books,' Rennie told her.

They laughed, too, the sound of it like cool, fresh air after stepping from a sauna. In the end, a whole life was too long for Joanne to work with. She said she'd keep working Rennie's shifts at Skiffs through the New Year . . . and then see.

Rennie wasn't ready to make a decision, either. Until the moment she'd stepped from the hospice, every choice she'd ever made had been based on survival. She'd never allowed herself to imagine 'forever' in Haven Bay. She'd never decided to stay - she just hadn't left. Now she was on the first page of a new story and she wasn't sure what it was about yet.

As Jo turned off the expressway for the last twenty-minute stretch to Haven Bay, Rennie let the final chapter of her last story filter through her mind with new eyes.

Naomi went into early labour three days after she discovered her husband was a monster. On the night of the confrontation at the point, she heard about the gunfire and when two uniformed police knocked on her door, she thought James must have somehow been caught in the crossfire. The reality buckled her at the knees and prompted the cops to call a doctor to the house.

Rennie went to see her two days later. Not to discuss the how and why of it all but because Naomi had been her friend when she'd needed one. She figured a cup of tea and toast was the least she could offer.

Naomi's parents and a younger sister were with her, as shocked and exhausted as Naomi. Rennie made tea and toast for all of them then took Naomi to the nursery and helped her assemble the cot that'd been in the back of James's car just hours before he tried to kill three people. They put sheets on the mattress, hung mobiles and organised nappies, laughing at how small they were and crying for Naomi's loss.

She'd had no idea of James's plans or the money he'd taken or the year-long affair and Rennie wondered if Naomi's need to find the good in every story had only deceived her - or whether it would protect her when the whole truth came out.

The contractions started the next day and Naomi rang Rennie to ask if she'd sit with her at the hospital. She didn't just sit though. She held her hand through the sweating and pushing, stunned by the process, honoured to be included. Rennie had no idea what it took to care for a newborn baby, she just knew Naomi's little girl was coming into a tough new world and she'd need her mother to be strong and capable.

Pav had nothing to do with Max's disappearance and chastised himself for asking for the loan, figuring he was the catalyst for the violence. Rennie had felt guilty about suspecting him after the full story was out - now she hoped the guilt was a sign she was learning how to be a friend.

At Max's urging, Pav and Trish took steps to come out from the shadow of their own past. Rennie introduced them to Evan Delaney, who introduced them to someone in Immigration. Pav hadn't done anything wrong in Australia but the Department was interested in his information. So were the Serbian police.

Evan had turned up like a surrogate parent and, as he'd done before, filled in some of the missing detail. Notification of Anthony's release had been sent to their solicitor just days before Nathan Bruce-Allen died of a heart attack, leaving his partner in the throes of a major extradition case and his practice in disarray. The letter was presumed to be a duplicate for his files, got listed as non-urgent and five months later was still waiting for attention when Evan started asking questions. Rennie wondered what would have happened if she'd received the details five months earlier. Would she have searched for Max when he went missing or just believed the weight of evidence? Would she have told him about Anthony or kept the secret and hoped Max never had a chance to see her father's DNA at work?

Then yesterday, she caught up with Eliza for the first time since the shooting. She'd given Rennie a business card, told her the man who'd rung the cafe while Max was missing had come in. He owned a small art gallery in Newcastle. He wanted to talk to Rennie, said there was no hurry in light of what had happened but to give him a call if she was interested in meeting him. Nothing like the call from her father she'd imagined.

'I'll be a couple of hours,' she told Joanne as she pulled into the driveway.

'Will it take that long?'

Rennie glanced up at the house, the dark grey of the timber looking cool under the midday sun. 'There are things that need to be said. It'll take as long as it takes.'

It was cool in the hallway after the heat outside. Brenda and Mike's car was gone and the silence gave her hope that they'd taken Hayden with them. She didn't want to do this with an audience.

She went to the bedroom first, pulled the backpack from the wardrobe, carried it through the house and propped it by the wall inside the back door. The smell of gardenias reached her on the light breeze as she watched Max in his veggie patch, holding his injured side as he stretched to reach the tomato stakes.

His weight loss was obvious even at this distance: five and a half kilos in two days then another as he recovered from surgery. Rennie had worried that James's deceit and violence would damage him more than the physical injuries, crush the optimism that the mine accident had almost destroyed. But while James was still an open, stinging wound, Max knew he'd come between his son and a gun and that somehow made it okay for him.

As she stepped onto the deck, he turned and smiled.

'Should you be doing that?' she asked, nodding at the vegetables.

'Gardening therapy.'

'For you or the veggies?'

He shrugged, wincing at the movement. 'Both. The lettuces aren't looking too good but check this out.' He pulled two plump Lebanese cucumbers from the back pocket of his shorts and grinned. 'We're eating from the garden tonight!'

She laughed a little. Last week she thought he wouldn't stay for cucumbers, but maybe he would.

'You just missed Phil Duncan,' he told her, taking the steps up to the deck cautiously. He had broken ribs on one side, with a shoe-shaped bruise where James had stomped him, and stitches front and back on the other where the bullet had passed right through him.

'What did he have to say for himself?'

'Some of the forensics are back. They confirmed the blood in the back cab of James's ute. Mine.'

She nodded. James had attempted to clean it in the days Max was missing, picking up the cot and storing it there to keep the stain out of sight. Rennie figured the thud on the back gate was him too, trying to get at the computer and destroy Max's files when she went out to pick up Hayden. Not that James was talking about any of it. He'd been charged with attempted murder, fraud and a bunch of other crimes but he wasn't admitting to anything. Rennie wondered how his patronising, arrogant smirk was going down with the cops.

'And he said you won't be charged,' Max told her as she helped to lower him to a sun lounge. 'Phil still thinks the gun was yours but he can't prove you ever had it.'

'I wonder how hard he tried.' After being so categorically wrong about Max, the detective didn't seem too interested in her previous crimes now.

'Maybe you don't need that solicitor in Sydney after all.' He patted the cushion, an invitation to snuggle in beside him.

She faced him instead, perching on the edge of the sun lounge. 'We didn't see a solicitor, Max. We saw my father.' After all the secrets, Rennie had wanted to tell him everything but he'd been drugged and hooked up to fluids, trying to remember and forget. And there'd been a stream of visitors and worried parents and Naomi's baby being born on the floor above. Now they were here and she needed to put her secrets to rest.

'Phil Duncan asked me about your dad,' Max said. 'He said he was in hospital. How is he?'

'He's dying. He didn't recognise us.'

'I'm sorry.'

'No. Don't be.'

She told him the story of her life then, starting from the brutal beating that prompted her mother's flight and finishing the day she arrived in Haven Bay with a gun in her backpack. It took a long time and when it was done, they sat in the hush of the summer afternoon without speaking.

'I didn't want to be that person anymore when I came here,' she finally said. 'I thought I could remake myself, paint over the ugliness with brighter colours. I thought I had but Katrina Hendelsen is still in here.' She held a hand to her chest. 'And you need to know that.'

'You're Renee Carter, too,' Max said.

'I'm more like a hybrid now. An artist with violent tendencies.'

'Van Gogh cut off an ear.'

'It was his own ear.'

He smiled. She smiled back.

'I know who you are, Rennie. You found me and dragged me out of a tunnel and stopped James from . . .' He glanced away.

'I wanted to kill him, Max.'

'So did I.'

'I almost did. I thought hard about pulling that trigger.'

'You protected my son and kept him safe.'

She nodded. She felt good about that. Maybe a little like Max and the bullet in his gut. 'You asked me to marry you last weekend. Is that what you want?'

He hesitated, maybe wondering what she wanted to hear. Whether 'yes' or 'no' would be the deal-breaker. 'I thought I was going to lose everything. I thought James was going to leave a bloody mess. I thought it would make you go and I wanted you to stay.'

It wasn't the answer to her question but she understood. When he'd seen it was all about to go to hell, he didn't want to be there without her. She understood what that meant now. 'Is that what you need, to be married?'

He reached for her hand. 'I've got everything I need right here.'

She wanted to smile but there was more before she could get to that. 'I've never put down roots, Max. I told you from the start I wouldn't stay. Until today, I thought I had no choice. Until the last two hours, I haven't let myself think about it.'

'Rennie . . .'

'Please, let me finish.' She took a breath. 'All I thought I'd find here was a place to sketch. I didn't expect to find you. I didn't know what it was like to be happy. I won't marry you, Max. I don't want a signature on a piece of paper to be a reason to stay. But I *want* to stay. I want to be here with you for as long as you'll have me.'

His fingers tightened around hers as something sweet and moist filled his eyes. 'Just to let you know, babe, that'll be for a long time.'

She smiled then, cupped her hands around his bruised face and pressed her lips to his dry, cracked ones. Let them linger there for a while, telling herself this was what it felt like to belong.

He winced as they parted, his fingers clutching at a twinge in his ribs.

'You should rest,' she said.

'I was hoping we could seal the deal with more than just a kiss.'

'Not in your condition, buddy,' she grinned as she stood and started for the door. 'But don't worry, we've got plenty of time.'

'Where are you going?'

'Jo's at the cafe on her own this afternoon. I told her I'd help close up.'

'What's with the backpack?'

She glanced at the worn black strap she'd picked up, looked back at him from the house. 'I'm throwing it out.'

'Are you sure? I mean you've had it a long time. It's taken you a lots of places.'

'No point keeping it. I can't fit my life in it anymore.'

ACKNOWLEDGMENTS

There are people without whom this book couldn't have been completed. Many thanks to:

Random House for first publishing this book, especially to Bev Cousins, for her enthusiasm and her input - even if some of it nearly sent me insane! To Virginia Grant and Elena Gomez, for not letting me take short cuts, and to the rest of the team that helped make this project come together.

My agent, Clare Forster, and Kate Cooper in London, for making sure I get to keep writing.

Cath Every-Burns, who walked me around Wangi Wangi on the shores of Lake Macquarie and even braved the spider-webs at the gun emplacements to show me the creepy places underneath.

Grant Every-Burns, for his engineering and underground advice.

For research: Sam Findley once again, for his police expertise, Lachlan Jarvis, Dean Grant and Dr Shaunagh Foy.

Chris, Isolde, Elizabeth, Kandy, Carla, Carol, Simone and Melinda - couldn't do it without you!

Wendy James, fellow crime writer, for chewing over ideas.

Dayle White for sharing her story and being happy to be inspiration.

Nikki for her die-hard support - and for wanting to *be* Rennie!

Mum and Les, Joan and Brian - my cheer squad.

And to my family - Paul, Mark and Claire. You keep me sane, make me laugh and understand what it takes. You are my safe haven - even on the other side of the world.

For those of you who have read this far, the World War II gun emplacements exist, although I've renamed the point where they sit, added to their number and moved their position to suit the story. There are bunkers underneath (and lots of spider-webs) but as far as I know, that's all.

KEEP READING FOR A SNEAK PEEK OF THE NEXT JAYE FORD THRILLER

DARKEST PLACE

Chapter 1

Carly scrambled from bed, stumbling and snatching at the darkness, caught between fight and flight.

Where? Where was he?

Listening, straining for sounds, she heard the thump of her heart, the dry gasp of her breath. No taps, no knocks, no bumps. That didn't mean a fucking thing.

Her mobile was in her hand. She didn't remember picking it up. It took three tries to dial the numbers. Forever for a voice to answer. She wanted to shout, managed to pull it back to a hiss. 'There's someone in my apartment.'

'Newcastle police. We received a call about an intruder at this apartment.'

Carly pressed her mouth to the intercom. 'Me. From me. I don't know where he is.' She hit the release for the security entrance. Finally heard deep, hushed voices in the corridor outside. A thump on the door. She cracked it open and saw two uniforms. Men, waists bulky with equipment, chests heaving from the run up the stairs. Both swept their eyes over her – bare feet, flannel pyjamas, clutching a hair dryer.

'Are you hurt?' one asked. Stiff shake of her head.

'Is there someone in the apartment with you?'

'I . . . don't know.'

He shot a look over Carly's shoulder into her hallway. His partner checked back the way they had come. A radio crackled with static and Carly's stomach clenched.

'Can we come in?' he asked.

Please. She pulled the door wide, saw guns and handcuffs on their belts. The one who'd spoken found the panel of switches on the wall and flicked on the hall lights. Carly squinted in the sudden glare, her feet itching to run.

'I want you to wait here while we check the apartment,' he said. Close to the exit, behind cops with guns. 'Okay.'

His partner unclipped a radio mic from his jacket, speaking into it quietly as he passed. Carly stayed by the door as the single bulb in the living room came on. Two more officers appeared in the corridor, a man and a woman, barely acknowledging Carly as they hustled in.

She edged along the wall behind them. There were no drawn guns, no hand signals. One took the stairs to the loft, another turned the key in the handle of the French windows and stepped out. The others shoved at the panes on either side. Had he come in there?

'How long since you saw him?' It was the first guy, back from the loft.

'I . . .' Carly cleared her throat. 'What time is it now?'

'Three twenty-two.'

'It was three something when I looked at my mobile. And that was . . . a minute, I guess, since he'd . . . since he'd been . . .' She touched her throat.

'Okay. Wait there.'

He turned away, speaking fast, indistinct words into his radio.

There was a brief conference with the other officers, nods and exchanges and pointing.

Carly pulled her pyjama top tight around her chest and listened to the words they threw around: perimeter search, a car, acronyms she couldn't catch, something about a slow night and more officers turning up for a search of the other floors. She turned her face to the dim night-time lighting beyond her front door, the black void on the other side of the railing. Five stories of old warehouse covering an entire block. There were a thousand places to hide.

'You can come in now,' the first cop said. 'There's no one here.'

Carly walked to the kitchen on shaky legs, turned on the tap and gulped straight from the faucet. The wetness barely touched the dust-dry lining of her mouth. She scrubbed at her cheeks, her neck, snatched up a tea towel, buried her face in it and burst into tears.

'Are you cold?' First Cop asked.

She was shaking all over. It wasn't from the chill in the air but she nodded.

'Can I get an officer to find you some warm clothes? A dressing gown? Socks?'

She saw the motley purple of her feet before registering that they were almost numb. 'There's a dressing gown on a hook upstairs. Uggs near the bed.'

'What's your name?' He was in front of her now, arms slightly raised as though he might need to catch her.

'Charlotte Townsend.' No, she didn't want to be Charlotte tonight. Charlotte was pathetic. 'Carly. Call me Carly.'

'Carly, I'm Dean, okay?' Dark hair little more than stubble, eyes like black coffee. Not a young hotdog: mid-thirties, something kind in his straightforwardness.

'Okay.'

'You want to put down that hair dryer now?'

She was holding it like a huge red handgun, muzzle up, power cord trailing on the floor. It felt stupid now but she couldn't let it go. 'It was all I could find for a weapon.'

'Sure.'

'If I had to hit someone.'

'You could do some damage with that thing.' He took it by the muzzle end, slipped it from her trembling fingers as though he was disarming her and laid it on the kitchen counter where it couldn't hurt anyone. 'Why don't we sit down?'

She walked through the sea of dark uniforms to the single small sofa, feeling anxious and wobbly and pathetic in her green pyjamas with their fat white sheep – thirty-three- year-old woman living alone and wearing a flock of sheep to bed. Dean spoke quietly to the other officers and they dispersed. He produced a notebook and pen and sat knee-to- knee with her.

'Can you tell me what happened, Carly?'

She rubbed at her thighs. 'I woke up and . . . and . . . I . . .' Her brain was buzzing with words, her mouth struggling to let them out. Fast forward and slow motion at the same time. 'He, uh, . . .' A hand fluttered around her neck and cheek. 'Touched me and . . .' She twisted her fingers into a knot. 'He left.'

'You were in your bedroom?'

'Yes.' The hand fluttered above her head in the direction of the loft room.

'He was touching you when you woke up?'

The memory of it – the pressure, the caress – made her shudder. 'He was standing beside the bed.'

'And then he touched you?'

She pressed the tea towel to her lips, trying to force down the pulsing and scrambling inside her. The memory was fuzzy and disorganised, but her throat and cheek burned as though she'd been scorched.

A soft touch at her shoulder made her jump. The female officer was back with Carly's dressing gown and slippers. She pulled it around herself, warmer but still shaking. Clamping her hands between her knees to contain the jittering.

'I'm going to ask some more about all of that in a minute,' Dean said. 'But first, I want to get some information out to our other patrols. Can you describe the man?'

Carly shook her head.

'I know it's hard, but a description is important.'

'No, I mean I can't. I couldn't see anything.'

'Take a second to think about it, Carly.'

'I don't need to *think* about it. It was *dark*.'

He nodded as though her anger made sense. 'You said he was standing beside the bed. How did you know that?'

'I *saw* him,' she snapped, then realised that was stupid. 'The shadow of him.'

'Can you tell me what the shadow looked like?'

She scratched the backs of her hands. Tucked them away in the pockets of her dressing gown. 'It was a shadow. It looked like a *shadow*.'

'It's okay, Carly. Relax.' He waited a beat. 'There are patrols driving around. If the intruder is on foot, there's a chance he could be spotted if I can get a description out. Okay?'

She nodded.

'So let's try this. Was the shadow tall?'

'It was . . .' *Think*. 'Tall enough to –' she held hands in front of her face, like she wished she'd done when he was there '– bend over me. And . . . and . . .' He'd breathed on her. 'Man-shaped and thin-ish. Not fat, anyway.'

'What about clothes? What was he wearing?'

'Everything was black. He was a black shape in a black room.'

'Do you think his clothes might have been black?' She lifted her eyes. 'Yes. That makes sense.'

'What about his head? Was he wearing a cap? Or a hood?'

'It was . . .' Carly used two cupped hands to make an arch over her head. 'A smooth outline. It must have been a hood.'

'What about his face?'

Blinking, trying to see it again, she got . . . nothing. Come *on*. The warm staleness of his breath had whispered across her face, he must have been close. Really close. She scrunched up her face. 'I don't . . . I just remember black.'

'Could there have been something on his face, like a balaclava?'

'Maybe.' That would explain it. 'I didn't think of that. Yeah, it must have been that.' She smiled a little with relief, until she remembered a man had been in her bedroom with a balaclava and a hood and his hand on her throat. 'Shit.'

'And you thought it was a man?'

'Yes.' Her voice was firm on that one.

'Okay. Wait here a moment.' Dean spoke to the guy he'd arrived with, the only other officer left in the room. He pulled the radio mic from his jacket, turning away as he spoke.

'We're getting a description out,' Dean explained, sitting again. 'How are you doing, Carly? Can you answer some more questions?'

She tugged the lapels of her dressing gown closer, ran a hand through her hair. The limb-jerking had eased up, something shivery taking its place. If answering more questions meant two burly officers would stay for a while longer . . . 'Yes.'

'Is there anything missing from your apartment? Something he might be carrying?' Her eyes scanned the room: slim pickings if he'd wanted to rob her. 'I don't know, I don't have much.'

'When he was touching you, did you try to push him away?' Her hands curled into fists.

'Do you think you might've scratched him? Caused some damage we could use for identification?'

She pushed to her feet, arms tight around her waist, stumbling as she got away from the confined space of the sofa and coffee table.

'Carly?' Dean joined her, something gentler in his words. 'I know it's difficult but I have to ask this, for your own sake.' He waited until she'd lifted her gaze. 'Did he hurt you, Carly? Maybe touch you somewhere else?'

She pressed fingers to her lips, her stomach wanting to rise.

He spoke before she could answer. 'I can request a female officer to be here, if you'd prefer.'

'No, it's all right. He didn't rape me, if that's what you're asking. I told you everything, it's just . . . I didn't . . . *do* anything.' She touched the hollow of her throat below the hinge of her jaw. Her fingertips were icy; his had been hard and rough and eager. 'Nothing. I just lay there and let him put his hands on me.'

'Fighting back isn't always the best thing, Carly. You might have saved yourself by keeping still.'

Doing nothing to help herself – she was an expert at that. A tear trickled from the corner of her eye. Dean cocked his head at the sofa, a suggestion she might be more comfortable there. She shook her head, couldn't sit.

'So he stopped touching you and left?' he asked.

'It didn't happen like that. He took his hand away and just . . . stayed there. Bent over me. Watching, I think.'

'You could see him?'

'Not after I closed my eyes.'

'Did he say anything?'

'No.'

'Make a noise?'

'No.'

'And then he left?'

She nodded. 'When I opened my eyes, he was gone.'

Chapter 2

'Tell me about your doors,' Dean said.

They were standing at the French windows, Carly peering cautiously beyond the balcony into the early morning. There was only one police car in the street now. The neighbourhood was asleep, the unrenovated warehouses hulking and dark.

'Do you usually leave the key in this door?' he asked, pointing at it.

'I've been leaving it there,' Carly told him, 'so I don't have to go searching for it every time I want to open up.'

'Do you usually lock it before you go to bed?'

'I've only been here three nights.'

He raised his eyebrows in a question.

'I've just moved in.' Two whole days, three nights; not long enough to be home, just the promise of somewhere better.

'Where were you before?'

'Out west. North-west really. Past Tamworth.' Eight hours' drive. Another life away. He glanced around the apartment. 'Is it just you?'

There was one sofa, a coffee table and a small wrought iron table with two matching chairs, meant for outdoors but arranged in her dining space. Maybe he thought there was a partner coming with the rest of the furniture. 'Just me, no baggage.' It was a lie; her baggage was itching under her skin like mites.

'Did you go out last night?'

'I walked around the corner to the supermarket in the afternoon. Cooked dinner, watched a DVD and went to bed.' She'd stood on the balcony, too, and toasted her new life. Maybe a little hasty. 'I locked this door earlier in the night.'

He tried the handle. It was secure but he gave it a shove, testing how hard it might be to force. It didn't budge. 'Did you check it before we got here?'

'Was it unlocked?'

'No. Do you think you might've come over here first? Made sure you were locked in before you called us?'

She hesitated, trying to catch the hazy memory. Remembered she'd thought about the doors when she was staggering on the stairs but her feet had gone the other way. 'I went straight down the hallway. To wait for you.'

'Do you leave a key in the front door too?'

'No, they're in a bowl on the kitchen counter.'

'Are they still there?'

Had he taken her keys? Carly stumbled in her hurry to find them, clutched the bunch in her palm with relief. Talked as she led the cop down the hall to the door. 'I didn't turn the deadlock. I thought it was dangerous to lock yourself in, you know, in case there's a fire and you can't find your keys. Besides, there's no handle on the outside, you need the key to get in.'

'Have you given a key to anyone else?'

'No.'

'Is there a chance the door might not have closed properly? Maybe you just swung it and it didn't catch when you came back from the supermarket.'

Did she have her hands full, fumbling for the keys? She couldn't think that far back now. 'I don't remember. It's not something that's happened before.'

'You've only been here three days.' Dean opened the door a little and gave it a light push towards the jamb. There was a soft metal clack as the bolt met the strike plate but when he pulled on the knob, the latch slipped out of the lock again.

Carly sucked in a breath. 'Shit.' She stared at Dean, then the lock, then back at the cop. 'I *let* him in?' She reeled away. She was a fucking idiot.

'Sometimes it happens like that. Offenders buzz random apartments from the security entrance until someone lets them in, then they wander around until they find a door they can open. You're not far from the stairs, maybe he didn't wander too far.'

Carly rubbed hands over her face. She'd let him in and she'd let him touch her.

'You're okay, Carly. That's the main thing.' Dean signalled his partner. 'And someone in your home is a serious matter, whether you locked your doors or not. Your information will be logged, we'll organise for fingerprinting to be done and a check of CCTV.' He paused to glance at the dark expanse of the warehouse beyond her door.

'Maybe a canvass of your neighbours. And I'll be recommending your case gets handed over to detectives. You should expect a call later today.'

It was something, but . . . she copied his glimpse at the corridor. 'What if he's still in the building?'

'The building has been searched and there's been a troop of cops through here tonight. That kind of thing usually scares an offender off.' Dean's partner moved between them into the corridor.

Carly glanced after him into the quiet gloom, lowered her voice. 'What if he lives here?'

Dean made a doubtful face. 'Is there someone you can call?'

'No.'

'A family member? A friend?'

'I don't know anyone in Newcastle.'

'What about your neighbours?'

She hadn't met them yet. She'd barely spoken to anyone since she'd moved in – and she wasn't about to introduce herself at four o'clock in the morning and ask if she could camp on their sofa. 'No, there's no need to wake anyone.'

Dean produced a business card. 'This is my mobile number. Call if you're worried. I'm working until nine but I keep my phone on during the day.' He was through the door by the time he'd finished, held out a hand to shake. It was warm and firm and calm, everything Carly wasn't. 'Lock your doors and try to relax, okay?'

Carly toggled the deadlock back and forth, gave it a firm tug and pressed her back to it. Held up her hands, eyeing the twitching and jerking of her fingers: her baggage was trembling and breathless inside her.

She didn't need to hide it now, so she let it carry her away, long strides down the hallway and through the living room, unlocking and re-locking the balcony door, keeping the keys in her fist as she moved about. Restless, fearful, searching. She didn't know what she what she was looking for, only that a man had made his way through the apartment to her bedside without waking her. He could have been here for hours.

Wishing she had more lights to switch on, she lifted the cushions on the sofa, looked in the kitchen cupboards, the half bathroom. Then up in the loft: under the bed, in the ensuite, inside the wardrobe. There was nothing except the anxious apprehension crawling under her skin.

She couldn't go back to bed. She was repulsed by the thought of him in her loft, and couldn't risk lying still when she was like this.

Hauling at the sheets as though they were infested, she tossed them over the rail for washing later. She wanted a shower to scrub off the memory of him but was scared he'd come back when she was wet and naked. She stalked the apartment instead, tired but wakeful, drained but hyper, turning on the telly, flicking aimlessly through the channels, shifting from the sofa to the kitchen counter to the wall of checkerboard glass that looked out onto the balcony.

A cup of tea kept her still for fifteen minutes. Another one made her doze fitfully for ten. At six forty, she stood at the windows and watched the sun lighten the sky, her body telling her she needed to be outside, pounding a path. Walking had been her physical and mental therapy for so long it was the first thing her body craved when the agitation started.

She zipped her mobile and keys into the pockets of a jacket and ran the four flights of zigzag stairs to the foyer, her breath steaming in the frosty air when she hit the street. She followed the route she'd taken both previous mornings, a flat, five-minute walk through the old industrial neighbourhood – long strides, arms pumping, focusing on walking, not thinking, like she'd done for years. But by the time she saw the harbour, she was puffing hard. When she reached the restaurants on the boardwalk her legs felt like lead weights and her bones were aching. Not from exertion, not in twenty minutes, but from the effort to keep the itching, scrabbling anxiety at bay. Freaking out could be exhausting, she reminded herself. She was only halfway to the headland but gave up punishing herself and ordered a cappuccino at the last cafe in the row.

She'd been there twice, it had gas heaters out front and a brew that made her blood flow. Today, she sat at a table with a warm cup between her palms, watching a tugboat rock and roll in the wake of a container ship and trying to talk herself to calmness.

It wasn't about her, she told herself. She'd paid for her sins. She couldn't change the past but she could begin again. It was why she was here. Why she'd walked away from everything she knew, the small town where her guilt and pain were a part of the collective memory. Where every day was a reminder of what she'd done and who she'd been.

'Perfect morning for soaking up C's and D's,' a waiter said as he collected her cup.

'C's and D's?'

'Caffeine and vitamin D, essential for good winter health. I'm Reuben, by the way. I'm here every morning.' He dropped the newspaper from under his arm onto Carly's table.

'Stay as long as you like, we're having a quiet one today.'

'Thanks.'

'Another coffee?'

Carly glanced at the path back, not ready to return. 'Yes, please.' Her lovely apartment in the renovated warehouse was meant to be inspirational, a metaphor for her own renewal. But the image wasn't so appealing now. Yes, it was her fault the door was unlocked, but that didn't change the fact that someone had pushed it open and walked in. All the way to her bedside. A man who had snuck past the security entrance, or a neighbour. Not your average *Oh look, that door's not closed properly* neighbour but someone who saw it and took advantage. A creepy guy she lived with.

ABOUT THE AUTHOR

Jaye Ford is a bestselling Australian author of five chilling suspense novels. Her first thriller, *Beyond Fear*, won two Davitt Awards for Australian women crime writers (Best Debut and Readers' Choice) and was the highest selling debut crime novel in Australia in 2011. When she needs a break from the dark stuff, she writes romantic comedy under the name Janette Paul. Her novels have been translated into numerous languages and recorded as audio books. Before writing fiction, she was a news and sport journalist, the first woman to host a live national sport show on Australian TV and ran her own public relations consultancy. She now writes fiction full time from her home in Newcastle, NSW, Australia where she loves to turn places she knows and loves into crime scenes.

To sign up for Jaye's newsletter click the link here, or visit her website the join up at www.jayefordauthor.com

Or connect on social media:

www.facebook.com/JayeFordauthor

www.instagram.com/jayeford50

CPSIA information can be obtained
at www.ICGtesting.com
Printed in the USA
LVHW031524091120
671184LV00013B/2596

9 780648 753254